D1130936

Barriers

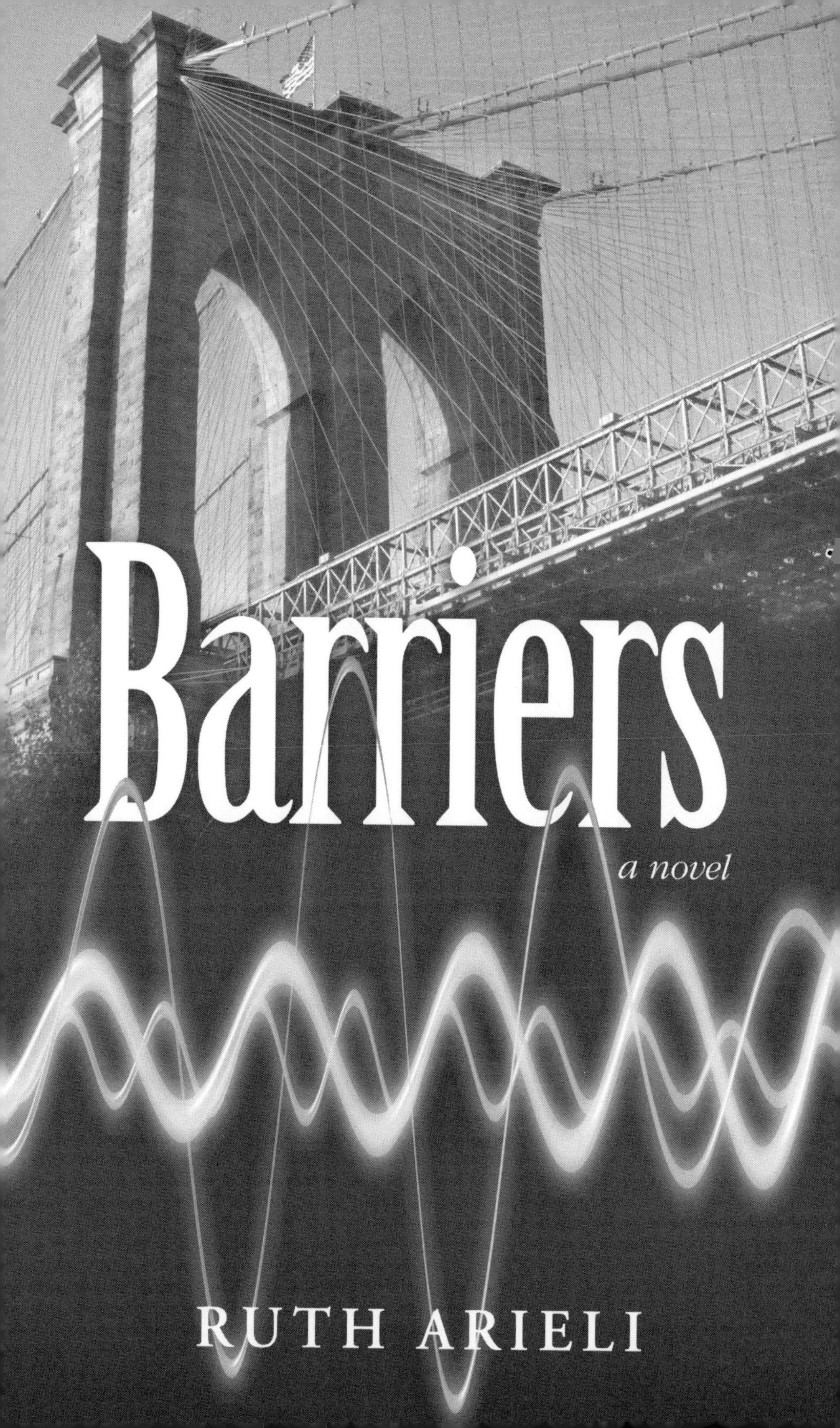
Barriers
a novel
RUTH ARIELI

First published 2007

Copyright © 2007 by Ruth Arieli

ISBN: 965-7375 10-X

All rights reserved.
No part of this publication may be translated, reproduced, stored in a retrieval system or transmitted, in any form or by any means, electronic, mechanical, photocopying, recording, or otherwise, without permission in writing from the publishers.

HAMODIA PUBLISHING
POB 1306 / Jerusalem, Israel

FELDHEIM DISTRIBUTORS
POB 43163 / Jerusalem, Israel
208 Airport Executive Park
Nanuet, NY 10954

www.feldheim.com

Printed in Israel

Cover design and typesetting: Zippy Thumim

Acknowledgements

We thank You, Hashem:

You make our hearts work in a wonderful rhythm; You give our brains the power to command and our limbs the ability to obey.

You empower our muscles, enabling us to be active; You open and close our eyes in wonderful rhythm; You allow us to hear and to speak, and You blow air into our lungs.

I thank You, *Ribbono shel Olam*, for my health and for my inner fire, which You created with Your wisdom. I thank You, Hashem, for it would be impossible to exist and stand before You without all of the above — even for an hour. I thank You for every day that my heart beats, my eyes see and my ears hear; for every day that my legs can walk and that my arms can work; for returning to me my *neshamah* each day, in Your great mercy.

I thank You, Hashem, for the faith you have planted in my heart, for the strength with which I am able to stand up to this world and its tests. For belief in You — that too You gave me, in Your great mercy.

Many thanks to my dear family for their encouragement and support throughout; for the listening ear and the supportive shoulder they provided for me, as well as for the characters of this book; for accepting me and them with affection, understanding and trust.

I wish to express my gratitude to the professionals who contributed to this book: to L.L., speech therapist; T.B. and A.Y., occupational therapists; and R.S., social worker, for their tremendous assistance given above and beyond the call of duty, their genuine interest and the expertise necessary for the book.

Many thanks to the staff at English *Hamodia* for providing me with the opportunity to present my story and who accompanied me throughout. Special thanks to Mrs. Dvora Kiel, the editor, Mrs. Channie Goldwasser for translating the story and to Mrs. Chavi Ernster for her warm feedback and encouragement.

Ruth Rappaport (Arieli)

1

New York 5751/1991

Naomi sat on the little wooden bridge. In her mind's eye, she saw cars of various sizes and colors whizzing past on a multilane superhighway that seemed to lead nowhere at all. It was a foolish notion; she knew that. Every vehicle would have a destination of some sort — but only the drivers themselves knew where they were headed.

She savored the imaginary scene. She loved seeing streams of cars whooshing by; the constant, never-ending motion fascinated her. As a child, she had often longed to stop her father mid-trip and settle herself in the middle of the Brooklyn Bridge, where she could count the cars and fantasize about where each one was going. A bridge is undoubtedly one of the best places to keep an active imagination occupied, and she'd been blessed with a very active imagination indeed.

She'd never realized her dream of sitting on the Brooklyn Bridge. Instead, she made do with the small wooden bridge that crossed the gully not far from her home. She would sit at the edge of the walkway while Shmulik, her older brother by just one year, played with his toy cars, zooming them up and down the center of the bridge. Of course, they were nowhere near as exciting as the real cars on the highway, but she enjoyed counting them just the same.

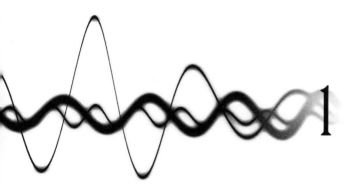

Blue ones, yellow ones, red ones. ... Shmulik had hundreds of model cars, and he never confused their color, make or number. He had an entire fleet of yellow cabs just like the kind in Manhattan.

From time to time, once every hour or two, a real car would approach, traveling in the direction of their bridge. It always surprised them when that happened, because they had made the bridge their plaything, and it seemed ridiculous to see a real car traveling on it. Every time a real car approached, she, from her vantage point, would call out, "Shmulik! Shmulik! Watch out, a car's coming! A car's coming!"

Shmulik would hurry and scoop up his large collection, and the car would drive by. It wasn't dangerous, because the cars, after driving down the bumpy dirt path leading to the bridge, were traveling slowly. Most of the time, Shmulik managed to collect his cars before the car actually reached the bridge. It was only on rare occasions that a driver had to stop and watch as the child picked up his toys.

Ah, Shmulik's cars. She was the only one who had ever shown any interest in his huge fleet.

Naomi rose and slowly traversed the bridge. How many years had passed? The bridge was shaky, her parents had grown aged and weary, and Shmulik had married and was raising a family in Eretz Yisrael. The desire to build a Jewish home in Eretz Yisrael had burned in his heart ever since his thirteenth birthday. She, the more sensitive of the two, had sensed her father's hidden pain when her brother had first verbalized this dream. He had not expressly forbidden him to travel there, but he had told his son he would never come visit him.

Now, symbolically, a small, broken car rested in the crack between two crossbeams. Crouching down, she picked it up, her fleeting smile filled with nostalgia. She could see her parents' house, low and red-roofed, in the distance. She began making her way over there, idly wondering why her father, who couldn't abide rustic scenery, had chosen to live in so quiet and remote an area, so far away from pulsating Manhattan. Or was it her mother who had been attracted to the bucolic nature of the area? Maybe ...

In any case, she was glad they had chosen this area as their place of residence. She wouldn't have enjoyed a childhood surrounded by skyscrapers. Now that she lived in Boro Park, she often longed for a quiet, village-like place like the one where she had grown up.

Rapping lightly on the door, she entered her parents' house.

"Naomi?"

"Yes, it's me," she replied.

Her father stepped out of one of the bedrooms.

"Hi there, daughter. Come to visit your elderly parents?"

"The way I do every Monday."

"Every Monday and every Thursday," her father corrected. "So how are you? How's Shlomo? How's Yanky?"

"*Baruch Hashem*."

Her eyes were on the small car she held in her hand, and her father, sharp as ever, noticed it immediately.

"What are you holding?"

"Oh. " She blushed. "Nothing really." But her heart did not allow her to toss the small, broken car into the nearby garbage can.

"You always loved cars," her father said with a smile, "and Shmulik even more than you."

"You knew that?" Naomi asked, sitting down. She ran her finger gently over the car, removing a layer of dust. "It's a shame Shmulik's name is not etched on it," she murmured.

"I knew," her father said in response to her first comment. "I knew you and Shmulik loved cars. But I didn't know Shmulik etched his name onto his cars. Did he always do that? He etched his name onto every single car in his collection?"

She nodded.

"Yes. I helped him," she said dreamily. "It was fun."

"I imagine it was." Despite their differing natures, her father understood her. "Those were the days, eh? Much water has flowed under the bridge since then."

"Yes," she agreed. "I was once a little girl."

Her father's gaze swept the walls, and he sighed. "You're not exactly an old lady now. But once – once these walls were adorned with the drawings of a small, enthusiastic artist."

"Didn't you like them?"

"Didn't I?" They were both surprised by the stiffness of their conversation, but the warmth of their nostalgia was tangible, as if they had been sucked forcefully through a time machine. Neither of them wanted to forgo the aroma of cakes baking, the sound of childish peals of laughter, or the feeling of paternal warmth. Naomi was young, but she'd always been more mature than other girls her age.

"I liked them, daughter; I liked them."

"Why?" she asked softly.

Her father chuckled. "You sound just like the psychologist you are," he said. "But I'm not your client. I'm ready to return to the present."

She made a final attempt to hold onto the past just a moment longer. "Really, Daddy, why?"

"Never mind. Shmulik loved his cars. He really did."

"I knew. I knew that. I always waited for him by the bridge when he came home from yeshivah. Even when I was seventeen and eighteen years old."

"Why did you like the cars so much? Cars are not really a girl thing."

"I enjoyed counting them," Naomi replied, aware that her reply sounded strange. "Funny, huh?"

"You liked to count cars?" her father asked in surprise. "Why?"

"Because ..." She paused, stuck. "To tell the truth, I don't quite know."

They returned to the present.

When Naomi's mother returned from a shopping excursion a quarter of an hour later, she found the two of them chatting and laughing together. There was no sign of the journey to the past her husband and daughter had taken. The small, dusty car in her daughter's hand was the only witness, and it was a silent witness.

When Naomi left the house, she stopped at the bridge again. Tears filled her eyes as she fingered the railing. How fleeting was the past! Though her childhood had not been riddled with crises, her memories were bittersweet. She sensed that her father had burned many bridges in his past. She had struggled valiantly against them, with no success. Her childhood, though happy, had been different. There was something in her father's past that he never spoke about; she'd sensed as much throughout the years.

She was surprised to discover tears filling her eyes. *Where did they come from?* she wondered, smiling to herself. Even the sweetest childhood memories are accompanied by tears. One feels a wistful sort of sorrow for the days now gone forever. *Stop! Stop! Stop!* an inner voice begs. *Let me look back at the carefree, happy-go-lucky life I knew as a child, a life that slipped away without even saying good-bye.* When the memories came, she longed to hold fast to all the things she had once loved. To feel like a small, innocent child again, leaning against a strong, supportive parent. To stop the passage of time that turned her into the strong, supportive one and her parents into the weak ones.

Sitting on the bridge, her emotions were so strong, her feelings of distress over the days gone by so acute, that she felt a physical ache in her chest. She was afraid of the future. She couldn't bear to think of seeing her parents in need of her support.

A short beep, followed by a long one, and then two more short ones interrupted her thoughts. That was Shlomo's beep. Shaking herself out of her reverie, she rose slowly and, brushing an invisible speck of dust from her skirt, made her way over to the car.

"Hi," Shlomo Mandel said. He waited for her to settle in and shut the door. "What's up?"

"*Baruch Hashem*, everything's fine. Why do you ask?"

"What's that car you're holding?" he asked, starting the motor.

"It's nothing. Just a fragment of childhood."

"Mmm." His wife's response was typical. "Shall I go say hello to your parents?" he asked, slowing down.

"No, it's alright."

"What do you mean 'alright'?"

"My father went to learn and my mother's resting."

"Okay." He picked up speed again and they drove off.

"Shlomo, are you in a rush?" Naomi asked hesitantly after a few moments of silence.

"What?" he asked, stopping at a traffic light.

"I asked if you have time."

"Time for what?"

"To drive to Manhattan."

"No problem."

"Thanks."

"You need to take care of something there?"

"No … er, yes."

He was silent. He was an expert at silences, believing them to contain magical, healing powers. The scenery outside the car window remained more or less the same throughout the ride: exhaust fumes, buildings, cars. From afar, he could see the skyscrapers, especially the Chrysler Building, the Empire State Building and the Twin Towers.

Naomi did not see them. Her mind was on other things.

"Where exactly are we headed?" he asked her as they drew closer to the city.

"Take the Brooklyn Bridge, okay?"

"Okay; I was planning to — but where are we going?"

"To the bridge."

"Huh?" He kept his eyes on the road, but surprise and curiosity were evident in his voice.

"I want to get out of the car and walk on the bridge."

This time, he turned to look at her. "Walk on it?"

"Yes, don't worry." She chuckled, and something in her tired eyes lit up. "If I'll need a psychologist, she'll be right there — for free. I'm alright. It's a childhood fantasy I've always wanted to fulfill."

"A childhood fantasy? And you still long to fulfill it?"

"Yes. Humor me, will you?"

"Can one really stroll on the bridge?"

"Of course, but that's not really what I'm after."

"What are you after, then?"

"You won't believe it." A smile illuminated her eyes.

"*Nu*, tell me," he coaxed. "What are you going to do on the bridge?"

"Take a power walk," she replied with a smile.

"The bridge is 1,500 feet long," Shlomo noted. "Doesn't seem like the right length for a power walk to me."

She was silent.

"Honestly, what is it you want with this bridge?"

"Wait another moment and you'll see."

The Brooklyn Bridge, rising over the East River in a huge, impressive arc, grew in front of their eyes. Shlomo climbed it in silence, wondering what had gotten into his wife. The Brooklyn Bridge, he knew, was a major thoroughfare through which traffic poured into the heart of Manhattan. At the time of its construction, it was considered an amazing feat of technology and architecture, and it had retained its place of honor ever since it was opened to the public in 1883.

None of these thoughts crossed Naomi's mind. She simply stood on the bridge and counted cars.

IT WAS ONLY when Benjy Kahaneman turned four that his parents became consciously aware of a phenomenon that had been nagging at their subconscious ever since the boy had been two-and-a-half. Only then did they put their fears into words. Benjy was a bright child, very talented and generous, but his attention span was incredibly short. It often took him more than an hour to get dressed in the morning, because various people and things distracted him from the task at hand.

"Do you see?" Benjy's mother said, clasping her son's hand in her own. Her expression was one of open distress, even fear. "The child can take a toy in hand, and instead of playing with it — he'll start acting wild." She coughed lightly. It was obvious she was alarmed.

"I know I'm not making myself clear. The doctors we went to entirely dismissed our fears, since Benjy behaved completely normally in their offices."

Naomi looked at Benjy's parents with interest. The mother was well groomed and classy, and the child appeared to be lacking nothing. Both parents exhibited love and warmth toward their son. The father picked him up and seated him on his lap, radiating sympathy. Like his wife, he, too, seemed alarmed. He tried valiantly to keep his fingers from trembling by toying with his son's short *peyos*.

"So we did something very simple," Mrs. Kahaneman went on. "We videotaped him." She removed from her purse a small videocamera cassette and handed it to Naomi. "I imagine you have a camcorder in your clinic."

"I do," Naomi nodded, "but first, I want to ask you a few questions. Is that okay with you?"

"Of course," the father replied.

"Does Benjy have any behavioral disturbances?"

"No," the mother shrugged. "Nothing out of the ordinary, as far as I know."

"Besides," the father said, "he's a little child, isn't he? How can you tell at this age?"

"It is hard to tell," Naomi admitted, "but very unusual behavior can be spotted. Is there something you haven't told me about? Does he, for example, ask loads of questions on one particular topic, or repeat a few particular questions over and over again, despite having already received answers?"

Benjy's mother nodded. "Yes, that's very obvious. He can ask the same question dozens of times in one day."

"Even after he's received an answer?"

"Yes."

"And it's not a complicated question?"

"No, not at all."

Naomi explained herself. "Sometimes, a child asks over and over again: 'Where is Hashem?' or 'Where does the *neshamah* go when a person dies?' or 'Why does the moon grow smaller?' He may ask such a question over and over again because he hasn't properly understood the answer."

"No, he asks simple questions," Benjy's mother said. "He asks how old he is and how old his siblings are, sometimes ten times a day."

"Is Benjy your oldest child?"

"No, he has an older brother and two younger sisters."

"Alright." Naomi deliberated for a moment, then asked for the videocassette.

"I think it would be best," she said quietly, "for Benjy not to be present while I watch it."

The father rose immediately, hoisting Benjy up in his arms. "C'mon son," he said, his voice warm. "Want me to buy you something good to eat?"

Naomi waited for him to close the door behind him before pressing "play." Her eyes squinted in concentration. The child seemed to be having an attack of some sort. Naomi threw a glance at the mother, who sat trembling in her seat, biting her lip. From time to time, she covered her eyes, trying to escape from the scene being played out on the screen.

Benjy writhed about, clenching his muscles and then relaxing. It seemed as though something unseen was pushing him to behave in this incomprehensible manner. In the video, the mother was trying to cajole him to stop, to relax, to put down the toy he was holding. The child seemed spaced out and inattentive, and he resisted his mother's attempts to stop him from what he was doing.

When the video ended, the mother's eyes filled with tears. "We thought he was autistic," she whispered, her voice broken. "He cuts himself off from us, stares into space and refuses to talk or communicate during these episodes."

"But he does talk and communicate most of the time," Naomi said encouragingly, "doesn't he?"

"Yes, but ..." the mother shattered completely, dissolving in tears. "We can't help him. Sometimes he cries and pleads with me to soothe him, and I'm so helpless. I ... I don't have the faintest idea what he wants. My child is locked up, withdrawn, suffering – and I can't help him. He's so miserable when he has these attacks. I know he feels very alone."

"Mrs. Kahaneman." Naomi's voice was soft.

"Please," she said, wiping her tears, "call me Yael."

"Yael, it's very clear," Naomi spoke soothingly, her voice filled with confidence, "that your son is not autistic."

"Well, then, what is he?" She was openly disbelieving. Perhaps she was afraid of the disappointment that would surely follow her initial spurt of joy, or maybe fear of the unknown was even worse than the certain knowledge of a specific problem.

Naomi smiled. "Most people are familiar with a few types of conditions, and they automatically try to connect unusual behavior of any sort to one of these conditions. It takes years of study to be able to draw the connection between certain sets of behavior and the conditions they signify."

"I need to calm down," Yael said, her pale lips curving into a slight smile. "'Soothe me,' as Benjy says."

"No problem. Call your husband in."

Mr. Kahaneman entered, somber and frightened. Like his wife, he was afraid of a diagnosis of autism, and if not that, of some other unknown condition.

"Your son has Obsessive Compulsive Disorder," she said simply. "Are you familiar with the term?"

They nodded slowly — the mother emphatically, the father hesitantly.

"OCD is when you wash your hands a hundred times a day, or

something like that, no?" Mrs. Kahaneman asked.

Naomi smiled pleasantly. "That's one type of obsession. The condition causes a person to engage in involuntary, uncontrollable actions dozens of times a day, and it's impossible for other people to stop him. Some people have an obsession with cleanliness: They wash their hands all day and spend hours cleaning imaginary dirt. Religious people suffering from this disorder sometimes daven Shacharis eight or ten times a day, certain their prayers 'didn't count' because they didn't have enough *kavanah*. Such behavior doesn't stem from *yiras Shamayim*. It's a disorder.

"Children with OCD often play with the same toy for hours on end or ask the same question over and over again. There are many types of obsessions, and the common denominator between them all is that it is impossible to put an end to them."

"That is," she added quickly, at the sight of their pale faces, "it used to be impossible. Up until the early 1980s."

Naomi believed in furnishing parents with detailed medical explanations. Medical conditions generally sounded less threatening against the background of a thorough explanation.

"Until the '80s, obsessions were considered rare disorders, psychological in nature. By 'psychological,' I mean that the source of OCD was believed to be in the mind rather than in the brain, and therefore not receptive to treatment."

Mr. Kahaneman's brow furrowed in concentration. His wife looked at Naomi questioningly.

"During this decade, however, research proved three of the medical world's previous assumptions wrong. First, the condition is not rare at all — it's rather common. One out of every fifty people suffers from an obsession of some sort."

Naomi saw the Kahanemans' faces relax as relief crept into their eyes. Somehow, the fact that so many other people suffered from a particular disorder made it less terrifying.

"Second, the source of the disorder is not psychological; researchers have found a link between OCD and levels of a neurotransmitter called serotonin in the brain. Third and most important, the disorder is treatable, both through medication and behavioral therapy." She paused for a moment, and they both used the opportunity to ask questions.

"Will he get better?" That was Yael.

"What is behavioral therapy?" her husband asked.

"Yes, Mrs. Kahaneman," Naomi replied. "With Hashem's help, Benjy will get better. Much, much better. With proper treatment, his disorder will be unnoticeable.

"Behavioral therapy is treatment in which the patient is gradually exposed to his greatest fear. For example, therapists will place the hands of a person suffering from a cleanliness obsession into a bowl of mud for an extended period of time. The patient will see that nothing happens to him. The amount of time the patient's hands remain dirty is gradually extended, until he completely rids himself of his terrible fear of dirt.

"When treating a child who is obsessive, like your Benjy, I allow him to play with whatever toy he likes, but I control the game. I do not allow him to grow wild and uncontrollable.

"Medication will solve the other problems. As a psychologist, I don't have the authority to prescribe medication. Judith Rappaport is a psychiatrist who's been treating such conditions since the '70s. She's the best in the country in the field of OCD. She can prescribe medication that will achieve the proper balance of serotonin in the brain."

"Medication? From a psychiatrist?" Yael sounded suspicious.

"Yes. The medication will level out the brain disorder. The brain is a marvelous thing. We're going to have Benjy's brain scanned before and after treatment. At the end of his treatment, you will see the difference in his behavior. And even though we haven't touched his brain, you will be able to see an actual physical difference in the scan."

The Kahanemans were silent, digesting the information.

"Benjy is a perfectly normal child," Naomi said softly. "He has a small problem with serotonin; that's all. After treatment, you won't recognize him. All the symptoms related to the disorder will disappear."

"But he's just a child!"

"The disorder surfaces in children, too — even in two-year-olds."

"And is it dangerous? The medication, I mean."

"No," Naomi said emphatically. "You'll see it isn't. Make an appointment with a psychiatrist and another one with me. We'll work together. Don't worry; everything will be just fine."

"Do you really think so?"

"I'm sure of it," Naomi said, nodding. "*Be'ezras Hashem.*"

"And Benjy will cooperate with you?"

"G-d willing. Most children cooperate."

"And he'll be able to concentrate? He'll be back to his old self?"

"He'll be back to his old self." Naomi stroked the little boy's head. Benjy, bored while his parents spoke to a lady he didn't know, had been playing with a newspaper he'd found, tearing it into small pieces and fashioning paper boats.

"Do you insist on worrying?" Naomi asked the parents, with a smile. "Look what a creative child *Hakadosh Baruch Hu* has given you. You ought to thank Him for this wonderful gift."

"Thank you," the Kahanemans said, rising. They still seemed overwhelmed and more than a little confused, but Naomi was not concerned. She knew they'd internalize what they'd heard from her and calm down.

"Are there any patients that medication is not effective for?" Yael asked.

Naomi pursed her lips. She nodded quickly, trying to downplay this small but significant piece of information. "There are such cases," she replied, "but only a small percentage."

Naomi paused for a moment, then plunged ahead. "Do either of you exhibit any signs of obsession?"

They both shrugged their shoulders. "No," they replied simultaneously.

"Ah." Naomi sat down in her chair again and made a notation in her notebook.

"Why do you ask?"

"OCD is usually hereditary," she said, hoping they wouldn't ask the obvious question: Would Benjy pass the disorder on to his children? It was likely that indeed he would.

They did not ask. They were too preoccupied to think of such questions.

"We'll let you know which psychiatrist we consult," Mr. Kahaneman said. "Thank you."

"Thank you very much," Yael echoed. Benjy merely waved his hand and said "'Bye," with a shy smile. Naomi handed him a candy. "Take it," she said. "You're a terrific kid."

"Aww," he said, waving his hand dismissively. His eyes sparkled with mischief. "That's silly."

2

Rome, May 1945

The war was over!

It was undoubtedly a day that would be recorded in the annals of world history. For six years the world had waited with bated breath for the day the Nazis would abandon arms and surrender. For six years the world had hoped and prayed for the war to end. Men, women and children had been slain in this cursed war, the worst in the history of humankind. Six years is not a long time in the eyes of history — the world has known many wars that have lasted far longer — but the scale of destruction and loss in this one was colossal. For six years, the world had longed for and prayed and waited for this day. Six years, six long years ...

That day was here!

Off in the Far East, battles were still being fought, but events clearly signified that there, too, the war was finally coming to an end. Looking down on the streets of Rome from the window of his hotel, Lt. Marty Katz pondered the vicissitudes of war. The breeze ruffled his hair, trying in vain to instill in him a sense of lighthearted joy. He was sad and gloomy, beset by feelings of responsibility, pain and loss.

He was still dressed in his camouflage uniform, his rifle slung over his shoulder. His backpack lay at his feet. He looked like a typical soldier returning from war.

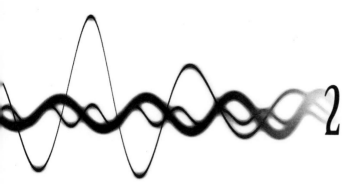

How the world had suffered from the war. Tens of millions of people had been killed or murdered as it ran its course. Tens of millions had been hurt, physically or emotionally. And what about the Jews? What had become of the Jewish race? What was left of it now that the war was over?

His eyes remained dry. True, everyone had longed for the war to end. True, the past six years had been difficult for the world at large ... but the world at large had had something to look forward to at war's end. For the Jews, it was too late.

Lt. Marty Katz, a loyal soldier of His Majesty's royal infantry, had returned from Bergen-Belsen a few days earlier. He had left the death camp reeling with anguish and suffused with tears. He had been there with his comrades in arms to liberate the infamous camp, but it had been all too obvious that for thousands of Jews, their arrival had come too late.

Memories, memories. They gave him no rest.

Marty smiled forlornly. Was it only the war memories that were troubling him? He was honest enough to admit that was not the case.

Home ...

His father's eyes had glowed with a special fire; the very air in his house had been saturated with sanctity. His home, built upon lofty principles and exalted ambitions, had glowed with holiness and purity. His home had epitomized untarnished faith in the Creator of the World. His home had radiated goodness and truth. The members of his family strove to attain ever-higher levels of spirituality; they had prayed to grow in Torah and service of Hashem. His home had been staunchly chassidic. The Rebbe's spirit had hovered between the four walls, guiding them in everything they did.

Papa. Mama. Yaakov and Dovid, Naomi and Hershel, Shaindel and Feigeh, Shimaleh and Toby ...

Gone — all of them. So good and pure, so precious and dear. Where are they all today? Where were my parents taken? Where are my brothers and sisters? Why have they perished while I've survived?

Why am I the sole survivor of my wonderful family? Why? Why me?

I'm not even called by my Jewish name anymore. I've crudely and brutally ripped my past out of my life, flung away Torah and mitzvos. I'm the rebel, the freethinker, the son who ran away from home and reached the shores of Palestine shortly before the outbreak of war. They were so righteous, so good — but they didn't survive. Since it was decreed that one member of our family survive, shouldn't it have been a worthier person than I? A holier one? One with loftier values? Someone to bear the family's name with pride and bring nachas to the neshamos on High? Someone who would perpetuate our family's legacy? Who would observe Torah and mitzvos with fiery zeal, like Papa used to, or pray with pure, hot tears the way Mama did? Someone whose children would study Torah with love and awe in the manner of my brothers, whose daughters would be modest and G-d-fearing like my sisters?

I'm the only one left.

He slammed the window shut angrily. It was 16:56. The train to Berlin left at 18:00, and he was counting the minutes. An hour and four minutes to go, according to the most accurate watch in the world. It was the watch of a soldier, for whom a delay of one split second could spell death.

I'm the only one left.

The hotel seemed surreal to him. Life outside the army did not exist for him; it had no meaning.

He had yearned to find someone from his family who had survived the nightmarish horror of the past six years, but there was no one. Misery seemed to seep from the walls of his room; he was enveloped by an almost tangible loneliness. The oppressive silence hurt his ears, so accustomed was he to the clamor of war — whistling rifle fire, exploding shells, booming cannons, roaring airplanes.

Though he had spent the past few years on the battlefield, Marty could not forget his past. Most of the time, his thoughts focused not on the war and its consequences, but on his family.

I thought I'd forgotten you. But he hadn't.

Slowly, Marty heaved his knapsack over his shoulder. He withdrew the bullets from his Enfield rifle and counted them slowly, over and over again. He reloaded the gun, locked the safety mechanism and went out onto the street.

He couldn't remain in the hotel any longer. His thoughts threatened to drive him insane. He preferred to wander aimlessly through the streets of Rome rather than allow his melancholy thoughts to overwhelm him completely.

In the streets of Rome, the signs of war were evident everywhere. Marty knew the war had achieved nothing. Europe was in shambles; the defeated soldiers of the Third Reich had nothing to show for their efforts.

At 17:30 he was already waiting in the train station. His eyes raked the area in all directions. He laughed scornfully at himself. He was acting as though he was still on the battlefield, keeping an eye out for ambushes, watching his back, checking and double checking.

The war was to have been just a brief respite before he'd decide what precisely he wanted to do with his life. After all, he'd already made the decision to leave everything behind and go to Eretz Yisrael before the winds of war had begun blowing. He'd been standing on the soil of that Land when the war started, and he'd volunteered to go to the front.

For six years he'd battled the Nazi beast until it collapsed, spent, at the feet of the Allied armies. Churchill, his prime minister, had fought the war with dogged persistence and accepted nothing less than unconditional victory.

Now he was unsure if he ought to return to Eretz Yisrael. The war had changed his perspective on life. His youthful zeal to subdue the Land and establish a Jewish State had waned considerably. He felt like a tired old man with a mature and wise outlook on life.

If only he hadn't abandoned his family during their difficult moments. ...

If you hadn't left, you'd most likely have joined them on one of the cattle cars to Auschwitz. There's no reason to think you would have survived this horrific war when they didn't. But I left them. I wasn't there when they needed me. How do you know they needed you? How would you have been able to help them?

Stop! Enough!

He shook his head wearily. Right now, his goal was to avenge their blood.

The train roared into the station, and Marty boarded it with eyes still misty with tears. He would take vengeance for them. That was the only way he could ever feel he had fulfilled the mission imposed on him by being the only surviving member of his family.

I'm the only one left. ...

There, in Bergen-Belsen, he had thought he was the only living Jew in all of Europe. In Bergen-Belsen ...

His memories carried him back to that day.

THEY'D BURST INTO the camp on April 15th.

The sky was a pale blue, free of clouds but full of smoke. The camp teemed with soldiers, both American and British, most of whom seemed to have nothing of pressing importance to do. Here and there, a soldier or two was helping the Joint and UNRRA representatives with their work: speaking encouragingly to the inmates, distributing food, spraying DDT, sending people to the hospital, sorting and organizing, counting people and sending lists of survivors to the Joint headquarters.

Marty was among those wandering aimlessly about. He was completely shattered by the sights that met his horrified eyes: walking skeletons, seriously injured people, piles of corpses. Even when he closed his eyes at night, he couldn't shake the horrific images from his mind. The war might be over, but he was still living it.

During the daytime, he sat on an empty TNT crate, eyes dull with despair, fingers tracing the words "*U'vehar Tzion tihiyeh hapleitah*" over and over again on the crate. When his buddies passed by, they clapped a hand on his shoulder and made attempts at humor, but he remained silent.

At night he slept fitfully, dreaming and waking, dreaming and weeping. Silent days; tortured nights.

His fellow soldiers, too, were shocked and deeply pained by what they saw. They also were somber and reticent, but they weren't as broken as he was. They would return home and forget about what they had seen or push the memories to the back of their minds and get on with their lives. But he could not stop weeping over the destruction of his people.

There was another Jewish soldier in his regiment who dealt with his pain and anguish by doing his utmost to help the representatives of the Joint. Throwing himself into a torrent of activity eased the ache in his soul. Marty found he was incapable of doing that.

One day, someone placed an emaciated hand on his shoulder. "Are you Marty Katz?"

Marty jumped, startled out of his meditation.

"That's me," he said to the former inmate. Though the man was no longer dressed in the striped prison garb the inmates wore under Nazi rule, the lifeless look in his eyes confirmed that he had been a prisoner at Bergen-Belsen. His body was frail; his eyes were dull, yet somehow fiery at the same time. It was the look in the survivors' eyes that horrified Marty most. "Why?"

"Your commander is looking for you."

"How did you know who I was?" Marty asked. It was the first complete sentence he'd uttered since his arrival in the camp. His buddies had already despaired of getting him to talk.

"They told me you were Jewish," the man said simply. He turned to go.

"Hey!" Marty called after him. "And so?"

The man turned around. Marty sensed his surprise and explained himself. "I mean ... I don't look Jewish."

"Oh, that." The former prisoner chuckled, a sound devoid of

joy. "You have Jewish eyes." He turned to leave again.

Marty caught up with him in a few strides. "What is it you see in my eyes?" he asked.

"I've seen a lot with my own eyes," the man said earnestly. "At this point, I can see things in other people's eyes."

Marty hesitated for a moment. There was something about the tall, emaciated man that entranced him. "Tell me, what's your name?"

"Shmuel," he said, extending his hand. "Shmuel Segal."

"This is kind of superfluous, since you already know my name," Marty said, extending his hand, "but allow me to introduce myself, anyway. Marty Katz."

"Katz? So we're a *kohen* and a *levi*." A smile spread over Shmuel Segal's face. "I hope we'll merit working together in the *Beis Hamikdash*."

Marty nodded.

"It's a blessing," Shmuel said gently. "Say amen."

Marty said amen. He went to headquarters, where his commander spoke to him about everything and nothing, about the past and the future. He took Marty to task for his lack of motivation and his failure to obey orders. He did his best to flush away infinite sorrow in a torrent of insignificant words.

He did not succeed.

New York 5751/1991

Naomi stood near the open faucet, rinsing carrots and cutting off their greenish heads with the deliberate precision born of deep thought. One small, scrawny carrot was still unpeeled. She gripped the peeler and swiped it forcefully down the length of the carrot. It wouldn't peel easily and she struggled with it for a longer time than she had with the nice, firm carrots, those that had radiated freshness and youth. For some inexplicable reason, she was drawn to the child who had aged before its time.

Why have you labeled this carrot a child?

Well, it's obviously smaller and skinnier than the others. It's different.

She finished peeling it, then sliced off its head and rinsed it.

From there she moved on to the scallions. Scallions added so much flavor to a potato salad.

She stirred the dressing for the salad with what seemed to be great satisfaction, but in truth, something was disturbing her. A cousins' get-together was being held that night and she'd have to go alone, without a sister or sister-in-law. Naomi grimaced at the thought, as if she couldn't abide such get-togethers. In fact, she enjoyed them greatly, but the last few days had been so full, so charged with memories from the past, that she had little patience for frivolity and merriment.

The idea for a cousins' get-together had arisen spontaneously. The cousins she'd be meeting that night were from her mother's side, not her father's. She had no family from her father's side; his siblings had all perished in the Holocaust. Her father had been spared the Holocaust; he had left Poland just before the war.

Had he fought the Germans? Naomi had no idea. Her father had never spoken to her about his past. Now, cubing the cooked potatoes for the salad she was preparing for the party, she wondered why that was. Strange! True, her father was introverted by nature, but wasn't it odd that he had never said a thing to his only son or only daughter? Never unburdened himself of the memories he bore in his heart?

It had never before occurred to her to analyze that fact. The thought had come to her unexpectedly while preparing the salad. Abba. He was such a special, wonderful person. Though very reserved by nature, he was, Naomi knew, deeply emotional. *What was your youth like, Abba? What experiences did you live through?*

Her mother's family lived in the States. Her mother had been born in America; she had lived through the war years in safety. Despite the difficulties involved in maintaining a religious lifestyle in America in those days, all her aunts and uncles were observant.

Of course, *siyatta diShmaya* played a large role in that, but Naomi knew her grandparents deserved much credit, too. They were strong, happy people — they had worked on themselves to become that way — and it was these two traits that had helped them and their children remain steadfast in their faith. Their strength of character helped them remain firm in the face of the difficulties involved in Torah and mitzvah observance during that period in the United States. And their joy enabled them to rise above feelings of self-pity that they, poor things, were obligated to observe Shabbos despite the fact that it meant missing out on so much. Their children never heard a word of complaint about the financial hardship the family endured because of their religious practices.

The phone rang shrilly. Startled out of her reverie, Naomi went to answer it. Her mother was on the line.

"Naomi?"

"Hi, Ima."

"How are you?" Ima sounded worried.

"Fine, *baruch Hashem*. Are you ready to leave?"

"To the party?"

"Yes," Naomi said, surprised that her mother was asking.

"No, I'm not."

Naomi knew that something was up. Her mother loved parties and get-togethers; she often initiated them. She was a very social, bubbly woman who thoroughly enjoyed meeting and chatting with others. What could have happened?

"Why not? What's wrong?"

"It's Abba."

"What's the matter?" Naomi's heart sank.

"He's not feeling well."

Naomi visualized the most recent test results her father had sent her as soon as he'd received them. They hadn't been very encouraging. His sugar was high; his cholesterol was high; his blood pressure was high. And Abba was so young!

"Something is making him very tense," the doctor had told her mother. Naomi couldn't do anything to help him, though, if she had no idea what it was. If it was the war, why had he suddenly become so sad and withdrawn only now, years later? If only she could do something.

Perhaps it was the situation in Israel that was causing him distress? But Ima had told her he was spending a lot of time looking at the few photographs he'd brought with him from Poland. He'd look at the photos and sigh deeply. No, his melancholy had something to do with the war he'd lived through, not the Iraqi threat in the Middle East.

Naomi added some salt to the salad and tossed it again. There, it was done. She transferred the salad from the mixing bowl to a plastic container and snapped the lid on, ready to begin preparing another salad.

Naomi sighed. Sometimes she was so overwhelmed with work that she only managed to get three or four hours of sleep at night, but things had been somewhat calmer at work of late. She had cut down her hours in order to be able to help her father and try to get to the bottom of what was causing his frequent headaches. She'd asked him endless questions but hadn't come to any conclusions. He'd been to numerous doctors, none of whom had found anything wrong with him other than slightly elevated blood pressure and considerably elevated levels of sugar and cholesterol.

"Nothing out of the ordinary happened," her mother said, bringing her back to the present. "You know, the situation."

"Of course I know." She thought about the situation in Eretz Yisrael. The ultimatum the United States had given Saddam Hussein, the crazed Iraqi dictator, had almost expired. Eretz Yisrael was in serious danger, and Jews in America were storming *Shamayim* with their prayers.

"Is there any news?"

"No, no news."

Naomi threw a quick glance at the newspaper on her kitchen table. It was filled with warnings and threats. The situation was far from simple. Shmulik, her only brother, the apple of their eye, was there in the thick of it. He lived in Eretz Yisrael and refused to jump ship while his country was in danger. He was keeping everyone's spirits up with his infectious optimism.

"Naomi?" Her mother sounded worried.

"Yes?"

"What do you think it is?"

"How could I know? Maybe he's worried about Shmulik."

"Maybe," Ima murmured.

"You told me he was looking at old photos a lot."

"Yes," her mother said after a brief silence. "At first I thought it had nothing at all to do with that war, but I don't know any more." She sighed deeply, concerned about the situation, worried about her husband and praying for the safety of her son and his family. "I still think they ought to come here, if only for Abba's sake. Alright, Naomi, take care. ... Enjoy yourself."

"It's a shame you won't be there, Ima. Maybe I should come by and pick you up?"

"Absolutely not!" her mother said emphatically. "Go and have a good time."

"Ima …"

"There's nothing to talk about, Naomi, 'bye."

Naomi looked out the window. Her taxi was waiting. She hurried out of the house. Placing her packages carefully in the trunk, she made a decision: Before going to Shaindy's, she'd stop off at her parents' house and check on her father. A glance at her watch as she settled herself in the cab, however, told her she was running late. She'd go to Abba after the party.

3

"I'm going to read answers aloud," Shaindy announced ceremoniously. "If you have the question, raise your hand. Whoever answers first, scores a point for her team."

"And what happens at the end?"

"Wait and see."

"What type of questions?" the cousins asked curiously.

"Boy, you're worse than my students," Shaindy said with a mock groan. "They sit quietly and listen until the end. If you must know now, though, the questions are on all kinds of topics, from general knowledge to facts about the family."

Naomi listened absentmindedly. Finding questions to fit the answers. First came the answers, then the questions. First came the strange behavior, and only then the question: What's making this child, this person act that way?

Take Abba, whose behavior was somewhat peculiar of late, and Benjy, the pint-sized patient she couldn't stop thinking about. Naomi had a tendency to submerge herself in every case she accepted. It would take time until Benjy became a little boy like others his age. The psychiatrist had to make an evaluation, then Benjy had to begin therapy with her, and then they would have to wait a while and see whether the therapy was indeed effective.

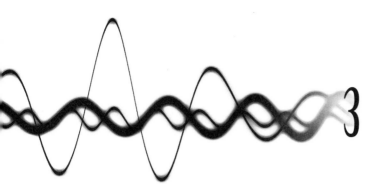

Naomi had purposely refrained from telling the parents that, years ago, people with obsessions were operated on. Brain surgery eliminated one problem, but often new problems cropped up afterward. People whose lives were miserable as a result of their obsessions had been willing to take the risk. Nowadays, thank G-d, that method was obsolete; today, OCD was treated with medication.

Naomi thought about Benjy Kahaneman. He was such a sweet, intelligent child. He was perfect, wasn't he? What was he lacking? Almost nothing. It was astonishing that such a tiny defect could be so significant, could affect so seriously his ability to function. How grateful we must be for every little thing, for every tiny part of the brain that functions properly and allows us to live normal lives!

Naomi knew many people whose lives had become unbearable as a result of obsessive behavior disorders. They would wash their hands dozens of times a day, pick up the tiniest crumbs from the floor, worry all day because they might have forgotten something or have failed to lock the door or have hurt someone, or have done some damage along the way. She hoped and prayed that Benjy would not join the short but real list of people who had not been helped by behavioral therapy.

Questions ... answers ... gnawing doubt.

She heard her cousin's questions — or, to be more precise, the answers and then the questions — through the haze of her preoccupation.

"Uncle Aharon to Avreimy," Shaindy announced.

"Oh, I know!" one of her cousins said enthusiastically, jumping up from her place. "I have the question: 'Who said to whom: You need to be small in age, not in the way you act?' Uncle Aharon said that to Avreimy"!

"Very good," Shaindy confirmed. It seemed a strange sentence, but it made perfect sense to those who were familiar with the expression and its background. Everyone chuckled as they recalled the event that had prompted the remark.

"Seventy C.E." Shaindy called.

"In what year was the *churban* of the Second *Beis Hamikdash*?" someone responded immediately.

In middle of the game, the phone rang. Shaindy, the hostess of the party and the game leader, went to answer it.

"I told her to take the phone off the hook," said Leah, one of the cousins.

"Naomi," Shaindy called, "it's for you."

Naomi rose somewhat heavily. Who could be calling her here? Maybe it was Mrs. Weiss, the neighbor who was babysitting two-year-old Yanky. She hoped so. She was thinking of her father, though. She walked slowly over to the telephone.

"Naomi'leh," she heard her mother say with overtones of alarm, "Abba's asking for you. He wants you to come over."

"What?" Naomi was taken aback. Her father had never before made a request like that. Something must be seriously wrong. Her father always ridiculed both the doctors' exaggerated interest in his condition and her concern — "obsessive concern," he called it — for his health.

"Abba apologizes for disturbing you, but he really wants you to come over after the party. He also said ..." She fell silent.

"What did he say?" Naomi pressed. "Ima, what else did he say?"

"That now is not a time for parties," her mother said, sounding flustered.

"Did something happen?"

"To him, or in general?"

"Either one."

"Well, in general he's upset because of the war. He says that the evening before the ultimatum expires is not an appropriate time for partying. He's very, very tense, and his blood pressure's very high."

Was Abba's concern unusual? No. He was afraid for his son; that was perfectly logical. Still, she sensed that something else was bothering him as well. Something she didn't know about and likely would never know about. He didn't tell her as much, but whenever he discussed "the situation" — and he often did — though he spoke about Shmulik and what was liable, G-d forbid, to happen in the

Middle East, she always saw the spark of an additional fear in his eyes. She had no idea what that fear might be.

"Are you worried about Shmulik?"

That was Naomi's first question when she arrived at her parents' house after the party.

Her father's head snapped up. There was a pained look in his eyes.

Naomi regretted having asked the question, though it seemed to her the most logical one to ask under the circumstances. War was about to break out in the Middle East, perhaps tomorrow, and his son in Eretz Yisrael was in the thick of it. Wasn't it perfectly natural for her father to be concerned that the Iraqi dictator might make good on his threat?

But he was pained, and it was she who had caused it. She had hurt him without knowing why or how. What was troubling him? He continued looking at her in silence. The stillness in the house was terrifying.

Her father had borne a lot in life, but he had always retained his cheerful disposition and been satisfied with his lot. Contentment had seeped from the very walls of the house. This was the first time she ever saw the father she knew and loved radiating deep sorrow.

Abba had always been somewhat fragile and weak because of the traumas he had experienced in his youth. It had always been necessary to protect him from unpleasant information, to trivialize problems, to minimize difficulties. Ima often said that Abba had endured terrible things in his life and that they had to try to make things easy for him as much as possible.

But he was a happy person! Definitely a happy person. Yes, she had sometimes seen a shadow pass fleetingly over his face, and she recalled a few occasions when his eyes had held a look of deep sadness for a moment or two. Now, however, he exuded sorrow, and Naomi couldn't fathom why.

"Yidden are in danger," she murmured, hoping to elicit a reaction. She knew her father had not personally endured the horrors of the most terrible of wars. Aside from a few black-and-white photographs he held dear, there was nothing in their home even remotely connected to the Holocaust. Her mother was American-born and -bred, and her father had escaped from Poland before the war. Nevertheless, his parents and all his family had remained in the Valley of Death. They had perished along with the rest of European Jewry.

Her father had not suffered physically during the war. He spoke about his parents and siblings the way someone who has lost his entire family in a horrific car accident might speak. He never mentioned Europe or what had happened there. Still, she knew that what she had just said would elicit a reaction, for he knew, more than many other people, the meaning of the words "Yidden are in danger." He had seen the refugees. He had tasted the fear of death, or so Naomi assumed, when he'd escaped from Poland. He had inhaled the atmosphere of war, had felt the ground burning beneath his feet. He had lost his parents in the war.

Once she had questioned him about the photographs, inquiring whether the people in the pictures were his parents, a brother, an uncle or a grandmother. He had answered all her questions with a short "no." His lips had been tight, and she hadn't asked again.

"Which ones?"

His voice cut through the silence, interrupting Naomi's thoughts. He sounded hesitant and weary.

"What?" The long silence had confused her and distracted her from what she'd said a few moments earlier.

"Which Yidden are in danger?" her father asked.

"The ones in Eretz Yisrael," she replied, puzzled. She sensed she was walking on unsure ground.

Her father sighed heartrendingly. "Eretz Yisrael is in danger."

"Eretz Yisrael?" she probed carefully. Could a piece of land be in danger? Yidden might be endangered if Eretz Yisrael were to shrink in size — but the land itself?

"Eretz Yisrael, daughter. Eretz Yisrael." He placed his head in his hands again, and she fell silent. Something peculiar was going on, though she hadn't an inkling what it was. For the next five minutes her father sat motionless, and Naomi thought he'd fallen asleep. Then he stirred suddenly.

"Come. I want to show you something."

Naomi followed him, burning with curiosity. Her father opened the drawer where "those" photographs were kept, but now he withdrew photographs she had never seen before. A desert, a beautiful desert. An oasis. Wild flowers, a large lake, birds, forests, groves. A variety of stunning scenery.

In one photograph, Naomi spotted a sign. She leaned closer to try and read what it said.

"Abba!" she called out in surprise. "It says something in Hebrew! This sign is in Hebrew! *Malon* ..."

"Yes," he said, interrupting her.

"But ... how can it be? Who wrote those Hebrew signs?"

"Only one very specific segment of the world population writes signs in Hebrew."

"Jews."

"That's right."

"Ah, I see. Many Jews wrote signs in Hebrew even though they lived outside of Eretz Yisrael."

"Yes," he said with a sad smile, "but this photograph was not taken outside of Eretz Yisrael."

"Wh-what do you mean?"

"This," he said, drawing a deep breath, "is Eretz Yisrael."

"Eretz Yisrael?" She was surprised for a moment, but then understanding dawned. Or so she thought. "Shmulik sent you these pictures?"

Her father chuckled sorrowfully. "No. I took the pictures."

"You? You were in Eretz Yisrael?" She was thunderstruck. "When were you in Eretz Yisrael? For how long? How come you never told me?"

Her father objected to the State of Israel with all his heart and soul. He refused to visit his only son there. He had never visited the Kosel, though he had been very moved when it was liberated from the Jordanians. Her father was opposed to the State of Israel, and now he was telling her that he had taken those lovely photographs?

"I was there," he said shortly, caressing the photographs lovingly. "I was there ... and how I was there."

"But why aren't you in any of the pictures? When was this? How did you come to have a camera?"

"I was a photography buff," her father replied, answering her last question first. "A camera was very expensive in those days, but I felt I had to have one in order to snap pictures."

"Pictures of what?"

"What do you mean? Of Eretz Yisrael! I was there. I inhaled the pure air; I discovered the wonders of creation *Hakadosh Baruch Hu* placed in this special land. I felt I simply had to freeze those moments and preserve them for the future."

His lips twisted into a bitter smile. "It didn't dawn on me then that my children would not see these things for themselves. I was sure, then, that you would lift your gaze to the Jerusalem mountains every day, that you'd breathe the mountain air and see the lovely stone houses with your own eyes. I never thought things would turn out the way they did."

Naomi held her breath as her father spoke. When he fell silent, she waited a moment or two for him to go on. When she saw he had no intention of doing so, she broke the silence.

"But Abba, you always say that ..."

"That what?" A sheepish smile played on his lips. "I know what you're about to say. That I always say I'm opposed to Israel. Yes, but not because I don't love it and not because I didn't want — no, long — to raise my children in its pure and holy atmosphere. But

Eretz Yisrael is far from me, daughter. Its sanctity could not abide my presence."

Naomi was stunned. Her father had never uttered anything of this sort before. He had never explained his opposition to the state, and she had always assumed it was the Zionist government he objected to. Now he had said something totally different.

"But Shmulik ... how come you?"

"I didn't want him to go because I didn't want to feel pressured to go there against my will," her father said candidly. "I didn't want my only son to live so far away from me. Eretz Yisrael can tolerate his presence, but not mine." His facial expression became resolute and Naomi knew he wouldn't say another word on the subject.

"And me?" she asked quietly. "Why don't you want me to travel to Eretz Yisrael?"

"I never said I didn't want you to go there," her father protested. "You never asked me!"

Naomi was taken aback. She had thought that the day's supply of surprises had come to an end, but now she saw that her father had opened a small window into his world and she was hearing many things she had never heard before.

"But ... I never dared ask you because I thought you were vehemently opposed. And I ... I didn't want to hurt you."

Her father smiled wanly. "I'm sorry, my dear," he said. "It never occurred to me. I thought you'd ask me if you wanted to go. I hadn't realized you honored your parents to such a degree. That's something I never merited."

Feeling uncomfortable, Naomi sought to change the subject. "Abba," she asked hesitantly. "Will you ... will you ever return to Eretz Yisrael?"

"Look." He ignored the question and withdrew the last photograph.

Her breath caught in her throat. A small rectangle, pale in color. The photograph, with its zigzag edges, was creased and torn at the corners.

But she was looking at the Kosel.

"Abba!" she cried, moved to the very core of her soul. "Abba, it's the Kosel! Where did you get this picture?"

Her father had been to the Kosel? And yet he'd said that Eretz Yisrael could not tolerate his presence!

"You've never been there," her father said with a smile. "How do you know that's the Kosel?"

"Oh Abba, come on ... it's the Kosel! Where did you get this picture? Did you take this one, too, when you toured the country?"

"It's a long story, darling." She was listening attentively, but his expression was distant. "Allow me not to tell it."

Disappointment struck forcefully at Naomi's heart.

"When will you tell me?" she pleaded. She felt like a little girl, but her eagerness overcame logic. As a psychologist, she could tell that her father was unprepared to open up to her.

"I don't know." He gently stroked the picture of the Kosel. "Maybe never."

"Abba, you were there," Naomi said quietly. "You were there, in Eretz Yisrael. ... How was it able to tolerate your presence then? If you were there — if it did tolerate your presence — why did you leave? When did you leave? What happened to change your outlook so radically? I see your concern for Eretz Yisrael, your love for it. What caused you to make up your mind never to return there?" Her eyes were fixed upon him expectantly, pleading.

"Naomi, Naomi," her father said levelly. "You're a psychologist, and you want to arouse my old dreams in order to understand the present through them." He smiled. "You know, you can learn a lot about a person and his desires from what he remembers from his past. But life is more complex than that, and these are not just the dreams of an old man."

"You're not so old," she protested, attempting to lessen the barrier that had sprung up between them.

"No, it was just a figure of speech." He smiled again and his eyes grew soft. "Naomi dear, let us decide that we're leaving the topic entitled 'Eretz Yisrael' aside for the time being, okay?" His voice was pleading, and Naomi felt uncomfortable.

"Okay," she said reluctantly.

Her father replaced the photographs in their leather case and returned the case to the drawer. He sighed deeply. "Those days are long gone."

"You've been very nostalgic lately." There was a hint of warning in her voice.

"Yes," he admitted. "I don't know why."

"Tell me something, Abba, please!" she pleaded. "I know you don't want to talk about it, but something ... at least one sentence!"

"Alright. I'll tell you one thing." Beads of perspiration glistened on his forehead. His breathing grew heavy. "I'll tell you one thing now and that's it. Please don't beg me for more, because I won't be able to handle it. One thing I will tell you: My heart is bound to Eretz Yisrael with more than one strand of love, more than one strand of self-sacrifice."

4

It was raining outside.

Naomi watched from the window as the fat droplets fell to the pavement, a feeling of pleasurable warmth spreading inside her. She hugged two-and-a-half-year-old Yanky and planted a kiss on each of his chubby cheeks.

"Wan' Ima," her little boy announced.

Naomi hugged him again. She was only mildly concerned about his rather limited vocabulary.

"Don't you want to go to Shuli?" she asked in surprise. Shuli was his most favorite playgroup teacher in the world. He ran to her joyfully every morning.

"No," the little boy said. "Wan' on'y Ima!" He encircled her neck with his plump arms, and waves of warmth and love engulfed her. She had almost decided to keep him home for the day when Shlomo walked in, tallis bag in hand.

"Hi there, son!"

Shlomo placed his tallis bag carefully in the closet and turned to his son. "How are you, little tyke?"

"Look," Naomi said resignedly. "What can I do with him? He doesn't want to go to playgroup."

"He's just playing pretend," Shlomo said, smiling at Yanky. "It's all a game, eh, Yanky? Why are you playing games with Ima? Come to playgroup!"

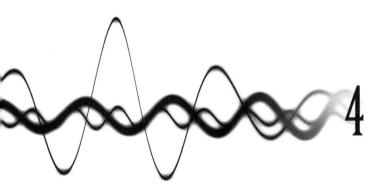

Yanky shook his head stubbornly. "Don' wan'!" he insisted. "Wan' on'y Ima!"

"You have too limited a vocabulary for a kid your age," Shlomo said. "Did you know that?" He placed the siddur he was holding on the table, crouched down, and lifted his son from the rug where he was standing. Bare feet, curls unkempt from a night's sleep, light-brown eyes reflecting all the innocence and sweetness in the world. His pajama sported little ducklings splashing in puddles of water.

Yanky writhed in protest in his father's strong and loving arms, but Shlomo did not allow him to wriggle free.

"'Bye, Ima," he said to Naomi. "Have you ever seen a sweeter child?"

"No," she said, laughing.

Shlomo smiled as he bounded upstairs to the second floor, his "battle cries" competing with her son's desperate wails of protest. A moment later, the wails stopped.

Naomi smiled. She was familiar with the stages: First came a moment of haughty silence as Yanky realized he'd been defeated, then full cooperation. Yanky could never resist his father's suggestions for fun games.

Sure enough, Yanky's tinkling laughter was soon echoing through the house, filling Naomi's heart with love.

Yanky went to playgroup. Despite his declarations that he would refuse to go in and refuse to play, the moment the door opened, he burst inside like a tightly-coiled spring set free. Yoni and Duddy greeted him happily, and he grew absorbed in building a tower with Lego.

"Big tower! 'Til da sky!" he promised his father.

"Really? Won't it get burned by the sun?" Shlomo asked with mock seriousness.

Yanky shook his head. "Fire burn," he said.

Shlomo understood what he meant to say – the sun doesn't burn; fire burns. He said good-bye to Yanky and left the building, shivering in the chilly morning air. The rain had stopped, but his entire body trembled. He was empty-handed; he had deposited his treasure with a stranger. His gait was alternately slow and quick. An onlooker might have wondered whether this particular pedestrian was completely sane.

But no one saw him. It was 9:30 a.m. on a blustery day. Most people were already at school or work; he was the only one in the street. The drivers of the few cars on the road did not go to the trouble of glancing at the pedestrian and the clip at which he was walking.

The streetlights glowed dimly. A light fog made for poor visibility, and Shlomo was glad for the relative darkness. His heart was aglow; his eyes shone. He trembled from the abundance of contradictory emotions he was experiencing. Fear and hope; longing and tension. Explosive happiness and clammy apprehension.

Arriving home, he warmed up the car and sounded his trademark honk. Naomi entered the car and they drove off.

The car stopped outside a large building. Shlomo and Naomi exited the car and quickly made their way through the large, imposing gate.

Shlomo prayed fervently, hoping and longing for good news. If only the heavens would be illuminated with blinding light, with warm rays of sunshine. If only the earth would absorb the tiny seedling. If only the rain would water it gently so that it would grow tall. If only the air would be saturated with dew drops. If only ...

Two rays of sun penetrated the cloudy sky.

Twin girls were born.

SHMULIK, NAOMI'S OLDER brother, lifted the receiver of the ringing telephone.

"Hello?" The voice on the other end of the line was weak and somewhat choked. Shmulik hoped that could be attributed to the caller's fatigue and a faulty international connection.

"Yes?" he replied, his voice trembling slightly.

"*Mazal tov*, Shmuel! *Baruch Hashem*!" The caller burst into tears, and Shmuel, gripping the receiver tightly, responded with a hearty "*Mazal tov*!" of his own.

"Abba! What's the *mazal tov*?" Shmulik's children wanted to know. Only Chani, the baby, continued sleeping peacefully.

"Give me the phone!" Shlomit, Shmulik's wife, exclaimed excitedly. "Give me the phone!"

"Twins! Twin girls!" His mother's voice sounded steadier now. She was a strong woman; Shmulik knew that.

"*Mazal tov*!" he cried again. "*Baruch Hashem*!"

The children were cavorting around the room, begging to be let in on the news. "Abba, what's the *mazal tov*? Tell us already!"

"Naomi had twin girls!" Shmulik announced.

Exclamations of joy and excitement filled the house.

"Abba, when are we going to America?" asked six-year-old Yossi, the eldest, pulling at his sleeve.

"Ima, we need to pack!" exclaimed five-year-old Racheli, ever the practical one.

"Are they yellow?" Yossi wanted to know.

"Why do you ask?" Racheli asked, mystified. "What difference does it make what color their hair is?"

"I'm not asking about their hair, silly," Yossi snickered. "Girls don't know anything!"

"Yes they do," Racheli said, pouting. "You don't know what you're talking about."

"You don't know that if they're yellow, they might have to postpone the *kiddush*," Yossi said smugly.

"The *kiddush*?" Shlomit's lips curved into a smile.

"Yes," Yossi said impatiently. "The *kiddush* for the baby."

"Why 'baby'?" asked Racheli. "Babies! There are two of them!"

"Whatever," Yossi said with annoyance. "Will they push off the *kiddush*?"

"A *kiddush* doesn't get postponed," his mother explained. "A *kiddush* is not like a bris."

"Why should they push it off?" Racheli asked. "Ima, why did Yossi think it might be postponed?"

"We're going to America?" asked Yanky, who had been playing with the phone wire until now.

"Of course," his siblings said encouragingly. "For sure we'll go!"

"Ima, how come they have twins already and we don't?" Yossi complained suddenly, forgetting the *kiddush* for the moment.

"You're not allowed to be jealous," Racheli told him self-righteously.

"Abba, right it could be that the *kiddush* will be postponed?" Yossi suddenly recalled that he hadn't quite settled the issue.

"Ima, when are we going?"

Shmulik raised his hand. "Quiet! Quiet! Quiet! I can't hear a thing!"

He listened attentively, a wide grin on his face. "Okay," he said after a moment. "I'll talk to her later."

He hung up the phone.

"Abba!" The chorus of voices started up again.

"Here's the scoop," Shmulik said, waving his arms dramatically. "Naomi gave birth to twin girls. They each weigh about four pounds."

His children stared at him, their eyes huge with curiosity and excitement, and he laughed.

"They're adorable, I'm sure. The *kiddush* will not be postponed even though they're both kind of small – 'preemies' is what we call it. They're in incubators in the hospital, but baby girls don't go to shul for their *kiddush* even if they're home and not in the hospital."

"See? I told you there was a chance they would postpone the *kiddush*!" Yossi interrupted.

Shmulik held up his hand. "No interruptions, please," he said. "As far as our trip to the United States, we'll try to get tickets for two days from now."

"It's a good thing it's Sunday today," Shlomit said. "There's plenty of time before the *kiddush*. I'd like to help Naomi."

"Naomi will most likely be in the hospital."

"Yay! Hurray!" The children shouted and whooped for joy. "We're going to America! We're going to Sabba, Savta, Naomi and Shlomo! We're going to Yanky! We're going to Sabba and Savta Katz!"

The Katz children had already been to the United States numerous times. Shmulik's father had invested in real estate as a young man and now enjoyed substantial returns on his investments. He longed to see his grandchildren from time to time, so he paid for tickets for the entire family. He would not set foot in Eretz Yisrael under any circumstances. He never explained why, but his beloved grandchildren accepted his "veto" of their country of residence as fact.

A few hours later, when the children's excitement had died down and they had dispersed to cheder, kindergarten and playgroup, Shmulik said quietly to his wife, "I'm off."

"Where to?" Shlomit asked sharply.

"The Kosel."

She froze. "The Kosel ..."

Two months after their marriage, Shmulik had gone to the Kosel for the first time in his life. He had torn *kriyah* and wept. Later, he told her he had experienced a sense of spiritual elevation like never before. When he told his father about the supremely moving experience, he received a wholly unexpected reaction.

"You were at the Kosel?" His father's voice had been casual, and he'd fallen into the trap.

"Yes, why?"

"You were at the Kosel!" His father's heart had begun pounding wildly, but Shmulik couldn't have known that.

"Yes." Shmulik suddenly sensed that something was up, and he injected a happy note into his voice. "The huge stones, and the doves ... I davened like never before." He paused, suddenly aware that the line had gone dead. The dial tone sounded angrily in his ears.

His mother had called back a few minutes later, apologizing profusely. "He grew overly excited. I found him staring at the receiver in his hand, pale as a ghost. I asked him who had called, and he finally told me five minutes later. What did you tell him?"

Shmulik had felt guilty. "Nothing, just that I'd been to the Kosel."

His mother reacted as expected. "How nice! Did you take any pictures? Can you send us pictures of yourself at the Kosel? Even a postcard with a picture of the Kosel would be nice. Describe to me exactly how it looks."

He'd answered her questions, but his heart had remained with his father. Something strange was happening. His father had "vetoed" the Kosel as well. What was going on there at home in America? It was an enigma.

The bus dropped him off near the Kosel. He walked alone, his head lowered as he communed with his thoughts. He'd been to the Kosel a few times since then, but each time he imagined an accusatory finger pointing at him from *Shamayim* for disregarding the commandment of *kibbud av*. Wasn't it bad enough that he lived in Eretz Yisrael against his father's wishes? His guilty conscience prevented him from achieving the same state of spiritual exaltedness he had experienced on his first visit.

But now he had to go. His sister had given birth to twin girls! He had to express his gratitude to Hashem for that. He had to thank Him for the past, pray for the present and plead for the future.

He rested his head upon the Wall and his eyes filled with tears. The stones seemed to disappear as the *Beis Hamikdash* rose majestically in front of his eyes. His heart throbbed with emotion. Sobs burst from his throat. Abba, Naomi, Shlomo, Yanky. Ima, Shlomit, their children. The faces of his nearest and dearest blurred together in his mind's eye and he felt a stab of pain and fear. Would they all be safe and happy a day from now? A week? A month? A year? Who knew what the future held in store?

He felt foolish. *Be happy! Say thank you! Dance with joy for the sweetness of the present!* He prayed with all his might for the future. Ambiguous splotches of color spun before his eyes, fading in and out. He tried to stabilize his eyes and mind and track the ever-changing shapes as they spun. Black — blue — gray. He closed his eyes, trying to concentrate on the image taking shape in his head.

It was a toy car. Small, blue and helpless. It was traveling on a huge bridge full of real cars and trucks, and it was small and fragile.

New York 5758/1998

SHE STOOD NEAR the road. She had no desire to count the cars; they afforded her no enjoyment at all. On the contrary, they scared and confused her. She was too frightened to move a limb. The busy road with cars speeding in both directions was overwhelmingly large, and she was so small. She wasn't even six years old yet.

No one noticed her. She was short and inconspicuous. It was no wonder that the busy drivers hadn't paid any attention to her. She didn't hear the noise of the cars whooshing by, but the sight of them was intimidating enough. A moment passed, then another, and another. When the middle number on her digital watch changed, telling her that she'd been standing there for ten whole minutes now, tears sprang to her green eyes.

What will be? she thought fearfully. *Will I ever cross this street? Will I ever reach home? Will anyone ever see me and help me cross? I can't cross on my own, and I can't ask for help either.* The tears in her eyes threatened to spill over onto her cheeks.

In her vivid imagination, Becky already saw her parents calling the police. She saw her mother sobbing into the phone, saw Abba frightened and worried, running through the streets in search of her.

But he wasn't calling her name.

She pictured her mother, weeping copiously, and Yanky, the best brother in the world, biting his lip to keep from crying. Yanky didn't cry easily, she knew, but his anguish was stamped clearly all over his face. She saw Sabba and Savta, faces pale and drawn, whispering *Tehillim*. She pictured her mother joining the police officers as they combed the city.

Weren't they suffering enough as it was?

She didn't want to add to their pain. The tears burst from her eyes and dripped quietly down her cheeks.

That was how a woman walking briskly down the street found her. When she saw the weeping little girl, she hurried over and stopped near the curb.

"Why are you crying?" she said. "Are you lost?"

The child did not reply. She wiped her eyes vigorously and looked up at her benefactor. Then, with a courageous tip of the chin, she pointed to the road.

"You want to cross the street?" The question was superfluous.

The woman took the little girl's hand, and the two crossed the street together.

"Why didn't you ask someone to cross you? You're a big girl already! There's no reason to be shy, sweetie. You look very mature to me."

The little girl smiled. Her lips mouthed the phrase "Thank you," but the words were inaudible.

Understanding suddenly dawned on the woman. She watched with misty eyes as the little girl disappeared into one of the buildings. Then she nodded slowly. It was simple, really. The sweet, shy little girl could not hear!

BECKY DID NOT attend preschool. No preschool wanted her. No preschool would have her. That was why she had to stay home. Maybe forever.

Her high forehead sported furrows not usually seen in a child her age. Smooth brown hair framed her refined-looking face. Her large green eyes, always questioning, were her most striking feature. Becky knew that people liked to describe her as a china doll. She didn't fully understand the expression, but the words *china* and *doll* seemed to her to signify fragility. *Am I fragile?* she often asked herself. *Or am I just a scaredy-cat?*

Becky did not always know how to respond to the questions

adults asked her. “How did you understand what I said?” was one question she was often at a loss to answer. “Why didn’t you say that it bothers you?” was another. Her own questions, though, were the toughest of all.

And now she had no preschool.

She lay in bed, dreaming, and gazed at the pretty picture she’d drawn a few days ago. It hung precisely above her bed, and she examined it carefully. Yes, it was definitely a lovely picture; its bright colors were so vivid. And yet, even though she drew such beautiful pictures — no one wanted her. No one was interested in having her join a preschool. Why?

She tossed and turned in bed but could not fall asleep. Mindy lay near her. She knew her sister was breathing ... but how was she breathing? Were her breaths short or long? Slow or fast? Shallow or deep? Becky had no idea. She had never heard her twin sister breathe.

No one in the world loved her. No one! Well, Abba and Ima did. And so did Yanky, the best and kindest brother in the world. But they, too, would have preferred that she had been born different.

She pounded her pillow, causing it to drop off her bed. Becky froze guiltily. If Mindy woke up ...

By the dim light of the nightlight, she saw Mindy shift in her sleep. Her eyes were still closed. *Baruch Hashem*!

Her face twisted with anger and pain. Everyone wanted her to be different. No one wanted her to be deaf. But she was deaf, she couldn’t hear and she never would.

No one wanted her in any preschool. No one!

Becky was smart. Very smart. “Above average,” a man had once told her parents. “I’d go so far as to say gifted,” the man, a professional evaluator (what did that mean?), had said. “The question is only whether her intelligence will find expression or be locked up forever between her silent lips. That depends solely on you.”

Abba hadn’t been pleased with that long and complicated sentence; Becky could tell by his facial expression. His lips formed a thin line and something in his eyes dimmed.

No one had noticed that she, who'd been playing with dolls, building towers and completing puzzles as per the man's instructions, was now leaning on the table and listening, in her own way, to the strange conversation. She'd sensed that the discussion had great import on her life.

"Solely on us?" Abba had protested. "There's a G-d, Dr. Allen. There's a G-d!"

What a peculiar declaration. Of course there was a G-d; why suddenly state it? Becky didn't ask any questions. She just placed her small hand in Abba's large one, and they left. Many papers were sent back and forth between the man and her parents. Becky, who had learned to read at a very young age, read them all but didn't understand a word.

She understood only one thing: Someone in the government or city council was displeased with the fact that she was five and a half years old and not attending preschool. She'd attended preschool for a few days, but Ima hadn't been pleased. She and Abba had long discussions with all sorts of important people, but nothing had come of it all. Becky, tired of the whole to-do and the talk of an appropriate school that might be established the following year, preferred to withdraw into her own world and stay out of the adults' problems.

"They're saying that they can't put you in a school with retarded children," Yanky had explained to her. "'Cause you're normal. But no school wants to accept a deaf girl. Until you were four years old, no one argued with Ima, and with some help from your speech therapist, Jenny, we were able to teach you more at home than you would have learned in any kindergarten. But now you're supposed to go to preschool, and there's no place for you to go."

"What happened last year?" Becky asked, thinking hard. "Last year I also switched from one school to another. Why didn't I stay home?"

"Because the government said you had to go to school. I think they called it 'an educational framework.' They forced Ima to send you, so she had no choice but to send you to a school for children who aren't normal. You switched from one school to another, but you didn't fit in anywhere."

"So what will I do?" Becky's eyes filled with tears, the tears of a little girl who feels frightened and different. "Will I stay home when it's time for me to go to grade school, too?"

"I don't think so," Yanky said. "I'm sure you'll go to school."

"I don't want to switch schools all the time!" Becky protested. "I don't want to!"

"The important people Abba and Ima speak to all the time don't want you to, either. That's why everyone's arguing so much with everyone else."

"And what will be the end of the argument?" Becky asked, hugging her doll protectively. "How come no one wants me? What's the matter with me?"

"C'mon, you know," her brother said. "You know you're deaf."

"So what?" Becky said. "You see I can talk to you. What's the problem?"

Yanky shrugged. For the first time in her life, Becky "read" him saying, "I don't know."

Becky knew that Ima spoke to lots of people and explained the situation, and Abba asked questions and demanded to know why his daughter couldn't attend a "normal" school. Becky herself didn't want to think too deeply about it. She just wanted a place where no one would ask so many questions, where she'd be accepted with love and understanding. A place that would provide what she lacked so sorely: peace and quiet and the opportunity to learn. No one gave it to her.

In the mornings, when she woke up late because she had left yet another school, and the school her mother wanted her to attend was still unwilling to accept her, she would look at Mindy's empty bed and sigh to herself.

Are you jealous of Mindy? she'd ask herself wonderingly.

No. She didn't want to be like Mindy — but she definitely envied the steady routine her twin sister enjoyed. Wake up, eat breakfast, go to school, recess, school, eat lunch, return home, do homework, go to bed. Becky had none of that. She switched schools every week, and the strain of meeting new girls and a new teacher so often was taking its toll. Shy and reserved by nature, she felt that she was standing in an invisible corner, looking out at the world with her large, sad eyes and wondering why it was this way.

Jenny, her speech therapist, was concerned. She did her best, trying each time anew to help Becky become integrated with the other children. At this point, though, Becky was thoroughly tired of adapting to a different set of classmates every week. Well-schooled in disappointment, she had lost the will and capability to make the effort to adjust. Her mother's heart went out to her.

"The child is suffering," Naomi said to her husband. "She's so pathetic! She's lost interest in everything. Maybe we were wrong to have pulled her out of the special-ed preschool. At least she had some sort of routine there, and she saw familiar faces every day."

She didn't notice Becky sitting on the floor, playing quietly with her dolls, eyes fixed on her parents' faces. They spoke in hushed tones, but that was no obstacle for her. She read lips.

"She didn't make friends with them," Abba reminded Ima. "They're not on her level. She's on a very high level — way above average. It was a crime to put her into a school with special children!"

"But no teacher in a regular preschool is willing to have her," Ima sighed.

Becky trembled.

"What can we do, Shlomo?"

"I don't intend to give up or give in," Abba said determinedly. "She's our daughter, and I won't accept anything less than the best for her."

"Bureaucracy," Ima sighed. "Don't they understand that even though our child is deaf, she's perfectly normal?"

Silence reigned. A furrow or two in Abba's brow deepened significantly. Becky saw them forming in his high forehead.

It's a pity, the little girl thought to herself. *It's a pity I am the way I am.*

Becky remained at home for a long time. Jenny came to teach her at home, and she made wonderful progress. On good days, when she knew her work perfectly and Jenny complimented her sincerely, Becky felt like embracing the world and forgetting completely about the threatening thing called "preschool." Who needed it? She got along wonderfully without it.

But letters came to the house that made Ima cry, and Becky realized that she was too small to understand the complexity of the situation. What could be done? The government wanted her to attend preschool.

Why did they care? Becky wondered. Why should the mayor or the governor of New York or even the president care whether she attended school or not? What had they to do with her? They could send their children to whatever school they felt like, as far as she was concerned. They could register their daughters in any preschool at all. What difference did it make to the man in the gray suit and tinted glasses if she went to school or stayed home? Why did they want to test her so often? Why did they keep checking what she knew and what she didn't yet know? What business was it of theirs?

Becky was growing tired of the constant testing. Every time Ima dressed her in her nicest clothes, she felt like crying. She knew she was going to yet another "evaluator" who would ask her lots and lots of questions. She didn't mind answering, but nothing was worth the fear in Ima's eyes and the furrows in Abba's forehead. Those things terrified and saddened her. She hated to think that she was causing her parents so much pain.

And they're sad enough about Mindy, as it is, she thought.

She wanted to burst into tears like a little girl and run to them and tell them that she was their daughter and she loved them more than she loved anyone else in the world, but she was afraid she would ruin everything and someone would yell at them for not sending her to school. Maybe they would even be sent to jail. Maybe they would be forced to pay a big fine and then they'd have no more money left. Maybe ... maybe they would take her away from Abba and Ima and send her to a school terribly far away.

"I don't like them," Becky said to her mother one day.

"Who?"

"All of them!" Bitterness burst from her throat. "All those evaluators and important people that want to force me to go to school. I don't want them to take me from you and put you in jail!"

"What?" Ima was shocked.

"Yes! They'll get angrier and angrier and pretty soon they'll send you to jail. They'll do it in the end, because you're not doing what they say!" The tears poured forth uncontrollably. "I'm afraid they're going to take you away. I don't want to be here alone! I want to be at home with you! I want to be with you, only with you! I don't mind going to a school with girls who are not normal; just so long as no one is angry at you!"

Ima stared at her in shock, utterly speechless. "You're completely wrong, my Becky," she said quietly, caressing her daughter's smooth hair. "Becky darling, it's a shame you didn't tell me sooner that you were frightened we'd be sent to jail. It's not true at all. Those people are not fighting with us or angry at us, and they certainly won't send us to jail. Everyone wants what's best for you."

"Best for me?" Becky hid her face in her mother's dress and wept bitterly. "They want me to be happy? I don't want anything. I don't need anything. All I want is to stay here with you and not go anywhere."

"But Becky," Ima pleaded. "Becky, sweetheart, you have to learn somewhere. We're looking for a school where you'll have fun and enjoy yourself."

"And every day people check to see if I'm smart or not! And you're afraid when they test me! You are!"

Sabba entered the room, holding his watch in his hand. "What happened? It's getting late! Naomi, I want to take you there. Shlomo left twenty minutes ago already."

He suddenly noticed Becky's tear-streaked face and stopped short. "What's wrong, little girl?" he asked softly. "I see something's worrying you. Want to tell me what it is?"

She didn't go to any evaluator that day. Instead, Sabba took her to the park and they played ball. It was very peculiar: She didn't tell Sabba anything at all, but she felt much, much calmer by the time he brought her home.

5

En route from Rome to Berlin, 1945

Marty rose from his place near the window and began wandering aimlessly about, looking for something to do. He smiled to himself. *As if I have nothing to do!*

He paced up and down the aisle, until one of his fellow passengers grumbled, "A little quiet, *bitte*." He moved on to another car, where he continued to play the part of a restless man to perfection. When the passengers in this car, too, became disgruntled with his behavior, he moved on once more.

In the sixth car sat a man drinking a mug of tepid coffee. The strong scent of coffee dominated the entire car. Most passengers were Germans or Italians. A few were Allied soldiers. Marty began the same routine he'd performed in the first five cars — sitting down, rising a moment later and pacing restlessly back and forth.

"Can't you sit still?" a balding man asked angrily.

Marty stopped short, affecting a guilty expression, then sat down opposite the man with the mug of coffee.

"Coffee?" he inquired curiously. "Where did you get coffee?"

"In the cafeteria," the man replied shortly, pointing a weary thumb at car No. 7.

"Can you order some for me?" His English was perfect.

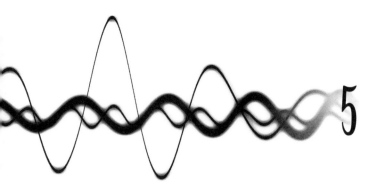

The man nodded, angry impatience written all over his face. "Don't you speak German or Italian?"

"No, I don't," Marty said, ignoring the fact that he had spent most of his life in Germany. He spoke German fluently.

The dour man rose, went to the cafeteria and returned with a mug of coffee. Some coins changed hands, and Marty thanked the man profusely.

"Where are you going?"

The man did not appear to be inclined to conversation. "Berlin. Where else can one be going if he's on this train?"

"Is it a direct train?" Marty asked.

"Don't you know where you're going, young man?"

Marty smiled sheepishly. "No."

"Then you've got a problem." The man turned to look out the window.

"Have you ever been to Berlin?" Marty was determined to talk to the man.

"Yes." "Laconic" was this fellow's middle name.

"Can you describe its scenery and tell me a little bit about the customs of the people there?"

"Right now, it looks like a bombed-out city. The only scenery you'll see is rubble. You can ask the survivors about their customs. In a word, the national hobby is murder."

Marty was taken aback by the man's frigid tone. "Still ..."

"Listen, would you leave me alone?" the man asked in annoyance, turning back to the window again. "G-d in heaven," he mumbled to himself. "Scenery! Customs!"

Marty was silent for a moment. "Sir, what's the value of the British pound against the German mark?"

"I have no idea."

Marty sighed. The man was obviously not one for conversation. He withdrew a folded newspaper from his pocket and spread it on the table. His nationality was clearly exposed, as was the name of the paper he was reading: *The London Times*.

"What's your name?" the dour man asked suddenly.

"Marty Katz."

"Marty!" the man spat bitterly. "Don't you have a Jewish name?"

"I do. Meir."

"Why don't you use it?"

"With all due respect, sir, you don't look like the type of fellow who cares about Jewish names."

"Ah," the man said, patting his bare head. "You mean this?"

"Yes. Bareheaded, no *peyos*, beard or tzitzis."

"I'm not religious, but I'm a proud Jew. Why don't you use your Jewish name?"

"It's wartime," Marty replied, stating what he felt was obvious.

"Wartime? The war is over." The man drank the last drop of coffee in his mug and grimaced. "Name's Shaul. Last name isn't important. You have something to tell me."

Marty's eyebrows shot up in surprise. "Me? I only received a letter."

"Alright, alright," the man interrupted. "Yes, that's right. Someone suggested you meet me, and you accepted his advice. That's a sign you have something to discuss with me, isn't it?"

Marty was forced to admit that the man was right. His silence encouraged Shaul to go on. "You have a rich military background, but a weak background in intelligence."

"Yes."

"You drink strong Turkish coffee. Your cigarette of choice is Golf Lights. You wear a size forty-two shoe. Your blood type is O. You don't drink alcoholic beverages. You come from a religious family, of which you are the sole survivor. You resided in Palestine until the war. You waited for the establishment of a Jewish regiment but grew impatient. You traveled to England to help in the war against the Germans and joined His Majesty's infantry. You served in the Fifth Regiment. Your commander is Major Jim Stuart, a friend of yours. You rise at six o'clock every morning and take a one-and-a-half hour walk. Military exercises for two hours. You retire at midnight. You were in Bergen-Belsen and what you saw affected you deeply. I imagine it aroused the Jewish spark within you. You have a 32 mm automatic in your right pocket and a German Lilliput in your left. You've been trained to use Shpanden and Schmeisser submachine guns; you have trouble with automatic carbines. You're a superb shot. Dark brown eyes, blue contact lenses. Brown hair dyed blond, to lend you an Aryan appearance. Am I right?"

"Completely." Marty was shocked. "How do you know all that?"

"We investigated you. You're right about aid. You're the man we need, but we have a different goal in mind from the one you set for yourself."

"A different goal?" Marty's chin lifted defiantly. "What different goal? Is there anything more important? What's your goal in life?"

"To rescue Jews." Shaul's tone was emphatic.

"And my goal? You said, 'We have a different goal in mind from the one you set for yourself.' How do you know what my goal is?"

"We know." The shadow of a smile crossed Shaul's lips. "Revenge."

"Revenge." His lips tightened with helpless rage. Pain and anger mingled in his eyes. "Revenge against one particular nation. Until there's not a single German, not a single cursed Nazi who feels safe."

"You're getting carried away," Shaul said, dampening his enthusiasm. "Our avengers started their work long ago, but our arm is not as long as you think. The Nazis do feel compromised when we're around, though," he said candidly. "I was an avenger. Killing did not satisfy me. In my opinion, that is not the way to take revenge. I have an eye to the future. There's a greater revenge than killing Nazis."

"That's not the way to take revenge?" Marty said, nearly shouting.

Shaul silenced him, and Marty lowered his voice to a pain-filled whisper. "That's not the way to take revenge? Did you see the gas chambers with the words, '*Yidden, nekamah!*' written on them in blood? Did you see the Jews being led to their slaughter? Did you see your brothers, your family, murdered in front of your eyes as you stood helplessly by? Have you lost your entire family? Have you?"

Shaul shifted his gaze to the window. He was a tough person; tears never sprang unbidden into his eyes. After a long moment, when he trusted his voice to remain steady again, he slowly rolled up his shirtsleeve and said calmly, "Yes. I have."

Marty froze. A blue number was tattooed on Shaul's forearm, below his elbow. He felt a stab of guilt, because he himself had not seen his brothers slaughtered. He had left Poland earlier. It was only after his regiment had liberated Bergen-Belsen that he visited the various death camps. He stared at the man in shock.

"How?" he whispered weakly.

"Auschwitz. I was there for a year before I escaped. G-d helped and I made it to Palestine. Now I'm returning to this bloodthirsty country, my heart aflame with the desire for revenge. But I'm planning to take revenge by returning the Jewish people, with renewed Jewish pride, to Eretz Yisrael. There, only there, will our battered, shattered people rise to glory once more. That's my revenge.

"And you — you haven't witnessed the war with your own eyes. You are not like me. You heard about the horrors of the war, but you haven't experienced them firsthand. I'm the one who felt it on my flesh — and yet I tell you that murder is not a life purpose. Which is more important: blood, destruction, and loss for the Germans, or resuscitation for the Jews?"

"Both are important," Marty said. "Let each man do as he sees fit."

"No. We need people like you: You're eloquent; you know Palestine like your own backyard; you have a military past and connections with the authorities. We need people with organizational abilities. We need soldiers, strong, healthy men. In short, you have many of the qualities we need."

"The goal?"

"The goal ..." he echoed.

The train stopped and people began rising. Shaul rose as well and donned his lightweight jacket. "Eleven o'clock. Timer Cafe," he murmured. "See you there."

And then he was gone, merging with the crowd. Marty glanced at his watch. His commander, Jim, had promised to wait for him at the station and lead him to the hotel. He scanned the crowd in search of Jim's blue eyes. There was no sign of him.

It was only once the platform had emptied completely that Jim came running up, panting noticeably.

"I'm sorry, Marty," he said. "Public transportation here is for the birds."

"It's okay," Marty said dismissively. "Where's the hotel?"

Jim took Marty's backpack. "Come with me," he said.

Marty looked around him. Throngs of people, golden sunshine, vendors and shoppers, dizzying noise, teeming squares – life that had returned to normal so quickly. Was this the city where the Final Solution was born, the city where genocide had originated?

Yes, this was Berlin.

New York 5758/1998

"YOU SHOULDN'T HAVE done that," Yanky told her firmly. "You know how sad Abba and Ima are about Mindy. What did you do that for? Why did you tell Ima that you were so sad? Why did you tell her you didn't want to go to the evaluation?"

Becky prickled defensively. "But it's true, Yanky. I didn't say it for nothing. I was really feeling awful."

"It doesn't matter," Yanky said angrily. "I try my best to make Abba and Ima happy, and you should too. Never, ever tell them that you're sad because you don't have a school to go to, understand? They're worried enough as it is!"

Becky wasn't certain that Yanky was right, but he assured her he was.

"I'm older than you, and I understand things better," he said authoritatively. Yanky was such a good brother that Becky believed him.

"But Ima said I should always tell her when I'm afraid of something," she pointed out.

"Well, of course she would say that," Yanky said sagely. "Ima always wants the very best for you. But we — you and I — need to think about what's good for Ima. When Sari gets bigger, she will, too. Ima has it very, very hard with Mindy; I see that. She's always sad, and it's up to us to try and make her happy."

"I do try to make her happy," Becky protested. "But is it my fault I'm deaf?"

"No, it's not your fault," Yanky said soothingly. "I'm not upset at you, Becky. I also want what's best for you, but you're not Mindy's mother, and you're not terribly worried about her and about what will be with her when she grows up. We need to try to always be happy, for Abba and Ima's sake."

"I don't think Ima would be happy if she knew you were keeping things from her."

"She wouldn't," Yanky conceded, "but as long as she doesn't know, she is happy, and I'm going to make sure she doesn't find out."

Becky thought about what her brother said. "So I should have kept quiet and been scared forever?"

"No," Yanky said decisively. "I'm your big brother, and I can take care of you. When something bothers you, tell me, and I'll take care of whatever you need. Alright?"

"What would you have done today? How would you have soothed me?"

"I would have read the letters. I'm sure I would have understood them better than you. And in the worst case, I'd have asked Sabba. You can also talk to Sabba and Savta."

"Okay." She felt relieved. "Look, you may be nearly three years older than me, but you're still a child. But I can tell Sabba and Savta instead of Abba and Ima the next time I have a problem."

"You can tell them, if you prefer," Yanky said, "but you should know that I'm always glad to hear what's bothering you, and I'm always glad to help you."

"Always?" Becky said doubtfully.

"Yes. I like to help you. I think you're a *tzaddeikes*."

"Who, me?" Becky shone with delight at the compliment. "Why do you think so?"

"Because you behave like a regular girl even though you're deaf. You're not spoiled. There are some people who, just because they're deaf, do nothing all day besides feel sorry for themselves. You're much better than them."

Becky smiled with pleasure. "I'll tell you about things you can help me with," she said by way of compromise, "and the rest I'll tell Sabba and Savta."

"Okay," he conceded. "Just try not to upset Abba or Ima."

Yanky's such a good boy, Becky thought. *He's so concerned about everyone!*

The following morning, Becky woke up bright and early, but she remained in bed for quite some time, gazing dreamily at the dust particles dancing in a shaft of sunlight streaming into her room through the window. She smelled the aroma of the hot chocolate Ima was preparing and smiled happily.

A glance at the bed near her dampened her mood. Mindy wasn't awake yet. Mindy, Mindy, Mindy. Becky saw her sister's name on her parents' lips all the time. It seemed to Becky they were always talking about her twin sister. Their eyes were sad and their brows were furrowed when they spoke about her.

Becky thought to herself angrily that Mindy wasn't being fair. Here she was, deaf, struggling to cope with a silent, suspicious world — and yet, Abba and Ima did not concern themselves with her nearly as much as they did with Mindy.

It isn't fair! she thought to herself, kicking her thin quilt and sitting up in bed. Mindy took the lion's share of their parents' concern for herself without making the tiniest effort on their behalf. Becky couldn't bear to see the furrows forming on Abba's forehead. No, she couldn't stand it! Nor could she tolerate the sorrowful look in Ima's eyes. She tried so hard all day to please them, to avoid causing them distress, and so did Yanky. She struggled to prove to them that she was just like everyone else, that they didn't have to be so sad that she was deaf. Sometimes, she came very close to making them smile a real, happy smile — the kind that not only curves your lips but illuminates your eyes too — but then along came Mindy and ruined all her hard work.

Mindy was autistic. Mindy didn't try to give Abba and Ima *nachas*. She lived in a world of her own and cared about nothing. Nothing at all. Why should Becky be the only one to care about Abba and Ima? Wasn't Mindy their daughter, too? Didn't she worry about them? And they were so sad because of her. Mindy didn't deserve such an Abba and Ima. She didn't!

Becky knew that was a foolish way of thinking. Mindy was autistic — that was why she didn't think about anyone or anything. Mindy was absorbed in a world all her own — a strange, remote, foreign world. She lived in a thick bubble, perceiving the world differently from the rest of the human race. Her world was not only as terrifyingly silent as Becky's own; it was completely detached from the regular world. What kind of life was that?

Becky dressed quickly and went downstairs to the kitchen to stave off the tears. Mindy was pitiful in her own way. She never cried or smiled at anyone; all she knew how to do was screech and kick, bite and throw fits.

Becky was not afraid of Mindy. She was her twin, after all. It was decidedly unpleasant to be in Mindy's company when she was having one of her fits of rage, but Becky wasn't afraid to extend a hand and caress her twin sister's long, smooth hair, so much like her own. Mindy never bit her. Becky felt Mindy softening when she drew near. Ironically, when Becky felt overwhelmingly upset and went to hide in her room to cry about nothing in particular and everything together, it was Mindy, her wild, thrashing sister, who helped her calm down. There was something in the appearance of her twin sister, so different from that of others, that helped her relax.

She and Mindy played together sometimes in utter silence. Mindy knew how to make eye contact, so Becky played with her from time to time. Of course, the games they played were different, without the benefit of a single spoken word, but they were still games of a sort.

When Mindy was not around, a certain knot of tension in Becky's heart loosened. Becky felt the need to protect her sister. She was relieved when Mindy went away because then she could let her guard down. "Becky, you don't need to protect Mindy," her mother often told her. "Mindy's feelings don't get hurt the way yours do. We take good care of her. Don't worry about her so much!"

But Becky did worry. How could she not worry about her twin sister — the only one in her family who could truly understand the difficulty of being different?

Becky tied her shoelaces. She was proud that she could do so all by herself. Yanky, her older brother, still had difficulty tying his shoes. She had good hands. She drew beautifully, had nice penmanship and handled scissors with great proficiency. Ima took the pictures she drew to the evaluators she met with, and all of them said she had "superb coordination."

No one was in the kitchen now. The kitchen was on the ground floor, and it had two doors. One opened to the stairs leading to the second floor, where the bedrooms were, and the other opened to the hall leading to the dining room. Apparently, at the very same moment that Becky crossed the dining room on her way to the kitchen, Ima had climbed the stairs to the second floor.

Becky sighed. She pulled a chair over to one of the cabinets, clambered up and took a box of her favorite breakfast cereal. Then she took a bowl and spoon from the dish drainer and leaped lightly down from the chair with the entire armload. She poured some cereal into the bowl and added milk.

Yanky entered the kitchen. He tapped lightly on Becky's shoulder to draw her attention.

"Hey," he said cheerfully. "You're up early today."

"I wanted to see you off," Becky replied.

Yanky's eyes clouded. "Alright," he said shortly. "Mindy will be down in another minute. Be careful."

Becky didn't like it when he spoke that way. "Don't forget she's your sister," she said, trying to express her feelings but not really succeeding.

"And don't you forget that she's autistic," her brother shot back.

Becky ate in angry silence until her twin sister burst into the kitchen as though shot from a cannon. Ima was directly behind her, looking utterly spent. Mindy was wearing an outfit identical to Becky's, but there was a major difference: Becky had dressed herself, while Mindy had to be dressed.

Ima fed Mindy carefully, placing her soft hand on Mindy's rigid one. Mindy pulled her hand away from Ima's, and Becky averted her eyes. Ima looked so sad that Becky felt the need to climb under the table and place her head on her knees.

Ima felt Becky's small head on her knees and stroked her tenderly. Becky was sorry that she couldn't see her face. Was she happy? Becky hoped so, but she knew it was a vain hope. Ima would never be truly happy. She would never smile happily at Becky or Yanky. Even when Mindy was not around, her spirit hovered around them and cast a pall over their house.

Every day before Mindy came home from her special school, Ima became sad and tense. "Turn off the dishwasher, please, Shlomo," she said to Abba. "Put the vacuum cleaner away, Becky," she asked Becky. "Yanky, can you close the pantry door? Shlomo, it might be wise to lock the door to the shed."

There were electrical appliances in the shed. Becky knew that Ima tried to clear away all the expensive objects before Mindy came home, because when she was around, Mindy destroyed everything.

Mindy had broken many costly appliances. Vases that had survived baby Sari's small, mischievous hands were no match for Mindy's strong, destructive ones. That's the way it was.

Once, when Sari broke an expensive vase, Ima had sighed and then chuckled. "No, no, no," she said, wagging her finger for Sari's benefit. When Sari lifted her laughing gaze to look triumphantly at Ima, Ima had scooped her up and hugged her. "I ought to know better than to leave such things where Sari can get to them," Ima had said, her eyes merry.

When Mindy broke an expensive flowerpot, Ima's response had been similar, almost identical. Only the order was different. In Mindy's case, Ima first chuckled and then sighed. She didn't say, "No, no, no," to Mindy, but she hugged and kissed her the way she had little Sari. Becky had been glad, in her young heart, that Ima was not angry or sad about the flowerpot and that she laughed the incident off the way she had with Sari. When she'd lifted her eyes to meet Ima's, though, she had discovered there was a difference after all. As she hugged Mindy, Ima's eyes were filled with tears.

6

The month of Cheshvan arrived, bringing fierce winter winds and thunderstorms along with it. The city was a blur of scarves, hats, umbrellas and windshield wipers. Becky, who had been waiting eagerly for some news about her preschool situation, was bitterly disappointed.

After everyone left the house one morning, she was feeling terribly lonely. Yanky and Mindy had gone to school, Sari was at playgroup, and Ima had hurried to her clinic. Becky sat alone near the window, waiting for Jenny, her speech therapist.

She wanted so badly to have friends. She saw two little girls walking to the bus stop together. She knew who they were: Esther Nechama and Baily from the building next door. Both girls were her age, and they attended preschool. Why did only she have to stay home? Why? Wasn't she as good as the other girls? How come no one wanted her? How come no preschool teacher in the world loved her? Would she never go to preschool?

And what about elementary school? Would they force her to go to a school like Mindy's, with children who weren't normal? She didn't want to. Not at all! She wanted real friends who talked and laughed, friends you could have a good time with — not girls who didn't speak and who threw fits, like Mindy. She wanted friends. Why shouldn't she have them?

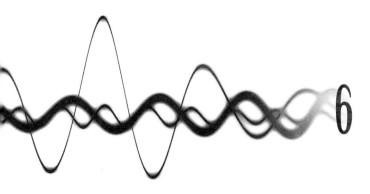

Her green eyes filled with tears and her lips trembled. A group of little girls with lunch boxes passed by under her window. *They hear and they go to school, too. How come I don't get to do either? They have friends*. The stab of envy in her heart grew stronger and stronger, and she burst into tears. Why am I like this? How come no one is happy with me? How come everyone wants me to be different?

"Becky, I want to speak to you." Abba had entered her room.

Becky dried her eyes and lifted them so she could read her father's lips.

"Yes, Abba?"

"Come." Abba helped her into her coat as if she was a little girl and fastened the buttons. "Let's go on a trip."

"It's raining," Becky replied logically.

"Even so. I need to make a trip to a large shopping mall. You'll come along, okay? You can also choose a different place to go, too. The mall opens at nine, and it's only ten past eight now."

"What about Jenny? She's s'posed to come at 8:30!"

"We'll give her a day off, too."

Abba opened the car door, and Becky settled herself in the back where she could see Abba's lips in the mirror. Becky fastened her safety belt, Abba revved up the motor and they were off.

"So, Becky, where would you like to go?" Abba asked softly. "Where do you want more than anyplace in the world to be right now?"

"I want to go to school," Becky said immediately. She saw Abba's teeth come down hard on his lower lip.

"No, ack-shully, I don't want that," she said. "I don't want to go to school at all."

"Why not?"

"Cause I don't want you to be sad."

Abba burst into laughter. He gripped the steering wheel and turned it sharply, having nearly lost control of the car. "You're so cute," he said, making sure to raise his face to the mirror so she could read his lips, though it was more difficult to drive that way. "And you're such a good girl, too."

"Not good enough," she said bitterly.

"Why do you think that?"

"Because no one wants me in their school."

Abba grew serious. He didn't look her in the eye as he asked, "And you want to go to school?"

"Yes."

"How come? There was a time when you didn't really want to go. You said you were fine with Jenny and Ima and Yanky."

"Because I want to have friends."

"Ah." He was silent. Becky peeked at his lips to see if he was saying anything else, but they were still. His forehead was furrowed and his eyes were thoughtful.

The rain continued pounding on the car windows. Becky used her finger to draw pictures on the glass. She wrote her name and then played tic-tac-toe with herself. Abba smiled when he saw and offered to play with her. "I'll tell you where to draw my O," he said.

"Okay."

They played for a while, and then Abba parked the car in the parking lot next to a large mall. "You didn't tell me where else you wanted to go, so I came directly here. I think there might be a few interesting stores that open before nine. Later, we'll go buy what we need," he explained. "Come, darling, let's see which stores are open already."

The pet shop opened for business at 8:30. Abba and Becky watched the animals with great interest.

"Do you like animals?" Abba asked.

"Of course!" Becky declared. "They're so cute!"

They stood together, watching in silence. Abba held Becky's hand in his own warm one. Every few minutes, Abba glanced at his watch. Finally, he said, "Becky, it's nine o'clock already. Do you want to come with me to do some shopping, or would you rather stay here?"

"I want to stay here," she replied decisively.

Abba left her looking at the silent fish and bouncy rabbits. A moment later, he was back. "This is a large mall, and I'm afraid you might get lost," he said worriedly. "Maybe you should come with me, after all?"

She hesitated, then shook her head. She wasn't a baby, nor was she Mindy. Why couldn't she stay and look at the fish while Abba did his shopping? She'd show all those evaluators that she could, too!

"I prefer to stay."

"Alright. But don't move from here until I come for you, okay?"

She nodded, and Abba left.

The hamsters huddled in a corner of their cage. The puppies yipped excitedly. She watched their mouths open and close, and the sight amused her. She didn't hear them barking, of course. There were fluffy kittens who scratched their cage with their claws and ducks who watched her with large round eyes. The array of sights fascinated her, and she stood rooted to the spot.

Ten minutes passed, then fifteen. The numbers on Becky's digital watch kept jumping and changing, but Becky wasn't concerned. Abba had told her he'd come back for her, and the fish were swimming in interesting circles.

A store employee holding a crate containing two barking puppies approached the store. "Little girl!" he shouted above her head.

She didn't move from her spot.

"Little girl, I need to go inside the store an' you're blockin' my way. Can you move over a bit, please?"

Becky remained where she was. The employee looked at her strangely.

"Hey, Charlie, what's holdin' ya up?" asked another employee, coming up right behind him with another crate.

"Look," Charlie said quietly. "She seems to be autistic or somethin'. She's not reactin' to what I'm sayin'."

"So what? Move her aside and go in. This crate is heavy!"

Becky was oblivious to the conversation going on behind her back at a rather loud volume, but the owner of the pet shop heard the commotion and stepped out of the store to investigate.

"What's going on? Come on in with those crates!"

The employees pointed to the little girl standing rooted to the spot. "Hey, you!" the storekeeper said aggressively. "Let these men pass! Move!"

This time Becky noticed that the storekeeper was talking to her. "Pardon?" she said. Her guttural, unpolished voice could barely be heard above the barking of the dogs.

"You heard me," replied the storekeeper. "Move, y'hear?"

The man's bushy moustache made it hard for Becky to read his lips, and she felt confused and frightened. She didn't understand what he wanted from her, but he looked threatening, so she instinctively took a few steps back, intending to run away. Charlie, who had been following the exchange with great interest, failed to notice that Becky was moving backward, and the box he was holding fell down and tipped over. The two puppies made the most of the opportunity and escaped.

The mall was a sea of commotion. The puppies scampered rambunctiously about, and the employees gave chase. The storekeeper, who stayed behind to man the store, looked helplessly about him. Becky fled the area and began to run. Where to? She had no idea. She ran and ran, unable to think rationally and figure out where Abba might be. *Run! Run! Run! They're going to blame you for the dogs' escape.*

Lots of people attempted to stop her and ask her why she was crying and where she was going, but Becky didn't hear a thing. All she saw was that they were pointing at her and talking. They thought she wasn't normal. They thought she was like Mindy. It wasn't true! She was normal! She was a perfectly ordinary girl!

Becky's frightened eyes searched for a place to hide. She found a large flowerpot and crouched behind it. She couldn't hear the sound of people approaching, but a moment later, she was surrounded by a group of people.

Becky could not follow the conversation of the people surrounding her, but she did make out a few words. "Retarded," she saw one woman say. "Autistic," said a man.

She wasn't autistic! How could she prove it to them? She wasn't autistic! No!

Shlomo left the electronics store with a brisk step. It had taken him twenty-five minutes to complete his purchase, and Becky was waiting for him. He lengthened his strides and approached the pet shop.

The store was empty.

"Becky?" he called. He knew she couldn't hear him, but it was human nature to call the name of the person you wanted. "Excuse me," he said to the man behind the counter. "Did you see a little girl? I left her here watching the pets."

"Yes, of course!" the storekeeper replied. "She stood here like a wooden log. Are you her father?" He suddenly grew flustered.

"Yes." Shlomo was apprehensive. "Where is she?"

"She caused quite a commotion and fled," the man said. "See, we asked her to move because she was blocking my employees from entering the store, and she didn't respond. Then she suddenly moved back and overturned a crate with two puppies. It took us a long time to catch them, and in the meantime, she ran away. You ought to teach her to listen when people talk to her."

"I'm afraid it's not that simple," Shlomo murmured. "She's deaf."

"Oh!" The storekeeper's hand flew to his mouth. "How come I didn't think of that! I'm so sorry."

"Did you see where she went?"

"She hasn't left the mall," the storekeeper assured him. "I've been watching the exit. She's still here somewhere. I suppose it won't be much help if we call her over the PA system, eh?"

A shadow passed over Shlomo's face. "No. Thank you, in any case."

Shlomo began running through the mall, looking out for his little girl or a small crowd. Oh Becky, Becky! His shy, quiet daughter had found herself in the center of a crowd on more than one occasion.

Where are you, darling? Where are you, light of my life, my heart, my soul?

Shlomo was not totally terrified, because he knew that, unlike Mindy, Becky wouldn't hurt herself. Becky was a mature, responsible girl. If only he could take the storekeeper's suggestion and announce her name over the PA system. Shlomo smiled wryly to himself. If Becky could hear, they never would have gotten into this situation to begin with. She'd have moved aside as soon as the employees had called her name.

As he had expected, Shlomo spied a small crowd at the end of a corridor. His daughter was standing in its center, her eyes filled with tears and her lips clenched tight. She was gripping a flowerpot so tightly that her knuckles were white.

"Becky!" he called, hoping to attract the attention of the people surrounding her.

They saw him and made room for him to pass. Becky ran to him with outstretched arms, crying with relief.

"Becky, Becky," her father murmured softly, pressing her to his heart. "Why didn't you talk to them, explain what happened?"

"They ... didn't ... give me a chance," she wept, her voice choking up.

"Were you scared, darling?" He stroked her hair lovingly, trying to impart his love, support and empathy, though he knew he could never really understand the *nisayon* Hashem had given his small daughter.

She shook her head. "I knew ... you would come," she said through her tears. "I wasn't scared."

"So why are you crying?" he asked softly.

"Because ... because ... they thought ..." The initial flood of tears had abated, but profound pain now colored her words. "They thought ... I wasn't normal."

YANKY WAS DASHING down the stairs on his way to the kitchen when he heard the phone ring. Since Becky never spoke on the telephone and Ima hated to be disturbed in middle of cooking, Yanky knew it was up to him to answer it.

"Hello?" he said somewhat impatiently. Ima and Becky were in the kitchen, and he was eager to talk with them after his long day at school. The telephone call had interrupted his plans, and he hoped it wouldn't delay him a lot.

"Yanky?" It was Aharon, a boy in his class. "I'm glad you answered the phone. Reuven and Bentzion want to come play at your house. Is that okay?"

"And you too?" Yanky asked hopefully. Aharon was a popular boy and Yanky was pleased he had called. "D'you wanna come, too?"

"Yeah," Aharon replied confidently. "Me too."

A moment of silence followed as Yanky strained to hear what was going on in the kitchen, where Ima and Becky were chatting. *Becky!* he thought to himself. He played with her every afternoon. No, he couldn't have friends over. He had to play with Becky. Who would play with her if not Yanky? He knew his sister never played with anyone else. She was afraid of other children, afraid they would talk to her and she wouldn't hear, and afraid they would laugh at her. Becky was very suspicious of her surroundings and he, Yanky, had been chosen by Hashem to be her brother and help her.

He always smiled at her and never complained when she didn't understand things right away. He played with her and never refused her requests. It was up to him to make her and Ima happy. He had to prove to his parents that life was good despite it all, despite deaf Becky and autistic Mindy. He was Yanky, their perfectly healthy, ordinary son, and he had to help them.

And he was the one who had told Becky that she mustn't worry Ima. He'd promised Becky he'd take care of her. Could he break his word just because a few friends wanted to play at his house? What was the promise he had made to always be a help to Becky worth, if he disregarded it whenever it suited him?

Becky was lonely. He was her brother. He knew that his mother would be sorry if Becky felt lonely and bored. He'd give up the pleasure of having Aharon, Reuven and Bentzy come over to his house. Some things are more important than playing with friends.

"Listen, Aharon," he said finally. "I'd really like to, but I can't today, alright?"

"So how about tomorrow?" Aharon asked in the tone of voice of someone who won't take no for an answer.

Tomorrow. What was the difference between tomorrow and today? Yanky knew nothing would change by tomorrow. He had to stay with his little sister and help her. He couldn't just go and play with friends from cheder when he was needed at home to be company for Becky.

"She's completely detached from society," he'd once heard Ima say to Abba. Yanky trembled as he recalled the conversation he had overheard. "Completely detached! Shlomo, do you realize how lonely she is? She has no one, not a single friend, not a single child her age to play with! How much longer can she go on this way? We must do something."

"There's Yanky," Abba had said in a completely unconvincing tone of voice.

"Yanky is her brother. He can't take the place of a friend!"

"Yanky is excellent company for her, and you know it. You're right, it's not enough, but it's good that she at least has him. Another boy might completely ignore a sister like that. Thank G-d for Yanky. He's such a sensitive child, so understanding and responsible."

Hearing that, Yanky, the "sensitive and responsible child," had accepted the burden of responsibility for Becky as an established fact. He knew then that he would never be able to go anywhere without feeling guilty for having abandoned his sister. Wherever he went, he was accompanied in his mind by a small figure who chastised him for playing with someone else while his mother wept over her daughter's loneliness.

"No!" he said aloud, his voice aggressive and angry. "I can't. I told you I can't, so I can't!" He didn't care that it was Aharon, who could make the whole class laugh with him no matter what he did. His mother's happiness was more important. He'd show her he was a devoted brother to Becky, a sensitive and understanding brother who had no interest in anyone but her.

"What are you getting all worked up about?" Aharon said. "'I can't,'" he continued, mimicking Yanky scornfully. "Whatsa matter, you have a meeting with the president? Every day you can't? Whaddya think, you're the king of the third grade that you can be such a snob?"

Yanky swallowed. "I'm not a snob," he said firmly. "Is it against the law to not be able to have friends over?"

"No, it's not against the law," Aharon said, "but it's not nice to tell us no every single day. You're just a snob, and you should know that the entire class says so, too."

"The entire class says what?" Yanky demanded to know.

"That you're a snob who thinks it's beneath his dignity to go to any boy in the class after school or have anyone over to your house. You think we're not worthy of seeing your beautiful house?"

Yanky clenched his fist so tightly that his knuckles turned white. No, he would not reveal his secret!

"No one wants to be friends with you anymore," Aharon declared. "I'm going to make sure that no one in the class talks to you anymore."

This was too much. Yanky didn't dare to remain silent in the face of such a threat.

"You don't understand," he said pleadingly. He threw a glance toward the kitchen and then said quietly, "I have to play with my sister."

"Your sister? Why doesn't she play with her friends?"

Yanky couldn't just say, "Because she doesn't have any." That would be *lashon hara*; Becky would be dreadfully embarrassed if she heard. "Her friends can't come," he said, shrugging. Was that a lie? No – they couldn't come because they didn't exist.

"Fine," Aharon said, resigned. "Never mind." And he hung up.

Yanky gripped the receiver tightly. Piercing regret spread slowly throughout his body, overtaking him completely. *Why are you so sad?* a voice inside him asked. *Aharon accepted what you said in the end; he's not angry with you. Are you upset with yourself for having turned down the offer? No way! You know you can't go anywhere; you've got to stay with Becky. You had no choice!*

Ah, Yanky mused, *maybe that's why I feel so sad.*

ON TUESDAY, A reply came in the mail. For Becky, the day began like any other, but the moment she entered the kitchen her mother greeted her with sparkling eyes.

"Becky, guess what!"

"What happened?" Becky's heart skipped a beat. She didn't really like surprises. The world was frightening enough as it was. Every sentence people uttered was a surprise for her, an unknown variable she could never be certain she would solve correctly.

"You've been accepted!" Ima embraced her lovingly. "Becky, darling, you've been accepted into preschool, to Morah Devorah's class."

"Preschool? Morah Devorah?" Becky asked hesitantly.

"Yes, and she's a wonderful teacher. The very best there is."

"How do you know?" Suspicion, her constant companion, reared its head.

"I know her. I've spoken to her many times; I've told her all about you. She's a wonderful person. I hoped and prayed she would be given permission to accept you into her class, and *baruch Hashem*, permission was granted."

"Permission? Whose permission did she need?"

"Becky," Ima chuckled, "you're acting like a police investigator, asking so many questions. She needed permission from the supervisory board. It's a complicated issue you don't need to trouble your head with. Just be happy."

"But Ima, what kind of preschool is it?" Becky pressed. She absolutely had to verify this point, no matter what Yanky said about protecting Ima.

"Pre-1A!" Ima announced dramatically. "Pre-1A, Becky!"

"What does that mean? Is it a regular preschool? Are there regular girls there? Normal girls?"

"Of course! It's a perfectly ordinary preschool class. Isn't that wonderful?"

"Pre-1A?" Becky asked doubtfully. "Are you sure, Ima? An ordinary preschool class? A real, real pre-1A class?" It sounded too good to be true.

"A real pre-1A class," Ima assured her, scooping her up in a huge bear hug. "Stop worrying so much, dear girl. *Baruch Hashem*, you were accepted into an ordinary school and everything will be just fine. After you attend a regular preschool, you'll continue to a normal grade school and everything will proceed smoothly." Ima often used big words. Becky knew lots of words like "proceed smoothly."

Yanky burst into the kitchen. "Hey, Becky," he whooped, "I knew that's what would happen in the end! I knew you'd win 'em all!"

"But I didn't fight with anyone," Becky countered logically.

Yanky laughed in the manner of a wise adult. "Abba and Ima fought the battle for you," he said dramatically.

"When do I start?" Becky was short of breath from excitement.

"Tomorrow!" Ima announced. "Tomorrow our Becky goes to preschool."

For a moment a hushed silence reigned in the kitchen. Becky's eyes sparkled with joy. She was going to a regular preschool, with regular girls, and she'd be completely regular herself. She'd be like everyone else: She'd draw and cut, paste and color. She'd learn to write (she already knew how to read perfectly) and stick stickers onto exactly the right shapes. She'd learn so many things.

Joy surged up inside her. She'd have friends! She'd laugh and talk and play with regular girls, girls her own age. Yanky wouldn't have to play with her all afternoon and tell his friends that he couldn't spend time with them after school because of her. What fun it would be; how totally wonderful!

She'd play jump rope and "house" and "school" and all sorts of games Yanky didn't really know how to play. Yanky preferred to play things like ball and cars. (Ima chuckled at Yanky's fascination with cars; she said Uncle Shmuel used to have a huge collection, too.) Yanky was a boy after all, and even though he meant well, there were some things he just didn't know how to do — jump rope, for example, or swap stationery.

He could swap, of course, Becky noted to herself, *but he doesn't have a collection. And even if he did, it would be just like mine, because Abba and Ima would buy two of the same of everything, and Yanky wouldn't swap his with his friends.*

The stationery Ima once bought her had remained in the closet, untouched. What good was stationery if you didn't have anyone to swap with? But tomorrow — tomorrow she'd have friends. She'd swap stationery and have a fantastic time.

Tomorrow! Tomorrow she was going to preschool!

7

After such a lengthy struggle, after endless meetings and countless bureaucratic procedures, Naomi's and Shlomo's dream had come true. *We've endured so much for our little girl's sake, and we will undoubtedly endure much more in the future,* Naomi mused.

After Becky left, Naomi raised her eyes heavenward and whispered a prayer of gratitude. She asked Hashem to grant her strength — lots of it. Every mother needs strength, but she – she needed strength to raise all her children, and an inexhaustible supply to raise her two handicapped daughters.

Naomi walked slowly to the mailbox. She had taken the day off, and she made a conscious effort not to think about her clients' deep and painful problems. Naomi had enough of her own. An occasional day off was not a luxury for her; it was a necessity.

She reached into her pocket to withdraw the key to the mailbox. From habit, her breath grew short and shallow, the way it had for the past few months every time she collected the mail. Naomi had been living in fear of receiving yet another letter informing her that yet another institution had closed its doors in her deaf daughter's face.

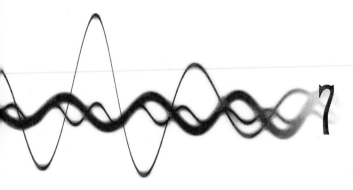

No one was willing to accept part of the responsibility involved in raising a deaf child. Naomi so badly wanted her to grow up in the company of healthy, normal children her own age. She had no idea at first how difficult that would turn out to be. *My daughter is such a good girl, so refined. She won't cause problems in school; she won't bother the teacher. I know plenty of super-rambunctious children who were accepted into preschool without a hitch. My Becky, on the other hand — such a smart, good girl — had to fight for years to get into preschool.*

This particular struggle is behind us, thank G-d. But there's so much still ahead.

The mailbox held five letters. One was from the telephone company, two were wedding invitations, the fourth an invitation to a bar mitzvah. But wait – what was that? The envelope bore the logo of the institution Mindy has been attending for the past three years.

"Flowers in the Garden — Educational Center for Children with Autism or P.D.D." the fancy script letters read. Naomi's knees buckled. Did they want to tell her that Mindy would no longer be allowed to continue in her school? Was a new struggle about to begin?

Ribbono shel Olam, Naomi found herself whispering quietly. *Please, I have no strength now. I have no ko'ach anymore. We've only just completed one struggle; I need time to gather strength before the next one begins. Please, please ...*

Stop! She commanded herself. *Sit down, open the envelope and read. You've never heard of an institution for autistic children throwing out a student in the middle of the school year. What reason could they possibly have for doing so? Rowdy behavior? Failure to complete homework? Disrespect to teachers?* Naomi smiled sadly and took a deep breath. The letter was decorated with balloons, flowers and pictures of children holding hands.

"Dear Parents," the letter began. "We would like to inform you about a number of changes with regard to birthday celebrations. Please answer the questions below and return this letter with your daughter tomorrow.

1. What is your child's Jewish birth date?
2. What is her favorite activity?

3. What is her favorite sweet?

4. Would you be able to participate in a birthday party conducted by our staff on the day of your daughter's birthday? If it falls on Shabbos or Yom Tov, or on a day you are not available to join us here at Flowers in the Garden, please select an alternate date."

After the questions came a detailed description of the birthday parties that would be held, G-d willing, on the students' real birthdays or as close to the real date as possible. Family members were invited. It was preferable to coordinate the parents' arrival with the staff a week before the event. The birthday parties were going to be especially festive this year.

"Thank you for your cooperation," the letter concluded.

It was signed by Nicole, teacher of "The Roses," the class and the entire staff at Flowers in the Garden.

"Thank you for your cooperation." When would Mindy be able to cooperate with them? When would Mindy cooperate with anyone?

So that's all it is, you paranoid woman! Mindy's school wants to celebrate her birthday with a special party, and her family is invited. Does that include Yanky, Becky and Sari? A birthday party for Mindy. That means Becky's birthday is coming up, too. They're twins, after all. Happy birthday, Becky and Mindy. Happy birthday ...

It all began six years ago. We were a happy family before, and then everything changed. No, that's not quite accurate. We are a happy family still, baruch Hashem, despite the difficulties. Our children are more mature, more responsible, more understanding and sensitive. I wonder if Yanky would be as sensitive as he is if he were part of a different family. When we were first hurled into the depths of this nisayon, I had no idea what our family would look like six years down the road. Today I thank Hashem for every step we take with His help and kindness. We observe so much siyatta diShmaya that only a blind man could fail to see it.

Six years have passed since that day. Their birthday is 24 Cheshvan. Today is 16 Cheshvan. It's nice that her school is taking the initiative to celebrate Mindy's birthday on its Jewish date.

Naomi's mind swept back to an altogether different date, some three years after the twins' birth. She and Shlomo had been running from doctor to doctor for a year or so, trying to figure out what was wrong with Mindy. It was just past her third birthday that her condition was diagnosed officially.

The memories came rushing back.

Smooth brown hair, green eyes and a pale face. An exact copy of her twin sister.

"Your daughter is autistic," the doctor said, his eyes compassionate. "Do you know what that means?"

Naomi gripped the chair she was sitting on, out of her mind with fright. Of course she knew what that meant – she herself had diagnosed many autistic children. "But ... but ... how can that be? You told me they were deaf."

"I'm not saying that diagnosis was wrong," the doctor replied, coughing uncomfortably. He tried to retain his composure, but his sensitive heart melted before the Mandels' panic-stricken faces. "But there's an additional problem."

"How come you didn't know it until now?" Helpless rage mingled with unfathomable pain. And yet, she, too, should have realized.

"It's not easy to diagnose autism," the doctor said quietly. "She was too small for me to be absolutely sure. Autism can only be diagnosed from the age of two or three."

"But she's small now, too, isn't she?" Shlomo asked.

"She is small," the doctor agreed, "but it's pretty clear ..."

"So perhaps you're mistaken," Shlomo interrupted.

The doctor sighed. "I don't think so. We took extensive tests, and she's already three years old. There is still a chance I'm mistaken, but it's highly unlikely. After all, you yourselves saw that something was not quite right with your little girl. That's why you came to see me, isn't it?"

"Is there any treatment for autism?" Shlomo was groping for a piece of solid information that would help them deal with the thunderbolt in a concrete manner.

"Yes, of course," the doctor said, his voice deep and steady. "But it's rather complex."

"Treatment for autism? I don't think such a thing exists," Naomi said, her voice riddled with pain. Emotion from the depths of her heart surfaced in her eyes. Shlomo sat motionless, staring into space. Their dream to help the twins lead normal lives despite being deaf was disintegrating. Naomi's eyes brimmed with tears – the very essence of a Jewish mother's broken heart – and the precious liquid was gathered into *Hakadosh Baruch Hu's* cup.

Naomi wept uncontrollably, and Shlomo felt miserably helpless. Pain sliced his heart, but he had to be strong and supportive for her sake.

"There are methods of treatment," the doctor insisted gently. "There are many schools for children suffering from such disorders that can be of great help. I've seen a few cases where schools of this sort have worked near-miracles. I personally don't know much about dealing with autism, I admit, but ..." He pushed a thin pamphlet across his desk to Shlomo, who took it reluctantly. "There's some basic information there that you should find helpful. I'll also provide you with a list of professionals in the field and their phone numbers."

He continued talking for another few moments, offering guidance and encouragement. They said nothing, asked no questions. They were too broken to talk, too shocked to respond. What was there to say? Their world had been shattered.

They left the doctor's office and took the elevator down to the ground floor. Outside, spring was flaunting its lovely colors. The hospital lawn was resplendent with lush green grass and vibrant flowers. A gardener was picking up litter from the well-tended paths.

It is not unusual to see a woman weeping copiously in a hospital. Death means saying good-bye forever, and no artist's brush can capture the depth of pain such a parting evokes.

Naomi was, in a sense, saying good-bye to her daughter. A diagnosis of autism meant they would not share the same world. She'd already known that Mindy lived in a world of deathly silence — she had learned that the twins were deaf shortly after their birth. Now she had learned that Mindy's world was one of abject loneliness as well. She knew the doctor's diagnosis meant her daughter would be unable to communicate with others, not even her closest family. Her daughter inhabited a cold, foreign world, devoid of emotion and love.

Who will love you, dear daughter? Who will press you warmly to his heart when nothing at all ties you to humanity? Who will whisper words of love into your ear when you don't hear? Who will smile warmly at you when you don't understand? Who will help you understand who your parents are?

I'm your mother, little angel. You've been born into a dark world I cannot illuminate for you. I'm your mother, my Mindy. Naomi hugged her daughter and wept bitterly. *How will you know that I love you? How will you hear the beating of my heart as I hold you close?*

Mindy had fallen asleep in the doctor's office, and Naomi had insisted on carrying her out despite her not inconsiderable weight. Now her tears fell on her daughter's face as she slept peacefully.

"Will you ever know who your mother is?" she whispered silently. Mindy shifted in her arms and opened a pair of expressionless eyes, only to close them again immediately. Naomi swept a gentle finger over the high forehead, pug nose, soft cheek and narrow lips. Mindy continued writhing, clutching Naomi's finger forcefully.

You're clutching me hopefully, precious, but I cannot help you. You have a Father in Heaven, dear child. Ask Him to help you. Pray! Cry! Plead! This is your life, beloved daughter, but your life is forever intertwined with mine.

The car sped off, traversing roads and highways. The sun's rays shone through the windshield, illuminating the car's interior. *Light and shade, light and shade. Hashem, give this child the strength to grow. Give me the strength to raise her as best I can. Send her the rays of light that do have the power to illuminate her life. Lift the light out of the shadows for her.*

Berlin 1945

Marty stepped out into the warm day. Late morning had brought with it mild gusts of wind and a sprinkling of clouds in a clear blue sky. He walked quickly, head upright, to the Timer Cafe. Ordering a cup of coffee and a slice of cake, he took a seat and spread *The London Times* on the table before him. The pungent aroma of coffee mingled with the scent of apple-cinnamon cake. Marty sipped slowly from his mug and crumbled his cake into tiny pieces.

"Meir?" The voice was deep and low, and Marty leaped from his seat in alarm. Shaul was already seated at one of the side tables. He held a cup of lukewarm coffee and wore the same expression on his face that Marty had seen on the train to Berlin.

"Hello," Marty said, relieved. "I was beginning to think you wouldn't show up."

"I'm never late, Meir. And I don't say things I don't mean." He paused. "You came. That means you're serious."

"Very much so," Marty promised.

For five minutes the two sat in silence. It was an unnatural, uncomfortable silence. Perhaps that was why Shaul smiled when he finally raised his eyes and looked at Marty.

"You know," he said, "there's another characteristic you have that we haven't yet discussed."

Marty's eyebrows rose and Shaul went on, still smiling. "You're patient. You have the ability to wait and wait and wait some more. That's a positive trait."

"Not necessarily." Marty was not pleased with the compliment. He didn't consider it a compliment at all. "It's not the trait of a warrior."

"Why do you say so?" Shaul asked in surprise. "Lying in ambush for hours on end requires infinite patience. A good intelligence agent must be painstakingly meticulous. A spy ..."

"A true warrior," Marty interrupted, "must be bold, quick to react and good at hand-to-hand combat."

"Well, perhaps. There is some truth to what you're saying. Obviously, both traits are necessary, but ..." A note of concern crept into Shaul's measured voice. "And you, aren't you a brave warrior? You aren't quick to react?"

Marty smiled, his eyes filled with pain. "I am a brave warrior," he said quietly. "I fought without fear. I was indifferent to death; I courted danger. I had nothing to lose, Shaul. I have nothing left in the world."

A spark of satisfaction glimmered in Shaul's eyes. "I imagined as much," he said.

"You understand me," Marty said, shocked at his own words. Although Shaul had captured his heart from the very first moment they met, Marty hadn't planned to bare the secrets of his soul to anyone just yet. "You, too, lost all you had in Auschwitz."

A shadow passed over Shaul's face. "All I had," he murmured. His eyes were pools of anguish; his voice tinged with pain. "All I had."

Silence hung between them once more. Shaul seemed lost in thought, his eyes staring expressionlessly at an unseen point in the distance. Then he snapped out of his reverie and smiled again. "And your goal in life is no longer revenge?"

Marty shrugged. "I'm confused," he admitted. "You've sown seeds of doubt in my mind. What have you to offer me other than revenge? You spoke of restoring the glory of the Jewish people, of the revival of our broken nation in Eretz Yisrael. Do you have a plan?"

"We have a plan," Shaul said quietly, "and I think we've found the right man to oversee it."

Marty was no fool. "Illegal immigration. Am I correct?"

Shaul shook his head slowly. "No, we have plenty of men working on that front. You are more suited to different work, no less important."

"I'm not suited ..." Marty began in protest.

"There are many people who can help us with illegal immigration. What I have in mind for you is something not many people can do — but you can. We don't want to waste your talent on something anyone can do."

"And what is it I can do that others can't?" Marty asked defiantly. A sharp-eared man would have detected the note of pride and hope in Marty's voice.

"You're a soldier," Shaul said. "You can fight. You wanted revenge, did you not? You wanted to take revenge on the Nazis. You wanted to fight. I want you to fight, too — but for the sake of building rather than for the sake of revenge."

"Building?"

"Building Eretz Yisrael."

"You want me to fight the British," Marty whispered, leaning forward and scanning the people in the cafe.

"Yes," Shaul nodded. "I want you to fight the British. I want you to fight for Eretz Yisrael in Eretz Yisrael. It's not Palestine; it's Eretz Yisrael, and it belongs to us."

Marty rested his head between his hands and attempted to think. Suddenly, his lips stretched into an ironic smile.

"What's so amusing?" Suspicion was evident in Shaul's eyes.

"I was a soldier in His Majesty's army," Marty said. "I put myself at his disposal. I gave Britain my blood, my strength, my capabilities." He smiled again. "Wouldn't the situation you're proposing be ironic?"

Shaul nodded angrily. "The British ..." he murmured. His voice grew stronger and angrier. "The British took everything we gave them when they needed us, and now they give us nothing when we need them. They took everything! We put our struggle against them on hold for the sake of the war. We offered them our blood, our lives. Our men fought shoulder to shoulder with theirs, and what do we ask of them now? Only what is rightly our due! And they ... they allow us to be slaughtered, they restrict us, arrest us, fight us mercilessly."

Marty looked at him in surprise. Shaul was a tough man, not given to outbursts. This display of sudden emotion surprised him.

"So, young man," Shaul said, his eyes raking Marty's face. "What do you say?"

A blast of cold and the smell of danger assailed Marty suddenly. In his mind's eye, he saw red lights flashing and heard wailing sirens and creaking tank turrets. Where had the smell of gunpowder and smoke come from? Why was he thinking of war?

Wait Marty; wait a minute! His sense of caution kicked in. Do you know Shaul? How do you know who this man is or what he's really after? You received an anonymous letter proposing a meeting on the Rome-Berlin train with a man who had a suggestion for you. Who's to say this is not a trap?

Shaul saw the hesitation on Marty's face. He smiled. The young man was very careful. That was another attribute to add to the already long list.

"I don't know," Marty said finally. "I'll have to think about it."

Shaul nodded earnestly. "I understand you. You want to verify how trustworthy I am, don't you?"

Marty did not move a muscle. The acrid taste of danger rose up in his mouth. He had survived six years of combat in one of the most difficult wars in history, but a hidden enemy could be his undoing. The route to jail was a short one indeed. No one could accuse him of anything yet, though.

"May I ask just how you intend to verify that?" Shaul's voice held a note of scorn.

Marty turned to him in fury, but Shaul went on unfazed. "You're completely alone in the world, Meir. There's no one at all you can trust. Your only friend, Jim, won't be able to help you here. He's British, after all. How can you confide in him?"

"Let's assume that is indeed the reason for my hesitation," Marty said evenly. "The fact that I'm not sure I can trust you. Is there anything wrong with that?"

"No," Shaul conceded. "In fact, your wariness is commendable. But tell me, Meir, is there anyone you feel you can trust?"

Marty suddenly became aware of the full extent of his loneliness. Until now, he had confided everything in Jim, but that was not an option now. Pain welled up in his heart at the thought of the friendship he'd have to give up if he accepted this mission. Jim was his only friend.

"My family perished in Auschwitz, as you know. I'm all alone."

"If that's the case, I'll use logic to persuade you. What reason would a British cop have to set up an elaborate trap for you? What would he get out of having you thrown into jail?"

Marty nodded and Shaul went on. "The policeman wouldn't gain a thing, Meir. If you were already a wanted activist, a known troublemaker, it would be worthwhile for the British police to catch you in a trap and arrest you. But now? What purpose would there be in baiting you?"

Marty nodded slowly.

"Alright," he said quietly. "I agree."

Shaul smiled, relief showing in his eyes. "Thank you, Meir. I feel certain you will never regret your decision. History will repay you, as will hundreds of thousands — even millions — of *olim* who will come to Eretz Yisrael once it is liberated from the British."

Meir did not return the smile. He was keenly aware of the burden of responsibility that had been placed on his shoulders, and traces of fear that this was a trap troubled him as well. Maybe one day he'd be proud of his success and maybe ... maybe he'd be able to forget a little bit. A shadow passed over his face.

Shaul looked at him worriedly. "Is everything alright?" His caring voice tugged at Marty's lonely heart.

He nodded. "Yes, thank you."

"Alright then, Meir. Good-bye. We'll meet here tomorrow at six p.m. See you."

Shaul disappeared quickly, the way he had the first time they'd met. Marty looked after the receding figure of his new friend with something akin to astonishment.

His new friend? His new friend! His new ... Wait a minute! What about his old friend? What would he tell Jim, his British friend? Should he stay away from the hotel and just not meet him again, or should he go to the hotel and say good-bye forever?

Jim was no fool. He'd connect Marty's sudden withdrawal with the fact that he, Jim, was British. What then? Would Jim tail him, investigate him? Jim had connections. If he decided to put a tail on Marty, he'd have no trouble doing so. If he went so far as to explain that he suspected a traitor to the British had turned up, Marty would be arrested in a flash.

Marty cradled his head in the palms of his hands. What should he do? What would Jim do? Would Jim sacrifice his personal friendship with Marty on the altar of his patriotism to England, or would the strength of their friendship prove stronger than his loyalty to his homeland?

He had to ask Shaul. But he wouldn't be meeting him until tomorrow. What should he do until then? *Calm down!* Marty scolded himself. *Why have you become so fearful and hesitant? How many years did you stare death in the face fearlessly? What's gotten into you? Have you become utterly dependent on a man you met two days ago? Stop being a child.*

Marty considered the facts. Right now, Jim knew nothing. He'd go to the hotel, meet Jim and chat with him the way he did every day. In the course of their conversation, he'd tell Jim his plans for the future: He wanted to travel to the United States to try and begin life anew there.

To allay Jim's suspicions if he decided to check up on him, he really would fly to the States. From there, he'd take a direct flight to Germany, Palestine, or wherever Shaul sent him.

Should he maintain a correspondence with Jim? Marty deliberated and decided in the end that he would not. He was an honest person, and he'd find it too taxing to pretend he was enjoying life in the United States when he was in fact miles away. He'd ask Jim for a "vacation" from his life and he'd promise to renew contact in a few months, after he'd had some time to recuperate.

What then? Marty hoped the war against the British would not last long. When Palestine became Eretz Yisrael, it would be easy for him to renew his bond with the only friend he had. Until then, his life's goal was more important than friendship, dear to him as it was.

He rose from his place with a sense of satisfaction. His plans were taking shape, growing clearer with every passing moment. He didn't have to cut off all contact with his friend; he'd renew their friendship when the battle was over.

As Marty tipped the waiter and prepared to leave the cafe, he became aware of a faint sense of unease lodged in his brain. Something was troubling him. What was it? The fact that Shaul was intimately familiar with his plans? The fact that he seemed to know him through and through? The fact that he had the habit of commenting on every character trait he noticed in Marty, as though he'd been a soldier in his unit for years? The fact that he treated him as a commander might treat a soldier? The fact that he'd been following him for some time?

No – it was none of these that made him feel uneasy now.

There was something else that echoed through his head over and over again, setting his heart atremble. He couldn't put his finger on it. He was intrigued by Shaul and his ideas. There was something aside from his personal charm that drew him to the man, however. Something that struck stubbornly at the rock in his heart and dug a tunnel through to the tender, loving part of that organ.

Oh, yes, that was it. Shaul called him Meir.

8

New York 5758/1998

The moment Becky entered the school building, she realized there was something she had completely forgotten to take into account. Dozens of girls of all sizes were running about, chatting and smiling to one another. It seemed that everyone knew everyone else. It was a happy, raucous tumult. Although Becky couldn't hear the din, she absorbed the atmosphere with her eyes and heart. Fear and apprehension gripped her.

Becky was a suspicious child by nature, or perhaps the trait was a consequence of her handicap. She always kept her eyes wide open and fixed upon the lips of the people around her, an expression of fear on her face. She was constantly afraid people were talking about her, making fun of her, pitying her, laughing at her.

Naomi felt that a person's circumstances affected his character, his inner self. The slightest deviation from the "norm" determined by the world at large causes the "different" person to be different by nature as well. She had noticed that heavy people tended to be especially sensitive, while short people often suffered from low self-esteem. Becky's deafness, Naomi felt, had caused her to become apprehensive, suspicious and shy.

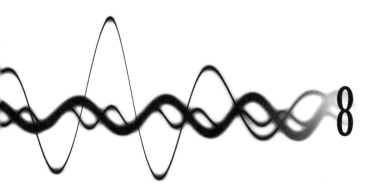

Now Becky's character worked against her. Becky paled. Everything was so confusing, so frightening. She didn't know whether the little redhead was laughing at her or whether the four tall girls chatting animatedly together were discussing her or something else entirely. The place she for so long had yearned to attend — the magical preschool of her dreams — lost its appeal in one fell blow. She had imagined girls sitting in neat rows, hands clasped in front of them as they listened with rapt attention to their teacher. The teacher taught them fascinating things, and then they went home. The whirl of action that greeted her now had never figured in the picture she had envisioned.

Loneliness came and stood at her side. Once again Becky felt how very different she was, how separate and apart from others her age. She took a few steps backward, intending to turn and flee; but then a strong, confident hand grasped her own and a pleasant-looking woman bent down so she was at eye level with her. "Becky?" she said. "Welcome to preschool!"

It was Morah Devorah, the teacher. Becky read her lips easily. Scanning her face, Becky saw that this was a woman she could trust. She had learned at an early age to discern whether someone was truly kind or not. Good people had laughter in their eyes and a soft expression on their faces. The teacher, Morah Devorah, was good.

Becky nodded. "I'm Becky," she said.

"Pleased to meet you. I'm Morah Devorah, the teacher. Jenny, your speech therapist, told me she'll be arriving a bit later. In the meantime, come with me and let me introduce you to all the girls."

She continued talking but forgot to turn her face toward Becky. Becky tugged lightly at her sleeve. "I didn't hear the last thing you said," she explained. "You weren't looking at me."

Morah Devorah smiled. "I see you know how to take care of yourself," she said. "Come, darling."

"Girls," Morah Devorah announced, "take your seats, please. I'm going to introduce a new girl."

Becky felt a shiver of apprehension run down her spine. She wasn't sure what she was worried about, but her highly developed sixth sense predicted trouble.

"Her name is Becky," Morah Devorah began.

"How come she didn't start the year with us?" interrupted the short redheaded girl Becky had noticed earlier.

Becky's face drained of color. Her lips trembled. Morah Devorah hugged her fondly and said, "Because she's a very special girl."

A current of excitement rippled through the class.

"What's so special about her?" demanded a tall girl.

"She can't hear."

"What?" a few girls asked incredulously. "How come she can't hear?"

"Because that's the way Hashem wanted it," Morah Devorah replied calmly. "But she has a very special way to —"

"So how can we talk to her?" the redhead interrupted again.

"Ruchaleh," Morah Devorah said, her tone a trifle annoyed. Becky saw her eyebrows draw together in warning, "I don't want to have to stop speaking every minute because of your interruptions!"

The redhead fell silent.

"Becky has a very special way of understanding what people say to her," Morah Devorah went on. "She looks at people's lips, and she can tell what they're saying by the way their lips move. But you have to look at her when you talk so she'll be able to understand you. Isn't that wonderful? Do any of you know how to do that?"

The girls stared at Becky incredulously.

"She's a very, very special girl," Morah Devorah concluded, "and she knows lots of things that you don't."

The girls crowded eagerly around Becky, who felt completely overwhelmed. All her life she had never spoken to even a single girl her own age, and suddenly dozens of girls wanted the pleasure of talking to her! She was too frightened to enjoy the attention. Her fear was more intense than her desire for friendship.

"Do you really understand what people say just by looking at their lips?" the redhead asked. Becky saw that she was curious about everything but had little patience to wait for answers to her questions. Her clothes were wrinkled and dusty and her socks were torn. Her skirt was worn; it looked old. Its red and blue stripes were faded and didn't match her pink blouse at all. Her long ponytail was messy and knotted.

"Yes," Becky replied. The girl's lips were somewhat difficult to read, but Becky managed. She wondered about the girl's clothing but felt too shy to ask.

"And if we cover our mouths?" demanded a girl who looked as though she ought to be in third grade. She was a head taller than Becky and wore glasses. "If we cover our mouths when we talk, you won't understand what we're saying?"

Becky did not understand the entire sentence, but she was accustomed to completing sentences by filling in missing words on her own. She shook her head no.

"So if we don't want you to hear something," the tall girl said sharply, "we can just cover our mouths!" She covered her mouth, said something, and burst out laughing. The girls all laughed and Becky felt utterly helpless. Tears sprang to her eyes and it was only with a supreme effort that she managed to stop them. Suddenly, a comeback sprang to her mind.

"When I whisper something to someone sitting near me, you can't hear me, but when you tell your friend a secret, I know what you're saying even if I'm across the room!"

"Never mind," the tall girl said dismissively. "It's a lot easier to cover our mouths than to whisper. Besides, I don't believe you can read lips from across the room." And she sauntered away.

Most of the girls turned their backs on her and joined the tall girl. Becky didn't even know what her name was. Ruchaleh, the small redhead with the strange clothing, remained at her side, staring at her with admiration.

"She doesn't know what she's talking about," Ruchaleh declared. "You can be my friend any time."

Becky shrugged. A friendship with the bubbly redhead with the messy hair and shabby clothes seemed very threatening to her. She was more attracted to the blond girl standing on the side and sucking her thumb, but when the tall girl called, "Shifrah Leah!" the blond girl sighed resignedly and followed the other girls.

"Let's not call Ruchaleh," the tall girl said. "She's messy and lazy and dirty. She can be friends with the crazy deaf girl. Why do they let crazy girls into our class?"

"But Raizel," protested one of the girls, "Why do you think she's crazy?"

"'Cause she can't hear," Raizel replied decisively. "Even the teacher said so."

"So what? Who says if someone can't hear, she's not normal?"

"Stop talking nonsense," Raizel grumbled. "You know very well she isn't normal. If she were normal, she'd be able to hear like everyone else."

The redheaded girl remained at her side. "Isn't she silly? You'll be my friend, and we'll see who won't want to be your friend. In the end, everyone will be our friends."

She leaned over and whispered something in Becky's ear.

Becky chuckled, her initial dislike of the girl dissipating. "Ruchaleh, I didn't hear you," she said.

Ruchaleh looked her full in the face and said, "No one wants to be my friend. They say I'm messy and dirty." She surveyed her worn clothes and sighed heavily. "That's why I have no friends." Tears filled her eyes.

Becky's heart went out to the little girl. She seemed so pathetic. "Want to be my friend?' she asked.

The vivacious redhead suddenly appeared weak and unsure of herself. Becky felt encouraged, though she wasn't sure why.

"Yes!" replied the redhead firmly, her gaiety returning. "We'll be best friends!"

"Great!" Becky was pleased with the signing of this unwritten pact.

"But remember," Ruchaleh said, "my clothes are old and torn

and my hair is not always brushed. Are you sure you want to be my friend?"

Becky's eyes filled with tears. For the first time in her life, her small heart filled with pity for someone else. Look at that – this girl, even though she heard perfectly, was worse off than she was! Becky looked down at her own neat and pretty clothing and stroked her smoothly brushed hair. True, Ruchaleh was not as bright or as clean as Raizel, but she had a much, much kinder heart. And who was to say which was more important?

"You know," she said to Ruchaleh seriously, "Raizel might be cleaner than you, but your *neshamah* is cleaner than hers, and so is your tongue."

"That's *lashon hara*," Ruchaleh said with equal seriousness. "My daddy says you're not allowed to talk *lashon hara* about anyone, no matter what."

"My *ima* says if you're doing it to teach another girl to be better, you're allowed to."

"You think we're allowed to tell Morah Devorah what Raizel said?" Ruchaleh asked. She shook her head doubtfully. "I don't think so."

"Ask your father," Becky suggested. "Tell him the story without names, and ask him if we can tell Morah Devorah the story."

"My father's not home a lot. It's better if you ask your mother."

"My mother?" Becky recoiled as if from a snake. "My mother? Oh, no. I couldn't do that!"

"Why not?" Ruchaleh wondered aloud.

"That's how it is," Becky said patiently, a note of absolute certainty in her voice. "My brother Yanky told me so, and I agree with him. We're absolutely not allowed to tell her things that will make her upset."

"Why do you think this will make her upset?"

"I want her to think everyone in the class is friendly with me," Becky explained. "If I ask my mother such a question, she'll know it isn't like that."

"Ah," Ruchaleh said. She sighed. "Alright, I'll ask my daddy."

"Good," Becky said happily. "That way, we'll know what to do."

"Come," Ruchaleh said, tugging at her hand. "Come to the sandbox. You can build wonderful castles there and live in gorgeous houses!"

"In the sand?" Becky couldn't believe it. "Can't be!"

"I mean that we imagine it," Ruchaleh explained, stating the obvious.

That was how Becky learned about one of her friend's most prominent characteristics. Her highly developed imagination was unlike any Becky had ever come across.

"My house isn't very nice," Ruchaleh explained, "so I pretend it's lovely. Every time something not so pleasant happens, I pretend something wonderful happened instead."

Becky was somewhat taken aback, at first, by this way of thinking, but she quickly discovered its advantages. "Can I pretend I'm not deaf?" she verified carefully.

"Of course!" her new friend exclaimed. "Come on, let's go to the sandbox."

Becky went out to the backyard and waited a moment for Ruchaleh to join her. Ruchaleh held a plastic bottle filled with water.

"What are you doing?" Becky asked, confounded.

"Making mud," Ruchaleh said happily. "You need mud to build nice things."

"Mud?" Becky was shocked. "Mud is awfully dirty."

Ruchaleh paused in middle of pouring the water on the sand. "Haven't you ever played with mud before?" she asked. Her shock was greater than Becky's.

"No."

"So what did you play with your friends?"

"Um," Becky said, flustered. Her smile was tinged with sadness. "I've never had friends."

BECKY STOOD ON tiptoe, peering out of the large window overlooking the spacious backyard. Sabba was there. Sabba often came to visit.

Ima was his only daughter and his only child in America; Uncle Shmuel lived in Eretz Yisrael. Savta came often, too, but not as much as Sabba.

Sometimes Becky had the feeling that Sabba was especially fond of her and Mindy. True, his face took on a strange expression whenever he looked at Mindy, but Becky knew he loved Mindy very much — even more than he loved her, Becky. It was strange. You couldn't talk or play with Mindy normally, but Sabba loved her more than "Yanky the *talmid chacham*," more than her, who attended a normal preschool and knew how to read already; more than Sari, their baby sister, whom everyone adored because she was so cute. Sabba loved Mindy. Face pressed to the windowpane, Becky watched her grandfather and her twin sister interact.

Sabba was playing with Mindy in the backyard. He was very determined. Over and over again, he tossed a ball in her direction and waited for her to catch it and throw it back to him. Mindy was curled into a ball in the middle of the lawn, refusing to cooperate. Sabba got up, went over to Mindy, and with a firm hand pulled her upright so that she faced him.

"I want you to throw the ball to me, Mindy," he said firmly. "You hear?"

Mindy stared at him blankly. Wriggling out of Sabba's strong grasp, she ran to a corner of the lawn. Sabba did not give up. Again he drew her upright and stated his request. Mindy raised expressionless eyes to meet his steely, determined ones.

Becky watched without moving a muscle. Mindy bent down reluctantly, picked up the ball, and threw it in his direction. Becky's breath caught in her throat. Sabba had succeeded! A small smile of triumph played at the corners of his lips.

"Good," he said, his tone still somewhat aggressive. "Again!"

"Sabba!" Becky ran to him breathlessly. "Sabba, you did it! You got her to throw that ball!"

"Ah, my flower. Were you watching us?"

"I wanted to come talk to you, but I saw that you were busy with Mindy."

"I have room in my heart for all my grandchildren," he said with a broad, inviting smile.

"Maybe so, but that doesn't mean you can give each of us attention at the same time," Becky replied logically. "If you're playing with her now, you can't listen to me."

Sabba chuckled. "You always have an answer for everything, little flower."

"It's Mindy who goes to 'Flowers in the Garden,'" Becky protested, "not me."

"*Baruch Hashem*." Sabba pointed to the ball. "Maybe you should try to play with her?" he suggested.

"With Mindy?" Becky made a face. Suddenly, she remembered what the girls had said about her. They said such things about Mindy, too, that she was crazy, that she wasn't normal.

It was sad, but in Mindy's case, it was true.

"Yes, why not?"

"Okay, but we don't usually play ball. She'd rather play with dolls."

"How do you know?"

"That's the way it seems to me."

"Alright, then," Sabba smiled. "If you say so."

The two of them were silent for a moment and then Sabba said, "You came to tell me something, didn't you?" He fixed a penetrating gaze on his granddaughter's face.

"Yes."

Sabba glanced at Mindy, who had curled herself up into a ball again. He sighed.

"See?" Becky said. "She doesn't like to play ball."

"Okay, let's leave her alone," Sabba said resignedly. "Tell me why you're not enjoying preschool."

Becky stared at her grandfather in surprise. "How do you know I'm not enjoying preschool?"

"You didn't tell anyone, right?"

"Right." Becky sighed like an adult. "Look how happy Ima is, now that I'm finally going to school. Don't you think she'd be upset if she knew I wasn't happy there?"

"Let me tell you something, little flower. Your mother is my daughter. I wouldn't want my daughter to hide from me things that happen to her, even if they're sad or hard."

"Did you ever have anything sad and hard happen to you?" Becky asked, looking at Sabba.

Sabba burst out laughing and hugged her tight. "My little flower, I do believe you're going to grow up to be a psychologist just like your mother!"

"Maybe, if people will have the patience to listen to me and hear what I have to say," Becky said, her tone despairing.

"Ah," Sabba said, stroking Becky's smooth hair as it billowed in the chill winter wind. "I understand that that's your problem at school."

"What?" She was confused.

"The girls don't have the patience to listen to you."

"But they didn't even try!" The tears came gushing forth. "They didn't try at all! Raizel ... she said I was crazy and that no one should be my friend."

"Raizel?" He raised an eyebrow.

"It might be *lashon hara*," Becky sobbed. "She's this really tall girl and everyone does what she says, except Ruchaleh. Promise not to tell Ima?"

"Why should I promise?"

"'Cause I don't want her to be sad!" She heard Yanky's warning ringing in her ears.

Sabba appeared displeased. "Alright."

"Only Ruchaleh wants to be my friend now."

"Great!" Sabba said happily. "So Ruchaleh will be your friend."

"But Raizel says Ruchaleh's lazy." She lowered her voice to a whisper. "She says she's dirty and messy."

"Ah," Sabba's smiling eyes turned serious. "And she also said that you're crazy."

"But I'm not!" Tears filled her eyes again.

"And who says Ruchaleh is lazy?" Sabba demanded. "I think she'd make a good friend for you. That way, you can show the class what happens to a girl who's a true friend and doesn't hurt other girls' feelings. Everyone's going to want to be friends with good girls who never say unkind things to each other. You'll see, Becky, in the end, all the girls will be your friend. It's going to take time, as it does for every new girl, but that's what will happen in the end."

"But Ruchaleh really is ..." Becky paused in mid-sentence. "Is this *lashon hara*, too?" she asked, looking at Sabba worriedly.

"I don't know her," Sabba said, "but I understand that she doesn't have such pretty clothes and her hair is not always brushed neatly. Am I right?"

"So you do know her!"

"No," Sabba objected. "I guessed, my flower, I just guessed. Raizel might be right on some counts, but she's not right on them all. She said you're deaf, and that's true. She said you're not normal — and that's not true. She said that Ruchaleh's not so clean — that may be true. She said she's lazy — that's not true at all."

"How do you know?"

"A lazy person is someone who doesn't try to do anything," Sabba explained. "Someone who tries to do the right thing but doesn't always succeed is not lazy at all. Maybe Ruchaleh has trouble understanding certain things the teacher says; maybe she can't remember the alphabet so well — but she's a good girl with a kind heart, and that's far more important."

"That's what I told Ruchaleh," Becky said proudly. "I told her she had a clean *neshamah*."

"That's a nice thing to say," Sabba said seriously. "It was the right thing to say. The two of you are going to be good, good friends — the best friends in the class — and once everyone sees that you're friends, they'll all want to talk to you."

"That's what Ruchaleh said." Becky seemed a tad more cheerful than before. "But I don't want only one girl to be my friend."

"So maybe you ought to speak to Raizel," Sabba suggested. That idea was downright frightening.

"But she purposely covers her mouth so that I won't be able to read her lips!" Becky wailed. "I don't want her to laugh at me!"

"Ruchaleh can listen for you to Raizel and all the others and tell you what they said. In exchange, you can teach her what she doesn't know."

"Who told you she doesn't know things?"

"I have a hunch," he said, avoiding a direct response. "I think that as a team you can do lots of mitzvos and also become friendly with other girls in the class."

Becky considered the idea. "You really think it will work?" she asked doubtfully.

"You can always try," he said softly.

"I'm not sure I can suggest it to Ruchaleh," Becky said hesitantly. "We'll see. But you say I ought to be Ruchaleh's friend?"

"For sure."

"And afterward everyone will be friends with us?"

"I hope so," he sighed. "Little flower, I can't promise you that."

"Okay. But ..." — she looked at him warningly — "don't tell Ima."

He shook his head with displeasure. "Why not?"

Becky looked at him reprovingly. "Sabba, I already told you. Because I don't want her to be sad."

"Ah." He nodded. "Okay, I won't tell her, because I promised. But you should know that it isn't right to keep secrets from your mother."

"Yanky told me to," Becky said. "After I cried because I didn't want to go to another evaluator, Yanky was mad at me. He's never mad at me; that was the only time. He told me that Ima's sad because of Mindy and we're not allowed to tell her anything that will make her sadder, no matter what."

"Yanky said that?"

"Yes."

"He's a good boy."

"Don't you think he's right?"

"No, not at all. *Imas* always have the strength to hear the things their children want to tell them, even if they're not happy things."

"I'll wait until I have something happy to tell her," Becky declared.

"Come tell me something happy," Sabba said, pinching her cheek lovingly. "It's going to be your birthday soon. What would you like for a present?"

Becky wasn't sure if the experiment would work. The girls in preschool didn't like her; that was a fact. Raizel had stopped telling the other girls not be Becky's friend; she simply paid her no attention at all. It was as if Becky didn't exist. The other girls took their cue from Raizel. Who had the time to speak slowly and clearly to make sure the deaf girl understood what you were saying? Who had the patience to listen to her somewhat guttural, not perfectly clear voice? No one did, except for Ruchaleh.

Ruchaleh spent a large part of the day with a different teacher, not Morah Devorah. During circle time, Ruchaleh often leaped up from her seat. Morah Devorah had to tell her over and over again to sit down.

Sometimes Morah Devorah's rebuke helped, but most of the time it didn't. Sometimes Ruchaleh went outside to play in the sand in the middle of circle time! On rare occasions, Morah Devorah went so far as to punish her. After Ruchaleh ripped up the new poster in anger when she didn't get the doll she wanted, for example. Most of the time, though, Morah Devorah made an exception for Ruchaleh and didn't punish her, even when she did things that other girls certainly would have been penalized for.

Ruchaleh was a bubbly, merry girl. Despite her learning difficulties and the punishments she received, despite her worn and shabby clothing and unkempt hair, despite the fact that she brought only a plain slice of bread for lunch — she was always laughing and happy.

For sad, withdrawn Becky, Ruchaleh was like a ray of sunshine, like a butterfly. Becky loved being in Ruchaleh's company — and not only because she was the only girl who would play with her.

Once, when Ruchaleh went to the other teacher, Becky followed her and peeked through the keyhole of the room they went into. The other teacher spoke to Ruchaleh and played with her. Becky, who was personally familiar with the concept of private tutoring, understood that the teacher was helping Ruchaleh understand the material that Morah Devorah taught the class.

Why is Ruchaleh like that? Becky wondered. *Why can't she understand what Morah Devorah teaches, just like everyone else?*

The answer occurred to her almost immediately. *For the same reason I'm the way I am. Everyone has a different job in this world, Ima says, and Hashem makes everyone be the way he has to be in order to do that job.*

In the meantime, though, when Ruchaleh went to the small room with the other teacher, Becky was left alone. So very alone.

9

Naomi asked that Mindy's birthday party be held a day early so that the next day would be free for Becky. Becky needed the excitement and celebration of a party more than her twin sister. Becky would be celebrating her birthday in school the next day, and Naomi wanted to be there.

Naomi deliberated long and hard over whether to take the children to Mindy's school. On the one hand, she wanted them to see what Mindy's life was like, where she spent the better part of her days. And she knew Mindy would be glad if they came. On the other hand, Naomi was reluctant to expose them, especially Becky, to Mindy's life.

Especially Becky? Not quite. Yanky, too. Sometimes Naomi thought that the day the twins were born, Yanky aged. His back bent to receive the burden of his special sisters. His intelligent eyes were constantly seeking out ways to help. Yanky was a son to be proud of, but Naomi didn't want him to be the way he was. She didn't like it at all.

Naomi's father had spoken to her. He told her that Becky was unhappy in school, that she was having trouble making friends.

"I can't tell you the details, daughter," he said softly. "I promised Becky I wouldn't tell. I gave her advice, but maybe you should try to draw her out."

Naomi nodded. "You said there was something you wanted to

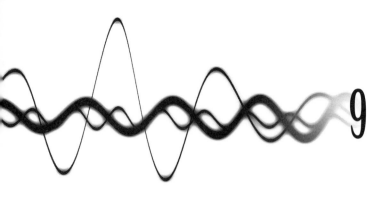

discuss with me," she reminded him. "What is it, if not Becky?"

"It's Yanky."

"Yanky?" Naomi's eyebrows shot up in surprise. "Yanky's my only regular child!"

"No, that's not true," her father said firmly. "You've got Becky and Sari, too."

"Becky?"

"Becky's a regular girl, Naomi. She may be deaf, but you'll agree with me that her intelligence matches and even surpasses that of your average regular girl. She's extremely bright and talented."

"*Baruch Hashem*," Naomi agreed. "She even attends a regular school."

"*Baruch Hashem*," her father echoed, a note of rebuke in his voice. "You shouldn't say that, Naomi. Becky sometimes thinks that she really isn't normal, and such thoughts are naturally very disturbing to her. If you send her that message as well, she'll be sure it's like that. You know what I mean?"

Naomi nodded silently.

Her father continued, his voice low, "You know, Naomi, children absorb the messages you send them."

"What is it about Yanky that you wanted to tell me?"

"Yes, you have Yanky, as well. Did you know that the child has taken the burden of responsibility for his sisters onto his own shoulders? It's very unhealthy."

Naomi sighed deeply. "Yes," she said, "I know. What can I do about it?"

Her father drummed his fingers on the tabletop, still covered with crumbs from lunch.

"I understood from Becky that Yanky told her she mustn't upset you."

Naomi said nothing.

"I think you have to speak to him, Naomi. A child shouldn't have to bear such a burden on his own, without the help of an adult."

Naomi nodded. "Thank you, Abba," she said in a choked voice. "I'll speak to him."

"This might be connected to what I told you before."

"About what?"

"About any messages you might send your children. Maybe if you were a bit more optimistic, happy; if you sent them the message that everything was fine and in order, that you aren't sad at all, they'd relax, do you see?"

"How can I send them such a message?" Naomi whispered. "How can I show them that I'm not sad when I am? How can I radiate optimism and happiness when I'm in so much pain?"

"I don't know," her father said heavily. "I don't know."

They were both silent for a moment, and then her father said, his voice soft and pleading, "Naomi, I don't want to hurt you, you understand?"

Naomi nodded. "I think I'm capable of handling this," she said. "I'll try. I'll see what I can do about the two matters you mentioned. They might very well be connected."

"Will you do that?" Her father's furrowed brow relaxed.

"Yes," she replied. "It will be okay. I'm not a little girl, Abba."

"I know," he said with a sigh. "Oh, my little girl, how you've grown. ..."

And matured, Naomi thought to herself. *Life has forced me to mature quickly and painfully.*

Shlomo and Naomi decided that only they and the baby would attend Mindy's party. Sari wouldn't ask any questions. She'd look at the students in the institution Mindy attended with round, curious eyes. She'd see their beautiful souls and accept it all with the healthy understanding of a pure, innocent baby.

Naomi waited for Shlomo. He was supposed to return from davening and drive them to Flowers in the Garden. The institution was located quite some distance from their home; it would be a forty-five minute drive if there was no traffic.

Becky and Yanky had not yet left for school, but Naomi thought she could trust her almost-nine-year-old son and six-year-old daughter to get ready on their own. She had prepared their sandwiches the night before and left them on the kitchen table, and before the children went to bed she hugged them and asked them to dress and go to cheder and school this morning on their own. Yanky's bus stop was close to the house, and Becky's preschool was just one block away.

A long honk, two short ones, then two more long ones. That was Shlomo's honk. He was signaling to Naomi that he had arrived. He still had to come in to take the cake, but he wanted her to know he was home. Naomi was about to leave, the bag of candies in one hand and Sari in the other, when someone grabbed her legs in a giant bear hug. Small hands clutched her and a sleepy voice said, "Ima? Are you going to Mindy's school?"

Naomi turned around to answer her. "Yes, Becky darling, and Abba's honking for me. I have to leave now, sweetheart."

"I didn't hear," she replied impishly. "I didn't hear anyone honking," she repeated, laughing. She was clearly pleased with her joke.

"Becky!"

"What?"

"I need to leave. Please let me go." But Becky held her mother so tight, Naomi couldn't break free, not with Sari on one arm and the bag of nosh on the other.

"So, you're going?"

"Yes. Do you need something?"

"I think Mindy will be happy if I come."

"I don't think so," Naomi replied, without thinking. She bit her lip. Illogical as it sounded, considering the severity of Mindy's handicap, there was a tenuous bond between the twins, and she didn't want to destroy it.

"Why not?"

Naomi crouched down and kissed her daughter's forehead. "Becky, I don't think it's a good idea for you to come. Besides, you're not dressed, and we're in a hurry."

"So I'll dress really fast!" Becky insisted.

A key sounded in the lock and Shlomo walked in. He hurried to the fridge to take the birthday cake Naomi had prepared for Mindy.

"What happened?" he asked, his voice somewhat on edge when he saw Becky, still in her nightgown, looking at her mother pleadingly. "What's the problem?"

"Becky wants to come to the party," Naomi explained, her face toward Becky's. Becky raised her eyes to her father's face, looking apprehensively at his lips.

Shlomo hesitated for a split second, a furrow forming in his brow. "No," he said decisively.

Becky sighed. She knew that her father was not one to categorically refuse requests, but when he did, nothing in the world would change his mind.

"What a shame. I wanted so badly to come along," she said quietly. "Why can't I?" she asked in a subdued tone of voice. Without waiting for an answer, she turned on her heels and climbed the stairs to her room. Shlomo caught up with her in two quick strides.

"If you'd like," he said softly, "you can come with us instead to the Chanukah party in Mindy's school. But think about it carefully first and decide if you really want to come."

Becky nodded silently.

Shlomo returned to the kitchen, picked up the cake carefully, and went out to the car. Naomi waved good-bye to Becky and left the house as well.

"Why did you say no to her?" she asked Shlomo, once they were on our way.

"Because you and I had discussed the matter already and reached a decision. Becky and Yanky were told that we don't want them to come to Mindy's school. I don't want Becky to think that we give in to her every request just because she's deaf," he replied firmly. "Yanky wanted to come, too. You refused quite firmly, right?"

Naomi had to admit he was right.

"Becky's got to grow up like a regular child. As it is, there are too many instances where we go easy on her because of her situation. I don't think it's healthy for her."

"What about the Chanukah party?"

"We didn't hand down a final decision on that yet. Becky senses that if she pleads with you, you'll eventually give in because you feel sorry for her. I don't want her to get the impression that we're wishy-washy with our decisions. We'll discuss the Chanukah party as a separate issue."

Naomi thought about what Shlomo said. It was true; she wasn't firm enough with Becky. Her handicap caused Naomi to look the other way and give in far more than was good for her. It was wrong; Naomi knew it. *You're hurting her*, her brain said. *You've got to stop*, logic dictated. Somehow, though, her heart refused to cooperate.

Shlomo and Naomi arrived at Flowers in the Garden. Shlomo parked the car and they got out.

Flowers in the Garden was a nice place. Every time Naomi saw it, she was impressed by how noninstitutional it looked. Both the floor and the lower part of the walls were carpeted so that students who banged their heads weren't hurt. The windows were high up, out of reach of the children. Various sports equipment for play and therapy were attached to the wall. Still, there was a certain beauty to the place. The designers met the challenge of creating a pleasant atmosphere despite the special requirements of the building's inhabitants. Soft colors, good lighting and pleasant music helped a lot.

"Are you Mindy's parents?" Nicole, Mindy's teacher, greeted Shlomo and Naomi with a broad smile. "Come, Mindy's waiting for you. Is this her little sister?" She chucked Sari under the chin and received an adorable toothless grin in response. Naomi held her baby tight, seeking her unstinting support. She was as afraid as a child of what she was about to see.

It was almost like a regular party. Balloons, a birthday cake, nosh. Fragmented, hesitant singing. Most of the singers were staff members; a few children joined in. Mindy watched it all expressionlessly, not reacting to the collective cries of *mazal tov*.

"Come, Mindy, open the gift we prepared for you," Nicole told her. Mindy rose and approached the gaily wrapped box. As she opened it, a large helium balloon floated to the ceiling. The script letters read "Happy birthday!" Mindy tried to catch the balloon, but it slipped away from her eager fingers. She fingered the attached string, looking for what she had lost.

Slowly, with surprising gentleness and patience, she tugged at the string until the shiny, round orb was within reach. With a seemingly indifferent motion, showing no sign of happiness that her efforts had been crowned with success, Mindy grabbed the balloon. She gripped it hard and hugged it tightly to her. The balloon burst, and Mindy's face remained completely expressionless as she toyed with the torn pieces. Naomi averted her eyes from the scene.

What was it the teacher had said? *Mindy's waiting for you.*

Mindy's waiting for us?

Maybe someday.

"TODAY," MORAH DEVORAH told her preschool class, her facial expression and tone of voice indicating that she was about to impart sensational news, "today we're going to start learning songs for our Chanukah party!"

A ripple of excitement spread through the class. "A Chanukah party! A Chanukah party!" Tzili clasped Yaffa Tovah's hand, and together they twirled around the room.

"And guess what every girl who behaves nicely and sings and dances will get?"

Twenty-four pairs of eyes were riveted to Morah Devorah. You could have heard a pin drop.

Morah Devorah smiled and withdrew from her briefcase an assortment of fascinating and beautiful things: red and yellow crepe paper and crowns with candles made of colored paper. "Every girl will wear one of these hats, and we'll tie crepe paper streamers to our wrists. Won't it be gorgeous?"

The girls looked at the accessories with awe.

"And there are more surprises," Morah Devorah went on dramatically. "Can you guess what they might be?"

"Dreidels!" Shiffy and Chani called out.

"That's right," Morah Devorah confirmed. "What good memories you have! You remember everything from last year. What else?"

"Menorahs! Latkes!" The six-year-olds were indeed old enough to remember their impressions of Chanukah — that happy, joyful festival filled with light and song — from the previous year.

"So, girls, what do you say we need in order to have a lovely party?"

"Nice songs," called Rivkah Brachah.

"Good. What else?"

"Decorations," Nechami said, glancing at the crepe paper and colored-paper candles.

"Wonderful. What else?"

"Dancing!" Raizel thundered.

"Latkes! Candles!" The suggestions came thick and fast, and the teacher smiled.

"Girls, your ideas are all wonderful. But I'm waiting for one answer that's the truest and nicest of all, one that will teach us what we actually have to do on Chanukah."

"What do you mean?" Raizel asked. "We light candles on Chanukah."

"Yes, that's true. You're getting close. Chanukah is called the Festival of Lights, so we want to have lots of light at our party. What makes the brightest, strongest type light?"

"Lightbulbs!"

"What makes an even stronger light than lightbulbs?"

"The sun! The sun is a lot brighter than plain old lightbulbs,"

Gittel Devorah said indignantly. "Look how dark it is at night when there's no sun. Even when you switch on the light, it doesn't become as light as when the sun shines!"

"The moon," Esther suggested.

"No way," protested Gittel Devorah. "The sun's a million times brighter than the moon. It's dark at night even though the moon is out then, isn't it?"

"What gives off even more light?" Morah Devorah asked.

"More than the sun?" Gittel Devorah asked skeptically, determined to be the sun's advocate. "There's no such thing."

"And I say," said Morah Devorah with sparkling eyes, "that there is something that gives us even more light than the sun."

"I know!" Fraidy said, leaping up from her chair. "The mitzvos! The Torah! Doesn't that make the most light?"

"Yes, Fraidy, you're right. That's the answer I was looking for." Fraidy sat down, flushed with pleasure.

"Mitzvos," Morah Devorah said dramatically. "Mitzvos create a super-bright light in the world, light that enters the saddest corners of people's hearts. Can light from a lightbulb or the sun light up a person's heart? Is there any light in the world that can cheer up someone sad? No. But when we share with a friend, we light up her heart; when we're careful not to fight with a classmate or a younger brother or sister, we add light to the world. Hashem takes all these lights and guards them carefully. They're extremely precious to Him."

Becky dwelled on Morah Devorah's words. She could share with Sari, help Ima with Mindy. Might the girls in her class be friendlier to her now that they wanted to do more mitzvos? *But*, she wondered, *do you want them to be your friends just because it's a mitzvah?*

Unsure, Becky weighed the matter in her mind.

"And so, girls," the teacher went on, "what are we going to do to create a lot of light in the world?"

"We'll share! We'll be careful not to hurt anyone's feelings!"

Morah Devorah withdrew from her bulging briefcase a rolled up oak-tag poster. She unrolled it and hung it on the wall for everyone to see. It was a chart bearing the names of all the girls in the class.

"Every time a girl shares nicely or helps a friend, we'll light one candle next to her name," Morah Devorah said, showing the girls a package of candle-shaped stickers. "Before we know it, the chart will be filled with candles, and our class will make a light so strong it will light up the whole world," she concluded festively.

"And now," she said as the girls looked admiringly at the mitzvah chart, "let us begin learning a song for the party."

The girls took their seats and the teacher began singing the first song:

Al hanissim,
We thank you, Hashem,
For the miracles that you do,
Every day, morning, noon and night
For that we say thank you!

Morah Devorah thought to herself with amusement that she had never thought she'd sing aloud in front of others. She wasn't much of a singer, to put it mildly, but ironically enough it was she, not the nightingales of her seminary class, who was using her singing voice every day. Miriam Glick, who had starred in every choir and concert during their school years, was now a saleswoman in a clothing store. Did she use her lovely voice to persuade potential customers to buy? Zeesy Pinter, another top soloist, was a math teacher in a high school. Did she sing the rules to her students? And here she, always one of the weakest in all things music-related, made use of her voice all the time. Her students loved singing, and she was not ashamed before them of her poor singing ability.

Becky stood on the side, as always, her green eyes large and questioning in her pale face. Mitzvos. Sharing with a friend was a mitzvah. If only she could do that mitzvah! Which of the girls would want her to share with her? Which of the girls was willing to take the time to talk to her and listen to what she had to say? Maybe Ruchaleh?

"Come, Becky," Jenny said, tugging gently at her hand. "Let's try and do what everyone else is doing."

"No," Becky said firmly. "I don't want to!" Did Jenny think she would try to sing with girls who could hear and who would make fun of her? No way!

"Why not?" Jenny asked in surprise. Jenny, Becky's speech therapist, spent two hours a day with Becky in school. For the first two hours of the day, Becky managed on her own. Jenny joined her for the next two hours, and at noon, the two of them left school together and went to Becky's house, where Jenny spent another three hours working with Becky on important things such as lip reading and speech. Sometimes, when her help was very important — like today, for example — Jenny came to school for the first two hours as well. She maintained daily contact with Morah Devorah in order to know when her presence would be necessary.

"Because it's funny," Becky said sharply, "and I don't want anyone laughing at me."

"Why should they laugh? You speak almost exactly like everyone else."

"Almost ..."

It was true. Becky's voice was guttural and heavy, its tone somewhat unnatural. Nevertheless, although most of the time the difference was barely perceptible, Becky, who couldn't hear what she sounded like, thought her voice must sound very different from that of other people.

Jenny studied Becky's face as she stood silent and still. "So you don't want to sing with the others," she said, summing up the situation. She had seen how Becky's eyes had sparkled at the sight of the hats and streamers and how that sparkle had been extinguished when Morah Devorah had begun to sing.

"I don't sing nicely. I don't sing like everyone else. I can't learn the tune properly and I'll sing off tune and I have an ugly voice," Becky said. "I'll ruin the party if I sing."

"Ruin the party? Who's going to ruin the party?" Morah Devorah asked, coming up behind them. She put her arms around Becky's shoulders. "You're going to ruin the party? Do you remember what we said about the strong light of mitzvos lighting up the world? About what's the most important part of our party?"

Morah Devorah leaned forward and whispered something in Becky's ear.

Jenny smiled. "Becky can't hear you," she pointed out. "You forgot."

Morah Devorah smiled sheepishly. She turned her face to Becky and, speaking in a low voice that reached Jenny alone, she said, "You don't have to be in the choir if you don't want to. You'll be in the dance for sure, and you'll even have a solo dance. I know you dance beautifully. But you should know that if you do decide to be in the choir, you won't ruin it at all. Even if you sing a bit more slowly than the others, it doesn't matter. It's the light of our mitzvos that's important, not the songs. For me, the choir will be all the more beautiful if you're in it." She smiled warmly at Becky and went over to the other girls.

Becky's eyes lit up. "Morah Devorah likes me," she said to Jenny. "I don't want to disappoint her. Maybe you can teach me one song today instead of something else?"

"Sure, Becky," Jenny replied immediately. "I'll learn the song and the motions and we'll practice that today instead of your speech lessons, okay?"

Becky's eyes shone. "Okay!"

Jenny turned to Morah Devorah quietly.

"Thanks for encouraging Becky. Your every word is worth its weight in gold."

"Like Becky herself."

Morah Devorah adored Becky. Most adults who came in contact with her did. People couldn't help but admire her drive to understand and learn everything without missing a single detail. She was incredibly mature for her age.

"We need to leave now. How can I teach Becky the song?" Jenny asked, thinking aloud. "Would I be able to pick up a copy of the tape from you this afternoon? Wait, I have a class today. You wouldn't happen to have a spare copy with you?"

"I do, actually," Morah Devorah replied, taking a cassette from her briefcase. "It occurred to me that you might want to practice the songs with Becky at home, so I prepared an extra copy for you right away."

"You're incredible," Jenny said admiringly.

It's one thing to agree to accept a deaf girl into your class — a step that includes having the girl's speech therapist sit in your class and listen to what and how you teach your students — but it's altogether another to carry that girl in your heart all day and think constantly how you can make things easier for her.

"Becky told me that she wants to learn one song for your sake, so as not to disappoint you."

"She's an angelic child. She's so refined, so full of charm. ... I can't believe she's only six years old."

"Yes," Jenny agreed.

"Keep me posted, okay?" Devorah asked. "It's important that I know where things stand with her."

"Okay, I'll let you know about every bit of progress or, G-d forbid, regression."

"What do you mean, regression?"

"If she refuses to sing, for example, or becomes withdrawn, or rejects our opinion with regard to her dancing and singing." Jenny smiled sadly. "We can't foresee everything. I hope everything goes smoothly."

"Yes, me too."

Jenny opened the classroom door, grimacing as its rusty

hinges emitted a series of agonizing squeaks. *Why don't they oil this thing?* she thought in annoyance. *I must remember to tell Devorah.* She glanced at Becky, who was smiling contentedly. She hadn't heard a thing, hadn't recoiled from the unpleasant noise. The squeaking of rusty hinges didn't bother her. Jarring sounds didn't disturb her quiet world.

On second thought, Jenny mused, *maybe they should leave this door the way it is. That way, it will serve as a reminder for me every time I leave with Becky not to underestimate the difficulty of her struggle. I need to remember what she's up against. She deserves my admiration for coping as well as she does.*

10

Poland, the early 1930s

Meir Katz was born on top of the mountain.

His father, Harav Shmuel Katz, was a *Ram,* and his mother ran one of the Bais Yaakov schools established by Sarah Schenirer. Meir was a brilliant child, brimming with energy and he had a fiery temper. Blessed with a natural charm and grace, he excelled at his studies and was popular with his friends.

Meir's sense of self-worth increased as he grew older. When he looked into the waters of the river not far from his home, he saw the reflection of a talented, righteous, G-d-fearing youth, beloved on High as well as on earth. Whatever he lacked in personality — and he lacked very little — was more than made up for by the prestige of his family lineage.

When Meir was twelve years old, a year shy of the age at which it was generally accepted for the boys of his hometown to enter *yeshivah ketanah*, his father was summoned for a meeting with the righteous *melamed*, Reb Ber, who was known for his subtle perception.

"You have a very talented son," the *melamed* said. "Perhaps you should consider sending him to yeshivah."

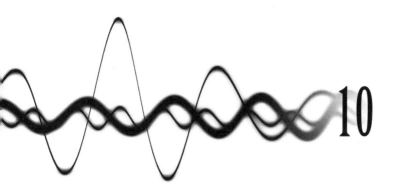

"He still has time, another year at least. He's only twelve years old," said Reb Shmuel, puzzled by the suggestion. True, his son was very capable, *baruch Hashem*, but was that any reason to send him off to yeshivah at a young age? His older children, Yaakov and Dovid Hershel, were very talented as well. Reb Ber hadn't made the same suggestion for them when they were Meir's age. Something was up.

"But he's suited for yeshivah, as far as his level of learning is concerned, that is." He fell silent. Reb Shmuel sensed the tension in the air despite Reb Ber's efforts to hide it.

"What do you mean?" he asked, trying to understand what Reb Ber was getting at. What did the *melamed's* words — or rather, his manner — intimate? Why did Reb Ber seem so acutely uncomfortable? "My older children were suited for yeshivah as well, weren't they?"

Reb Ber grew even more flustered. "Yes," he said stroking his luxuriant beard and averting his eyes from the worried father's. "But he's not like them. Haven't you noticed?"

"In what way?" Reb Shmuel demanded.

"He's different."

"I know," Meir's father nodded. "He's very sociable, energetic and hot-tempered. He's more excitable than they are, quicker to emotion. He loves action, adventure. His older brothers are more laid back, more reserved. So what?"

"It would seem there's no harm in those traits," the *melamed* agreed.

Reb Shmuel went on. "One of my daughters is like Meir. Full of energy, brimming with life, a social butterfly. My wife says she'll make a phenomenal teacher. She predicts she'll run a school singlehandedly at a young age," he said proudly — and a trifle defensively. "I think such a personality is an advantage."

"I'm not saying it isn't," Reb Ber said. "His friends adore him and he's very successful in all areas."

"And yet ..." Reb Shmuel attempted to draw out the elderly *melamed*.

"And yet ..." Reb Ber echoed. He was unsure of how to proceed.

He hoped dearly that he was wrong and the last thing he wanted to do was cause a Jew needless distress. "There's something ..."

"Reb Ber," Reb Shmuel said pleadingly, "please tell me what you're getting at."

"Look, Reb Shmuel, the fact that he's so effervescent and sociable does indeed contribute greatly to his popularity, but he is very excitable and that's a slightly dangerous trait, especially in our times, with so many youth groups and movements eager to trap our best and our brightest."

Reb Shmuel paled. His knees threatened to buckle under him. "Has ... has the rebbe seen anything wrong?"

"No, not exactly," Reb Ber said.

"Please," Reb Shmuel pleaded. "Please tell me, what fault have you seen in my son's behavior?"

Reb Ber sighed deeply. "Something about him isn't sufficiently ... G-d-fearing, perhaps. He doesn't concentrate intensely enough on his learning. I sometimes find him daydreaming. All this has begun only recently."

Reb Shmuel was white as a ghost. "Rebbe, is there any hope for my son?"

"Reb Shmuel," the *melamed* protested, "I didn't say Meir was off the *derech*, G-d forbid. I can't even tell you exactly what has changed about him. It's just a feeling, you see, Reb Shmuel. I sense a change. I don't see anything yet. My advice to you is to send him to yeshivah."

"And what will that accomplish?"

"In yeshivah he'll have worthy competition. Over here he lacks the motivation to throw himself into his learning; he can be the best without half trying, so his mind is open to mundane matters. He likes to be the best in everything, but being the best here is no challenge at all. No one here is as talented as he, so he has time to idle. It is my hope that when he has serious competition to contend with, he'll invest his energy in Torah."

Reb Shmuel was silent as he pondered Reb Ber's words.

"I wish you lots of *nachas* from him," Reb Ber said quietly. "Let us hope that he will develop into a great *talmid chacham* like Rav Meir Shapiro of Lublin."

Reb Ber's blessing indicated that the meeting had come to an end.

ON HIS WAY home, Reb Shmuel was pensive. He replayed his conversation with Reb Ber in his mind over and over again and realized the aged *melamed* had not pointed with certainty to any specific fault of his son's.

Let us hope that he will develop into a great talmid chacham like Reb Meir Shapiro of Lublin, he had said. *Let us hope ....*

In other words, there was a problem of some sort. It wasn't that Reb Shmuel had ever really anticipated that his son would become a towering *talmid chacham* and *gaon* of the caliber of Reb Meir Shapiro. Nothing would afford him greater pleasure, of course, but his Meir could still be worthy of the title *talmid chacham* even if he did not reach so exalted a level. So what was the problem?

Reb Shmuel was not one to take Reb Ber's words lightly. Although the elderly *melamed* had not been able to point to any specific changes in his son's behavior, he had sensed something. His sharply honed perception had never betrayed him.

Fear and frustration welled up inside him. What could he tell his son? What could he do in order to change his behavior if there was nothing specific he was doing wrong? Should he take the *melamed's* advice and send him off to yeshivah in the hope that it would transform him into a serious *talmid chacham*?

He called for his son immediately upon arriving home. "Tell me, Meir," he said. "Would you like to go to *yeshivah ketanah* already?"

"What?" The boy was shocked. "Abba, I'm only twelve years old."

"Yes, I know that." Reb Shmuel smiled tiredly. "Your *melamed* feels you're up to it."

"Me?" Meir was amazed. "What makes him say that?"

"I think he's right," Reb Shmuel said, looking into his son's dark eyes. A fierce, protective love filled his heart.

"Really?" Meir, still incredulous, sank into a nearby chair. "Listen, if you and Reb Ber both feel that way, who am I to differ?"

"You don't have to, Meir," Reb Shmuel said. "I'm asking what you think."

Meir hesitated. "Maybe," he said halfheartedly, very unsure of himself. "Maybe. I'll think about it."

Meir left the house and began pacing about, lost in thought. If word got out that he had left for yeshivah, his reputation would blossom. He'd be known as a genius who had been sent to yeshivah a year early at the suggestion of Reb Ber, whose opinion was greatly respected. If Reb Ber felt that he, Meir, was an *ilui*, no one would dare challenge that supposition.

On the other hand, here in his hometown cheder, he took first place easily. In yeshivah, he'd have to struggle to earn a place somewhere in the middle. He knew he was no match for the geniuses over there.

And what about the exhilarating news he read with such fascination every week? A Jewish uprising. The idea ignited his heart and soul. Jews were rebelling! No longer would they be downtrodden and oppressed, subservient to non-Jews who worked them to the bone. No more would they suffer the oppression of *galus* and the tyranny of despots. No more! Jews were bearing arms and going out to battle! Jews were fighting for their homeland! Jews were ascending to Eretz Yisrael.

Once a week an Orthodox newspaper came to their town. Meir read it secretly, relishing the sweetness of stolen waters. There was nothing improper about reading the paper, but as the *ilui* of the local cheder and the pride of his parents, he could not afford to do so openly.

No one knew that he read the paper with such enthusiasm. The articles condemned the Zionists for their war against all things holy, for rising up against the gentiles against Hashem's will, for trying to create an artificial redemption — but Meir's imagination was fired by what he read between the lines. He loved Eretz Yisrael dearly and thirsted for news of what was happening there.

Sometimes Meir managed to get his hands on a Zionist newspaper. That was a huge step out of bounds. He had to employ real war strategies to read it. If anyone were to catch him reading that paper .... There were no secrets in his village; he'd lose his standing in a heartbeat. His desire to know what was happening in the world was so strong, though, his longing to be a part of the history taking place around him so fierce, that he took the risk. Besides, reading a newspaper like that in secret was an adventure of the highest order.

The articles in the Zionist paper were filled with passion and enthusiasm. Meir was completely swept up by the movement's allure. He wanted to go to Eretz Yisrael, wanted to join the battle, wanted to bear arms and fight the battle of the Jews that hadn't been fought for thousands of years, wanted to participate in the social and political revolution, wanted to bind himself to the history taking place in his generation. Most of all, he wanted to be one with the Land he loved so.

In yeshivah, he knew, no one read newspapers. Not the Orthodox ones and certainly not Zionist ones, G-d forbid. Woe to him if he inadvertently mentioned the name of the paper he read to one of the *bachurim*. In yeshivah, they scorned the Zionist warriors, prayed they would abandon their alien ideas and return to their Father in Heaven. In yeshivah, they considered the Zionists heretics.

Longing burned in his bones. The vision presented in the paper ignited his heart and thrilled his soul. *A Jewish State for the Jewish people,* he thought. In yeshivah, he'd be cut off from news of the battle.

What should he do?

Meir did not want to be exposed, after all. He just wanted to remain up-to-date, to know what was happening and maybe – maybe – one day he would join the movement as a Torah-observant Jew. A different possibility never even entered his mind. But in the meantime, everyone around him opposed the Zionists and their ideas. What should he do? On the one hand, he wanted to study Torah and remain a G-d-fearing Jew, but on the other hand, he wanted to be a part of the commotion of battle. He wanted to feel the sense of Jewish pride that was finally awakening. Most of all, he wanted to go to Eretz Yisrael.

Meir sat down on a bench to think. What could he do? Establish a chareidi youth movement to fight the British? Nonsense! No one would ever agree to such a plan. First of all, they'd tell him it was *bittul Torah*. Second, it is forbidden to rise up against the gentiles so long as we're in *galus*. *Klal Yisrael's* redemption would be heralded by Moshiach, not by anyone else.

And would they not be right? Isn't such a war bittul Torah?

But it's a milchemes mitzvah, a voice inside him protested.

Don't be stupid, his conscience replied. *In a milchemes mitzvah, the warriors are completely free of sin, and they fight on Hashem's command only.*

Meir sighed. It was true. This war was forbidden, but they'd been waiting so long for redemption ...

And what about Eretz Yisrael? Hasn't it been promised to the Jews? Haven't Yidden throughout the generations prayed for its redemption from the hands of enemies? We can do that now! Why is everyone so indifferent to the fate of Eretz Yisrael?

Someone sat down next to him.

"Meir?" It was his mother. "Did Tatte tell you what Reb Ber said?"

"Yes." He looked at her. "Mama, what do you think?" he asked.

"Go, *mein kind,*" his mother said quietly. "Go where you will grow best. Exile yourself to a place of Torah."

He went.

But three years later, he was no longer there.

LIFE IN YESHIVAH was much harder than it had been back home. Spiritual toil is physically and emotionally taxing, and Meir was not up to the struggle. Too often, his *yetzer hara* won out and slowly, gradually, he began to change. He couldn't overcome his overwhelming desire to read the news. From time to time he left the yeshivah and through devious tactics obtained the newspapers he thirsted for. The battle for Palestine was heating up. Jewish fighters were raising their heads. Meir's heart roiled with excitement and emotion. He couldn't concentrate on his learning the way he used to. Many times he found himself daydreaming in front of his open Gemara, snapping out of his reverie only when his *chavrusa* called, "Meir!"

War. The smell of fire and smoke ... the glory of battle ... the pride of triumph. How could he sit tucked away in yeshivah when, outside, the winds of war were blowing? His brief excursions out of yeshivah in order to read the paper grew more frequent, and at the same time, the warmth of his *Yiddishkeit* began to wane. His *tefillos* grew shorter; his interest in Gemara decreased. He was completely absorbed in the Jewish battle for Palestine, the country that would become Eretz Yisrael once it was liberated from the oppressive British mandate.

His yarmulke did not shrink in size, G-d forbid, nor did he touch his *peyos*. The changes were more subtle: He still spent every minute of the official study hours in the *beis medrash*, but when he studied, his swaying was less vigorous than it had been, his gesticulations as he posited a *svara* less enthusiastic. He no longer caressed the *sifrei kodesh* lovingly when he put them away after davening or learning. He never lingered a moment or two after *seder*; he left the *beis medrash* whenever possible.

The *mashgiach* was the first to notice the change taking place in the boy. He summoned Meir for a talk.

Meir was nervous as he entered the *mashgiach's* study.

"Hello, Meir'l," the *mashgiach* said, smiling fondly at him.

"Hello," Meir replied, waiting.

"I wanted to talk to you. What do you think of the yeshivah?"

"What?" Meir grew flustered. "What does the *mashgiach* mean?"

"The learning, the boys," the *mashgiach* elaborated.

"*Baruch Hashem*, everything's fine."

"Is there anything that's disturbing your learning?" the *mashgiach* probed.

Meir shook his head.

"Are you sure?"

Meir was silent and thoughtful. "The *mashgiach* wants to tell me something," he said, raising his black eyes to meet those of the *mashgiach*.

"Yes," the *mashgiach* confirmed with a smile. "You're very perceptive, Meir'l, but are you willing to listen and accept?"

"Yes." *Yes?*

"Not only to listen," the *mashgiach* emphasized. "To listen and accept."

Meir was silent, unsure of what to say.

"You have a passionate nature. Your passion, however, is not directed to Torah study, and for that I am sorry. When you first arrived here, you impressed me greatly. You studied with love, with enthusiasm. Passion is a wonderful character trait when used for Torah study and fighting the *yetzer hara*. But lately, you've been using it for other things."

"Such as?" Meir furrowed his brow. There was no way the *mashgiach* could know anything of his secret exploits. He had been exceedingly careful to cover his tracks.

"You tell me," the *mashgiach* said directly. "Is it the Zionist cause that's attracting you?"

Meir paled. His hands trembled uncontrollably. "Yes," he said quietly. "It interests me. Is it forbidden to take an interest in what's happening to our land?" he asked defensively. "It's our country!"

"That's the root of your mistake, Meir. It will be ours," the *mashgiach* said, maintaining his calm. "*Vechitisu charbosam le'itim*," he went on. "*Lo yisa goy el goy cherev velo yilmedu od milchamah*." He paused. "Do you know which time period these *pesukim* refer to?"

"What kind of a question is that?" Meir was insulted. "*Yemos haMoshiach.*"

"Yes," agreed the *mashgiach*. "Eretz Yisrael will be ours only when Moshiach arrives. I'm sure you're familiar with the *gemara* in *Kesubos* 111: '*Hishbati eschem bnos Yerushalayim bitzvaos ube'ayelos hasadeh ... Rabi Yosi berabbi Chanina d'amar: gimmel shevuos halalu lamah? Achas shelo yaalu Yisrael bechoma ve'achas shehishbia Hakadosh Baruch Hu es Yisrael shelo yimridu be'umos ha'olam, ve'achas shehishbia Hakadosh Baruch Hu es ha'ovdei kochavim shelo yishtaabdu beYisrael yoser midai.*'"

A smile played on Meir's lips. "And if the gentiles violate their promise?" he asked. "What if they do rule us too harshly? What then?"

"That is no business of ours," the *mashgiach* said firmly. "'*Verabbi Levi d'amar: Shesh shevuos halalu lamah? ... Shelo yigalu es haketz veshelo yircheku es haketz.*' Do you know the end of this *gemara*? '*Bitzvaos ube'ayelos hasadeh — Amar Rabi Eliezer: amar lahem Hakadosh Baruch Hu leYisrael im atem mekayemim es hashvua mutav, ve'im lav ani matir es besarchem ketzvaos uke'aylos hasadeh.*'" The *mashgiach*'s voice grew increasingly stronger until he sounded to Meir like the *neviim* of old prophesying the advent of the *churban*. Perhaps the wise *mashgiach* foresaw the demise of Zionism, or perhaps he was lamenting the spiritual *churban* the movement was causing at its peak.

"It is forbidden to incite the British, Meir. It is forbidden to fight them, forbidden to fight the Arabs living in Palestine. They're the sons of Yishmael, and they have a certain claim to it, too, until Moshiach grants it to us."

"But *Mashgiach*," Meir cried out, "How does that same *gemara* end?"

The *mashgiach* looked at him in puzzlement.

"*Amar Rabi Elazar*," Meir quoted, "*Kol hadar be'Eretz Yisrael sharui belo avon.*"

"*Belo avon*," the *mashgiach* said ironically. "Are the Zionists living in Eretz Yisrael *belo avon*? Woe to us from them and their opinions! They're freethinkers, in the fullest sense of the word!"

"Freethinkers?" Meir's eyebrows rose.

"Yes, freethinkers. They desecrate Shabbos; eat forbidden foods. They don't observe the holidays; don't observe anything. They're like the *maskilim*, Meir. It is forbidden for us — for you — to think of joining their ranks. We may only pray for them and wait for Moshiach."

But nothing could diminish Meir's fierce love for Eretz Yisrael. He read with avid interest the news about the war against the British. He prayed every day for the success of the underground fighters and longed for the collapse of the mandate.

Meir studied the Ralbag's poetry about the great man's love for Eretz Yisrael. He read books about *Gedolei Yisrael* who pined for the Holy Land and felt they corroborated his position. He didn't see the difference between yearning for Eretz Yisrael and fighting for it. He could not differentiate between what was forbidden and what was permitted. He failed to see why something that Yidden throughout the generations had longed for was forbidden to him.

Aschalta degeulah, he thought. *This is the beginning of the redemption. The Jewish nation is returning to Eretz Yisrael!*

For two years his heart was in the East while he remained in the West. And then one day, he heard that a boat of illegal immigrants would be leaving in a month's time from the coast of Romania to the shores of the Promised Land. He packed his things, left a note on the door of the study of his beloved *mashgiach*, and slipped out of the yeshivah.

Outside, the cold night greeted him. He made his way to the train station on foot and purchased a ticket to the nearest large city. It took him a week to reach his destination, but when he did, he was ecstatic. He didn't have a ticket, but he knew the organizers would be thrilled with every additional illegal immigrant. He hoped they would allow him to join them in their work one day.

Three weeks later, the boat set sail with Meir on board, his eyes raised heavenward in gratitude.

Palestine was in a state of prewar chaos. Adolf Hitler, the insane German chancellor, was saying the most preposterous, blasphemous things — and getting away with it. He'd legislated numerous laws that humiliated and restricted the Jews residing in his country.

Meir ignored the rumors that war was imminent and threw himself into the backbreaking labor assigned to him on a Jewish settlement in the Galilee. His youthful zeal and appetite for battle did not diminish; his blood still boiled inside him, eager for action. He made contact with the mysterious men who visited his settlement occasionally and asked to join the Haganah, a group that expressed its opposition to the British mandate in a most physical manner.

The men were reluctant to induct him because of his young age. They told him they'd give him their answer in a month's time.

And then Meir began to change. Everyone around him made fun of his opinions, his outlook, and his religious faith. Desperate for acceptance, Meir was prepared to do anything to win his friends' favor.

His yarmulke grew gradually smaller until it disappeared completely. He stopped davening. He threw away his tzitzis. He simply could not withstand the *nisayon* he was facing. The secular Zionist company he kept was too pervasive, too overbearing.

One Shabbos, Meir entered the dining room to find it shrouded in darkness. Instinctively, he reached for the light switch and flipped it on. Light bathed the room, and Meir found himself looking into a mirror where he saw plainly what he had become: a bareheaded, *treifah*-eating, Shabbos-desecrating Zionist.

Surprisingly, rejecting his old beliefs did not help him find his place. The further his spiritual situation deteriorated, the worse he felt.

In the meantime, war clouds billowed across Europe. Slowly,

the noxious fumes rose and spread across the entire continent. Meir went about his work biting his fingernails in frustration. He couldn't go back home the way he was, but he couldn't remain in Palestine, either: The rumors were driving him crazy.

The Zionist leadership declared it was prepared to place the Jewish fighting forces at the disposal of the British. Meir followed this tidbit of information hopefully. He hoped to be able to join the fighters and somehow reach his family. And even if he didn't actually reach them, perhaps he'd be able to make contact with the right people, who would help him extricate his family from an area that was growing more endangered all the time.

But a Jewish regiment failed to materialize. A friend explained to Meir that the leadership wanted the British to do away with the White Paper or at least freeze it temporarily in return for the regiment, but the British had no intention of cooperating. Also, the Zionist leaders hoped the Jewish regiment established by the British would eventually form the basis of the Jewish army they'd been dreaming of establishing for years.

The British understood as much and preferred a "don't do us any favors" policy. They did not favor the idea of a Jewish army that would later push them out of Palestine. In addition, they feared the reaction of the nearby Arab countries, which were openly hostile to the strengthening of the Jewish settlement in Palestine. The last thing the British needed was an additional front while battling the mighty German army. Maintaining quiet in Palestine was of paramount importance.

"That's why they're delaying their answer," his friend explained. "Personally, I think they've already made the decision to reject our offer. They're just waiting as long as possible before telling us so."

On 17 Elul 5699, just one day after Hitler declared that the Sudetenland would satisfy his appetite for conquest, he violated his word. His soldiers broke through the undefended Polish border and stormed into the panic-stricken country. Wehrmacht pilots bombed Poland mercilessly. War had broken out.

Meir followed the reports coming in from the battlefield with mounting horror. Although he had no inkling yet of the crimes the Nazis were perpetrating against the Jews, he was frightened for his family, caught as they were in a war-torn country.

With no clear goal in mind, Meir, not yet seventeen years old, left the settlement. His hope that a Jewish regiment would be formed to aid the British was disappointed. The Jewish and British leadership couldn't seem to work together, and the British declared that they were prepared to accept young Jewish volunteers into their regular army on an individual basis only.

Left with no choice, Meir offered his services to the British army. To his chagrin, they proposed he serve in a rear unit that wouldn't be doing any real fighting.

Angry and disillusioned, Meir left Eretz Yisrael that he loved so. As a British citizen, he reasoned, it would be easier to be assigned to the front units. He changed his name from Meir to Marty and applied for British citizenship. His request was approved sooner than he expected. The moment he received his papers, he visited a draft office.

His calculation proved right as he was accepted into the army immediately. His many talents served him well, and he quickly rose in rank. His passion was now directed to fighting the Germans.

As a soldier, Marty retained his custom of following the news closely. The experience was vastly different from what it had been in the past. Then he had worn a yarmulke; he had been a believing Jew. Then he had read the paper secretly and davened openly. Now he was bareheaded and completely secular. Now he read the paper openly and whispered prayers for his family and friends in secret.

11

New York 5758/1998

Jenny and Becky sat in a small room in Becky's house and practiced speech exercises. Jenny hoped the day would come when Becky would no longer require her guidance and would be able to live among people without the help of an intermediary. But achieving that goal would require much hard work, and she knew it.

Becky was making progress in preschool. She absorbed the material quickly, answered questions without hesitation and was far and away the brightest child in the class. Sometimes it seemed to Jenny that Becky didn't belong in preschool at all — she was more suited to first or second grade, maybe even third.

But then recess proved to Jenny how wrong she was. Becky had no friends save for Ruchaleh, the bubbly redhead. When Ruchaleh was in the resource room with her remedial teacher, which was quite often, Becky was on her own. She played on the slide alone, climbed the monkey bars alone, built sand castles alone, played with dolls alone. Alone, alone! Completely alone.

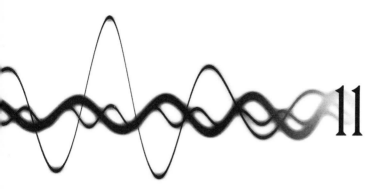

Jenny understood that Ruchaleh came from a very poor family. The child's gaiety and joie de vivre stood in sharp contrast to her clothing and poor social standing. Jenny felt a wave of pity for the sweet little girl. Ruchaleh was really a darling; she was pushed into a corner for such a trivial reason, one so easily correctable.

When Ruchaleh couldn't participate in a game, Becky asked Jenny to play with her. But Jenny refused. If Becky grew accustomed to the company of adults only, how would she stop her dependence on them when she wanted to? Jenny knew she mustn't allow her charge to play and form relationships only with those who understood her well. She needed to cope with girls her own age, on their playing field. It would take time, but if she helped the butterfly emerge from its cocoon by tearing it open, how would its wings be strong enough to fly later?

Jenny knew the story well. A man saw a butterfly, metamorphosed from a caterpillar, trapped inside a cocoon. The young butterfly was beating its wings frantically against the walls of its prison, trying to overcome its barrier to the free world. The onlooker's pity was aroused and he cut the cocoon with a pair of scissors. The butterfly was now free — but it couldn't fly! A butterfly's wings grow strong from its struggle to emerge from the cocoon surrounding it. This butterfly hadn't struggled, hadn't toughened its wings, and now it couldn't fly. Ever!

When would Becky be able to fly on her own?

The lesson in lip reading came to an end, and Jenny began to prepare for Becky's speech lesson. She withdrew from her purse the cassette Morah Devorah had given her and inserted it into her Walkman. She'd listen to the song while Becky completed her writing homework. Becky had to learn reading and writing differently from her hearing peers. A child who can hear the letters he pronounces has a much easier time learning to write than a child who can't.

Becky raised her head from her work. She didn't hear the song, but she noticed that Jenny was wearing earphones and swaying slightly.

"Jenny, what about the motions Morah Devorah's going to teach everyone? How will you learn them in order to teach them to me?"

"It'll be okay. Don't worry. First you've got to learn the song, and then to keep to the beat."

"Keep to the beat of a song?" Becky trembled. "I'll never be able to do that."

"Yes, you will. Don't worry. We have plenty of time. We'll work on it together until you can join in with the rest of the class."

Jenny listened to the song intently, paying careful attention to the rhythm of each line.

The door burst open. Yanky walked in holding little Sari, who was bawling loudly.

"Becky, where's Ima?"

"I don't know. What happened to Sari?"

"Look," Yanky said, pointing to Sari's knee. "It's bleeding, and I don't know what to do. Can you help me?"

"Sure." Becky rose from her place. She could do her reading and writing homework on her own. If Jenny was listening to the tape, it was okay if she did something else in the meantime. She was glad for the opportunity to prove how helpful she could be.

"Come," she said to Sari. "I'll wash the blood and put on a Band-Aid so it won't bleed any more, okay?"

Sari continued wailing.

"Why are you talking to her?" Yanky scolded his sister. "You know she's too small to understand. She's only a year old, for heaven's sake! Quit talking and take care of her, will you!" Yanky was clearly anxious.

Becky brought Sari to the sink and gently washed the scrape. She sterilized it with iodine and applied a Band-Aid. The baby looked at the Band-Aid on her knee and tried to scrape it off.

"No," Becky warned her sister. "That's to stop the bleeding."

"There you go, 'splaining things to her again," Yanky sighed. "Just like with Mindy. Stop talking to them! There's no point! Sari will be able to understand you in another year or two, and Mindy never will."

"You never can know what they understand," Becky said earnestly.

"You don't remember what you understood when you were a baby, after all. Ima talks to Sari all the time. You don't know how much Mindy absorbs or what Sari understands."

As if to prove her right, Sari stopped picking at the Band-Aid and smiled brightly at her sister. She was calm now.

Jenny, watching from the side, smiled to herself with satisfaction. Becky was just like any other kid! Well, actually, not quite.

BECKY TIED THE crepe paper to her wrist hesitantly. Jenny nodded and gave her an encouraging smile. They had practiced taking a deep breath before starting, over and over again. The melody was beyond Becky's grasp, and she struggled mightily with the notes.

"Right hand," Jenny instructed. Becky obeyed. Most of the time, Becky did not sing the words of the song at all; she just performed the accompanying motions. She joined in the singing only during certain parts where the tune was simple and slow. Her halting speech had grown far clearer after dozens of sessions spent practicing the same few words over and over again.

"The miracles that You do." Her eyes shone brilliantly and Jenny's heart surged with a combination of love and pride. "For that we thank you."

Becky's hands went up and down, in and out. Her feet stamped to the beat. There never was a beat in Becky's silent world, but the large clock on the wall helped her do the motions at the proper time.

The days grew ever shorter as winter settled in, and so did the hours Becky spent with her family. She spent most of her time practicing with Jenny.

Becky did not complain even once. She repeated the motions hundreds of times, sighing quietly to herself each time she made a mistake and had to start over again. The clock was her loyal helper. It ticked at a steady, monotonous, reliable pace, never stammering or making a mistake.

Now Becky performed the motions from beginning to end with perfect precision. When she was done, she flopped to the floor, overjoyed.

"No mistakes, right?" she asked.

"No mistakes," Jenny confirmed. She threw a worried glance at the clock. Her course was starting soon; she had to hurry. "Let's do it one more time," she said. "Then I've got to leave, sweetie."

Becky did her best and once again completed the song with no mistakes.

"Bravo!" Jenny applauded. "You're wonderful! See you!"

"'Bye, Jenny. Thanks for the extra time you spent with me today. Good luck with your course."

"Thanks, Becky."

As Jenny left the room, a new worry began to form in her mind. After all her effort, Becky would be participating in just one song. What about the solo dance Morah Devorah had promised her? Jenny didn't want her to forfeit that! Inside her coat pocket Jenny's fist clenched. *Oh, Becky, what is it about you that touches the hearts of so many people? Why do I feel such a surge of emotion every time I think about you?*

Wait a minute, she said to herself, trying to organize the thoughts speeding through her mind. *Maybe I should skip going in to preschool with Becky tomorrow? I can spend the time finding a tune that's easy to catch onto. If I send it to Devorah by tomorrow afternoon, maybe she can still make up a simple dance to it. Then Becky can dance part of the dance on her own and the rest of the girls will join in. Becky will be conspicuous for what she can do just as well as everyone else.*

Not quite, Jenny. She can't dance just as well as anyone else, because synchronizing dance steps to a melody will take her hours! The choir will be child's play compared to having her star in a dance.

Jenny went down the stairs slowly. The halogen lights on either side of the steps glowed brightly, a sign that Becky's grandmother had already arrived. On days when Naomi took her autistic daughter for treatment, Naomi's mother came to be with the children.

"Mrs. Katz?" Jenny called hesitantly.

"Ah, Jenny." Becky's grandmother stepped out of the kitchen. "Thanks. Have a pleasant evening. We'll see you tomorrow."

Jenny closed the door behind her. My, it was cold out! She turned up the collar of her coat, her thoughts still on Becky. She had to have that solo dance!

Jenny started her car. She had a long drive ahead of her, and her course was starting in just five minutes. She stepped on the gas pedal, trying to put Becky out of her mind for the time being. She still had courses to take, tests and assignments to complete before she earned her degree. She had to relax her involvement with one deaf girl if she hoped to work with hundreds like her throughout her life.

When Jenny left, Becky remained in her room. Her eyes swept over the furniture and came to rest on the two beds. She frowned. Mindy's bed was still empty. When would Ima be back?

She lifted her doll from the floor and danced with it to the beat of the second hand on the clock.

Becky loved her doll, for it did not seem to mind sharing her world of silence. The doll's golden curls brushed against her own smooth brown tresses as she danced.

The door squeaked open and someone entered the room. He took a giant step toward Becky and gripped her hands between his own.

Becky started in alarm. She hadn't heard either the squeak of the door or the approaching footsteps.

"Sabba," she breathed in relief.

"Yes, it's me." He distanced his face from hers so she could read his lips. "How are you today?"

"I'm going to sing in school," Becky said proudly. "Jenny taught me the motions, and I'm going to do them like everyone else!"

"And that's wonderful, eh?" He stroked her cheek tenderly.

"Yes."

"Good, good. What else do you have to tell me?"

"That's it."

"Who's that in the picture?" Sabba asked, examining a new photograph Becky had inserted into a picture frame on her dresser.

"Sabba, that's me!"

"Wow!" Sabba whistled in admiration. "How you've grown! I don't recognize you anymore."

"Really?" Becky looked at him in disbelief. "If I grow a lot and you don't see me for a while, you don't recognize me?"

"Nah, I was just joking, little flower," Sabba said, his eyes twinkling as he sat down on Becky's bed. "I'll always recognize you."

"Always?"

"Always."

"How do you know? What if I grow a lot? Have you ever tried?"

"I tried it with your brother Yanky."

"Ah, and also with Uncle Shmuel's children."

"Yes, that's right."

"Did your grandfather recognize you when you grew?"

"What?"

"Did your grandfather recognize you when you grew a lot?" Becky repeated innocently.

"No," he replied heavily, rising from the bed he'd sat down on. "My grandfather didn't recognize me."

Becky realized she'd said something that had made Sabba feel sad. "Why, did he pass away?" she asked.

Her grandfather looked out the window in silence. Silence was never a deterrent for Becky, however. She tried to make him turn his face to her. Maybe he was saying something and she couldn't read his lips? She climbed onto a chair in order to reach his face. His lips were not moving.

"Sabba, did you say something when I didn't see?"

"No."

"Why didn't you answer my question?"

Sabba did not reply. Outside, snow began to fall. Sabba's eyes remained riveted to the window for a long moment before he lowered his gaze to his granddaughter's face once more.

Sabba was strange sometimes, like Mindy. He embraced Becky, still silent, and she remained silent, too.

ON THE DAY of the Chanukah party, the butterflies in Becky's stomach woke her early. Glancing at the clock to see what time it was, she suddenly recalled the other job she had assigned the loyal timepiece: It was thanks to the second hand that she'd be able to participate in both the choir and the dance.

The butterflies careened wildly around inside her stomach. For a long while, Becky remained in bed, thinking. Mindy was still asleep, her hair spread loosely on her pillow.

All of a sudden Becky couldn't wait any longer. She sat up, shook off her blanket and walked to the closet. Climbing on a chair, she withdrew from the closet the black skirt and yellow blouse Ima had ironed carefully the night before. Ima never left Becky's clothes for the following day out on the dresser or over a chair because Mindy would crumple them. Whenever Mindy saw anything made of fabric, she pounced on it and toyed with it so much it grew creased and wrinkled.

Becky dressed quickly, her fingers trembling with excitement and nervousness. At the final rehearsal in school yesterday, Jenny had told her she was wonderful. Everything had gone smoothly. There was no reason to worry — and yet Becky couldn't stop worrying.

Ima tiptoed into the room. It was her habit to do things quietly in the morning so as not to wake anyone who was still asleep. Of course, not even a cannon shot could wake Becky or Mindy.

"All dressed already?" she asked Becky.

"Yup," Becky replied, her smile simultaneously happy and scared. "Ima, do you think I'll do alright?"

Naomi hugged her daughter fondly. "*Im yirtzeh Hashem*," she said. "I'm sure you'll be just wonderful." She squeezed Becky's hand.

Skin contact with Becky was important, Naomi knew. Becky loved physical contact because it helped make up for the sense of hearing she lacked. Mindy, by contrast, shied away from contact with people. She screamed when someone touched her.

Mindy's ride came earlier than usual that day. The driver honked his horn and Mindy boarded the van.

Yanky approached Becky with a shy smile. "You're leaving already?" he asked.

Becky, on her way to the door, stopped short. "Why?"

"Take this." He stuffed something into her hand and quickly walked away. Becky looked curiously at the little box, but Ima tugged her hand gently.

"Come on, little dreamer," Ima said. "Abba's waiting for us. I hear him honking."

Yanky's gift gripped in her hand, Becky hurried outside to Abba's car.

Jenny, smiling serenely, greeted her as soon as she arrived. Only Hashem knew how hard it was for her to maintain a calm facade. She hadn't slept a wink all night, so nervous was she that something would go wrong during the performance. The child had to succeed!

The hours of practice, the social difficulties Becky was experiencing, her fragile self-esteem — all these made success an absolute imperative. If Becky's classmates saw their "different" friend starring so successfully, there was a good chance their attitude toward her would change.

The tape recorder was playing merry Chanukah tunes. Mothers entered the classroom and chatted with one another as they took their seats and prepared to see their daughters perform.

They take it so for granted, Naomi thought, a lump rising in her throat. Had she known to appreciate, before the twins were born, the fact that Yanky was able to sing and dance without any particular effort? Did these mothers know what it meant to have a normal, healthy child? Even she would not know how grateful she had to be for Becky were it not for Mindy. Every child was a flower, a song. There are some children society does not realize are flowers, some children whose melody remains unheard.

Naomi glanced at Becky. She appeared to be shrinking into herself with fear. Her face was deathly pale.

Naomi tapped Jenny's arm gently. "Jenny, the child is terrified."

"I see." Jenny's lips were parched and dry. She had prayed a thousand times for Becky's success and promised a small fortune to *tzedakah* if all went well. If only it would!

Morah Devorah began the program. Most of the girls and mothers did not consider the choir the highlight of the day. The quiz with prizes for the children who solved the riddles Morah Devorah asked was far more exciting.

Becky, unusually bright and sharp-witted, usually excelled at solving riddles, but she was too nervous now to think clearly. She averted her eyes from Morah Devorah's face so she couldn't read her lips and could instead withdraw into her own silent world.

Suddenly, Jenny noticed that the chair next to hers was empty.

"Where's Becky?" she asked in alarm.

She found her in the backyard, eyes bright with tears. The child was trembling violently.

"Becky, what happened?"

"I don't feel well." Becky's speech had become nearly unintelligible. "I can't talk."

Her face was so pale it was nearly transparent.

"Becky," Jenny said gently, trying to remain calm. The choir would be taking place in about an hour, and Becky had to calm down. "Come inside and have something to drink. You don't have to participate in the quiz; you can rest in the meantime."

"No," Becky whispered hoarsely. "I want to go home."

"Home?" Jenny was surprised. "Why? Your mother is waiting to see you perform. ..." Her voice trailed off at the sight of the spasm that shook Becky's slim body.

"Becky, there's no reason for this," Jenny said, trying to be firm.

The child shuddered, her eyes glistening even more brightly than before. Concerned she might have come down with a fever, Jenny placed a hand on Becky's forehead.

Naomi appeared in the doorway, her face a mask of worry. "What happened?" she asked.

Becky, her head lowered, was not aware that her mother was there.

"Go back inside, Naomi, alright?" Jenny said. "I'll explain later."

Naomi obeyed and disappeared back into the classroom. Becky, unaware of the exchange that had taken place between her mother and Jenny, responded to Jenny's question: "I have a reason."

"What happened?"

"I don't want to be in the choir."

"You don't want to be in the choir?" Jenny couldn't believe she was hearing right. "Why?"

"Because," Becky said stubbornly.

"So don't be in the choir. You can be in the dance. You must be in the dance; you can't ruin it for the others!"

"Alright," Becky replied. "I'll be in the dance."

"So let's go tell Morah Devorah what you decided."

"Okay." Jenny was surprised by Becky's sudden surrender. Becky had worked for hours on the one song. What had happened now?

They entered the classroom together. During intermission, Jenny spoke quietly to Morah Devorah, who was as surprised as she.

"Should I try to pressure her?" she asked. "I can try to exert my authority."

"No," Jenny replied. "She'll have to suffer the consequences of her decision on her own."

The girls positioned themselves for the choir. Becky's eyes blazed as she stared at her classmates, her face a picture of longing. The first song began, and Becky's eyes became twin fires. Jenny feared the room would catch on fire from the intensity of Becky's gaze. Such yearning, such desire!

You can join them, a voice shouted inside Becky's head. *Go up there! Sing! Do the motions! You spent hours working to get them right!* The voices jumped wildly about inside her, and her little heart just barely withstood the heavy load of emotions. She shook her head firmly.

Naomi sat down quietly beside her. Becky, her eyes glued to the stage, did not notice. Naomi placed a hand on her shoulder. Becky turned around sharply and burst into tears.

It was only on the way home that Becky opened Yanky's gift. It was a small violin, and the attached note read, "Becky, I'm sure you sang nicest of all. Yanky."

"SHE DID DANCE," Naomi said to Shlomo. "Something prevented her from taking part in the choir."

"What was it?" Shlomo asked. He was far more upset about what had happened than she. "What could have deterred her after she worked for hours so she could join everyone else for one song? She learned one song and she couldn't sing it? So how come she agreed to be in the dance?"

"I don't know," Naomi replied honestly. "I wish I did. Believe me, this is not the first time I've wished I could enter her heart and see what's going on there."

"What did she do while the rest of the class performed?"

"Nothing," Naomi replied. "She sat there motionlessly, staring at them with all the longing in the world in her eyes."

Dinner was a grim, silent affair. Becky withdrew to her room and refused to allow anyone entry. Though Naomi praised her beautiful dancing, she was terribly dejected.

At six o'clock Yanky came home. He wanted to run directly to his sister's room, but Shlomo stopped him.

"How are you, son?"

"How was it?" Yanky asked. "How was the party? Did she like the present I bought her? How did she sing? What did the teacher say? What did they wear? Where is Becky, anyway? I must ask her. ..."

"Stop, Yanky," Naomi said tiredly. "Becky didn't sing today."

"What?" He was shocked and disappointed. "Why not?"

"I don't know." Fatigue crept from her heart to her brain. "She doesn't want to say. After supper she went upstairs to her room and asked that we not disturb her."

"So where's Mindy?"

"Right here," Naomi said, pointing to a small form curled into a ball near the oven.

"She doesn't care if she can't go into her room," Yanky said, "but I must hear what Becky has to say about my present."

"Your card was very painful for her," Shlomo tried to explain gently. But a nine-year-old boy who spent three hours looking for just the right present for his sister cannot be expected to develop such subtle sensitivity on the spur of the moment.

Yanky sank into a chair, his eyes filling with tears. "I wanted so badly to make her happy," he said quietly, "and I thought so hard about what to write on the card."

IN THE EVENING, Becky shuffled in slippered feet to her parent's bedroom. It was eight o'clock, and Becky knew they would both be downstairs now. Ima was cooking for tomorrow, and Abba was learning.

The bedroom was empty. Becky placed a piece of white stationery with a pretty border of red roses on her mother's pillow. She left the room hurriedly and entered Yanky's room, where he lay fast asleep. Another piece of stationery found its way onto his pillow, too.

She crawled back into bed and stared at the ceiling in silence.

Yanky opened his eyes the moment Becky left his room. She hadn't been particularly quiet when she'd entered his room; she didn't know the meaning of noise. Always a light sleeper, he woke up while she was still in his room, but from her furtive manner he understood she was preparing a surprise for him. He lay quietly, pretending to be asleep, until she left the room. Though burning with curiosity, he waited until the light in her room went dark. Then he flicked on his own night-light and read Becky's note.

Thank you so much, Yanky. I want you to know that you were the only one who made me happy today. Love, your sister Becky.

When Naomi came upstairs to change the linens in her bedroom, she was surprised to find a note on her pillow. Her eyes darted quickly over the lines of childish script. She was not surprised by the fact that Becky had written her a note — Becky had been writing from the age of five — but the content was nothing short of astonishing, considering the writer's young age. When Shlomo came upstairs a few minutes later, he found his wife staring at the sheet of paper in her hands.

"What's that?" he asked, interrupting her reverie.

The piece of stationery fluttered to the floor. "What?"

"What's that?"

"Read it." She still hadn't moved from her place.

Shlomo bent down and picked up the sheet of paper. His eyes jumped to the signature, though the wobbly letters were enough of a giveaway as to the writer's identity. If not for the familiar writing, he would not have believed that his six-year-old Becky had written the note.

Dear Ima,

I saw all the mothers and also you. I know you're sad because of me and Mindy and I knew that if I sang, everyone would see that I'm different, and if I didn't, no one would see and you would be happy.

Love,

Becky

12

New York 5751/1991

Life was different when the girls were babies. Naomi didn't come home from the hospital with two tiny babies swaddled in soft blankets like a typical new mother. She was different.

Naomi had always been a busy woman. Her clinic demanded all of her time. She couldn't tell a client "Not now," when a child was suffering from depression or something even more serious. She had to be available to her clients at unconventional hours, just like a doctor. She was a doctor for the soul.

True, Naomi was not a psychiatrist, but people did place a great deal of faith in her, often more than was reasonable. She spent a lot of time at the clinic and very little at home.

Yanky was an easygoing, obedient child and his personality allowed Naomi to invest most of her time and energy into building her practice. She tried to spend as much time as possible with him when she was home, but he spent most of his day at playgroup. Naomi's life flowed pleasantly along. The cleaning lady kept the house in order, the cook put meals on the table, and Naomi tended to Yanky with great love and warmth when she was with him.

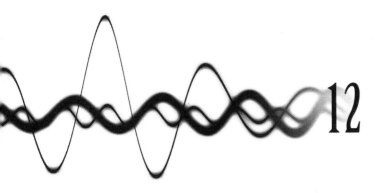

But then everything changed. Naomi knew she couldn't go back to her clinic. She had two deaf children at home now who demanded a lot more of her time than normal babies. Twins are a treasure that require constant care, and she didn't want strangers raising her children. Before she received the bitter news, Naomi was thrilled.

She intended to close her clinic for a full year, maybe longer, while she taught her darling daughters about the world into which they had been born. Naomi planned on investing all her time and effort into caring for them during the first and most significant year of their lives. She wanted them to be protected by an abundance of maternal warmth and love. She discussed her plans with great enthusiasm with her friend and colleague, Batsheva Klein. All Naomi's friends knew about her plans to put her career on hold while she raised her daughters.

All that changed in one day. After she learned her daughters were deaf, Naomi wanted to crawl into bed and never get up. The world seemed a hopelessly bleak place. She withdrew from it.

This was far more serious than postpartum blues; it was a failure to cope. How could anyone cope with news like that? How could Naomi accept the fact that she was the mother of two handicapped children — two children in whom she would invest her heart and soul but who would never be normal? Who knew what they would be capable of, what would become of them? What reason did they have to live?

Naomi didn't cry. Her eyes remained dry and glassy as she lay in bed, isolated from the world. An entire week passed. She signed the discharge form from the hospital like a zombie, allowing Shlomo to collect her things and transfer her to a convalescent home. The twins remained in the hospital for supervision. They'd been born rather small and a bit yellow, and the hospital didn't want to discharge them until they reached a reasonable weight of five pounds and until their jaundice disappeared. In contrast to all the other mothers of babies in the preemie nursery, Naomi didn't visit her children at all.

She sank into an abysmal depression. She didn't plan what to do the following day or even the same day. She gave not a thought to the future of her husband and small son, her twins or herself. Naomi didn't think about anything at all. She was silent and motionless, withdrawn into a bleak and hopeless world.

Naomi didn't want to see anyone, talk to anyone. Shlomo came to visit her every day, but she didn't react to anything he said. She just stared at the ceiling and said nothing. Sometimes she answered Shlomo's questions with a monosyllabic answer, but after half an hour or so of trying unsuccessfully to draw Naomi out, he joined her in her silence, looking dolefully out the window of her room. Naomi didn't take pity on him. She didn't pity herself, either. There was no room for emotion of any sort in the world she inhabited.

A few days passed like this. Unknown to Naomi, her husband and parents had consulted with professionals, who advised them to leave her alone and give her a chance to overcome the depression on her own.

"Do you want to see Yanky?" Shlomo asked gently one day. "He misses you."

Naomi burst into tears. That was the first positive sign she was still human since she'd learned the twins were deaf. "Shlomo, Shlomo," she wept. "What does he need me for?"

If Shlomo was shocked by the question, he didn't show it. "You're his mother."

"But he has deaf sisters!" Naomi cried. "Shlomo, what reason do I have to live? The rest of my life is going to be just anguish and pain. I'm going to spend my days worrying about them and trying to help them, and nothing will ever come of them anyway! What reason do they have to live, my babies? They'll never be able to marry and have families. They'll always be wretched objects of pity. What do they have to live for?"

Shlomo was silent for a moment. "And what reason does Yanky have to live?" he asked quietly.

Naomi stared at him in astonishment. Shlomo saw the shock on her face and said quietly, "I'm sorry, Naomi, but I think you're misinterpreting Hashem's intention in creating the world."

Naomi didn't quite understand what he was getting at, but as he spoke she sensed that the screen that had separated her from the rest of the world for the past few days was slowly lifting. She began to emerge from the deep, dark world she'd been inhabiting and to feel capable of contemplating the future. Naomi knew that Shlomo was overjoyed to be having this conversation, difficult as it was.

"What do you mean?" she asked through her tears.

"Do you think Hashem created the world so that everyone would be normal, marry and have families, and only then achieve the goal for which he was created?"

"Aren't children the purpose of this world?"

A smile played on his pale lips. Naomi knew his suffering was equal to hers, but his shoulders were broader and his faith more solid. "And if someone does not merit having children, does that mean he can't fulfill his assigned task? If so, why was he created?"

Naomi remained silent.

"Hashem created the world because He is good and He wanted to bestow his goodness upon us. He assigns each human being a *tafkid*, a mission in life, so that when the person arrives in the World of Truth he can enjoy his portion there with the feeling that he's rightfully earned it. The main point of this world is to get to the next, and that's why each soul receives a mission tailor-made for it."

"Becky and Mindy are different from most people," Shlomo went on. "They have lofty souls; various *Gedolim* have told us as much. They're here to accomplish a mission on earth and build for themselves a beautiful future in *Olam Haba*. It is quite possible that they will overcome this handicap and indeed marry and raise families, but even if they don't, G-d forbid, they will fulfill their *tafkid*.

"Their goal is to do Hashem's will in order to afford Him *nachas ruach*, satisfaction. They can do this better than we can. When, despite their struggle, they will be content with their lot and praise Hashem, He will have greater *nachas ruach* than when we healthy people do so."

Naomi's tears fell without letup. "But Shlomo," she sobbed, "how can I watch them suffer? How can I bear their pain over the fact that they'll never experience motherhood? How can I watch as they are rejected by society, as they experience difficulty with the simplest things, as they struggle through every step in life? How can I, Shlomo? My heart cannot withstand such pain ... it can't. Every child experiences difficulties of some sort during his lifetime, but the difficulties of a handicapped child are so great, and I ... I'm their mother! I want the very best for them, but I'll be forced to see them cry time and time again as they fail at whatever they try to do, as they're rejected by their peers."

Naomi covered her eyes with her hands, trying to blot out the terrible images of children making fun of her daughters that were taking shape in my mind.

We don't want to be your friends; you can't hear. You can't be my friend if you don't hear. Hey, you, whatsa matter, you deaf or something? I told you to move! You can tell she's not normal — why doesn't she hear? No one's going to be your friend ...

The voices echoed in Naomi's mind. At the same time, she heard the bewildered voices of her beloved children:

Ima, how come no one wants to be my friend? How come only I can't hear? Ima, she called me "you deaf girl!" Ima, I have no friends ... everyone ran away from the backyard when I came. ... Breindy said she won't play with a crazy girl. ... Leah'le said she doesn't like Monopoly, but then how come she played with Devorah yesterday?

And when they grew older their questions would become even more painful: *Ima, will I ever get married? Who would want to marry someone like me? Why am I the only one who's not getting engaged?*

Shlomo was silent. Through her tear-filled eyes, Naomi saw something she'd never seen before: A single tear trickled down his cheek. It was precisely because Shlomo's tears were so rare that this one touched her heart so.

Shlomo took a deep breath and said quietly, "Well, I don't profess to know Hashem's calculations, and I don't know why He saw fit to give us two deaf children. But one thing I do know: When a Jew is in pain, *Hakadosh Baruch Hu* is pained along with him. When a Yid suffers, his loving Father in Heaven suffers along with him. '*Imo Anochi betzarah*,' Hashem said to Moshe. Hashem loves you, Hashem loves Yanky, Hashem loves Mindy and Becky, and Hashem loves me, too."

Naomi looked at him and said nothing.

"Hashem sees your suffering, the suffering of a Jewish mother. He sees the suffering of His small daughters, *tinokos shel beis Rabban*, children who have never sinned. Hashem loves us far more than we love Becky and Mindy. There's a *midrash* in the *Zohar* that says that if people knew how greatly *Hakadosh Baruch Hu* loved *Klal Yisrael*, they would roar like lions and chase after Him. The human heart is incapable of feeling such a deep degree of love. Becky and Mindy are so small and helpless, you think to yourself, 'I must help them!' They are small and helpless compared to you, but how small and helpless are you compared to your Father in Heaven?

"Remember this: The *Ribbono shel Olam* thought about our children immediately on creating the world, when He foresaw all the generations of mankind. He thought of you and me, of Yanky, of Mindy and Becky. There are some things we are simply incapable of understanding. How long is a human lifespan — seventy years? Eighty? One hundred? Hashem is everlasting."

Things changed after that. The cry that burst forth from deep inside Naomi melted the wall of ice that depression had built around her heart and soul. She thought about what Shlomo had said and knew he was right. Finally, she was able to think again. The black screen lifted, and Naomi was able to breathe with less difficulty. She managed to look at the world around her.

Slowly, bit by bit, Naomi digested the idea. Yes, Hashem had given her two handicapped children. She was the mother of two deaf daughters; it was a fact. A sad, painful fact — but a fact nonetheless. She had the option of falling apart and sinking into a bottomless depression. A small, selfish, coddled voice inside her kept shouting: *You are fully entitled to do just that. You've been dealt such a miserable hand! You've been hurled into a world you want no part of.*

Slowly, another voice managed to make itself heard as well: *Yes,* it said, *you have the right to do that, but what will you gain? You also have another option: You have the strength and the ability to cope.*

For the first time since her world had fallen apart, Naomi dressed and traveled to the hospital. The twins were to be discharged from the hospital the following day. Shlomo planned to take them to Naomi's parents' house, where her mother had promised to raise them until Naomi recovered.

If you recover, the little voice reminded Naomi.

I will recover! she retorted bravely. *I will!*

Naomi arrived at the hospital feeling strangely calm. She climbed the three flights of stairs leading to the preemie nursery and was about to enter.

"Excuse me," a nurse said politely but firmly. "Only parents are allowed entry."

"I'm a parent," Naomi said, her voice sounding strange to her own ears.

The nurse looked at her, and Naomi knew what she must be thinking. It wasn't very complimentary.

"Only parents of the preemies hospitalized in this nursery are allowed in here," the nurse said slowly, as if she were talking to a six-year-old.

"Yes," Naomi replied in the same tone of voice, "that is what I am." *Just because your children are handicapped*, the little voice told her, *doesn't mean you have to behave as if you are mentally deficient.*

"I'm Becky and Mindy's mother," Naomi said briskly.

Oh! she could see the nurse thinking, *the one who's severely depressed. How do I know she won't harm her children?*

"It's okay," Naomi added. "I'm not dangerous. I admit I was a bit self-absorbed for a while, but I'm okay now. I would like to see my children."

"Is someone here with you?" The nurse's tone of voice had changed from what one uses when speaking to a child to what one uses when speaking to someone not quite normal.

"No."

"Does your husband or one of your parents know you're here?"

The nurse's tone of voice was infuriating.

"Ma'am, I'm not a minor. I'm past the age of twenty-one and responsible for myself, see?" Naomi tried to sound amused, but inside she was fuming.

The nurse hesitated, looking Naomi up and down, and then nodded. "Alright," she said. "Come inside with me."

Are those the regulations? Naomi wanted to ask. She bit her tongue, afraid the nurse wouldn't allow her in.

Naomi went inside and looked at her girls. They looked so much alike, sleeping in the same position, both of them sucking their thumbs. A tremor passed through her. Her lips trembled. She stood motionless for a moment, then reached out and caressed one baby gingerly. It was Becky.

"I love you," Naomi whispered to her. "It's me, Ima."

Becky's breathing was deep and even. Aside from her handicap, she was completely healthy. "Becky, I know I'm a little late. You've been here for two weeks on your own ... you forgive me, don't you? I'm ready to accept you as you are now."

Naomi stroked her tenderly, imparting warmth and love. "I ... I'm going to try and help you overcome your problem. I'm going to do everything possible for you, sweet girl. I promise."

She turned away and fled from the nursery. She couldn't handle the emotion. Naomi couldn't bring herself to say the same thing again to her other daughter. Mindy, lying near Becky, did not merit her mother's tender caress that day. Naomi couldn't bring herself to do it.

What kind of mother are you, she thought to herself, *abandoning your children when you hear they're not perfect? Why should they accept your apologies? Why are you treating them like strangers? What a far cry from the quintessential Yiddishe mamme you are!*

Despite the guilt, Naomi did not find it in her to re-enter the nursery and speak to Mindy, too. The following day, the twins came home, and Becky kept the secret of her mother's visit to the nursery to herself.

Later, when Naomi learned about Mindy's additional problem, it occurred to her that perhaps Hashem had orchestrated things so she wouldn't make her daughter a promise she couldn't keep.

The following day, the girls came home. Shlomo set up the bassinets in Naomi's parents' house. Naomi was weak and in need of both physical and emotional assistance. Her mother told Shlomo to put the bassinets in her bedroom, but he insisted he wanted the babies near him. In the end, they compromised: Naomi's mother took Mindy to her room and Shlomo took Becky to his. Every night, they would switch the babies. Both their grandmother and Shlomo wanted to bond with them both.

"I want to go home," Naomi said to Shlomo when he told her about it. "Now, immediately!"

"The twins came home just yesterday," he said hesitantly. "Are you sure?"

"Yes," Naomi replied firmly.

"Maybe," Shlomo said, still wavering, "maybe it would be a good idea if you first ..."

Naomi raised an eyebrow. "If I first what?"

"If you first see Yanky. He hasn't seen you in two weeks."

Dear heavens, Yanky! Her only son — Yanky! The severe, scolding voice kicked in again. *Is this the way a mother behaves to her child? You're not a coddled infant anymore; you're a mother!*

This time, Naomi silenced it firmly. This wasn't her mature, responsible voice; it was an obnoxious, derisive one that did nothing to augment her strength. She knew she needed every vestige of strength she still possessed, so she bade the voice be silent. She was allowed to be somewhat sad and withdrawn with such difficult news to digest. She wasn't an angel, after all, and even mothers have faults.

Poor Yanky, the voice managed to say before dying out.

He is not "poor Yanky," a different voice objected. *He may have suffered for a few days, not more.*

"Bring him," Naomi said to Shlomo, with great emotion. "Bring him now!"

Yanky came an hour later. His innocent, childish eyes were uncomprehending and mistrusting. Once again Naomi felt so selfish and inane. *Whatever the reason, you coddled little girl, you had no right to neglect your son and succumb to your emotions. You're a mother, Naomi, a mother!* That voice again!

Naomi cut it short and concentrated on her son. At first, Yanky stared at her in disbelief. "Yanky, come to Ima," Naomi pleaded with him. "Come here, darling." She tried offering him a candy and some chocolate, but he stuck to his father and wouldn't move from his place.

"Yanky," Naomi said to him, nearly in tears. "It's me, Ima!"

Perhaps she was too late for him, too, she thought sadly. Naomi nearly succumbed to the waves of bitterness and pain, but she made a supreme effort and kept her head above the water.

"Yanky, come listen to a story." Naomi opened the small book she'd bought for him and began reading. Slowly, gradually, he drew closer. By the end of the story, he was sitting at her side. Naomi gathered him into her arms and, despite his resistance, held him close. *Don't cry; don't cry,* she told herself over and over again. *Not in front of the child.*

Naomi didn't cry. She clamped her lips shut with an effort and smiled. She tickled Yanky the way he liked to be tickled, and by the end of the visit she had her child back.

Naomi packed her bags, left the convalescent home, and went to her parents.

She hadn't seen her parents since she'd heard the painful news.

Naomi hadn't wanted to see anyone, not even Shlomo, although he showed up every day. She was afraid to see the grandparents of deaf twins. Her mother was always a strong woman, but her father ...

Naomi's father had endured a lot in his life. She didn't know what exactly, but she knew his past was sad and painful. His past had turned him into a weak and fragile man.

How would he accept the news? How would he receive his deaf granddaughters? Naomi entered the house apprehensively. Her mother, glad to see her, chattered gaily as usual. Naomi's father entered the dining room when he heard she'd arrived. Naomi raised terrified eyes to meet his, and was shocked by what she saw.

He looked completely different from the way she remembered him. His eyes were twin torches of fire. His lips were clenched in the effort to contain his inner turmoil.

"What's wrong, Abba?" Naomi held her breath, waiting for him to answer. "What happened?"

"*Mazal tov*, daughter," he said calmly. "You gave birth to twin girls, didn't you?"

"But Abba ..." After seeing the way he looked, Naomi allowed herself to cry again. "You know they're not regular babies? You know they're deaf?"

"No," he said firmly, "they will be regular, Naomi, *be'ezras Hashem*. You'll see, little girl; your daughters will overcome their handicap. Nothing will stand in their way; they'll be perfectly ordinary in every way."

His eyes bore the look of stubborn determination Naomi knew so well. His chin was set, and she knew his decision had been made: His granddaughters would grow up like perfectly normal children.

And he was right — at least with regard to Becky. Naomi's father accomplished the incredible with Becky. From a very young age, it was obvious that she was extremely intelligent. She had an amazing understanding of human nature and was wise beyond her years. She learned to speak like anyone else and "hear" in her own way. She was completely regular. Naomi knew it, but she felt that knowledge was locked up within her own family. She wanted the entire world to know that her daughter was a normal, regular little girl.

When Becky was accepted into Morah Devorah's class, Naomi felt that Becky had emerged victorious. That they had won, that her father had won, that Shlomo had won. Yanky, her wonderful son, the most special boy in the world, was a partner in this victory as well. By sharing everything — time, effort, friendship, love — with his sister, he gave her her entire world, her entire life. He encouraged her when the going was tough, listened to her stammering speech when she first began talking, and complimented her every step of the way. He practiced lip reading with her and spent hours studying with her whatever she needed to know.

Whenever Naomi saw the two of them sitting side by side, bent together over Becky's never-ending drills, tears welled up in her eyes. Tears of gratitude to Hashem for the son He had given her and tears of joy for the bond Yanky shared with his sister. Rather than growing angry and jealous of his sister for dominating so much of his parents' time and attention, he willingly gave her his own time as well.

There was sadness, too, in Naomi's tears, but joy filled a greater area of her heart than sorrow.

Yanky was a full partner in this accomplishment. He was a partner with those who had made Becky what she was: an altogether regular girl.

Everyone admitted it: speech therapists and evaluators, special-education and regular-education teachers — everyone! It took time, but in the end, the world conceded what the family had known for a long time: Naomi's daughter was a regular girl in every way.

13

Eretz Yisrael 5705-5708/1945-1948

The blue sky spread above him in all its glory. Even the fumes of the farm machinery could not dim the brightness of the June sun that sparkled over the rivers and lakes. Birds soared overhead, tiny black dots in the blue, blue sky.

Spring was fast disappearing over the horizon. Butterflies fluttered gaily in the fields as farmers reaped their produce. Ripe wheat swayed in the hot summer wind as heavy, steamy air made its way from Eilat to Jerusalem with weary lassitude. The sun, positioned in the center of the sky, sent its warm embrace to the mortals below. Summer appeared to be warmer than usual this year, but the smell of hay and the produce coming from the fields took the edge off people's irritability.

They grew addicted to the pleasure of life on the kibbutz and refrained from thinking about the future. The war was over, but the Jewish fighters had not yet set down their arms. They were preparing for a war to liberate Eretz Yisrael.

Meir had accepted Shaul's proposition. He loved Eretz Yisrael so fiercely, why shouldn't he contribute his talents to expel the British and create a homeland for the Jews?

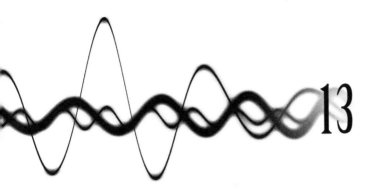

He'd ascended to Eretz Yisrael with the help of the Habricha organization, and it wasn't long before Shaul received confirmation that his assessment of the young recruit had been astonishingly accurate. Meir was a treasure, nothing less. His military ability and incredible prowess on the battlefield had turned one hundred and eighty degrees in another direction: From an outstanding, well-decorated British soldier of rank, he became a courageous warrior against the British. He was brave and stubborn, courageous and persistent.

Meir's appetite for battle was not yet sated. He was a formidable enemy with nothing to lose; he had sacrificed the love of his family on the altar of the new country he was now fighting for, and nothing else in the world mattered to him.

Meir soon earned a prominent spot on the British list of wanted men. He knew that he'd be hanged if they caught him. It was common knowledge that the British did not hesitate to mete out the death penalty to those who rebelled against them. Meir had heard about Jews the British had hanged, and he knew he could expect the same fate. *Meir*, he rebuked himself on more than one occasion, *you're the only one left from your entire family. You have to establish a family of your own and perpetuate the Katz name. You dare not risk dying without leaving behind any offspring!*

But he couldn't stop. The moment he entered the fray, he was hooked. He had changed his name from Marty back to Meir, but his outlook on life remained the same. Six years among gentiles had stripped him completely of the last vestiges of his erstwhile life. He had become a complete atheist.

Or had he?

Meir banished the doubt quickly from his mind. Yes. He was an atheist. He didn't believe in anything!

Really?

He forced himself to think about something else. What would Jim say if he met him now? Would he be angry with him? Hate him? Understand him? Fight him? How loyal would Jim be? How important was their friendship to him? What would he think of the friend who was undermining his native land and had become its sworn enemy?

As a rule, Meir avoided introspection. Thinking hindered his ability to act, and the work he did required constant vigilance.

Nonsense. That's not the reason I'm avoiding thinking.

A dim spark of faith flickered inside him. Occasionally, when he committed an *aveirah*, a voice inside him cried out in protest. He would be fidgety and restless for the next few hours until the cry abated.

Stop, Meir commanded himself as he entered the kibbutz through a rusted gate. *Concentrate on the task at hand.* The warm day illuminated the kibbutz with a pleasant light. Children wandered the dirt paths of the kibbutz with bare feet. He entered the waiting room of the kibbutz office and sat down on one of the chairs to wait.

His face remained calm and composed when he saw the door open and a tall British officer with a severe expression leave the office. He stared at the officer with contrived indifference, remaining motionless in his seat. The officer placed a hand on the doorknob and stood still for a moment. Meir's heart stood still as well; his blood froze in his veins. Not a muscle twitched in his face, but he was sure everyone could hear his pounding heart.

The officer fixed Meir with a penetrating stare and left.

Meir rose from his place and went to the door. He knocked and entered.

"You're on their Wanted List," Erez, the kibbutz secretary, told him. "Did you know that?"

Meir snorted. "Did I know that? What a question! What were you talking about?"

"About the Jewish fighters," Erez replied bitterly. "He gave me a list of wanted men. He said ..."

"He said what?" Meir asked. His hand instinctively went to his rifle. "Tell me, what was his threat?"

"He said that the day one of these men was found on the kibbutz, fifteen of our members would be imprisoned and tried. He warned that the very existence of the kibbutz was in danger."

Erez tried to avert his gaze from Meir's. "Meir, what is it you are accused of?" he asked.

"Why do you ask?"

"There's a long list of wanted men, but the soldier who was here before gave me a separate list of the ten most wanted. The others, he implied, wouldn't endanger the kibbutz if they were found; an arrest or two would suffice."

"I see." Meir thought for a moment. "Alright," he said finally. "If that's the case, my visit here is over." He extended his hand to the secretary. "I hope you won't refuse to see me once in a while, Erez, eh?"

Erez shook his head emphatically. "No," he said curtly. "I refuse."

Meir paled. His grip on the back of the chair tightened. Then he wheeled around and left the room without another word.

"Meir!" Erez called after him. "You misunderstood me."

"What is it?" Meir asked, stopping in his tracks. He didn't have that many friends here in Palestine that he could afford to lose one.

"I meant that I refuse to have you stop visiting here. I'm not afraid of the British or their threats."

"Oh, no," Meir said earnestly, shaking his head. "No, I won't endanger the kibbutz. I want to build up this country. Everyone has to do what he can. Your settlement here is playing an important role in building up Eretz Yisrael. Peace is no less important than battle. I won't come to visit anymore because I don't want to be responsible for the liquidation of a Jewish settlement in Eretz Yisrael —but I would like to continue meeting with you from time to time. Name a time and place, and that way we can continue our friendship."

"Let me walk along with you," Erez said. They walked along the dirt paths of the kibbutz, kicking up clouds of dust. Erez disappeared inside the stable and emerged a few moments later astride a black horse. He rode up to the steel gate at the entrance to the kibbutz, with Meir walking alongside him. Outside the gate, Meir's own big, noble horse was tethered. Its chestnut coat gleamed in the sun. The horse neighed restlessly, and Meir patted it lightly on the back.

"What's his name?" Erez asked.

"Guess," Meir said.

"It must be something connected to this land," Erez replied.

"That's right." Meir smiled. "Surprisingly enough, his name's Yisrael." He leaped onto the horse's back.

Erez looked at him in amazement. "You mean you succeeded in breaking him in at last? How in the world did you do it?"

"Of course I did." Meir pretended to be insulted. "Within two days."

"And you're riding him bareback, too," Erez said admiringly. "No one was able to ride him even when he was saddled. How'd you do it?"

"Secrets of the trade." Meir kicked the horse lightly in the ribs, and it set off at top speed. Erez bade his horse to break into a gallop as well, but it couldn't catch up with Meir's horse. *Meir ought to be dressed like a cowboy from the Wild West,* Erez thought to himself. The thought made him smile. Meir looked like he'd been born in Palestine. The wind had whipped his black hair around his head, and his black eyes burned with the strength and audacity of a Jewish fighter.

Meir slowed his horse and waited for Erez to catch up with him.

"What happened?" he asked. "Why are you smiling?"

"No special reason. I was thinking about you."

"I can't imagine what it is about me that makes you smile," Meir said gloomily. "What were you thinking about?" he asked curiously.

"I was thinking about your courage and daring. About the bravery of all fighters, in general."

Meir was silent. He raised his eyes to the sun, which had begun painting the sky with the vibrant hues of sunset. "You wouldn't understand," he said quietly. "We burn with love for this land. We know it is the land of our forefathers and we must inherit it, either peacefully or through war."

"Yes," Erez agreed. "I feel the same way, but I don't have your courage. Courage like yours is a rarity in today's world."

"A rarity? What makes you say that?" Meir looked at him, puzzled. "What about the Allied soldiers? Or even the cursed Germans? What about the people in the occupied countries, the various undergrounds, the partisans, the guerilla fighters? What about the courage of the Jews slaughtered in Europe? All that took place just a few months ago. The war in the Far East is not even over yet."

A shadow passed over Erez's face. "The Jews in Europe were not courageous," he said shortly. "Except for those who took part in the Warsaw Ghetto uprising," he added as an afterthought.

"What?" Meir asked furiously. "What are you saying?"

"Why didn't they try to fight the Germans?" Erez countered.

"You saw what their fighting caused," Meir said, the anger in his voice intensifying. "You saw what the Warsaw Ghetto uprising led to! You saw how people perished in the flames of that pointless battle!"

Meir was practically foaming at the mouth now. "The Germans starved them to death. And they tricked them! The Jews believed the Germans' promises and preferred to live rather than to die rebelling. They didn't know they would die in any case!"

Erez was taken aback by the degree of Meir's fury. "What's gotten into you?" he asked, trying to cool his friend's anger. "Who are you defending? The '*galus* Jews'?"

In answer, Meir snapped the reins sharply and galloped full speed ahead. In a moment, he had disappeared from view. Erez shook his head in bafflement and made his way back to the kibbutz.

Meir continued riding by himself. Night fell, and a carpet of stars unrolled in the sky, their sparkling light glowing softly. The night was warm and dark, and the wind rustled the leaves of the eucalyptus leaves. Meir stopped near one of the trees and stroked its thick trunk. "Thank you," he whispered. "Thank you for drying the swamps in my country." Piles of leaves that the tree had shed fluttered softly around his feet.

Midnight found Meir still leaning against the tree, eyes staring into the distance. Suddenly, he leaped up onto his horse again.

Yisrael, the horse, was tired; his gait was slow and weary. Meir, sitting erect on his back, allowed the animal to move at his own pace. He knew Yisrael would take him where he wanted to go.

Yisrael skirted the forest and trotted in the direction of a nearby city. Meir avoided sleeping in houses when another person was present because if the British found him, they'd surely arrest whoever was in the house with him. Meir knew that his picture and description had been circulated all over the country and that anyone who recognized him was supposed to hand him over to the police. No one did, however, despite the threat of imprisonment for not doing so. It was unthinkable that one of his friends would turn him in. Most wanted to welcome him into their homes, but he refused.

"There's no point in your getting arrested," he explained. "I manage on my own just fine."

Shaul had proposed that he come to live with him, as he too was high on the list of the Brits' most wanted men. Meir had refused.

The horse moved carefully, as if trying to make as little noise as possible. Meir looked apprehensively at the tall building. He thought he saw figures waiting at the door. Suddenly, he was sorry he hadn't accepted Shaul's offer.

He soothed the horse and dismounted carefully. Holding his rifle, he walked quietly toward the house. The figures he had seen were only coats left outside to dry in the wind. The *passuk*, *Venastem ve'ein rodef eschem*, "And you shall flee [even when] no one is chasing you," floated into Meir's consciousness.

He entered the building and lit a small lamp. The windows were shut tight; the dim light would not be seen outside. From a closet he withdrew an old, dog-eared siddur he kept hidden behind a bulky encyclopedia. That was the real reason he refused to sleep over at friends' houses. Every evening, Meir recited *Tikkun Chatzos*.

New York 5751/1991

Naomi began to grow accustomed to caring for the twins. Becky was a very easygoing child. Like Yanky when he was a baby, she was easy to care for. But Mindy – Mindy cried most of the day. Whenever she was awake she either screamed or writhed in discomfort, sobbing quietly. Naomi didn't know what to do. How could she help her? It was clear Mindy was suffering, and Naomi suffered along with her. What could she do for her?

Technically, Naomi could have taken on additional help so that she'd have another pair of hands to hold Mindy when she cried, but Naomi knew that would not solve the emotional pain she felt at the sight of her daughter's suffering. Besides, she didn't want a nurse. Naomi's mother loved babies; she worked as a volunteer in a convalescent home for new mothers during her spare time. Now, she quit her volunteer work temporarily and came to help Naomi instead. Shlomo was able to continue attending *kollel* as before. The problem was that Mindy cried inconsolably even when she was held.

Yanky went happily to playgroup every morning and ran to see how his sisters were as soon as he came home. He would climb the stairs to the second floor, where the babies' bassinets stood side by side, and call out: "Here are the dollies! I want to hold them. Ima, I want to hold the dollies!"

Naomi allowed him to "help" her care for them. She didn't know if he would be jealous of them, if he'd realize something was wrong with them, if he would love them. In the meantime, everything was normal in his simplistic, superficial, three-year-old world.

"You know what bothers me?" Naomi said to her mother one day as they sat down for a glass of post-midnight tea. Mindy was sleeping, for a change, but Naomi looked at her worriedly.

"Something's bothering the child," her mother said.

"Yes. I've reached the same conclusion. But something else is bothering me as well."

Naomi's mother brought a plate of Naomi's favorite chocolate chip cookies to the table. Naomi munched them, one after another, paying no mind to her recent declarations that she was starting a strict diet.

"What is it?" her mother asked.

"None of my friends called me to say *mazal tov*."

"Naomi," her mother said gently, "they did call, but you were unable to talk to them."

Naomi felt flustered. "So what?" she asked. "Do you mean to say that now they won't call me ever again? I mean, do they think I'm going to stay depressed permanently?"

Her mother thought for a moment. "No, I don't think so. But I understand them. They can't just call and chat as if nothing happened."

"Batsheva, at least, ought to call," Naomi grumbled. "To give me an update on my patients."

"I thought you left the clinic."

"I did," Naomi admitted, "but still, I thought she'd call to ask how I am, what's doing ..."

"You know your friends feel uncomfortable calling. If you think about it, you'll understand them."

Naomi nodded. "Yes. And now that they've heard I was depressed, they'll never call again," she said bitterly.

"You can't blame them," her mother said firmly. "I don't think you'd behave any differently, in their place."

A pretty painting of small cottages nestling in a valley hung in the dining room. Naomi stared at it intently for a moment. "What do you think I should do now?" she asked quietly.

"Maybe you should give your friends a call," her mother suggested.

The very idea made a chill run down Naomi's spine. "I'm afraid," she said simply.

"If that's the case, I understand them even more." Her mother rose from her place and went to the kitchen to place her empty mug in the sink. Naomi crumbled the last cookie on the plate absentmindedly.

Call her friends? If she didn't, she'd likely find herself cut off from all her friends. But so what? Wasn't she light years away from them in any case? What did they know of coping with hardship?

Ah, said the mature voice inside her. *And because they're fortunate enough to have been spared the pain you're suffering, you'll cut off all contact with them?*

No, Naomi replied defensively, *but they'll have a hard time identifying with me and I with them. What are their concerns? Financial difficulties? The baby is already ten months old and not crawling yet? The two-year-old wakes up every night and wakes the entire family? The five-month-old is teething and fusses all day? I'm so far from such petty worries. I couldn't possibly identify with them anymore.*

And they? They'll feel so uncomfortable in my company. They'll feel silly talking about their small concerns in the face of my tragedy. In addition to the pain I'm struggling with, I've got to suffer disconnection from society. I won't be able to discuss something neutral, such as childrearing, with them. I'm too wrapped up in myself, too absorbed with my personal mourning.

But when you'll be ready to let go, it will be too late. If you don't meet or talk to them for months, it will be hard to recapture the comfortable familiarity you once enjoyed with them.

The internal struggle made Naomi feel dizzy and weak. She didn't know what to do. She couldn't just call and chatter gaily about the hurricane the weathermen had predicted that never materialized, the snowy winter they were having, or the bargains at a terrific end-of-the-season sale at a well-known children's boutique. No, it wasn't for her. Not yet.

Naomi didn't call.

"Did you call Batsheva?" her mother asked her the following day as she folded laundry, carefully avoiding Naomi's eyes.

"No," Naomi admitted dejectedly.

"I don't want to tell you what to do, Naomi, but I don't think it's good for you to be so wrapped up in yourself."

Naomi made a face and said nothing.

"Do you feel up to traveling to my parents?" Shlomo asked her that evening, as if it was the most natural request.

"What?" Naomi stared at him in shock.

"I mean, if you've recuperated from the birth. We can wait a bit longer if you're not up to it yet."

"Shlomo!"

"Yes?"

"Travel to Eretz Yisrael – now?"

"Why not?" Was he pretending he had no idea why she was so shocked or was he truly so dense?

"Because ... because..."

"You know my parents are not up to flying. They can't come here."

"Yes," Naomi said shortly.

"Don't they deserve to see their granddaughters?" he asked. "That was our plan, originally," he added in a quieter voice.

Naomi wasn't sure whether he had said that to himself or whether he'd intended for her to hear. They had indeed planned to take a trip to Eretz Yisrael a month after the twins' birth. They had planned ... she had wanted to visit Shmulik, too. She had wanted ... Shmulik had planned to come here with Shulamit and the children as soon as he heard Naomi'd given birth. He'd planned ... After he heard about Naomi's situation, he had canceled their plans to fly in for the double *kiddush*.

"Originally," Naomi said in a chilly voice, "I didn't plan for them to be deaf."

"What are you afraid of? That they won't hear the safety instructions?"

"Shlomo! What are you talking about? You want me to just take them and go?"

"You want to hide them in a closet? Until when?"

"I don't want to hide them. I'm not up to such a trip, and that's that."

Shlomo was silent. "My parents want to see the babies," he added, trying one last time.

Naomi shot him a withering look. "No," she said. "Not now. Maybe in another few months."

He rose and left the room. Naomi felt awful. But how could she show up at her in-laws' with two deaf children as their granddaughters?

"I think you ought to leave the house a bit," Naomi's father told her. "Get some fresh air. You'll come back feeling rejuvenated."

"What happened to the lot of you!" Naomi cried angrily. "I can take care of myself, thank you!"

"You could've fooled me," her father said evenly.

Naomi didn't leave the house for an entire week. Her day revolved around Yanky and the twins, so it was easy to find excuses for staying home all day. She was busy from morning to night. Caring for twins is intensive work. Naomi ran from one to the other, changing diapers and feeding, soothing and holding, administering eyedrops and putting to sleep, rocking bassinets and patting lightly on little backs.

One day, when the babies were finally calmed, she sank into an armchair, totally spent. She had spent the past three hours running from one baby to the other. Her nerves were frayed and Naomi hadn't an ounce of strength left in her body. Her mother had gone shopping, and Naomi felt miserable and weak.

Shlomo entered the room with a cheerful hello.

"Where were you?" Naomi attacked him.

"In *kollel*," he replied, stating the obvious.

"You're late!"

He glanced at his watch. "Yes, you're right," he said. "By seven minutes."

"Do you have any idea how weak I am? Do you know that I'm utterly drained?" Naomi was on the verge of tears. "And I was so worried!"

"Because I was seven minutes late?" He wasn't the least bit sarcastic. He was sincerely apologetic, but Naomi exploded.

"Yes, seven minutes is a long time. I can't handle everything myself!"

To his credit, he refrained from reminding her that he actually helped a lot. He just stood there in silence.

"Instead of trying to be home a few minutes earlier than usual, you come home late?" Naomi ranted.

He lowered his eyes. When he raised them again, he spoke in a quiet voice. "I think you need to get out a bit."

"What?" Naomi fumed. "Why do I need to get out?"

""You've emerged from your depression, *baruch Hashem*, but you're still locked up inside yourself. You're caring for the twins and doing an excellent job at it, but you're cut off from society. Aren't you afraid the day will come when you'll regret that?"

"What does this have to do with your being late?"

"It doesn't," he admitted, "but if you'll be perfectly honest with yourself you'll admit that you're not caring for the twins entirely on your own. I think that what's bothering you is not the work involved in caring for the twins but the fact that you're indoors twenty-four hours a day."

Naomi nodded silently.

"And I also think," he went on, focusing his gaze on a single flower on the wallpaper, "that you should see a psychologist."

"What?" Naomi would have burst out laughing if it hadn't been so sad. "Me? See a psychologist?"

"Yes." He smiled wryly. "It sounds strange, doesn't it?"

"I have one right here, for free ..."

"A person can't treat himself," Shlomo said firmly. "I remember you once told me about a similar incident, where a woman who was a psychologist herself came to see you."

Naomi said nothing.

"I think you ought to think about it," Shlomo said, rising at the sound of Becky's cry. He lifted her from her bassinet and held her in his lap, admiring her tiny features. It occurred to Naomi that of late, Shlomo had been starting all his sentences with a wary, hesitant "I think." He was afraid of hurting her. He took great care when talking to her, the fragile, broken mother of the twins.

What about their father?

The thought struck Naomi with great intensity. Shlomo was the girls' father. He was suffering just like her; she'd noticed that a long time ago, but she had been focusing solely on her own difficulty, her own struggle.

Shlomo went to shul every day, three times a day. He continued going to *kollel* as usual, and she never heard a word of complaint from him. He continued meeting with his friends and acquaintances, learning with his *chavrusas*. On the outside, his life hadn't changed at all. How could that be? Hadn't he also become the parent of two deaf girls?

"Shlomo," Naomi called, coming out of her room to the adjoining one where he sat feeding Becky from a bottle. He looked up, surprised by the tone of her voice.

"Yes?"

"Tell me, how did everyone react?"

"Everyone? What do you mean?"

"You know, at *kollel*, in shul ... what did people say?"

He froze. The bottle trembled in his hand and fell from Becky's tiny lips. She wailed in protest. Shlomo recovered, gently replaced the bottle in her mouth, and raised his eyes to meet Naomi's.

"What makes you ask?"

"I'm sorry," Naomi said sincerely. "I only just now noticed how wrapped up in myself I've been."

"Let me tell you something," he said softly. "Society reflects the way you behave. People take their cue from you. The way you behave shows them how you want to be treated."

NAOMI KNEW THEY were right. Shlomo, Abba, Ima ... they were all right. Even Yanky, who threw his chubby arms around her neck and asked, "Ima's crying?"

"No," Naomi replied sharply. "I'm laughing."

She wasn't sure he was convinced. He went to play, murmuring under his breath, "Ima's laughing, Ima's crying; Ima's laughing, Ima's crying."

Shlomo's suggestion that she see a psychologist shocked Naomi completely. She, a respected psychologist whom people made appointments weeks in advance to consult – she should go to a psychologist? The idea seemed stranger than strange. The mature voice, which had been kicking in rather frequently of late, asked her relentlessly: *Tell the truth, Naomi. What bothers you about the idea? Is it your personal pride? Do you feel it's beneath your dignity to see a psychologist? What's the real reason you're resisting the idea?*

She didn't know how to respond. Actually, she knew very well what her answer should be, and that was why she preferred to remain silent.

"Is there any way I can make you give up on the idea?" she asked her husband as they enjoyed a quiet breakfast together one morning.

Shlomo poured milk into his bowl of cereal. "Which idea?" he asked, looking at Naomi in surprise. He didn't know what she had been thinking about before she shot her question at him, after all.

"*Nu*," Naomi said impatiently. "The idea you mentioned to me."

"What are you talking about?" He was truly confused.

"About seeing a psychologist."

Shlomo raised an eyebrow. "I'm not pressuring you to do anything you don't want to," he said.

"But you're not pleased that I'm not seeing one."

"Because I think it would be good for you."

"Can you think of anything else I could do to feel better? I'd really rather not have to see a psychologist."

"I can't understand why you're so reluctant."

"Because ... because ..."

"You always used to tell me what a shame it is that people foolishly refuse to help themselves by seeing a psychologist," Shlomo pointed out. "Now you're doing the same thing. Are you joining the circle of people who place pride above personal benefit? That's ridiculous! Even if people eventually find out, so what? Isn't it perfectly natural to want to help yourself after ... after ..."

"After becoming the mother of two deaf children?" Naomi finished bitterly.

"Yes, precisely." Shlomo didn't back down. "You've become the mother of two deaf daughters. It's a very complex job. Isn't it reasonable for you to want to learn a bit about it?"

Naomi said nothing.

They ate in silence for a moment or two, and then Shlomo asked her in a voice so low Naomi could barely hear him, "Tell me, are you happy?"

"No," Naomi admitted. "And I definitely think I would benefit from seeing a psychologist. But I would like to try a different way first. I want to try and overcome the problem by myself."

Shlomo grew pensive. He stroked his short beard. He was all of twenty-five years old, and he had so much on his shoulders. He was a young man who had matured almost overnight. "A different idea? Something other than a psychologist?" he said thoughtfully. "Maybe you should try to talk to your friends. Maybe you should take the twins out and show them to people."

Naomi decided to do it. She'd go for a walk with the twins.

She dressed them in identical pink and lavender outfits and adorable matching lavender socks. She put on their hats and attached pretty pacifier clips to their clothing. Mindy screamed in protest as Naomi dressed her.

Naomi loaded a diaper bag with bottles, extra pacifiers (just in case), small change, a small container of formula and a few rattles. Tissues, cloth diapers, wipes, four disposable diapers – there, she was done.

"Do you want me to come with you?" Naomi's mother asked when she saw her preparing to leave.

"There's no need," Naomi said decisively. "I'll be okay, Ima. Don't worry." She was talking more to herself than to her mother.

Naomi stepped out into the street.

Ah ... she felt the cold air on her face and inhaled deeply. Shlomo and her father had purchased the twin carriage on their own when they saw that Naomi wasn't going to be doing any shopping in the near future.

Actually, she had snapped out of her depression and gone shopping a few days later, Naomi thought. She smiled to herself. *Very good, Naomi. You're making progress. This is the first time you've complimented yourself since you received the terrible news.*

For the first time, Naomi took a good look at the carriage. The vibrant colors went well together: dark gray, yellow and orange. *It's a beautiful carriage,* she thought with pleasure. *I'm glad they chose this model. I like pretty things, and it would upset me to have to put my daughters in a carriage I don't like.*

Progress! the mature voice exulted. *Naomi, look what's happening. You've begun paying attention to external details. You're regaining your sense of aesthetics.* Naomi's heart swelled with joy. It was a long time since she'd felt so happy, so free.

She walked slowly, heading nowhere in particular. *Do you want to meet one of your friends?* Naomi asked herself as she strolled along. *Do you want to meet someone from "the past"?*

She couldn't say. On the one hand, Naomi was afraid of such a meeting. It would present questions she didn't yet know the answers to herself. It would leave her feeling frustrated and confused. It would make her feel sorry for herself, which was the last thing she wanted.

On the other hand, a part of Naomi longed to break the barrier she had erected. The twins were not yet one month old, but her life had changed completely. She constantly fantasized about what would have been "if," how wonderfully different life "could have been." Naomi hadn't yet fully made peace with reality.

And as long as she hadn't yet accepted reality, how could she meet her friends?

Naomi walked apprehensively toward the unknown. She crossed the street and turned the corner. She strolled for about half an hour before deciding that the twins had had enough. They were surely tired from the excursion.

Naomi hadn't met anyone. Slightly chagrined, she turned around and began walking back to her parents' house. She was sorry she hadn't bumped into one of her friends.

Just as Naomi was about to enter the house, a neighbor stepped out of a nearby house. The woman saw Naomi, stood stock still for a moment as if she'd seen a ghost, then turned on her heels and went back into her house.

Naomi's good mood plummeted. She had read about people who had a hard time dealing with uncomfortable situations and did their best to avoid them by crossing the street or walking quickly away, but she had never personally been on the receiving end of such treatment.

"Hi, Naomi," her mother greeted her happily. "How was your walk?"

"I met someone," Naomi said sharply. "Never mind who. It's *lashon hara*, I think. She looked at me in shock and fled."

Naomi's mother's lips curved into a smile.

"What's so funny?" Naomi demanded.

"The tragic expression on your face," her mother replied, tickling Mindy under the chin. Mindy responded with hair-raising shrieks, and Naomi's mother was alarmed.

"What's the matter, Mindy, darling? What happened?" she asked. "Look how she's screaming," she said to Naomi.

She bent over to pick her up, but Mindy's shrieks only intensified. Naomi's mother untied Mindy's hat and removed it from her head. She took off the baby's socks and loosened her outfit, and Mindy finally calmed down. Her breathing grew deep and even and she fell asleep.

"She's tired," Naomi said. "The walk tired her out."

"Did you keep an eye on her during your outing?" Naomi's mother asked in concern.

"No."

"A shame."

"Why?"

"Because you know she cries a lot. Babies don't cry for no reason. Maybe we ought to start paying attention to when she cries."

"I don't think she slept while we were out," Naomi said thoughtfully. "Strange, isn't it? Babies usually fall asleep in the fresh air." Becky was napping peacefully in the carriage, an angelic smile on her sweet face.

"That smile is not just a reflex," Naomi said, worried now. "You can tell she's content. Mindy isn't."

"A mother's heart senses when something's wrong," Naomi's mother said. "Let's try to keep a closer eye on her for the next day or two. If we see you're right, we'll take her to the doctor."

"I have no strength to even think of taking her to the doctor," Naomi said weakly.

Her mother looked at Naomi in surprise. "Why?"

"What if he finds an additional problem?"

"He won't," her mother said optimistically. "He'll just explain to you why she's so fussy. She might be suffering from stomach pain. It's very common at this age."

"But Ima, Becky is all of four minutes older than Mindy. How could it be that Mindy is suffering from something that Becky isn't?"

Naomi's mother chuckled. "It happens. Some babies are more sensitive than others. Becky and Mindy are not identical, although they do look very much alike. It's not at all farfetched to think that one of them suffers from something that the other doesn't."

"Mindy seems to prefer the bassinet or the carriage to my arms," Naomi continued thinking aloud. "Do you think that might be connected to whatever the problem is?"

"I doubt it," Naomi's mother said. "Babies usually like skin contact, especially with their mothers."

"Maybe she senses that I didn't accept her for what she was, at first," Naomi said apprehensively.

Her mother shrugged. "Psychology is your strong point," she said, smiling. "Maybe."

"Anyway," Naomi said, returning to the original topic of discussion, "that woman I met ... she fled when she saw me. Is deafness catching?"

"No, but maybe she thinks depression is," Naomi's mother said with a tired chuckle. "Naomi, to be perfectly honest, you are somewhat intimidating now, don't you agree?"

Naomi looked at her searchingly. "Even to those closest to me?" she asked quietly.

Her mother did not avert her gaze. She fixed her soft, wise eyes upon Naomi's face and said, "Yes."

"I'm sorry."

"Naomi, we always want the best for you — but there are some things that are beyond our control. I'm overjoyed when you're happy, and it hurts me when things are hard for you. You're my daughter; I carry you in my heart all the time. I don't want you to pretend to be strong in order to make things easier for me. I want you to be strong for real."

She left the room, probably so that Naomi wouldn't see her cry.

Naomi walked across the room to the telephone, with a determined step. She dialed Batsheva's number.

"Hello?"

"Hello, is Batsheva there?"

"Just a moment, please."

Naomi waited.

"Batsheva? It's me, Naomi."

Shocked silence. Did Batsheva think Naomi had become mute when she'd given birth to deaf daughters? Why was she so shocked to hear Naomi's voice? Perhaps she thought that depression was a condition that never passed.

"Batsheva?" Naomi repeated after thirty seconds of silence.

"Yes."

"How are you?"

"*Baruch Hashem*. And you?"

"Fine, *baruch Hashem*." What a fascinating conversation. Absolutely enthralling. And this was Batsheva, the friend Naomi used to talk to for hours. They used to spend ages on the phone talking about both the personal and professional aspects of their lives.

Silence.

"Are you home?" she asked.

"No, not yet. I'm still at my parents' house."

Silence.

"You know, the twins look more like me than like Shlomo," Naomi said, hoping a direct mention of her deaf children would break the ice.

"Ah," was Batsheva's response.

"They're very cute," Naomi assured her. "Why don't you come visit?"

"Maybe," she replied. "If I get around to it."

Ribbono shel Olam, Naomi cried silently. *If my friend is rejecting me because I'm the mother of deaf children, how will society treat the children themselves?*

14

Naomi looked at the calendar. The twins were one month old. A month had passed since the day she had been flooded with joy after giving birth to two healthy little girls. Her joy had lasted twenty-two hours ... no more. Tomorrow would mark one month since they had received the terrible news that hurled Naomi from sheer bliss into an abyss of misery.

Tomorrow, tomorrow ... How happy she'd been! She had hugged Becky, who hadn't needed an incubator, in her arms, covering her with kisses and pressing her to her heart. She had promised Becky that she'd always be there for her, that she'd help her through the rough spots in life.

What a pathetic promise. No one ever knows how much time he has in this world. Naomi's promise remained valid for nineteen hours. Then her daughter was taken from her to a sea of never-ending difficulty. Naomi remained standing at the edge of that sea, screaming bitterly and extending her arms as far as they could go in a vain effort to help her children.

Naomi's eyes filled with tears. The salad her mother had prepared for her before leaving the house tasted bland and bitter. Sadness wrapped its arms around her heart. Despite the progress she had made during the past two weeks, Naomi very nearly returned to the bleak world she had inhabited after learning the twins were deaf.

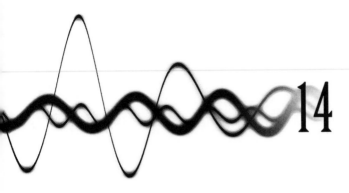

The telephone rang.

Distracted, Naomi lifted the receiver. She usually refrained from answering the phone. She never knew who the caller might be, and she didn't feel like talking to anyone. Naomi didn't know why she took that phone call. It was Hashem's merciful Hand that pushed her and made her do it.

"Hello?"

"Naomi? Hi, it's Shaindy."

Shaindy? Shaindy? Oh, of course! Shaindy, her bubbly, happy, always-energetic cousin. The one who arranged get-togethers for all the cousins. Shaindy always knew what to say, who to say it to and when to say it. As Naomi thought about her, she pictured Shaindy in her mind's eye.

"*Mazal tov*, Naomi. Sorry for the belated congratulations, but I absolve myself of all guilt. I called a few times but your family said you weren't accepting phone calls. I knew it was hard to get an appointment at your clinic, but I had no idea it would be so difficult to speak to you as a cousin!"

Though her humor seemed a bit tasteless to her at that moment, Naomi smiled wanly. She found the fact that Shaindy was making an effort to amuse her encouraging.

"I heard they're absolutely gorgeous. Listen, if they look like you, it couldn't possibly be otherwise. They look alike, right?"

"Right." What a heart-warming conversation. Maybe Naomi could try to be a bit warmer? Invite Shaindy over? *You're always complaining that no one comes to visit you, that no one calls you ... no wonder. Look how you're treating the one person who does call you. If you were in her place, you'd have hung up already. If she's a tad nicer than you, she'll spend another moment in conversation before giving up. She'll have fulfilled her obligation as your cousin, but you'll remain stuck in your misery. You'll remain detached from your friends.*

The pep talk sounded very convincing, but Naomi said nothing. *Ask her to come over*, the mature voice inside her nearly wept. Naomi remained silent.

"So what do you say, cousin, can I come over for a visit?"

For a moment Naomi's tongue caught in her throat. "Of course," she heard herself say. "I'd be so pleased if you did. Really."

They settled on a time and Naomi returned the receiver to its cradle.

Shaindy arrived two hours later, smiley as ever. She brought with her an abundance of inner joy and gaiety, a pleasant sense of humor and an open, generous heart.

"Look at that!" she exclaimed, leaning over a bassinet. "Is this one Becky?" she asked, trailing a delicate finger over the baby's cherubic face. The baby twitched sharply and burst out crying. "That's Mindy," Naomi replied, unable to stifle a sigh. "She's very sensitive. She cries a lot."

The other twin received Shaindy's cool touch with a sleepy smile. "So this must be Becky," Shaindy said. "She's a good girl, mark my words."

"Huh? Oh, yes, of course." Naomi wasn't concentrating.

"You're absentminded," Shaindy said. "When are you planning to return to work?"

"Not for the rest of the year."

"What? Why?" Shaindy looked at Naomi in surprise.

"That was my plan before ... uh, before ... before this happened. I mean, before I knew they were deaf."

"Why?"

"Because I wanted to devote myself to my house and children for this year. I wanted to give my babies everything. I wanted them to have a full-time mother. I didn't give that to Yanky, and now ... now I see I won't be able to give it to them, either." To Naomi's consternation, her eyes filled with tears. She had always been the strong, in-control type; she had never cried in front of someone outside of her immediate family. Something inside her had melted and disappeared since the heavy blow she'd been dealt.

"Why?" Shaindy asked again, looking at her placidly. Her eyes were filled with true understanding, and Naomi sensed that Shaindy was sincerely interested in her and her feelings.

"I wanted to give them a perfect childhood," Naomi said, wiping her eyes and trying to stem the flow of tears. "I wanted them to be happy children. I wanted to give them everything in my power. I wanted them to have it good ... I wanted it so badly, but ... that's not what happened ..."

"They'll have the happiest, most perfect childhood possible," Shaindy declared. "They will be happy; they will have it good. I'm sure of it. You're a very confident person. You'll be the best mother ever to your deaf children. True, you'll face difficulties as you raise them, but you're smart, warm and supportive enough to afford them complete protection from the things that are liable to hurt them."

Naomi stared at her. Where had Shaindy found the words she'd so badly needed to hear? If only Shaindy would go on talking, go on encouraging her and her ability as a mother. If only ...

Shaindy was speaking in a quiet, well-modulated voice. "No one is immune to difficulties with children. Every day when I send my eldest son to cheder, I pray: '*Ribbono shel Olam*, please, help my son to study Your Torah properly. May he find favor in Your eyes and in the eyes of the people he comes in contact with.'

"It's not always so simple though. More than once, he came home crying that someone hurt his feelings. Sometimes he fails a test I know he spent hours studying for. Once, he told me his rebbe punished him, and once his friends laughed at him when he didn't understand something. And my son is an altogether normal child, not learning disabled or handicapped or a social reject. A perfectly ordinary child. Do you know how my heart aches every time something like that happens?

"I have four daughters. The youngest will be starting preschool next year. The other three already attend preschool and elementary school, and they deal with various difficulties every day. Even the little one has to cope with hardship – she falls, occasionally, or can't reach something she wants. She cries bitterly when something like that happens.

"At that age, it's easy to soothe a child. You kiss and hug her, offer her a sweet and murmur endearments. It gets harder as they get older, though, because the difficulties are more serious. Did you think you could give Yanky a perfect childhood? There's no such thing."

Naomi said nothing.

"And something else, Naomi. Think of your mother. Doesn't she want the best for her children?"

Naomi remained silent. Acute pain must have been reflected in her eyes because Shaindy leaned over and grasped her hand apologetically. "I'm sorry, Naomi. I didn't mean to hurt you. I just wanted to explain that we have no control over what will happen in our children's lives. I'm sure you were occasionally hurt by your friends and teachers, too. It happens. It has happened, it happens and it will happen to your daughters as well. Don't be so frightened for their future. There's a Creator. He decides what's good for us and for our children. Maybe Hashem will grant your daughters an outstanding degree of personal charm so that they will be welcomed by society despite their handicap. Maybe He'll bless them with talent so astounding it will overshadow their deafness. There's no way to tell what the future will bring."

She changed the subject, asking Naomi if she had an idea for the graduation party Shaindy was in charge of arranging for her eighth-grade students.

"But it's only Kislev," Naomi protested.

"Yes, but my principal wants to plan everything in advance. The theme of the graduation party will coincide with the subject matter the girls will be learning all year."

"I see."

"They want me to choose a theme now so that they can plan contests and all sorts of special activities on the same theme throughout the year. I was considering 'Self-Control,' but I couldn't come up with an idea for a play on the subject. The highlight of the graduation party is a play performed by the students for their mothers and grandmothers."

"How about something like 'Aspirations,' or 'Reaching for the Stars'?"

"I'm not sure how that would be received. I'm afraid my principal will say it's too philosophical, not practical enough. She's a very down-to-earth woman, our principal."

Shaindy and Naomi spent the next two hours discussing the challenges of educating the younger generation in today's materialistic society. They each had their own ideas and they argued, sometimes heatedly. They felt hugely satisfied, as if they were the greatest educators of their time on a mission to stem the deterioration of Jewish values and restore Jewish pride in young people.

Naomi felt wonderful. Shaindy didn't treat her as "the mother of the deaf twins" or "an unfortunate woman struggling to raise handicapped children." She treated Naomi the same as always — as an intelligent woman with an analytical mind. For the first time in a month, Naomi completely forgot about her pain. She laughed at Shaindy's jokes, defended her position on various subjects with great passion, and objected vehemently to certain things Shaindy said.

This is the way it should be, Naomi said to herself. *This is the way society ought to treat me. People ought not to relate to my problem, but to me, the way they did before I had this problem.*

This is the way society ought to treat you, the small, childish voice said.

And this is the way you ought to continue living your life, the mature voice rejoined.

Shaindy rose to leave. She wished Naomi lots of *nachas* and an easy time raising the twins, and Naomi walked her to the door.

"It was a pleasure talking to you, as always. I really enjoy hearing your ideas," Shaindy said. "Bye, Naomi. See you soon. I'm planning another get-together in the near future."

"I enjoyed your visit," Naomi told her. "You can be sure I haven't enjoyed many visits lately."

"Really?" Shaindy looked at her somewhat sharply. "Have you had many visitors?"

Naomi thought for a moment, though she didn't really have to. She knew very well no one had come to visit her. "No," Naomi admitted, smiling suddenly. "Actually, no one else has come to visit me."

"Well, then, your compliment doesn't count for much," Shaindy said with a chuckle. "What a shame. I was about to pat myself on the back. If I had no competition, it's no wonder I was the winner."

"Tell me, Shaindy," Naomi said seriously, "why do you think people avoid coming to see me? Is it the twins, or is it me?"

"What do you mean?" Shaindy asked, the smile still on her lips.

"Is it because the twins are deaf and people are afraid of coming face-to-face with such a sad situation, or am I too intimidating?"

Shaindy's face grew serious, and she sat down again. "I would say it's you," she said. "The way a person accepts his pain and suffering has a strong influence on how society treats him."

Her words were familiar, very familiar – Shlomo had said the same thing.

"Of course, it will be hard for people at first. They'll be uncertain of how to behave with you and somewhat apprehensive about coming in direct contact with something other than the norm, but with your naturally pleasant disposition and sense of humor, you'll be able to overcome people's discomfort — or rather, you'll help them overcome their discomfort."

Did you hear that? Help them overcome their discomfort. You, Naomi. It's up to you.

THE JOVIAL ATMOSPHERE Shaindy brought with her remained even after she left. Naomi's mother had not returned yet, her father was in a morning *kollel* for older men, and Shlomo was in his *kollel*. Yanky was in playgroup, and only the twins and Naomi were home.

The twins were asleep. Even Mindy, who often writhed in her bassinet and moaned softly, was now slumbering peacefully. The house was still, and Naomi felt an urgent need to do something. It was a month since their birth, and she had done nothing since then but care for them. Should she bake something? Her mother would be glad. Maybe she should prepare dinner? It would be easier for her to sort out her thoughts while her hands were busy.

Naomi went into the kitchen. She decided to make *sufganiyot*, jelly doughnuts. The next day would be the first day of Chanukah. Her adorable Yanky had been singing "*Maoz Tzur*" in his high-pitched voice all day. Naomi's father had purchased wicks and oil for himself and for Shlomo. It was clear that they would be staying at Naomi's parents' house over Chanukah.

Naomi had always loved Chanukah. It was such a joyous holiday, so family-oriented, so warm. Outside, snow fell, the wind howled, and temperatures were freezing. Inside, in the warmth afforded by central heating, the family joined to kindle Chanukah *licht* and publicize the miracles wrought by *Hakadosh Baruch Hu*.

Naomi sifted flour and rolled out dough. Her hands worked quickly, deftly. She enjoyed baking; she found the kitchen a pleasant place to be. In the past, whenever Naomi needed to give serious thought to a client's case, she went to the kitchen and baked something. Cooking didn't appeal to her nearly so much as baking.

"What happened? What went wrong at your clinic today?" Shlomo would ask when he saw a beautiful cream cake on the kitchen table. Naomi would smile and tell him about the dilemma she had pondered over — without mentioning any names, of course.

NAOMI WAS VERY apprehensive about attending Shaindy's next get-together. She recalled the last such gathering, which had taken place nine months earlier. A mountain had sprung up between her cousins and herself in the interim. She knew they wouldn't whisper among themselves when she walked in — they were adults, after all — but she knew they'd lower their eyes in discomfort when they saw her, unsure of what to say.

Stay home, the childish voice advised her. *Don't ruin the party Shaindy worked so hard to prepare. Don't allow your troubles to ruin the evening for the rest of the cousins.*

Don't you dare think that way, the mature voice said angrily. *You're going to that party, same as everyone else. Staying home is not an option; is that clear?*

It was the first night of Chanukah. Naomi's father recited the first *brachah* in a ringing voice: *Baruch Atah ... lehadlik ner shel Chanukah.*

Naomi answered amen with more than a little apprehension. She knew that the moment was fast approaching when her father would break down and require support. She was too weak to offer support to anyone else, and she didn't know what to do.

"*She'asah nissim laavoseinu bayamim hahem bazeman hazeh,*" Naomi's father recited. Naomi suppressed the childish urge to flee from the dining room and hide in her room until the storm abated. She remained rooted to the spot in the dining room, looking at him in fearful silence.

"*Baruch ... Atah ...*" Her father's face turned gray. Shlomo was already familiar with the scene. He lowered his gaze. Naomi's mother took a small step forward. Naomi was always the one, with her gay and singsong voice, to encourage him to complete the *brachah*. She couldn't bring herself to do it now.

Naomi's mother looked at her pleadingly, but Naomi remained silent.

"*Shehecheyanu ...*" Her father stammered brokenly. "*Vekiyemanu ...*" He coughed, a heavy, hacking sound. "*Ve- vehi ...*" He couldn't get the word out. His lips trembled uncontrollably. His eyes blinked rapidly as he clutched his chest with his free hand.

"Sabba!" three-year-old Yanky looked at him in shock. "Sabba, what's wrong? Did someone hurt Sabba?"

His father stroked Yanky's head. "I want to light already," Yanky demanded.

Something in his voice penetrated the murkiness of his grandfather's memories. Naomi's father straightened with an effort and croaked hoarsely the end of the brachah. "*Vehi-vehigianu ... lazeman ... hazeh.*"

He kindled the flame with a trembling hand, stuck the *shamash* in place with difficulty, and collapsed in the chair his wife had prepared for him, burying his face in his hands. Shlomo took the matches and lit his *shamash*, his clear, pleasant voice banishing the thick, tense silence:

"*lehadlik ner shel Chanukah... she'asah nissim laavoseinu ... shehecheyanu vekiyemanu vehigianu lazeman hazeh.*"

No interruptions, no complications, no tortured memories. Shlomo kindled the flame and then helped his little boy recite the *brachos* as well.

"This is my menorah," Yanky said proudly. "Look, Sabba."

Children are a blessing. Children are a treasure. Naomi's father removed his hands from his face and regarded Yanky through eyes veiled with tears.

"Sabba's crying?" the little one asked in confusion.

"Yes," he did not deny it. "Yes, Yanky, Sabba's crying."

"Why?" Yanky asked. It was the same question Shmulik and Naomi asked at various occasions throughout their childhood. Every time Naomi's father recited the blessing of *Shehecheyanu*, he fell apart and wept bitterly.

"Sabba once had an *abba*, an *ima*, lots of sisters and brothers, cousins, aunts and uncles, a *sabba* and a *savta*," he explained quietly.

Naomi's heart leapt into her throat. She was flabbergasted. Her father was revealing the story of his life! She didn't dare move a muscle. Shlomo, too, remained frozen in place.

"And they did not merit to live and be sustained, and reach this occasion."

Naomi hoped that her father would forget they were there and tell his story, sad though it might be, to his uncomprehending grandchild. He could talk to Yanky without fear; Yanky wouldn't understand in any case, and would not be able to repeat what he heard.

As expected, Yanky did not understand. He gazed at his grandfather's face with wide, innocent eyes and announced, "So let's sing '*Maoz Tzur*.'"

"Okay, Yankeleh," Naomi's father said, hugging his grandchild and seating him on his lap. He cleared his throat. "*Maoz tzur yeshuasi, lecha na'eh leshabayach ...*"

Generation after generation, Jews all over the world sing this song. Everyone aches at "*ra'os savah nafshi*" and "*yevanim nikbetzu alai.*" Everyone hopes at "*ketz bavel zerubavel*" and "*naaseh nes lashoshanim.*" Everyone yearns at "*chasof zeroa kodshecha*" and "*dechei admon betzel tzalmon,*" and everyone pleads at "*hakem lanu ro'im shivah.*"

Everyone – except for those who are no longer alive.

On second thought, is not their prayer purer than ours? More exalted? They, the martyrs slaughtered *al kiddush Hashem* who now bask in the shadow of the *Shechinah* in Gan Eden, daven with greater passion, with a degree of understanding deeper than what mortal men can attain.

"Look," Naomi's father said suddenly, pointing to the dancing, flickering flames. "Look at these candles. They burn softly yet mightily; their light is pleasant, yet strong and daring. That is how Yidden lived throughout the generations – subservient to the gentiles by a G-dly command not to fight them until the arrival of Moshiach.

"And then a new generation arose. A generation of physical strength that overpowered the spiritual strength. A generation in which youth did not respect the elderly. A generation in which youth strayed from the light of Torah and disregarded the words of our leaders. A generation in which alien winds swept everything – everything – away. And then they defied that command. They rose up against the gentiles. And it was with them, those bold, daring heroes who had abandoned tradition, that I ascended to Eretz Yisrael."

Naomi's father had never spoken like this before. Something had influenced him to share part of his story. Could it be the twins?

"I went with them. I traveled to Eretz Yisrael, and I was the only one from my family to survive. I was a rebel, a freethinker, a heretic. I was strong physically but weak when it came to conquering my impulses and desires. I fought the gentiles and remained subservient to my *yetzer hara*. And I was the one who survived. Only I merited building a family. They, far better and more righteous than I, they did not merit ... they did not live, were not sustained, did not reach this occasion."

NAOMI LEFT THE house with a heavy heart. Although her father had donned his cloak of silence once more, she sensed that something inside him had given way. A hidden chord had vibrated and trembled, playing melodies Naomi dearly wanted to hear. She wanted to remain at his side and offer him support, hoping and waiting for another snatch of his memories to slip out and be told.

There was no point in saying, "But Abba, look at the family you've established! Perhaps you rebelled against Hashem for a brief period of time, but you've returned to Him wholeheartedly. Look at your children walking the path of the righteous. Your son and daughter and their spouses observe Torah and mitzvos and are raising the coming generation to do so as well." Naomi knew there was another secret her father was still keeping from her. She knew she didn't understand his words completely, so she remained silent.

The hour grew late, and Naomi's mother said it was time they went to Shaindy's house. Naomi's father and Shlomo remained sitting near the menorahs, Shlomo humming a chassidic *niggun* and Naomi's father listening intently. Yanky had gone to sleep, unaware of the emotional storm he had created with his innocent question. They say that grandparents are more easily swayed by their grandchildren's requests than parents are by their children's. Naomi saw that clearly.

Naomi, her mother and the twins took a cab to Shaindy's house. Naomi was feeling terribly distracted. Her heart remained at home, with her father.

She entered Shaindy's house, pushing the twin carriage. She saw some of her cousins exchange glances, and her heart stood still.

"*Mazal tov*!" Shaindy called out gaily. "And happy Chanukah!"

"Thank you," Naomi replied, not letting on that they had already met.

The other cousins took their cue from Shaindy. "*Mazal tov*," they wished Naomi and her mother, some with averted eyes, others with warm smiles.

The program went right over Naomi's head. She was too preoccupied with analyzing the reactions of those around her to be able to concentrate. Her tension gradually dissipated when she saw that everyone had forgotten all about her and the twins after their initial reception and was now engrossed in the program. Slowly her heart stopped pounding. It wasn't long before Naomi was able to relax enough to participate in the program as well. She played the game, conversed with her aunts, kidded the cousins and told stories. A small breach had formed in her barrier of misery.

Just as it had in her father's barrier of silence.

IT DIDN'T HAPPEN overnight. Naomi's acceptance of her situation ripened slowly inside her until it burst forth unexpectedly on various occasions.

She found herself humming again or laughing aloud and forgetting for a moment that she had two deaf daughters. Sometimes the laughter would freeze on her lips. How dare she laugh when her daughters would face such hardships? She felt guilty. Was she a bad mother?

Naomi began growing receptive to society. She phoned her friends again. They were surprised to hear from her, but the ice between them began to thaw. Something inside her that had wilted and withered began blossoming anew. She didn't know what to make of it. Didn't she feel her children's pain? How could she be so callous?

One day, Naomi burst out laughing at a joke she read in the paper. Almost instantaneously her muscles froze in guilt. How could she be happy? Her father saw it happen. His face grew dark. "Oh, you remind me of those times ... " he murmured to himself.

"What?" Naomi asked, turning to him.

"I was the same way," he said to himself.

"What are you talking about, Abba?"

"Naomi'le, you feel uncomfortable being happy, right?"

She nodded slowly. "How do you know?" Naomi asked, her lips white. "Abba, how did you know?"

"I was the same way," he whispered. "Being miserable won't help anyone," he explained, "least of all the twins. They need a happy, emotionally healthy mother. How do I know you're not allowing yourself to be happy? I once felt the same way."

Eretz Yisrael 5707/1947

"MEIR?"

The call was accompanied by a rap on the door. Meir never opened the door for people he did not know. He had an escape plan ready in case the British came calling.

"Yes." Meir opened the door for Menasheh, a novice fighter who had been trained for ground operations and had already joined Meir on a few missions. Meir admired the young man. He was the son of doting parents and had two adoring sisters. Unlike Meir, Menasheh had a large family and an abundance of relatives and friends. Still, he risked his life fighting for Eretz Yisrael on a daily basis.

"Meir, the guys are organizing a *kumzitz* tonight. *Ba lecha lehitztaref*?" Did he feel like joining in?

Among the things Meir had difficulty adapting to in Eretz Yisrael was the fast-paced, slangy style of speech the youngsters used. The sabra Hebrew was so different from respectable, formal, stolid Yiddish. Meir spoke Biblical Hebrew fluently, but he had trouble understanding the subtle nuances of the modern language.

"*Ba li lehitztaref*?" He repeated the question in his stilted, foreign, *galus* accent. Menasheh couldn't help but smile.

Meir smiled, too. His friends often imitated his accent, and he didn't take offense at all. He enjoyed socializing, and if someone wanted to joke about his accent, that was just fine with him.

"Yes, I'd like to join," he said finally. "When?"

"Tonight, at midnight."

"At midnight?" He seemed crestfallen for a moment. "Okay. Where? At Kibbutz Yaron?"

"Uh-huh. Bye, Meir."

At noon Meir set out for the shooting range to practice. He achieved satisfactory results and felt an enormous sense of accomplishment. Later, as he rode into the valley leading to the kibbutz on his horse, Yisrael, pangs of guilt attacked him. Tonight would be the first time he skipped reciting *Tikkun Chatzos*.

I might still squeeze it in, he assuaged his conscience. *I don't have to do it precisely at midnight.*

The campfire was already casting mysterious shadows on his friends' faces when he arrived. They sat around it, joking and singing, laughing and enjoying each other's company. The aroma of roasting meat and potatoes hung in the air. They hoped the smell wouldn't attract the British guard. They weren't breaking British law by having a campfire, but many of them were wanted men. Someone had brought a guitar and began singing in a soft, pleasant voice. Meir found himself humming the strange melody with great pleasure. He loved music and hadn't heard an instrument being played or another human being singing in years.

"Hey, guys, this man can sing!" Erez, the kibbutz secretary, declared, clapping Meir on the shoulder. "Meir'ke, how about singing for us?"

"Can you play too, Meir?" asked Mickey, the guitar player. "You can use my guitar."

"No," Meir said, rejecting both suggestions. "I neither play nor sing. It's better if you sing."

Eich ashir es shir Hashem al admas nechar? How can I sing Hashem's song on foreign soil? Foreign soil? Meir, what are you talking about? This is Eretz Yisrael!

Really? A bitter, demanding voice gripped his heart. *This is Eretz Yisrael? Treifeh food and bare heads? Where is your learning, Meir; where is your tefillah? Where is the sanctity of the land, and where is true love for all it represents? How come you don't travel to Yerushalayim or to the holy sites? Why do you make do with sowing, reaping and fighting? Is that the goal of Eretz Yisrael? You complete gentile, you!*

Meir shuddered, his face turning deathly white. By the dim light of the campfire, no one noticed his torment. *Will I never forget?* his heart wept. *Will I never forget what was and is no longer?*

Will you never remember? A different voice countered. *Will you never remember what was and is no longer? Why don't you reclaim your father's heritage and establish a new generation to perpetuate the beautiful legacy of your martyred family? Hitler murdered your entire family and you're cutting off the future generations.*

A slow, faint melody hovered in the air. Meir stared at Mickey as if in a trance. How could he play that melody? How did he know it? Meir was instantly swept back in time to his yeshivah days, when he and his peers sang songs like "*Mi kamocha be'eylim, Hashem*," "*Nakdishcha*," and "*Heyeh im pifiyos*." He recalled singing "*Al naharos bavel*" and weeping real tears over the exile of the *Shechinah.*

Meir snapped back to the present. *Stop right now! Don't allow the past to destroy the present.*

"Okay, I'll sing," he announced, ignoring the cries of his soul. "What would you like me to sing?"

His friends cheered. "Bravo, Meir! Way to go! Sing whatever you want."

"I don't know that many songs," Meir said hesitantly. "Certainly not those you know."

"What then? Just '*Veye'esayu kol le'avdecha*'?" a voice behind him asked.

Shocked, Meir looked behind him to meet Erez's laughing eyes. "Why are you so surprised? My father sings that song, too."

"You weren't you born here?"

"Yes, I was. So what?"

"And where is your father today?"

"*In Yerushalayim ir hakoidesh tibooneh vesikoinein bimheiru veyumeinee*," Erez replied, pronouncing the words with the chassidic inflection. His friends burst out laughing.

"And you came here? Alone?"

"Meir'ke, the past is gone. Only the future is important." Erez's voice sounded amused, but there was a serious note running through it.

Meir overcame his shock. So Erez had tossed off the yoke of Torah and mitzvos as well. He, too, had left a true Jewish home in order to fight for his country.

Feeling encouraged, Meir began singing an old English ballad about the bleak life of coal miners. His friends listened in admiring silence, and Meir felt gratified when he managed to move them to tears. When he was done, everyone cheered. Only Menasheh complained, "Meir, I don't think it's right to sing British songs now."

Everyone laughed, including Meir. His dark mood had lifted and he was enjoying himself again. The rest of the evening was spent singing. When Erez gave an off-tune rendition of *Veye'esayu*, Meir winked at him and said nothing.

For the first time since the conclusion of the war, since he'd lost his family, since he'd visited Bergen-Belsen, Meir felt happy. His friends were generous and loyal. Their friendship was a balm to his bruised soul, and he laughed and sang with them. He felt safe and loved, surrounded by these people. There was Menasheh, who had offered to die in his place during a recent mission. They had both survived in the end, but the offer had been made. There was Erez, who Meir knew endangered himself every time he met with him. There was Shaul, his commander and close friend, who was extremely devoted to his well-being. There were a few other truly loyal friends with whom he shared the bond of blood and war.

What did he need more than that? Soon the war would be over, soon his country would be liberated from foreigners. Soon, soon it would all happen and then he'd marry and establish a family. He didn't want to marry yet, lest he leave his wife a widow and his children orphans. Nor did he want to stop fighting for Eretz Yisrael.

Meir felt joy flood every cell of his body. He had made peace with his loss and was free to think about the future.

At 2:00 a.m. the joyous party broke up. Meir bid everyone goodbye and leaped onto his horse. Yisrael immediately began trotting in the right direction. Meir had trained him to obey immediately.

When he entered his apartment, Meir immediately went to the bookshelf, and groped for his siddur. It wasn't there.

Somewhat alarmed, Meir kindled the lamp and began searching frantically for his siddur. It was the only object he had as a keepsake from his parents' home, and he took it with him everywhere. The siddur wasn't there. His search proved fruitless.

Meir opened the window. He felt overwhelmed with guilt. All traces of gaiety were gone now. Images of his family floated before his eyes in accusing silence. They had taken his siddur because he wasn't worthy of it. He didn't deserve a remembrance of them. They were somber and angry, their lifeless eyes filled with deep pain and burning accusation.

You went to Eretz Yisrael saying you would rebuild rather than avenge our blood, but instead you spend your time partying. How can you? Aren't you sorrowful about the loss you suffered? How dare you rejoice when your family's been murdered? How can you enjoy yourself after witnessing such large-scale destruction? How can you be glad when we are dead? How can you laugh when we can't even cry? We went to our deaths, and you're not even sorry?

New York 5751/1991

"ON THAT OCCASION, my feelings of guilt were still in place," Naomi's father said as she stared at him in shock. He had never told Naomi anything about his past. She hadn't known that he had completely abandoned Torah and mitzvos!

"I have no doubt that my behavior at that time did indeed cause my loved ones great anguish. Even years later, though, after I had returned to my loving Father in Heaven, I felt it would be sacrilegious to laugh. I felt it was wrong to be happy after what had happened in Europe, that I couldn't laugh after so many Yidden had been exterminated.

"But I was wrong. It was only years later that I understood how flawed that way of thinking was. My sorrow was of no benefit to the dead. They wanted me to be happy and serve Hashem with joy. They wanted me to raise a happy family and teach my children to love Hashem.

"I don't mean to compare the Holocaust to your personal pain, G-d forbid," her father concluded softly. "But, Naomi, think about the fact that your anguish is of no help to anyone at all — certainly not the twins. They need a strong, happy mother, a happy childhood and a happy life. And you can give them that only if you're happy yourself."

15

Naomi returned home. She began to settle down, and she managed fairly well. Her mother came in the mornings to help her with the twins, especially Mindy, who cried constantly. In the afternoon, Naomi managed on her own, and she hired help for a few hours during the evening. Shlomo helped her the rest of the time.

They eventually settled into a semblance of routine. Mindy's constant crying and restlessness were now far more obvious and significant. Naomi began to compare Mindy's behavior with Becky's. She knew it's wrong to compare children, especially twins, but when they were so small, it was still possible to determine what normal behavior was. Even if Becky was a particularly easy baby, there was no question that Mindy was extremely demanding.

Shlomo saw Mindy's extreme fussiness as well. He and Naomi tried to pay close attention and see if they could figure out what triggered a crying jag, but they drew a blank. Mindy cried in her crib and she cried when she was held; she screeched when Naomi bathed her and howled when Naomi dressed her. She cried when Naomi fed her and when Naomi gave her to drink. She cried most of the day. Sometimes, exhausted after hours of nonstop crying, she slept.

Naomi made an appointment with a pediatrician. To tell the truth, she was rather apprehensive about the tests the doctor would take. It wasn't the tests Naomi was afraid of; it was the results.

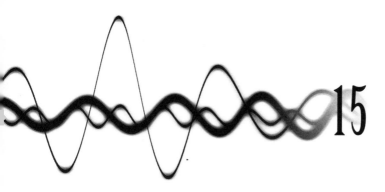

That morning, she dressed Mindy in a sweet outfit. She sent Yanky to playgroup and left Becky with her mother. Shlomo accompanied Naomi to the doctor. The doctor examined the baby and told them everything was in order.

"Her behavior is normal for her age. Give her time to grow and develop and learn about our world."

They returned home. They gave her time to learn about the world. Mindy developed nicely and made excellent progress. She recognized and identified things. She got to know the world but definitely did not get used to it.

A few more weeks passed and Naomi still felt uneasy. She knew something was wrong. They made an appointment with a top developmental specialist. Once again, Shlomo and Naomi took Mindy to a doctor. The specialist gave them a long list of tests he wanted Mindy to undergo. They were to return to him with the results.

When they saw him next, hearts pounding with fear, he glanced at the test results and asked in a haughty tone of voice. "Tell me, what brings you here?"

Naomi pointed to Mindy, who was sleeping soundly for a change. "She's not calm," Naomi said. "She cries for hours on end, even when I hold her in my arms."

"Are you familiar with the concept that a baby senses what his mother feels?"

Naomi knew what he was referring to, but it sounded wrong the way he put it. "Yes," she replied. She knew that babies could pick up on tension and restlessness in their mothers. That's why it was so important for a mother to be calm, accepting and, most of all, loving when holding a tiny baby.

"You're tense and anxious, Mrs. Mandel, that's all. You're making your baby feel that way, too. You're making a mountain out of a molehill."

"Doctor," Naomi said, trying to keep her anger in check, "this baby has a twin sister. How come I'm not making her sister feel that way?"

"Because you'd fall apart," he replied coolly, "if you had to deal with two such demanding babies. You wouldn't cope."

Naomi was speechless. The doctor had just about called her a liar!

"And as it stands, we're enjoying every minute," Shlomo said angrily. Unlike Naomi, he had found his tongue and reacted to the doctor's ridiculous pronouncement. He and Naomi looked at one another, rose and left without saying good-bye.

"Wonderful," Naomi said to Shlomo when she was sure they were out of the doctor's hearing. "We escaped his hurtful diagnosis — but we still don't know what's wrong with our daughter."

"He said the test results were okay," Shlomo said. "We'll wait a bit longer. Maybe it'll pass."

But Mindy's problem grew steadily worse. By the time she was a year and a half, they had already consulted a number of top specialists. They took her for neurological tests and, while Mindy's cooperation had been minimal, the neurologist had determined that there was nothing the matter with her physiologically. That is, they knew she was deaf, but aside from that she was completely healthy.

And still she screamed. They couldn't communicate with her; she wouldn't allow anyone to touch her. She'd run away from people and hide under her bed, so desperate was she to avoid contact with anyone. Naomi sensed that they were losing touch with her steadily. Mindy would have outbursts for no fathomable reason. She knew something was hurting her child, something terrible. And because Mindy was deaf, she couldn't tell anyone what it was.

Mindy's physical development was definitely normal. She crawled on time, stood up and walked even before Becky. Naomi and Shlomo didn't neglect her problem. They continued trying to figure out what it was that bothered the child. They did make eye contact with her, and sometimes she smiled disarmingly at them, but that was the farthest they got.

Since Naomi was a psychologist, she was familiar with various behavioral problems. Sometimes it seemed to her that Mindy was suffering from every existing behavioral problem in the book. Naomi recalled the conversation she had had with little Benjy Kahaneman's mother after Mrs. Kahaneman had shown Naomi the home video of Benjy writhing and hurling objects, looking as though an unseen fiend was driving him to inexplicable behavior. Mrs. Kahaneman, too, had been told by doctors that her son was perfectly fine. She'd had to video her son in order to prove that he had a problem. Naomi recalled how the poor woman had wept when the video ended, saying, "We thought he was autistic. He cuts himself off from us, stares into space, and refuses to talk or communicate during these episodes."

"But he does talk and communicate most of the time," Naomi had told her encouragingly. "Doesn't he?"

"Yes, but ..." Mrs. Kahaneman had dissolved in tears. "Something awful is hurting my son. We can't help him. Sometimes he cries and pleads with me to soothe him, and I'm so helpless. I don't have the faintest idea what he wants. My child is locked up, withdrawn, suffering — and I can't help him. He's so miserable when he has these attacks. I know he feels very alone."

"Your child is not autistic," Naomi had assured her.

"Well, then, what is the matter?" Mrs. Kahaneman had been openly disbelieving. Perhaps she was afraid of the disappointment that would surely follow her initial spurt of joy, or maybe fear of the unknown was even worse than the certain knowledge of a specific problem.

Naomi had smiled. "Most people are familiar with a few conditions, and they automatically try to connect unusual behavior of any sort to one of them. It takes years of study to be able to draw the connection between certain behavior patterns and the conditions they signify."

And now Naomi was on the opposite side of the fence. Her daughter had fits, threw things, cried inconsolably. Naomi knew Mindy didn't have OCD like Benjy, but she didn't know what the matter was. The terrible possibility that Benjy's mother had raised suddenly surfaced in Naomi's mind —could it be that Mindy was autistic?

She immediately rejected the thought. Mindy looked at people; she smiled sometimes. She wasn't autistic!

But what was it then?

In the meantime, they couldn't neglect Becky's needs. An angelic child, she demanded nothing at all, but her parents took her from one auditory institute to another, to a host of speech therapists and numerous hearing specialists. There wasn't much they could do for her; she had only a tiny percentage of hearing ability. Hearing aids would be of little help in her case. Jenny, her wonderful speech therapist, advised them to stop struggling to boost Becky's hearing ability and concentrate instead on teaching her to read lips. As soon as Jenny began working with her, Becky began to progress with meteoric speed. She read lips and began speaking fluently, communicating with her family easily and becoming a perfectly ordinary little girl.

The same could not be said for Mindy. She refused to cooperate with the professionals Naomi and Shlomo consulted in an effort to help her. She refused to communicate with anyone, growing more and more withdrawn each day. Mindy deteriorated steadily. Naomi and Shlomo saw it happening and could do nothing to help her.

"*Ribbono shel Olam*," Naomi wept. "Dear Father, You gave us this child. You gave her the difficult *nisayon* of deafness. You gave her the additional, mysterious problem she's suffering from. Please help us help her!"

But the barrier between Mindy and the rest of the world grew ever higher. She became locked into a world of her own, a world of uncontrollable outbursts and abstinence from contact with other people. They could no longer reach her.

New York 5754/1994

"IMA, IMA!" BECKY came running to Naomi one morning, shaking her awake. "Abba, Abba! Ima! Abba, Ima!"

Shlomo was the first to awake. "What's the matter, Becky?" he asked, instantly alert.

"Come, come see!" she shouted, alarmed. "Come see what's happening to Mindy!"

They hurried to the twins' room. As they approached the door, Becky burst into hysterical sobs. "She's bleeding!"

"What?" They stood in the doorway. Mindy was banging her head forcefully on the wall. She had a large bruise on her forehead and blood was dripping from an additional wound. The twins' room was painted with textured paint and apparently one of the tiny protrusions had scratched Mindy's forehead.

With two quick strides, Shlomo was at Mindy's side. He gripped his three-year-old daughter's shoulders and prevented her from dealing herself another blow to the head. She stared at him indifferently, blood dripping from her forehead.

Becky, horrified, sobbed in Naomi's arms. Mindy, in Shlomo's arms, was frighteningly somber.

Faced with the scene of one daughter's hysterical sobbing and the other's terrifying silence, clear understanding dawned in Naomi's mind. No one was going to tell her everything was fine. Let no one dare suggest Mindy's problem would pass. No one could convince her that such behavior could disappear without intervention. No one was going to tell her she was imagining things. Her daughter was suffering from something terrible. She'd been suffering for three years now, crying out for help in her own way, and they hadn't understood her. Now Naomi had clear proof that something was definitely wrong.

That was a turning point. Two months later they had a diagnosis. Mindy was not only deaf. To her parents' great dismay, she was also autistic.

"It can't be!" Naomi's father said firmly. "The child is not autistic! She makes eye contact with me. She smiles and laughs sometimes. She communicates. Not fully, not normally — but there is a certain communication between us."

"There are different types and levels of autism," Shlomo told him in a low but steady voice. "We received advice and guidance on how to deal with it," he added, as if to himself.

Naomi handed Abba the report and his eyes scanned its contents:

Mindy demonstrates abnormal social behavior. 1) Failure to communicate with children her own age. 2) Absence of spontaneous effort to share pleasure, interests or achievement with others. 3) Absence of social or emotional expression.

He raised his eyes. "What does this mean?"

"There are complex nonverbal behaviors most children this age are capable of, such as making eye contact, facial expressions, body language and socially accepted gestures," Naomi replied. "Mindy lacks that ability."

Her father was silent.

Eventually, they accepted the diagnosis as fact. Mindy had a serious communication problem; she would never be a normal little girl like her sister. Becky would cross the border, with Hashem's help, just as Naomi's father had predicted — but Mindy never would. Some things are immutable. This was a decree from *Shamayim*; it was not something they could reverse with love, warmth and supreme effort. For reasons unknown, Hashem had determined that they walk this path. Naomi's and Shlomo's job was to help one daughter overcome her handicap and become a regular child, and do their utmost to help their other daughter slowly break through the huge barricade surrounding her world. A barrier of ice could not be chopped down with an axe. It had to melt ever so slowly with the warmth of love.

THE NEXT FEW years brought no change in Mindy's situation. While Becky made wonderful progress, surpassing other children her age in intelligence, sensitivity and talent, Mindy gradually regressed. She was enrolled in Flowers in the Garden, one of the top institutions for children like her, but the dedicated professional staff there did not work the miracles her parents hoped for. Mindy locked herself in her own private jail and bolted its gates with her stubborn silence. Nothing helped.

Only two people maintained a semblance of communication with her: Naomi's father and Becky. Naomi's father would play with Mindy in his own way, stroking her and making eye contact. He'd smile at her lovingly and receive a real smile in return.

Becky played with Mindy, too — not the way one plays with an ordinary girl, of course, but in a very special way. They shared a certain understanding. Mindy would relax when she saw Becky. Sometimes she even greeted her with a fierce hug.

It was a strange bond they shared, a bond of blood and silence. They both inhabited a world of silence in which it was not necessary to speak in order to feel protected and loved. They accepted each other's handicaps naturally and simply. Theirs was a true friendship.

Naomi watched them play. They would toss a soft ball to one another in silence, smiling happily. Becky claimed Mindy liked only soft balls. They would dress and undress their dolls and pretend to feed and bathe them.

Not that this happened very often. It was actually a rare occurrence, because Mindy came home late in the afternoon and usually spent her time sitting in one spot, staring into space. On Shabbos and during vacations, however, they had the time to enjoy each other's company. Naomi would watch from the side, her eyes filling with tears.

Sari was born when the twins were nearly five years old. Naomi was the happiest woman in the world when Sari was born. She floated through a fluffy pink world of soft blankets and scented shampoo, of helium balloons and flowers, of chocolates and pacifiers, of stunning pink layettes and adorable hats. Naomi was as intoxicated with happiness as a first-time mother.

Stop it, she scolded herself as she left her room in the maternity wing of the hospital for the large baby store located on the ground floor. *You're behaving like a baby. Don't you know what the world is like? Don't you know what life is like? What are you so happy about, as if ... as if you don't know suffering and pain?*

Naomi's happiness did not hinge on the fact that she had given birth to a healthy child after Becky and Mindy. It was pure and unfettered joy, given to her from *Shamayim* as a balm for her aching heart. She didn't give a thought to the future, to the difficulties involved in raising a healthy child in the shadow of two handicapped older sisters. She didn't think about any of that. Naomi bought a beautiful pink outfit, a pretty bottle and an adorable pacifier.

She embraced her Sari, unaware of sadness or difficulties in the world. There was only her daughter, come to gladden her heart. Extensive testing showed that everything was in order. Her daughter was perfectly healthy; everything was the way it was supposed to be. Even her Apgar score had been perfect. Naomi was thrilled.

She dressed Sari in her new outfit. Naomi kept Sari near her bed most of the day, gazing at Sari's adorable face with an overflowing heart.

Shlomo arrived in the evening, smiling broadly. He looked at his daughter and stuck his finger into her clenched fist, reveling in the sensation of her tiny grip.

"The children are overjoyed," he told Naomi. "You should've seen how excited they were when I told them." He smiled, but Naomi knew him well enough to see that he wasn't perfectly calm. There was a furrow in his brow, a shadow in his eyes.

"Is something the matter?" she asked. "Are you having a hard time with the children?"

"No, why do you ask? Everything's fine."

Shlomo usually managed the children wonderfully. "So what is the matter?" Naomi pressed.

"Nothing's the matter. I told you, everything's fine."

Naomi leveled her gaze at him. "Shlomo," she said firmly, "I know something's wrong. Please don't hide anything from me. I can handle anything except not knowing."

Shlomo continued denying anything was wrong. "I don't know what you want," he insisted. "Everything is perfectly fine."

Naomi eyes filled with tears. "Shlomo, please," she said. "You see how worried I am. If you don't tell me what's wrong, I'm going to imagine all sorts of horrible things."

Shlomo sighed. "Alright. You really can read my heart."

"*Nu*?" Naomi's heart stood still.

"I'm not perfectly calm," her husband admitted quietly. "When Mindy was a baby, they said she was fine, too ... aside from her deafness, of course. I'm just having a hard time keeping calm and believing that everything is fine with Sari. That's all."

Naomi couldn't believe it. "You, Shlomo?" she asked incredulously. "You? You're always so happy, so calm, so optimistic!"

"I try to be," he said. "Don't say I'm wrong."

"Of course you're right," Naomi agreed, "but why now?"

He shrugged. "I'm just ... I don't know. Everything's fine; it's just my own personal feeling. The doctors have assured us everything's fine and that she hears perfectly."

"Look here, Shlomo," Naomi said. "When I had the same uneasy feeling five years ago, you put up with me and told me everything was fine. Now it's my turn to encourage you and assure you everything's fine. My maternal instincts tell me so."

"But everything was not in order then," Shlomo noted.

"Still," Naomi insisted, "you offered me encouragement when I sorely needed it."

He didn't smile. His eyes were very serious as he looked at her. "So what?"

"What's the matter now, Shlomo?" Naomi asked. "Then, when our world was shattered, you knew what to do and what to say to bolster my spirits. Now, when everything's fine, you insist on worrying. Why?"

"I don't insist on worrying," Shlomo said quietly. "I didn't want to tell you any of this so as not to worry you. I only told you because you insisted so strongly and you were afraid something awful had happened. Don't worry, they're just my fears, and I'll deal with them."

But he didn't.

Naomi returned home with Sari. The children received her with joy and delight, competing for the privilege of holding her, bringing her a bottle or pacifier, rocking her cradle and wheeling her carriage throughout the house.

Shlomo was not a partner to this joy. Naomi saw his sunken, lifeless eyes. His smile, usually so calm and happy, had become pale and weak. His tension did not dissipate. When he learned Gemara at night, Sari's carriage at his side, he would stroke her face and sigh deeply.

Naomi didn't know what to say to him. She didn't know how to encourage him. His fear was illogical, so logic wouldn't help.

"Look," she told him. "I'm going to conduct an experiment right in front of your eyes." Naomi placed Sari in her carriage and slammed the door of the room shut. The baby flinched and burst out crying. Shlomo hurried to gather her into his arms and rocked her until she quieted, but the triumphant smile on Naomi's face was not mirrored on his.

"That was a loud noise," he said.

"Becky didn't hear any noise," Naomi noted.

He said nothing.

Sari developed beautifully. She lifted her head early, turned over from her stomach to her back and from her back to her stomach, and one day, she reacted to Naomi's greeting with a joyous cry of her own: "Ah! Ah!"

"Did you hear that?" Naomi cried out. "She said 'Ah'!"

Shlomo nodded. "I heard. She wasn't imitating you," he said. "I mean, it's not like you said 'Ah,' and she copied you. I can't be certain she heard you."

Naomi despaired. What could she do? All the signs were there, but he was afraid to believe. Fear had his heart in an iron grip.

One night, Sari cried fitfully throughout the night. Naomi could barely keep her eyes open. Shlomo, who heard Sari start crying again just moments after Naomi had put her down, told Naomi he'd tend to her. He rose from his bed and went to Sari's crib. He rocked her gently and softly whispered words of comfort.

Naomi followed the scene. Why was he whispering if he wasn't sure she heard? Sari looked at him with her intelligent eyes. "Ah-bah," she said. "Ah-bah."

"She didn't mean to say 'Abba,'" Naomi said when she saw Shlomo's eyes grow wide with joy. "Don't get so excited."

"No," he told her joyfully, "she just wanted to calm me."

"Tell me one thing," Naomi said, sitting up despite her exhaustion. "There's just one thing I want to know. I've asked you this in the past but I haven't received a response. How come in the past, when our world was in ruins, you were so cheerful and optimistic, and now when everything is okay you've been so pessimistic and depressed?"

"I have not been depressed," Shlomo protested.

"Just about."

He cuddled Sari and lifted his eyes to meet Naomi's. His expression was inscrutable. "Because then everything was completely destroyed. If I hadn't picked up the pieces and continued to struggle for our family's survival, nothing would have been left."

New York 5756/1996

Naomi thought she was strong. She was placing the boxes of formula in the dairy cabinet when a sudden wave of dizziness engulfed her. She gripped the countertop, overcome with feelings of frustration and guilt.

Sari was crying in her crib. Five-year-old Becky was in the kitchen, her sobs echoing through the house. She was sick with the flu and the entire household was "on wheels" due to her illness. She'd been horribly whiny, infecting everyone else with her incessant complaints. Becky was usually a very pleasant, compliant child, but not today.

Yanky was due home from cheder any minute and Mindy in half an hour. The house was nowhere near ready to receive her. On top of everything else, there was a note on the refrigerator: *Please call me urgently. Zehavah.* Zehavah was the teacher of a kindergarten class to which Naomi was trying to get Becky accepted. Becky didn't seem to be fitting in, and the teacher thought she was having a negative influence on the other girls. Zehavah probably wanted to inform Naomi that she did not want Becky in her class.

Naomi swallowed hard and began doing the many things that needed to be done. She picked up Sari and tried her best to soothe Becky. Becky demanded to be put to bed. Naomi took her upstairs to her room.

"Read me a story," Becky whined. "Ima, sit near me. My head hurts. Put Sari down and come to me."

Dinner was not ready yet, and Shlomo would be home soon. Naomi was like an automaton, working mechanically through a haze of exhaustion. She felt like crying. She was utterly spent; she had no strength to go on. Finally, now that their lives were more or less organized, she was just so tired. Tired of running around, tired of visiting various auditory and speech clinics, tired of caring for Mindy, tired of the never-ending visits to communication specialists with both Becky and Mindy, tired of struggling to run a normal household while holding down a demanding job.

She sat on a chair near Becky's bed and showed her a picture book. Naomi felt drained of strength, of life.

"Hello!" Shlomo's greeting rang heartily through the house. Naomi threw a glance at the large photograph hanging in Becky's room in which Shlomo was holding one-year-old Yanky in his arms. His face bore the proud, dazzling smile of a young father. How everything had changed!

She wasn't functioning properly. She couldn't run her home properly – she, Naomi Katz-Mandel, who had always been the most talented, popular girl in her grade. When she started working as a psychologist, Naomi was in great demand. Life was once so rosy and promising. Shlomo had once been a young man filled with hopes and dreams like hers. Life had proved stronger than both of them.

Naomi rose shakily and made her way to the kitchen despite Becky's cries of protest. She wanted to say hello to her husband and organize the kitchen a bit. Becky leaped from her bed and chased after her.

"Hello, Shlomo," Naomi said. "Come, sit down."

"What happened?" Shlomo asked, taking in the huge mess. Becky and Sari began wailing again. Shlomo stared.

"Children, calm down," he said firmly. Becky grew quiet, but Sari was unimpressed by her father's command.

Naomi hugged Sari fiercely. Shlomo glanced at her sidewise. "Maybe you should go rest a bit?"

"Me? How?" Naomi was on the verge of tears. "The house is upside-down. Yanky will be home any minute and there's no dinner for him to eat. Mindy's due home in half an hour and her room is a mess. All the electric appliances are still out. Sari's hungry and edgy. And listen to Becky wailing!"

Shlomo remained calm. "Go," he said pleasantly but firmly. "I'll take care of everything."

Too tired to argue, Naomi gave in to his soothing voice. She knew she was losing control and she didn't want to explode at her children, who had done nothing wrong. She dragged herself up the stairs, Sari in her arms. Sari finished her bottle by the time they arrived in Naomi's bedroom. Naomi was seized with guilt for having let the poor child be so hungry. *She's so helpless,* Naomi scolded herself. *How can you starve her like that, when she can't even explain to you what she wants? Wait a minute, isn't Mindy helpless, too? Can she explain what she wants? And what about Becky? And Yanky?*

Sari fell asleep as soon as she finished her bottle. Naomi placed her gently in her crib. The bedroom was neat and clean, but Naomi couldn't forget about the mess downstairs. *You have a sick child and you're ignoring her. She's deaf and she struggles so hard; doesn't she deserve an extra bit of love and attention? Your son will be home from school soon. He's been away for the past ten hours and you don't even have a hot meal waiting.*

Tears welled up in her eyes. A blurry image of Mindy surfaced in her tired mind. *And what are you doing to help your deaf-mute-autistic child? You didn't even prepare a good dinner for her. You haven't given your children a drop of maternal love today.*

Naomi buried her head in her pillow and burst into tears. Feelings of guilt and frustration buried her desire to rise again and continue struggling. How could it be that life had once been so cheerful and free of serious concern? What would be with Mindy? What would be with Becky? Would her other children grow up normal, or would the scars of the past remain etched on their hearts forever?

I'll never be a normal mother, her heart wept. *I'll never be able to give my children what I'd give them if I were a normal mother. What will be, Ribbono shel Olam, what will be?*

Naomi didn't know how much time passed before a shadow fell on Sari's crib. The shadow waited silently but she sensed its presence. Naomi raised her head and looked at Shlomo, who was gazing at her with a concerned look.

"Yes?" she asked.

"Everything's fine," he reported. "Mindy and Sari are asleep, and Yanky and Becky are in the kitchen, eating."

"What?" Naomi asked in shock. "What time is it?"

His eyes sparkled with amusement. "Eight o'clock."

"Impossible," Naomi said, a pleasant sensation of vitality in her bones. "I slept for two hours?"

He nodded, the sparkle in his eyes growing more pronounced. A smile lit up his face.

"What's so funny?" Naomi wasn't insulted. Something about his lightheartedness banished the last vestiges of gloom from her heart. "How did you manage?" she asked.

"Look," he admitted, "I won't say the house is in tip-top order, but everyone's happy. I ordered pizza for supper, and I canceled eight appointments you had in your book for the next two weeks."

"What?"

"You must rest. Sari's only three months old. I think you came back from the convalescent home too early. Sari needs her mother just as much as the other children. I can understand that you wanted to come home, but why did you have to return to work so fast? You haven't yet recuperated from the birth, haven't gathered your strength. What was the rush to go back to work?"

"These were urgent appointments!"

"Nothing that couldn't wait. If you don't rest at home, I'll send you to a hotel."

"What a threat!" Naomi smiled for the first time that day, but it was an empty smile that did not reach her eyes. "With such a threat hanging over my head, I really have no choice but to try and rest more. Who dressed the kids in their pajamas? Who put them to bed? Who cleaned the mess? Poor Yanky. He comes home from cheder so tired, but he helps at home far more than most boys his age. He carries too heavy a burden on his young shoulders. And Becky is sick, poor thing. And we're not seeing any progress with Mindy. What will be, Shlomo? What will be?"

"Yanky should not have to help in the house immediately when he comes home. That's the only logical thing you said."

"Well, what other choice do I have? Should I leave everything for you to do?"

"You have a five-year-old daughter, remember? There are lots of things she can do. Yanky helped a lot more at that age than you demand of her."

"What?" Naomi was taken aback by everything Shlomo said, but at this last pronouncement she sat up in bed. "What? Becky?"

"Yes, Becky," he replied. "Why not?"

"But she's sick!"

"Today she's sick," my husband conceded. "But you never ask

her to do anything in the house. Why not?"

"But she's always so busy with such important things."

"Such as?"

"Such as her lessons in lip reading and proper speech. How will she cope in life if she can't speak properly?" Naomi asked furiously. "Do you want it on your conscience that she won't speak fluently or that her development will be compromised? That's what's going to happen if we prevent her from practicing these things."

"And you think that if she studies and practices all day and doesn't do any of the things normal girls her own age do, she will develop properly?" Shlomo asked. "That's a mistake. Life comes first, then accuracy in speech."

"But Shlomo ..."

Shlomo sat down on the chair opposite Naomi. His humorous manner was gone; his demeanor was now serious and thoughtful.

"Becky's a little girl, and we're in charge of guiding her. We try our best, and Hashem helps. We need to remember not to allow Becky's deafness to define who she is and what she can do. That's a mistake we'll never be able to undo. Focus on what she can do. Someone who spends all day with something he doesn't do well becomes embittered, withdrawn and sad. I think those words describe Becky. I've been keeping a close eye on her ever since we began our efforts to have her enter preschool. I've noticed that she's become more withdrawn than she used to be, and I wondered why. And then it occurred to me: How will she gain self-confidence if we constantly send her the message that she's got to strain and struggle to be like everyone else? It's important that she live a healthy, happy life. That's what will make her strong in the future."

Naomi was silent.

"When you went to sleep, I called her over and we quickly organized the house. Yanky was tired so I let him rest, but in the meantime the little angel was keeping an eye on Mindy without my even realizing it."

"He really is an angel." Naomi's smile traveled a considerable distance but still did not reach her eyes.

"After Mindy came home, I ordered pizza."

"Did Mindy like it?"

"I think so," he replied, shrugging. "She finishes anything you give her."

"But Shlomo!" Naomi exclaimed. "We'll never be normal parents! We'll never be able to give to our healthy children what they need in order to grow up normal."

"Really?" He smiled. "And just what is a normal parent?"

"I don't know ... ordinary people ..."

"Everyone has *nisyonos*. Some people have financial problems and the father comes home late at night when the children are already asleep. Do those children have a father? No. Do they live a normal lifestyle?

"Some families have an elderly grandparent living with them, and the parents are very busy caring for him. Some children have a sick or weak father or mother. Some children are orphans. Some families are so poor they live off *tzedakah* and don't have even their most basic needs met. There are countless types of *nisyonos* in this world and each person, each family, must deal with the *nisayon* Hashem has given. There is no such thing as normal parents, just as there is no definition of a normal person.

"Each individual is what he is, with his own tools, capabilities and difficulties. Every parent raises his children differently. If you were the mother of healthy children, but you were less sensitive to their needs, or less warm, would they be happier? Hashem gave our children an especially warm and understanding mother with extensive knowledge of psychology. There's no doubt you understand your children better than most mothers. Hashem also wants them — yes, them, too, not just you — to raise a special sibling. Becky has received a double task: to deal with her own serious handicap and a sister with a serious handicap as well. We help her bear the burden to the best of our ability, but it is not our job — nor is it possible

— for us to take the *nisayon* away from her. Hashem loves us more than we can fathom."

"What about their future, Shlomo?" Naomi whispered, tortured. "What about their future? Will Becky ever marry and have a family? Will Mindy have a warm, loving place to be when we won't be here to provide it for her?"

"Look, I'm not a prophet, and I certainly can't feel exactly what you feel, but I'm also the parent of these children, and I'm concerned with their welfare just the same as you. I trust my Father in Heaven Who is bigger than us both. Don't take the burden of your child's future on your own shoulders; leave it in the hands of our Father in Heaven. Does Becky bear the burden of this household on her shoulders? Why are you taking the burden of our handicapped children's future on yours alone?"

"But look at what happened today! Everything fell apart. Becky was sick, poor thing. Yanky was tired. Mindy is pathetic — that's undeniable. And Sari ... do you know how hungry she was by the time I got to feed her? *Ribbono shel Olam*!"

"You just said *Ribbono shel Olam*," Shlomo replied quietly. "Did you think about what you were saying? There is a *Ribbono shel Olam*. There is a Creator Who designed this world, and every *nisayon* we or our children struggle with has been designed by Him with the purpose of us helping us accomplish our true mission in life."

Shlomo pointed to Sari, who was still sleeping peacefully. For a moment, her deep breathing was the only sound in the room. "Look at her. She's so tiny, a little chick hatched from her egg a mere three months ago. What is she compared to you? Nothing. Is she worried? No. She's totally dependent on you; she trusts you completely. She doesn't think; she just cries and asks. Learn from her. Ask your Father and trust Him. You fell apart, plain and simple. Rest up and know that Hashem doesn't give a person a *nisayon* he cannot withstand."

He rose and left the room.

Naomi felt a wave of weakness surge over her. She was too

fatigued to move a limb. Rather than struggle pitifully against them, she allowed the waves of weakness to wash over her unchecked. Someone whispered into her ears at that moment: *Let go, my child. Stop fighting so much. Relax. It's okay to be weak.*

That Someone was big and strong; Someone Naomi could lean on. He wrapped her in His protective arms, and she felt happy and at peace with herself for the first time since the twins were born. Naomi felt that Hashem was with her. She didn't just know it; she felt it.

And Naomi was no longer scared.

16

New York 5758/1998

One day Ruchaleh didn't come to school. Becky knew it was going to be a nerve-wracking day right from the beginning. She ignored Morah Devorah's cheerful greeting and inquiry as to how she was feeling and sat down, anxious and sullen, at the table.

Morah Devorah began distributing craft supplies and explaining what should be done. Becky brightened somewhat. She was one of the best in the class in arts and crafts. Becky didn't focus intently on the teacher's lips as she demonstrated and explained. Sometimes, Morah Devorah moved a bit too far to the right or left and Becky couldn't see her lips at all, but she was impatient to begin.

Morah Devorah usually remembered to turn her face to Becky when she spoke. Jenny, Morah Devorah and Becky had agreed together that when Morah Devorah forgot to do so, and Becky didn't understand something or couldn't read Morah Devorah's lips, Becky was to raise her hand and ask respectfully that the teacher repeat what she had said.

That day the plan didn't work. Becky didn't feel like stopping the teacher and delaying the arts and crafts project. Her fingers burned with a desire to use the craft equipment, the glue and the scissors.

"Is everything clear?" Morah Devorah asked.

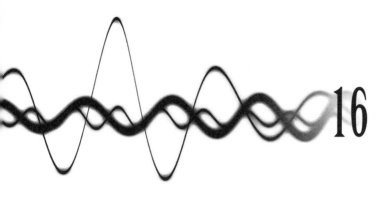

"Yes," the girls chorused.

Becky thought she understood better than everyone else what should be done, maybe even better than the teacher herself. She began by cutting the black oak tag with careful precision and then started on the red paper.

"Becky!" Morah Devorah remembered belatedly that Becky couldn't hear her. She approached her and tapped lightly on her shoulder. Becky started.

"What?"

"Why are you doing that?" Her tone of voice was severe. Becky couldn't hear it, but she saw Morah Devorah's eyes narrowed in anger, her eyebrows drawn together with displeasure.

"What's wrong?"

"Did I say to cut? I said to trace the picture, not to cut."

"Oh ..." Becky was flustered. "I didn't hear you."

Morah Devorah was not about to let the incident pass without comment. Jenny had warned her repeatedly not to give Becky preferential treatment.

"She's a child," Jenny had explained. "It's only natural for her to try and get away with as little effort as possible. It's up to us to be alert and sense when she's trying to take advantage of her situation. There will be times when you should be forgiving and look the other way, but for the most part, you've got to treat her as you would any other student. Preferential treatment will ruin the child's chances for a future as an ordinary girl."

"You didn't hear?" she asked with annoyance. "Why didn't you hear?" She winced inwardly at the sound of her own words.

"You turned your head a bit," Becky whispered fearfully.

"But we agreed that if you don't hear something you should tell me. Now you've ruined your arts and crafts project."

Becky looked miserable. "I'm sorry," she said quietly.

"Alright," Morah Devorah said forgivingly. "I'll give you new supplies, but this is the last time I'm letting you get away with not hearing what I say. Is that clear?"

It was very clear. None of the other girls cared that Becky's project was ruined. They hadn't even glanced her way when Morah Devorah had scolded her. It was as if she was invisible. Becky swallowed her tears and kept them deep in her heart. No one cared about her. Not one girl shared her distress; no one offered her a soothing word.

Once she'd received new supplies, Becky hurried to catch up to the other girls. She was still finishing up the final stages of her project when everyone else had finished. In her haste, she couldn't work as neatly and carefully as she would have liked, and the end result was somewhat sloppy. Morah Devorah hung up her work, but Becky had a sour taste in her mouth. Her project could have been so much prettier.

It's all because Ruchaleh didn't come, she thought to herself in frustration as she filled her pail with sand. *When she doesn't come I don't have a single friend in the whole class. Not a single one.*

IN THE EVENING Becky told Yanky about what had happened in school. "Instead of complaining," Yanky scolded, "go visit Ruchaleh. Maybe she's sick."

"She lives far from us," Becky said doubtfully. The thought of making her way to an unfamiliar house terrified her. Her natural diffidence, combined with her mistrust of society, caused her to be quiet and withdrawn.

"Not so far," Yanky said, studying a map in the phone book. "I think you can go there yourself. You're six years old already."

"Yes," Becky said gloomily, "but I'm afraid to go there."

"There's no reason to be afraid. Ruchaleh's your friend, your true friend," Yanky said. "C'mon, *bentch* and we'll go."

"We'll go? You'll come with me?"

"Yes. I'll walk you over there."

"Ah." She recited Birkas Hamazon slowly and with great *kavanah* while Yanky waited impatiently. They received their mother's permission and left the house. Yanky walked her down the block and then showed her how to proceed. She had to keep walking straight until the end of the block, turn left, and then right at the first turn. That was the street she needed, and then she was to walk until she found Ruchaleh's house.

Simple. All the evaluators she had been to said that Becky's spatial orientation was excellent. She walked confidently, trying to quell her fear. She found the house easily. She considered standing outside until someone happened to open the door, but she was afraid she'd balk and run away first. Yanky would be so disappointed in her if she did that.

She knocked on the door, quietly and hesitantly. Later she'd be able to say that she'd knocked and no one had answered. But someone did answer. A tall woman opened the door. Becky assumed the woman said something, though she couldn't be sure because the woman's face was not turned toward her.

"Hello," Becky said to the tall woman, who she assumed was Ruchaleh's mother. "My name is Becky. I'm in Ruchaleh's class. I'm deaf, so if you want me to hear you, please turn your face to me so I can read your lips." It was a long speech that she had rehearsed with Jenny countless times.

"Just tell it like it is," Jenny had told her. "You'll spare yourself lots of embarrassment, mistakes and confusion. Tell people right away that you're deaf but you can understand them if they look at you."

The woman leaned toward her. "I'm Ruchaleh's mother," she said, smiling broadly. "Ruchaleh talks about you a lot. She likes you."

Becky's heart expanded. "I like her, too, and I'm sorry she wasn't in school today. Is she home?"

"Yes," Ruchaleh's mother replied. "She's sick. You can come inside."

Becky entered the house, her heart pounding. The house was simply furnished and rather neglected looking. Becky thought in her heart that Ruchaleh's home looked somewhat like Ruchaleh.

"Becky!" Ruchaleh leaped from her bed. She was very pale, but her brown eyes shone. "How nice that you came."

Ruchaleh's bed was very messy, and the walls in her room were scribbled up. Ruchaleh had been coloring in bed, but she dropped the crayon the moment she saw Becky. Becky's heart could barely contain her joy. She had never heard such kind words from a friend before.

"I was sorry you weren't in school today," she said simply. "What were you drawing?"

"My family," Ruchaleh replied.

"Can I see?" Becky asked eagerly. She liked drawing.

"This is my father," Ruchaleh said, pointing. "This is my mother. And these are my brothers and sisters: Moshe Ze'ev, Chaim Aryeh, Tzilah Nechamah, Sarah Goldah and Betzalel Yehudah. Then comes me. After me comes Baila Sheina and Hershel Menachem. That's my whole family."

"We're only four children," Becky said, "and you're eight. That's double."

"Yes," Ruchaleh agreed. It was obvious she was very proud of her family.

"Let's play something," Becky suggested. Her shyness had disappeared in her friend's company.

"What can we play?" Ruchaleh's eyes swept the room. The house was a mess. A few of her siblings were making a ruckus playing hide-and-seek. The baby was wailing in his crib. Two older sisters were studying in the dining room, and two of her brothers were playing "war." The noise was deafening. Becky sat calmly at the edge of Ruchaleh's bed, completely unperturbed by the noise.

"We can play anything," Becky replied.

"No, I can hardly hear you," Ruchaleh said, making a face. "What a mess! What noise! I can't hear a thing."

Becky smiled. “Neither can I,” she said mischievously.

“Lucky you,” Ruchaleh said enviously. “Right now you’re lucky you can’t hear.”

“Don’t ever say something silly like that,” Becky said firmly. “Let’s play a card game.”

Ruchaleh took out a card game. She shuffled the cards and counted out four cards for each of them. “When you ask me if I have a certain card, tell me the color of the card, not what it says, okay?”

“What?” Becky asked, her mouth opening in surprise. “Why?”

“Because,” Ruchaleh said defensively, “I can’t read yet, even though I’m seven years old already. I’ve been left back.”

“You’re seven?” Becky looked at Ruchaleh admiringly. She was too young to understand the significance of Ruchaleh’s having stayed back a grade.

“Yup.”

“Well, you don’t have to know how to read as long as you’re still in preschool. You learn to read in grade school. I know how because Jenny taught me.”

“But I’m big already. I’m supposed to be in first grade already, but I’m stuck in preschool with girls younger than me, and they call me ‘Dummy.’” Her voice oozed bitterness.

Becky stared at Ruchaleh in surprise. Ruchaleh was always so bubbly and happy. Becky had never seen her sad before, but now. ... Maybe it was because she was sick. Or maybe in the protective surroundings of her own home she dared open her heart to her friend.

“And you know what else they say?” she asked, her voice dropping to a near whisper.

“What?”

“That I ... that my clothes are old and not very clean.” Her eyes filled with tears and she burst out crying. Becky, still stunned, did not know how to respond to the sudden turn their conversation had taken. She held Ruchaleh's hand and squeezed it warmly.

"But, Ruchaleh, I'm your friend. I like you no matter what."

Ruchaleh continued sobbing. Once she'd started she couldn't stop. She tried to smile through her tears, but she couldn't say a word.

"And I'm deaf," Becky said, trying to console her. "Everyone has something else. Don't be sad, Ruchaleh. Be glad you can hear. I would be happy to be in preschool instead of in first grade so long as I could hear, and I wouldn't care if people said my clothes weren't clean."

Ruchaleh stopped crying and stared at Becky incredulously. "Even if you were dumb?" she asked. "Even if the girls said you were ..."

"Yes," Becky replied firmly. "And I think you're a really great girl, Ruchaleh, just so you know."

Ruchaleh's eyes lit up. "Really?"

"Yes," Becky declared passionately. "And I'm going to teach you how to read." Her first meeting with sadness and difficulty other than her own moved her deeply. She was prepared to move mountains in order to help her friend.

"No!" Ruchaleh shouted angrily. "You won't teach me anything!"

"And in exchange, you'll help me with something else," Becky said pleadingly, reluctant to let Ruchaleh's hurt feelings get in the way.

"Me? How can I help you?"

"You can hear for me," Becky replied quietly. "When I don't hear something, tell me what I missed."

Ruchaleh' eyes began to sparkle again. She took a step toward Becky and extended her hand. "Okay," she said. "It's a deal."

BECKY'S PRESCHOOL CLASS was going on a trip tomorrow.

Becky was very excited. She had already filled her blue canteen with mango juice and placed it in the refrigerator. Yanky had helped her find a backpack in the basement, and Ima had filled it with nosh. Abba had gone to the grocery to buy her a special snack she liked. The whole family was excited along with her.

Becky felt her heart beat strongly. A trip! She'd be spending the entire day with her classmates in a park with a huge playground. She wouldn't hear if someone came up behind her on the slide and she had to hurry to clear the way. She'd swing high and wouldn't hear her friends call, "Careful, Becky! Shiffy's right under your swing. It's dangerous."

Becky was aware that when she played in the yard in school she couldn't maintain the high level of concentration she had in the classroom. Her ability to read lips was diminished, and she was almost completely cut off from the world. If she had so few friends when she made a supreme effort to be a part of things, what would it be like when she couldn't concentrate at all?

Becky was afraid. Very, very afraid.

"You're just a scaredy-cat," Yanky said soothingly. "You'll have fun. I wish we had a trip like that. We just spend the whole day learning."

"But Yanky," Becky protested, staring at him with eyes wide with astonishment. "You're learning Torah."

"Yes, I know," Yanky said. He was old enough to appreciate the importance of Torah study. "But the park you're going to has the most amazing fun things."

"But it's just a regular park," Becky said. "There aren't any rides, Yanky."

"I know," her brother replied. "Still, it's a beautiful place. The slides are really tall. And they're not like regular slides; they're sort of round."

"Round?"

"Yes, they're built like pipes, so you have a roof over your head. You go inside and it's too dark to see anything. It's so scary, it's delicious. You slide down without seeing anything."

Becky narrowed her eyes. "Yanky, if there really is such a slide, I'm not going on it."

"Why not?" He was disappointed in her. "You're not a scaredy-cat like most girls. When Abba took us to the amusement park, you weren't scared at all."

"A minute ago you said I was a scaredy-cat." Becky smiled, tired of arguing. "I'm not afraid of rides, but at the amusement park there was plenty of light and I could see what was happening. The type of slide you're telling me about is different, because it's scary not to be able to see or hear. I can never hear, but when I'm afraid that something might surprise me, I make sure to keep my eyes peeled. If I can't do that either, I'll be completely lost. Don't you understand, Yanky?" She sighed. "No, no, you'll never understand because you can hear."

Yanky considered what Becky had said. "I think I can understand," he said, "but I still think you should go on those slides. They're so much fun. Can't you have someone wait for you at the bottom? Ask your friend Ruchaleh to wait for you. That way, you won't be afraid."

"Maybe," Becky said doubtfully. "We'll see."

Becky went to bed early that night to gather strength for the coming day. *She needed strength to face every day*, Naomi thought to herself as she tucked her daughter in, kissed her on the forehead and wished her good night and sweet dreams, but a class outing would require maximum concentration and exertion of her healthy senses. Jenny had felt it would be best if Becky was given the chance to cope alone on trip day. She would not be accompanying Becky on the trip. "Becky needs to be able to manage on her own in society," she had explained.

Manage on her own? Becky's heart pounded so hard she thought it might fly out of her body. Could such a thing really happen? She trembled uncontrollably under her thick blanket. She knew she wasn't cold and there was no point in calling Ima to ask for another blanket. The cold she felt was the result of a deep, terrible fear gripping her with icy claws.

You'll fall and hurt yourself because you won't hear them warn everyone that a certain slide is broken. You'll get lost because you won't hear them calling after you that you're going in the wrong direction. You'll be left behind because you won't hear the teacher announcing that everyone should return to the bus.

Maybe Jenny should come along? No, no. Becky shook her head forcefully. She didn't want that. She didn't really like it that Jenny came to school. The girls giggled and pointed at her every time Jenny came. Tomorrow she wanted to be just like everyone else.

She couldn't fall asleep. She had gone to bed early, turned off the light and put on her favorite nightlight, but she couldn't relax enough to let slumber overtake her. The nightlight cast a dim yellow-blue light through its teddy-bear-shaped cover. The glow-in-the-dark hands of the wall clock showed it was nearly ten o'clock. Ten o'clock! She'd gone to bed at seven. Three hours had passed already.

It was tempting to imagine that tomorrow a warm and pleasant sun would shine, and everyone would be her friend and ask her to join them on the playground. Everyone would smile at her in welcome and be glad she was with them. Becky knew that in reality the girls would play hide-and-seek and tag and not offer to include her at all. "But you can't hear," they would say if she ever worked up the courage and asked to be included. "How will you know who is out and who isn't?" Why should she ask anything of the girls if they never agreed to anything anyway? No one wanted to be her friend. No one would ever want to be her friend.

Her green eyes filled with tears. The hands of the clock grew blurry and the teddy bear's head drooped sadly. She tried to console herself with the thought of Ruchaleh's friendship, but it offered scant comfort. *It isn't worth anything,* she thought bleakly. *Nothing at all. One friend out of an entire class?*

Becky didn't know it, but the tears she cried were good for her. They made her grow tired and close her eyes despite her intense fear of social rejection.

THE FOLLOWING DAY dawned bright and clear, just as the meteorologists had predicted. The winter snow had already melted, and spring was just around the corner. Morah Devorah had decided to take the girls on a trip to a large park just before Pesach vacation.

Becky slipped her hands through the straps of her backpack, hung the canteen around her neck, and said good-bye to her mother. "Have a good time! Don't be afraid," Yanky called out after her as she set off for school.

A large bunch of girls from two kindergarten classes milled around near the school gate. Becky hesitated for a moment before forging her way into her classroom. "Morah Devorah," she called. "I came."

Morah Devorah extricated herself from a mountain of picnic coolers and insulated bags. "Hello, Becky," she said with a smile. "I'm glad you came. Why don't you wait outside with everyone else."

Becky went obediently outside and stood quietly near the gate. Suddenly, someone squeezed her hand hard. Gasping with pain, she raised her eyes to see who had hurt her and why. It was Ruchaleh, her freckles sparkling in the sun, a happy smile on her face. "Isn't this fun?" she asked.

"Sure," Becky said, though she wasn't sure at all.

The girls boarded the bus in an organized fashion, two at a time. They sat down on the upholstered seats and listened quietly as their teacher took attendance and made sure everyone was on the bus. Then the bus took off, and the girls began to sing spiritedly. Becky did not join in. She looked out the window, her hand clasping Ruchaleh's.

The bus came to a stop, and Morah Devorah issued instructions for the trip. The girls disembarked from the bus and waited on the pavement. Morah Devorah crossed the street with them and took them into the park. Then she gave the sign that it was okay to go play, and the girls made a beeline for the playground.

It was wonderful. Becky had never seen such a large and impressive playground in her life. It was such fun to sit down on the large round wooden seat, grip the rubber wheel, and go flying down the steel wire. The line waiting for this ride, which the girls called a "chairlift," was longer than the line at any other. Becky's face turned red from the heat and excitement. Yanky was right. This park had really scary and fun things to do.

Ruchaleh disappeared almost as soon as they arrived, but Becky didn't care. She climbed and slid, jumped and ran, enjoying herself thoroughly. A large crowd of girls near one of the slides caught her attention, and she went to investigate. It was a long, long slide, enclosed on all sides, just as Yanky had described. The girls lined up to take turns on the slide. Raizel went first. She slid down. Once at the bottom, she called the name of the girl just behind her on line.

"Yocheved! Yocheved! Yocheved!" she called. Becky felt sure she was chanting the name in a special, gay, singsong voice.

She joined the line and watched as the circle of girls waiting at the bottom of the slide and calling the name of the girl who was sliding grew and grew. "Dina Chaya! Dina Chaya! Dina Chaya!" a group of eleven girls chanted. "Esther Leah! Esther Leah! Esther Leah!" seventeen girls thundered. Ruchaleh was number eighteen, and she, Becky, who had discovered the slide somewhat belatedly, was last on line.

Everyone stood near the slide and called out the name of the girl who was sliding. They even called Ruchaleh's name. "Ruchaleh! Ruchaleh! Ruchaleh!" Becky's heart pounded with joy. Soon it would be her turn, and everyone would stand and call her name. Her name! True, she was scared of sliding down the dark, completely enclosed slide, and she wouldn't even hear her name being called out as she slid down, but it was worth it.

With a smile of anticipation, Becky entered the large pipe-shaped slide. None of the girls in the class had ever called her name, but now they would all call it out together. Her smile widened as she neared the end of the twisty slide, and she leaped up, her eyes sparkling, as soon as her feet hit the ground.

The girls were gone. All of them. They had left without waiting for her. No one had called her name. No one had noticed that she hadn't had her turn yet. Or maybe they had noticed but had left anyway so as not to call her name. Not a single girl waited for her.

With tears in her eyes Becky dragged herself to a nearby bench. She was suddenly aware of a pounding headache brought on by a long stay in the sun without a drink. She sipped some mango juice from her canteen and wished she could go home.

"IT'S YOUR FAULT," Yanky argued heatedly. "If you were friendly with them they would have waited for you."

"What should I do?" Becky asked him. "What could I have done? You tell me. They waited for everyone – everyone, even Ruchaleh – but not for me."

"Because you're not their friend, so why should they wait for you? You're like a girl who's not in their class, like a girl they don't know at all. Why should they wait for you and call your name?"

Becky's eyes blazed. "If you're so smart," she said angrily, "tell me what you would do with those ... those horrid girls."

"They're not so horrid. It's your fault that you don't make friends with them, not theirs."

"It is too their fault. Raizel told them not to be my friend on the first day I came and everyone listened to her, just like that."

"But Becky, you said yourself that the reason they're not friendly with you is not because of Raizel but because they don't have the patience to hear you out, so you don't even bother talking to them."

"That's right. So what does that help? They really don't have patience for me."

"Have you ever tried to make friends with anyone?"

"No, because they don't have patience for me. Yanky, stop yelling at me. I've explained it to you already."

"But who said it's true? If you didn't try, how can you be so sure?"

"Because," Becky said, sighing heavily. "Yanky, I've told you a thousand times already: There are some things you can't understand."

"Maybe. But you've got to understand that you'll never have friends this way. If I were you, I would keep trying. In the end, I would make friends with someone. Besides, I wouldn't let them go before they called my name."

Becky's eyes remained dry. Her anger was greater than her hurt. "You wouldn't let them? I didn't even realize they'd left."

"Yes, but I told you, they didn't wait for you because you're not their friend. I wouldn't stop trying until they were my friends."

"How?"

"You told me you asked Ruchaleh to hear for you. Is she doing that?"

"I forgot about that," Becky admitted.

"You can't forget such things. You can't allow such a thing to happen again. You have to be friendlier with all the girls."

Becky was silent. At first she was too hurt to think. Then the pain was replaced by fury. But now Becky knew that she had to make a supreme effort to ensure that such a thing didn't happen again. Did no one care about her? It couldn't be. She couldn't allow the situation to continue.

Ruchaleh will hear for me, she said to herself with the steely determination that had helped her survive six years of deafness. *I won't let anyone get away with it any more. No one.*

Becky was not familiar with the expression "the straw that broke the camel's back," but the words "never again," etched themselves on her heart with fiery letters.

Maybe everyone in preschool already knew her as the type of girl you could ignore. There was no way she would let the same thing happen in first grade. No one would know she was deaf. It would be a secret she would guard with all her might. Becky knew she was smart, and she planned to invest all her brains into ensuring that not a single girl would know she was deaf. She'd go to a different school from all the girls in her preschool class. A faraway school where she didn't know anyone and no one knew her.

She'd show them. She'd prove how far a deaf girl could go.

17

Eretz Yisrael 5707/1947

"It's going to be a moonless night," Shaul, Meir's commander, said to a group of fighters. "Our target is a British munitions storehouse. We are suffering a severe shortage of arms."

There were four of them. The storehouse they intended to raid was poorly guarded. The plan was to overtake the guards quickly and seize the arms. The entire operation had to be over within fifteen minutes, before the forces the guards would surely alert arrived on the scene.

Meir was tense as he listened to Shaul. He knew that the tiniest mistake could cost him and his friends their lives, not to mention jeopardize their important mission. The Jews needed weapons if they were to continue fighting for their homeland. After the heist, the Brits would step up security and future attempts at penetration would be doomed to failure.

Shaul spread out a map and the fighters pored over it. They examined the road leading to the storehouse, the various possible approaches, its distance from the nearest British post, the deployment of the guards, and the location of the arms.

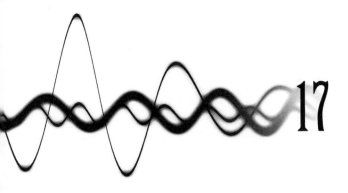

"It could be fatal if we don't locate the ammunition store," Shaul said. "Remember, we must carry out this operation without firing any weapons. No grenades or shooting at all. If the ammunition explodes, G-d forbid, you'll pay with your lives."

"May I ask a question?" Meir asked. He leaned forward and gripped the butt of his rifle with one hand.

"Go ahead." Shaul's gaze swept over the impassioned young man with more than a touch of admiration. "You know you're always welcome to ask. Your questions are always appropriate and are usually of benefit to us all."

Meir did not blush at Shaul's compliment. "If we see that the operation is failing," he said in the same matter-of-fact voice, "will we have the option of taking our own lives?"

"What?" Shaul was stunned. Meir's three fellow fighters stared at him in shock. "What are you thinking of?"

"Suicide," Meir said evenly. "Will we be able to commit suicide? Or rather, will I be able to?"

Shaul stared at him. "But Meir," he protested. "The mission ..."

"Yes, I know," Meir smiled. "The mission can't fail. But what if it does? What if we discover we erred in calculating the amount of time it will take the British forces to arrive? What if we suddenly realize our intelligence was wrong and the guards aren't where we thought they'd be?" Earnestness and responsibility were mirrored in his black eyes. "I don't want to be captured alive by the British. I don't want to give them the pleasure of killing me."

"But ..."

"Shaul, I'm among their ten most wanted men," Meir said, a note of pride in his voice. "They'll kill me the moment I fall into their hands. I don't want them to hang me the way they have many of my friends."

"But what will you gain from committing suicide?" Shaul asked heavily.

"Destruction," Meir replied quietly. "Destruction of the entire British armory. Confusion and unrest in the enemy camp. Isn't that a worthwhile goal?"

"How will you accomplish that?"

"It's very simple." Meir turned and withdrew from behind a tree a black square box. "Know what this is?"

They nodded silently.

Only Shaul spoke. "A time bomb," he said.

"Precisely." Meir smiled triumphantly. "I don't know about you," he said to his friends, "but I plan to use this. I will not fall into British hands alive."

The men were silent and pensive. There was nothing shocking about Meir's idea; it was just that it underscored the danger of the mission they were undertaking. Fighting the British was not child's play.

The three other fighters were not nearly as experienced as Meir. They had hours of training under their belts and were earmarked as rising stars in combat, but this was the first time they would actually be carrying out a mission. They were all aware that it might very well be their last as well, and the thought gave them pause.

Meir was different. He had already overseen dozens of operations and was indifferent to death. He welcomed the thrill of battle.

"Menasheh, Alon, Mickey — what do you think?" Shaul's voice was low.

"I agree with Meir," Menasheh said slowly, "but there's no point in all of us dying. If something goes wrong, Meir and I will create a distraction so the rest of you can get away." He glanced at Meir. "Alright?"

"Fine." A broad smile played upon the veteran fighter's face. This was not the first time Menasheh had offered, with complete calm, to place himself in danger in order to save others. "It's a good plan. But I have a slight improvement: Menasheh, you join the others. There's no point in two fighters being killed."

"No …" Menasheh began, but Shaul cut him off.

"Meir's right. He'll create a distraction and you make your escape. Of course, I hope there will be no need to implement such a plan. I hope the mission will be successful." He looked at them fondly. "Dismissed."

The men rose and began to leave the small, desolate clearing in the forest to return to their homes in various kibbutzim in the area.

"Meir?" Shaul's voice stopped him in his tracks.

"Yes?" He turned and, at Shaul's indication, returned to his place.

Shaul waited for the others to disappear from sight. "You know something, Meir?" he said forthrightly. "I envy you."

"Why?"

"Your love for our homeland is fiercer than ours. You have rare courage."

"I've heard that before." Meir's face grew thoughtful. "I don't mean to brag, but you're not the first to tell me that."

"I'm not surprised," Shaul said warmly. "You're prepared to sacrifice your life for your friends, for this country. You make such statements with such ease, with such simplicity."

"I know what I'm doing," Meir said, straining to see the stars beyond the foliage covering the sky.

"I know that," Shaul agreed.

Meir nodded and began to walk away.

"*Behatzlachah*, warrior," Shaul told him, his voice a mixture of admiration and love.

As MEIR'S FIGURE grew distant, Shaul wondered what it was the young man had that the others did not. What was it about him that made everyone speak so admiringly of him? Why was there talk of making him a commander when he was all of twenty-three? What was it about him that captured commanders' hearts and made them see him as the future leader of the State of Israel or at the very least of the Israeli army?

The golden-haired, black-eyed youngster had a certain mysterious, magical charm. Did he have any family in Eretz Yisrael? Why did he love the Land so fiercely, more so than the other fighters? Who was Meir Katz? Why had he come to Eretz Yisrael?

There were so many unanswered questions. Meir never spoke about his past. He spoke at great length about his journey by ship to the shores of Eretz Yisrael and about the military operations he carried out, but he never mentioned his life before that. Shaul knew many people who preferred not to discuss their past because the memories they bore were too painful. Meir, however, hadn't been in the Nazi valley of death. He'd spent the war years in the British army, fighting the Germans. He'd been a soldier in Jim Stuart's regiment, liberating Bergen-Belsen. He'd merited seeing the enemy's defeat with his own eyes. He'd wounded and killed Germans; he'd seen them taken prisoner by the British. He'd merited what many other Jews had not. He was not a death camp survivor; he wasn't haunted by horrific memories. Perhaps he was mourning the destruction of his home and family. On the other hand, if he'd had a warm and loving family, why had he abandoned them and sailed to Eretz Yisrael?

Shaul watched as Meir leaped astride his horse and rode off. He rose with a sigh and began walking toward the path leading to his car. His medical license was in his pocket, and he had a cover story ready about providing emergency care for a sick man in one of the nearby kibbutzim. He looked nothing like the picture of himself that the British had circulated, so there was no reason to fear arrest. His papers were excellent forgeries.

The car sputtered to life and Shaul drove slowly away from the area. He hoped he wouldn't meet any Brits. Tired of circuitous, roundabout routes, he stared danger in the eye and drove directly to his destination.

Danger did not materialize. A British military car passing his on the road did not even stop. The hour was late and the British were tired. Night shifts were not very reliable; experience had taught him that. Unless the guard was eager to prove himself, as his fighters were.

A smile played on his lips as he thought about his soldiers. He admired their love for Eretz Yisrael and he loved them dearly.

After half an hour's drive he parked next to a house and slipped quietly inside.

Switzerland 5758/1998

BUTTERFLIES FLITTED GAILY through the air. The elegant hotel the Mandels were staying in was surrounded by greenery. Becky and Yanky took little Sari by the hand and went to explore. Switzerland was a very inviting place to be.

They decided to stop and rest in a stunning flower garden. Becky cited the names of the flowers she recognized and Yanky helped her with those she didn't. The hotel management had given them permission to pluck one flower of each type so they could make pretty scrapbooks.

They chased butterflies and caught them with a net for Yanky's collection.

"You know," Becky said with sparkling eyes, "the butterflies in Switzerland are different from those in America."

"Maybe they migrated," Yanky said. "Like the birds."

"Didn't you learn about the life cycle of butterflies in school?" said a familiar voice behind them. Yanky and Sari turned around to see the speaker, who tugged lightly at Becky's shoulder so she turned around as well.

"Sabba!" the three of them cried together.

Meir smiled and sat down beside them on the grass. Spending time with his grandchildren was a most pleasurable activity for him. This was the first time he'd left the United States since he'd arrived there years ago, and he was enjoying the change of scenery. His son's family would be joining them the following day. Flying from Israel to the United States was too difficult for Shmulik with his family of six children. Switzerland was a good meeting place for them all.

The idea was born spontaneously. Shlomo and Naomi had heard about a renowned expert on communication disorders. They wanted to bring Mindy to see him. Maybe, just maybe, this man would be the right *shaliach* to help their deaf, autistic daughter.

At first they planned to leave their other three children in the States under the supervision of their devoted grandmother, but later they decided to take them along and spend Pesach at a hotel in Switzerland. When Shmulik heard about the change in plans, he jumped at the chance to have his family spend time with their cousins and grandparents. Switzerland was not so far away from Israel as the United States. He suggested to his parents that they join the Mandels and he would fly in with his family to meet them.

"After Pesach we're continuing on to Eretz Yisrael, right?" Becky chattered happily. "Why don't you come with us, Sabba?"

"What?" he asked distractedly. "What did you say? Ah, yes, I know. You're continuing on to Eretz Yisrael."

"Why don't you come along, Sabba?" Yanky wanted to know, winding a blade of grass around his finger. "It will be so nice if you come. We'll go to Shmulik's house. Do you know we were never there? We've never been to Eretz Yisrael before."

"Actually, Yanky, you have been to Eretz Yisrael," her grandfather said. "When you were a baby. But since you were born, Becky, your mother hasn't been there. Your father flew there on his own twice."

"And you? How many times have you been to Eretz Yisrael?" his grandchildren inquired.

Meir paled. Vague, blurry images from the past danced before his eyes.

"What's the matter?" Becky asked in alarm when she saw the expression on her grandfather's face. "What happened, Sabba?"

Yanky, who was not as well schooled in the art of reading people's expressions as Becky, looked at the two of them in surprise. "Why do you think something's the matter?" he asked.

"Sabba, are you sad?" She wrapped her arms around his neck. "Don't be sad. We just want you to come with us. We didn't mean to make you sad."

Meir smiled wistfully. His grandchildren had misinterpreted his expression. "You're good children," he said tenderly. "It's not you. It's Eretz Yisrael."

"Eretz Yisrael?" The children were surprised. "What do you mean?"

"Eretz Yisrael, children." His eyes focused on an unseen point in the distance. "Hashem watches over Eretz Yisrael 'from the beginning of the year until the end of the year.' It is more precious to Him than any other country in the world. In Eretz Yisrael, the sun shines brilliantly and the flowers are intoxicatingly beautiful and vibrant. The fields are full of top-quality produce; the fruit trees give off an irresistibly delicious scent. The sky there is ... oh, the sky of Eretz Yisrael ... what can compare? There's no such sky anywhere in the world: deep blue, pure and lofty. Just looking at it is therapeutic; it makes you feel calm and relaxed.

"The streets of Yerushalayim are filled with children and adults who heed Hashem's laws, and the sanctity of Eretz Yisrael can be seen on their faces. The special air they inhale makes them smart. The narrow, ancient streets smell pleasantly of the past. That is where our forefathers walked, our prophets, the *Tanna'im* and *Amora'im*, towering Torah scholars from every generation. And the Kosel, the Kosel. ..." He fell silent. Yanky and Becky looked at him expectantly, their eyes ablaze with childish passion.

"And the Kosel?" Yanky asked breathlessly. "Tell us about the Kosel, Sabba. Tell us, please!"

"The Kosel ... the path to the Kosel twists through the streets of the Old City. Here you feel your Jewish heritage with all your senses. The cobblestone streets are very slippery, worn smooth by thousands of pairs of feet over many generations. The Old City was built by truly righteous Yidden who lived in the times of the *Beis Hamikdash*. The houses are built in an old-fashioned style you don't see anywhere else in the world nowadays. The stone walls are thick and cool; if you enter such a house on a hot summer day you feel a certain pleasant coolness between the ancient stone walls. Walking down the street you might meet up with Arab men in kaffiyehs or

Arab women in head scarves. And then you enter the Kosel Plaza."

"You need to tear *keriyah* when you first see the Kosel, right Sabba?"

"Right," he nodded. "Whoever sees Yerushalayim in its state of destruction must tear *keriyah*."

"If he hasn't seen it for thirty days," Yanky noted.

"*Talmid chacham*." Sabba pinched his cheek.

"*Nu*, go on," Becky said, annoyed at the interruption.

"The Kosel stands there, still and silent, tall and regal, as befits *Shaar HaShamayim*, the Entrance to Heaven. All the *tefillos* of Yidden everywhere enter *Shamayim* through the Kosel. The stones are huge and smooth, waiting for the touch of Jewish hands throughout the generations. And these stones, these very same stones, were grasped by poor Jews in the times of the *Beis Hamikdash*. And you can touch this remnant of the *Beis Hamikdash* Hashem has left for us. Small bushes blossom between the stones and doves coo softly. The air is saturated with *kedushah* and the Kosel radiates purity. And you pour your heart out in prayer. ..."

Sabba closed his eyes and held his head in his hands. He swayed softly, as if in prayer, and the children stared at him in fascination.

"So you were there," Yanky said after a few moments of awed silence. "You described it so well, you had to have been there yourself."

"Yes," Sabba said, removing his hands from his face. Becky saw that his eyes were damp. "I was there. I loved Eretz Yisrael; I loved Yerushalayim; I loved the Old City. Most of all, I loved the Kosel."

"So why don't you come with us?" Becky asked, puzzled. "Sabba, why don't you come? You can see it all again."

"It sounds like you miss it," Yanky said.

"I do."

"So come!" the children chorused. "It will be such fun if you come too." There was such longing in his granddaughter's voice that he almost gave in to her pleas. Almost.

Don't be ridiculous, he said to himself. *He knew he would never set foot in Eretz Yisrael again. Eretz Yisrael had spit him out because of his sins; he was not worthy of walking on its soil, though Hashem knew how dearly he longed to.*

"No," he said quietly but firmly to his grandchildren. "I won't be joining you on your trip to Eretz Yisrael. I can't."

"Why not?"

"Because I can't." He sighed deeply. He would see the land he longed for from afar, but he would not draw near.

18

New York 5758/1998

Becky was about to graduate preschool and be promoted to first grade.

Naomi and Shlomo were on their way to a meeting with Morah Devorah and Jenny, Becky's marvelous speech therapist who accompanied them through every milestone in their deaf daughter's life. She had helped the Mandels fight to have Becky admitted into a regular preschool class and had helped Becky immeasurably once that goal had been achieved. Shlomo and Naomi trusted her and valued her input greatly.

There was to be another participant in the meeting: Moshe, an evaluator from the Department of Education. He, too, had followed Becky's progress throughout the year. The five of them could easily point out changes that had taken place.

Naomi's heart was pounding as she knocked on the door of the office.

"Come in," a voice called.

They entered and were received cordially. The table was set with a cold drink, an open box of cookies and a plate of sliced cake.

"Hello," Moshe said pleasantly. "Please sit down."

They took seats and Moshe offered them refreshments.

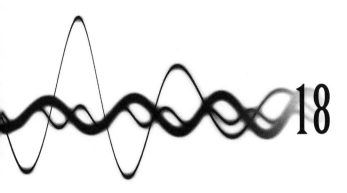

"Okay," Jenny said, getting straight to the point. "I think we can say we've come a long way together. Becky has progressed much faster than we expected her to. She is an absolute genius; she has an incredible mind. She's on par with her peers, and there seems to be no reason not to promote her to first grade."

"I agree that from a scholastic point of view, everything is in order," Morah Devorah said. "Becky's far smarter than most girls her age. She won't have any trouble with the first-grade curriculum."

"But there's something else you feel might give her trouble," Shlomo was quick to understand.

Morah Devorah coughed lightly and gathered her courage, which always seemed to fail her when facing frightened parents. "Yes," she replied. "From a social point of view, I'm not sure she's ready."

"What do you mean?" The furrows in Shlomo's brow deepened.

"I've noticed it as well," Jenny said. "Becky hardly communicates with her peers. What little communication there is between them is done with my intervention. She hasn't initiated a single conversation with anyone in the class except for one girl."

"So," Moshe summed up the situation, "we're talking about an unusually bright child whom it would be wrong to prevent from attending first grade but who doesn't bond with other children her age."

"I think," Morah Devorah said slowly, "that scholastic level in no way influences a child's ability to integrate socially, which means first grade won't be any different from preschool. The question is why Becky hasn't progressed socially."

"I'm not sure I understand what you're getting at. Can you explain?"

"Yes. What I mean is that there is no need for us to discuss whether or not Becky should be promoted to first grade. She is ready for first grade; she is extremely bright and talented. Her social difficulty will remain the same whether we keep her back or promote her."

There were nods of agreement all around.

"Involving additional professionals will only make Becky even more withdrawn," Naomi said. "The only professional she formed a bond with is Jenny. Anyone else is impossible. We've tried."

"She's failed so many times," Shlomo said, "that she's lost her trust in children. The adults in her life concern themselves with her welfare all the time, so she trusts them."

Silence reigned once again. Moshe doodled on the pad in front of him, unsure of what to write. Becky was highly intelligent; the teacher's report made that clear. But she wasn't communicating with her classmates.

He raised his head. "What about her speech?"

"That's okay," Jenny replied. "She speaks quite normally. Not perfectly, but almost. And she's learning to read lips extremely quickly and with nearly no mistakes."

"So as the teacher says, there's no reason she shouldn't be promoted to first grade," Moshe said slowly. "As for her social problem, we'll have to find a solution. Fast."

Becky was starting first grade. It was an exciting day, no doubt about that. It was perhaps one of the most exciting in Naomi's life. Becky, her deaf daughter, had overcome many obstacles and stepped over so many rocks strewn in her path. She was about to start school. A regular school, a regular class.

Will she be successful, the apple of my eye? Will her friends receive her with love and respect? Will she forge her way with difficulty, with pain and tears — or easily, with happiness and joy? What will her day be like? What will happen in school?

Much to Noami's surprise, Becky asked her to enroll her in a different school from the one her parents had planned to send her to. It was a most surprising conversation. She made her request the day after her class trip, from which she returned gloomy as midnight and told Naomi she'd had a nice time.

The day after the trip, she approached Naomi, sat down on the chair opposite her mother and told her that she had "something very, very important" to say.

"Yes, Becky," Naomi said with a smile. "I'm listening."

Becky did not smile. Naomi could tell she was very tense. "Ima, is it already time to register for first grade?"

"Why are you thinking about first grade already?" Naomi asked in surprise. "It's only Nisan now."

"Because I want to go to a different school from the one near our house. I want to go to a school where not a single girl from my preschool class will go."

"What?" Naomi asked in astonishment. "Why, Becky? What happened?"

"Nothing," she repeated, refusing to provide additional details. "Alright, Ima? Please enroll me in a different school, one far away from our house."

Naomi thought about the schools in the neighborhood and also those farther away. The other schools in their neighborhood were not in line with their *hashkafos*, and that was something she and Shlomo would not compromise on, of course. There was a different school Shlomo approved of, but it was located quite some distance from their home. It would take Shlomo an hour, an hour and a half with traffic, to drive Becky to school each day.

"Look, Becky," Naomi told her, "I'd be glad to help you if you tell me what the problem is with the school you go to now. It will take Abba more than an hour to take you to the other school each day. If we know the reason, we might decide that it's worth it. Do you see?"

Becky was silent. She bit her lip hard and said, "Alright, so Abba doesn't have to take me."

"So how will you go?" Naomi wondered.

"I'll take the subway."

Becky? Alone? On the subway? If Naomi hadn't heard it with her own two ears, she'd never have believed it. Becky was terrified of busy areas teeming with people. She always clung to her mother or her father for dear life when they traveled by train. She once explained to Naomi that she was afraid because she didn't know when the train was coming. Most people hear a steadily advancing rumble that tells them the train is approaching. Since she couldn't hear, she had an irrational fear that the train would arrive suddenly and run her over. Naomi tried to explain to her that it was forbidden to step beyond the yellow line regardless of whether or not one could hear, and that the train traveled only along the tracks and didn't jump up onto the platform — but nothing helped. Becky remained fearful. And now? What could frighten her more than traveling by train on her own?

"You?" Naomi asked Becky incredulously. "Alone? On the subway?"

"Please, Ima." Her eyes were fixed pleadingly on her mother's face. "It means so much to me."

If Becky was prepared to ride the subway alone, there had to be a reason.

"Alright," Naomi said slowly, "but I still want to know the reason. Becky, Ima wants to know what's bothering you, darling."

Her eyes filled with tears. Naomi sensed that she longed to reveal her secret to her but was afraid of something.

"Becky," Naomi said, embracing her protectively, "you don't have to be afraid to tell me. I won't tell anyone except Abba."

Becky's taut lips relaxed. Her eyes darted nervously all over the room and she spoke hesitantly. "The girls in my class are not so friendly with me because they know I'm deaf," she said. "In my new school, nobody will know."

Naomi was silent. Becky continued looking at her pleadingly.

"You think it's a good idea that no one should know?" Naomi asked quietly.

"I'm not sure," she said, "but I'm sure it's not a good idea that they should know."

Although her words were interlaced with pain, Naomi appreciated her daughter's intelligence. She hugged her tightly and said, "I'll discuss it with Abba and we'll decide."

Her eyes lit up. "Thank you!" she exulted. "I'm so happy."

And off she went, skipping and dancing, to play hopscotch with herself or cards with Yanky.

Naomi turned to her beloved refuge, her *sefer Tehillim*, which received her tears with loyal silence. "Please, *Ribbono shel Olam*," she prayed from the bottom of her heart, "help Rivkah *bas* Naomi Chayah find favor in the eyes of her friends and teachers. Help her do well in her studies and make friends. Make them give her a chance as an equal. Help her find acceptance. ..."

When Shlomo returned home, Naomi told him about her conversation with Becky. He listened attentively, his brow furrowed. When she finished, he sighed and then nodded.

"Alright," he said thoughtfully. "She's right that it's worth a try. Even if her friends do find out that she's deaf, she'll at least have the chance to turn over a new leaf socially."

"But don't you think it's unhealthy for her to bear such a secret?"

"Apparently, she feels it's worth it," Shlomo said. "I don't want to deprive her of the chance to conduct her experiment. If I do, she'll always be sorry that she never got to try it."

Naomi relayed Shlomo's positive response to Becky. Her eyes lit up.

"Don't worry about me, Ima," she said sweetly. "I'll study hard and be an excellent student."

"Will you?" Naomi bent down and kissed her, transmitting all her concern, love and hope, her prayers and wishes. She searched Naomi's face with her intelligent eyes.

"Why did you cry, Ima?" she asked. "Is it because you want me to be happy in school? I will be, Ima; I'm sure. I'll have lots of friends."

Naomi averted her face from her daughter.

"Don't be sad, Ima." Becky took her mother's large hand in her own small one. "Yanky says that Hashem loves children who are not regular, best. He loves them for sure! He told me his rebbe at cheder said so."

"When?"

"The boys in his class laughed at a boy they saw from the window of the school bus. He had Down syndrome. Do you know what that is?"

"Yes."

"Yanky was very angry at them. He didn't laugh, and he and three other boys yelled at the other boys."

"And what happened next?" Naomi was surprised that Yanky had never mentioned the incident. Why hadn't he shared it with her?

"The boys laughed at them too and stuck out their tongues. Yanky didn't give up. He went to the rebbe and told him the whole story, without mentioning names. Later, the rebbe explained to them all about children who are not like regular children. He told them that such children have special holy *neshamos* and that Hashem loves them very much."

"Yanky didn't tell me about it." Was there a tinge of hurt in Naomi's voice?

"Maybe he didn't want you to think that kids sometimes laugh at Mindy," Becky said simply.

Naomi had never been so shocked in her life. "What?" she asked, staring at Becky in astonishment. "What did you say, Becky?"

"Yanky's very worried," she replied, releasing some of the pent-up emotions in her little heart. "He doesn't want you to be sad because of Mindy."

Aha! Naomi recalled the conversation she had had with her father. He had told her that Yanky was shouldering the burden of his sisters. Naomi hadn't really understood him then. But now, suddenly, the curtain parted and she understood the reason for her son's unusual maturity and sense of responsibility. How much he had taken on himself! She felt a wave of weakness engulf her, and her head began to spin. Surprisingly, Becky didn't notice the change in her mother's expression. Maybe it was the excitement and happiness that accompanied her parents' positive response. She continued chattering merrily.

"Get dressed and come downstairs," Naomi instructed her. After she had left the room, Naomi leaned back against the wall and allowed the sentence to pound away inside her, over and over again.

Maybe he didn't want you to think that kids sometimes laugh at Mindy. Maybe he didn't want you to think that kids sometimes laugh at Mindy. Maybe he didn't want you to think that kids sometimes laugh at Mindy.

Stop it, Naomi scolded herself. *Put a stop to that choir.*

Yanky, my firstborn. Why did he take so much upon his young shoulders? Why did he feel responsible for me? In a general sense, something had changed in our house. Becky didn't tell me what she was going through, either. My father claimed Yanky gave her strict instructions not to. What was going on in my house? What had gotten into Yanky? How could I extricate him from the narrow place he'd gotten himself wedged into? What could I do to ease my son's burden? How could I help him if he didn't even confide in me?

Naomi raised her eyes heavenward. "Dear Father," she whispered. "You gave me the twins. You gave me the tools to raise them, these precious, holy *neshamos*. Give me the wisdom to understand and the strength to accept and raise their nonhandicapped brother too. Please, help me to help him."

"HELLO? IS THIS Naomi?"

Naomi replied in the affirmative.

"Am I disturbing you?" It was Reilly Rosen, the social worker from the hospital who had accompanied Naomi on her journey through depression. She was a warm, hearty woman who had helped a great deal — not so much emotionally as technically. She had assisted Naomi with the bureaucratic procedures related to the girls' treatment. Doctors, therapists, experts on lip reading, speech therapists – she'd been her liaison with these professionals. She helped Naomi form connections in the right places in order to help the twins' progress.

"It's Reilly, right?" Naomi wasn't absolutely sure, since they hadn't spoken for a few months.

"Yes. Naomi, I have a proposal for you."

Naomi gripped the receiver hard. "A proposal? What is it?"

"Do you know what a support group is?"

Naomi nodded, realizing a split second later how foolish the gesture was under the circumstances. "Yes."

"I've organized a support group for Orthodox mothers of deaf children with normal intelligence. Naomi, are you with me?"

"Yes." Her voice was heavy and low.

"When I first began to organize the group I thought of you. Your Becky's doing wonderfully, right? How do you feel about joining?"

"Thanks," Naomi said, biting back the words, "but it's not for me." But maybe it was for her? *Why should I reject assistance that might prove invaluable?* "Thanks for thinking of me."

"Wouldn't you like to join?" Reilly sounded suddenly hesitant.

"I'll speak to my husband about it. When can I give you an answer?"

"I'll be in my clinic at nine tomorrow morning. You know my number, right?"

"Right."

"Alright, then. Bye."

A support group? Naomi paced the house like a caged lion. *A support group?*

Stop it. Would it be good or bad? Naomi wanted someone else to decide for her: yes or no, a good idea or not a good idea. A wry smile spread across her face. *I want someone else to decide for me ... how atypical. Me, the quick decision maker, the one who couldn't stand dillydallying. I have changed over the years, like every woman and mother.*

When Shlomo came home, Naomi presented the question to him.

He furrowed his brow. "Are they Orthodox women?"

"Yes. Reilly wouldn't have suggested it to me otherwise."

"I see."

Naomi looked at him pleadingly. "What do you say? Should I go?"

"I think so," he said slowly. "What do you say?"

"Me? I keep thinking of Yanky. Maybe this will help me help him. He seems to me to be becoming more and more withdrawn lately. I davened to Hashem to help me help him, and along comes this support group. I think Hashem sent it to me for his sake."

THE GROUP OF women Naomi met the following day was diverse. There were twenty-seven women, all of them Orthodox and all of them mothers of deaf children, but there the similarity ended. During the brief period of time in which the women mingled and chatted before Reilly began her talk, Naomi discovered many differences between herself and the other women. While her daughters were six years old, one woman there had a seventeen-year-old deaf son. Another lady had a six-year-old daughter who, aside from being deaf, also had crippled legs. A third woman's son did not know how to lip read at all; he had a hearing aid.

There were other differences, too. Some women were educated professionals; others were homemakers with a high school education. Some were obviously wealthy; others were of limited means. Some were chassidic, some yeshivish. They were a motley group.

The women sat down in a circle, still somewhat uncomfortable about being there. Reilly, the instructor, introduced herself with a smile.

"It's really a bit silly and rather unnecessary, since everyone knows me," she said, "but I'll introduce myself nonetheless. My name is Reilly Rosen and I'm a social worker. I met all of you through my work in the preemie nursery of the hospital where you gave birth to your handicapped children, and it struck me that it would be a good idea to have you meet one another and help each other cope. I have six children, two of whom have asthma. I know that might sound trivial and insignificant compared to what you're dealing with, but I can tell you countless stories of hardships these children endure. I and they."

She took a deep breath and went on. "I believe that every individual faces hardships of some sort in life — some more, some less. Having a handicapped child increases the hardship of dealing with life's daily difficulties, though some would say it increases the challenge."

Reilly paused and smiled. "I think it would be nice if you each introduce yourself and tell us a little bit about your child." Reilly's eyes swept over the crowd, looking for a volunteer to go first.

A short, kerchiefed woman with soulful eyes looked up. Reilly nodded at her and she began to speak.

"My name is Malka Tova. I have twelve children, *bli ayin hara*. Meshulam, my deaf son, is my third. When he was born I was a young woman who knew nothing about dealing with a handicap. Everyone in my family was perfectly healthy and normal; everyone, including me, fit the same mold. I wasn't the type to think deeply about things, certainly not exalted concepts such as *Hakadosh Baruch Hu* or the purpose of creation."

Naomi stared at her in surprise. Had she "misdiagnosed" her? As a psychologist, Naomi was fairly good at reading people's faces, and she had never seen such soulful eyes in her life.

"And then Meshulam was born. He was born perfectly healthy. He was a regular child who developed beautifully — until he came down with meningitis. He was only a year old and he was very sick. *Baruch Hashem*, Meshulam got better, but then we learned what the disease had done to him. Both of Meshulam's ears were affected and he was now completely deaf."

Malka Tova fell silent for a moment. The memories were so close, so tangible. Her breath caught in her throat.

"I reacted to the news with complete shock. I didn't know what to do. A hurricane had struck my peaceful home and I was afraid.

I was afraid it wouldn't hold up, wouldn't weather the storm. I had two other children at home, a three-and-a-half-year-old and a two-year-old, and I was coming home with a serious problem I couldn't see the end of. I knew for sure that I would do everything possible to help my son progress, but I hadn't the faintest idea how to go about it. I felt as though something was gripping me in its claws, tearing me away from everything I knew and loved and leaving me exposed to the merciless wind in just a light summer dress, trembling with cold and utterly helpless. Before I went home from the hospital with Meshulam, I gave birth to my fourth child.

"That was my breaking point. I hadn't had the chance to recover from the reeling blow I'd been dealt and here I was in a weakened state after birth, knowing I had four little children to care for, one of them deaf. What do I do? How? Why?

"Over and over again I asked myself: Why did this happen to me? And over and over again I replied: Because that's what Hashem wanted.

"To my dismay, I saw that the answer didn't make me feel better. What was I, an atheist? Didn't I believe in Hashem? I rebuked myself severely: everything is preordained; everything is from *Shamayim*. I didn't expect myself to be happy; you have to be on a very lofty level to accept hardship with love and joy, but I did think that telling myself everything was from *Shamayim* ought to have calmed the storm in my heart somewhat.

"'Everything is from Hashem,' I murmured to myself over and over again. But why me? And why is that answer not enough for me?

"And then I had a flash of insight. I understood that if a person fails to see Hashem in everything throughout his life, he has a hard time accepting a real *nisayon* with true faith that everything is for the best. True *emunah* is not engendered spontaneously at the time of a test. It's true that you get special strength from *Shamayim*, but a person has to live with *emunah* all his life. When you live with faith you feel protected, enveloped with love and mercy, and you understand that everything is from Hashem and everything is for the good. When the blow is dealt, you understand that it is from your loving Father. Nachum Ish Gamzu said '*gam zu letovah*' all the time, not just when he saw that the treasure he was supposed to give the king had been stolen."

Her eyes swept over our faces, and she suddenly seemed a bit shy. "I'm sorry, Reilly," she said. "I didn't mean to take up so much time."

"Go on," Reilly requested. "Please, Malka Tova, go on."

"I can't say I'm glad about what happened, G-d forbid. I feel Meshulam's pain and try my best to cushion him. But since then, I feel connected to Hashem. I feel that 'the King has brought me to His chambers.' I feel Hashem's true love every step of the way. My life has changed as a result of this challenge, changed for the good.

"Some people tell me, 'So you chose to cope rather than collapse.' I say I chose to rise, to ascend, to move upward and forward rather than to stay in the same place. And as the mother of such a child, who I know has a special *neshamah*, I feel I have a special privilege. This dear, pure child helps me achieve goals I would never reach on my own: meaningful prayer, a powerful bond with Hashem, and love, indescribable love."

When Malka Tova finished speaking, one could have heard a pin drop. She was a very dynamic woman. Naomi wondered if she managed to imbue her strong *emunah* into her children and others who came in contact with her. Naomi wondered if she had a career and if so, what it was. She wondered to what extent Malka Tova utilized her potential to inspire others.

"I have a problem on my hands now because of you," Reilly said to her with a broad smile after five minutes of silence.

Malka Tova looked flustered. "What's the matter?"

"Usually, everyone feels a bit shy about opening up to a bunch of strangers, but one brave woman volunteers to speak first and then everyone else finds it easier to follow suit. I appreciate that you volunteered to be the first to introduce yourself, but you spoke so powerfully that no one wants to speak after you."

Malka Tova blushed. "I'm sorry," she murmured.

Reilly's eyes swept over the group again. "Does anyone volunteer to go next?"

"I'll introduce myself," Naomi offered. She told the group a little bit about Becky and Mindy. She related that she learned they were deaf shortly after they were born but that she didn't know about Mindy's additional problem until she was three years old.

Reilly thanked Naomi. Her words weren't as electrifying as Malka Tova's. Then, one by one, the other women told their stories. Some mothers had two or three deaf children. Everyone identified with everyone else, and it was a good, pleasant feeling to be with others who were familiar with what each woman was going through.

"The most difficult thing for me," said a woman who had given birth to a deaf little girl four months previously, "is the reaction of my other children. My oldest son refuses to accept it. He insists the doctors have made a mistake and we'll see that the baby really can hear. My younger son cries all day, and my seven-year-old daughter doesn't stop asking questions."

"My parents refused to accept Shainy," another woman said, a pained expression on her face. "They couldn't accept that a grandchild of theirs was different from everyone else. My father kept calling me with names of different specialists who he felt sure would prove the doctors' diagnosis wrong. My mother couldn't bring herself to look at the child."

At first the women were shy and hesitant with one another, but gradually the stories began to flow. Real-life scenes were related with pain and anguish, on the one hand, but with optimism and hope on the other.

"I have a problem with my son," one woman said. "He's the second in the family. My oldest is a girl, then comes Yossi, then two more boys, two girls, and then Kreindy, who is deaf. Yossi is already ten years old, and he really ought to be helping out in the house a lot more than he does. He always wriggles out of his responsibilities, especially the ones involving Kreindy. Kreindy's only three and she needs lots of help in every area. The kids take turns helping her with the homework her speech therapist assigns her, and they really take pride in her progress. They also help out every time we travel with Kreindy to treatment sessions or to specialists all across the country.

"'Ima, don't worry,' my daughter once told me. 'Any time you think someone might be able to help Kreindy — go. Don't hesitate. We manage just fine.' And it's true. Everyone pitches in and helps, except for Yossi.

"Yossi comes home late from cheder and hurries out to play with his friends. He comes home to eat and sleep, that's it. Even his meals are wolfed down really quickly. I get the impression that he does his best to avoid spending time at home, especially when Kreindy's awake. When he comes in, the first thing he asks is, 'Where's Kreindy?' When he hears she's sleeping or that she isn't home, his face lights up. It hurts me, because they're both my children. It's hard for me to see such discord between two of my children."

"Your son is simply afraid," Reilly said. "He's afraid to become involved; he doesn't think he'll be able to handle it. He sees Kreindy as a threat to the peaceful home he dreams of, so he prefers to stay away, where he can pretend his house is normal, rather than to be home with reality staring him in the face. Of course he prefers to have her sleep when he's home — that way he can erase her from his consciousness. It's hard for him to digest the change that has taken place at home, and he's afraid you're going to saddle him with a burden he feels unready to accept."

"But I've never asked anything of him," the woman interrupted. "I see that he doesn't like to help at home, so I try to give him as few jobs as possible at home and send him on errands outside the house instead."

"Could it be that his older sister demands from him things he can't live up to?" Reilly asked.

The woman thought for a moment. Naomi's eyes swept over all the women in the group as she did. Some women were attentive and empathetic; some seemed pained and withdrawn. Some were smiling in understanding and some were nodding sympathetically. There was only one woman who seemed indifferent to someone else's pain. Most really cared, and Naomi suddenly felt proud to belong to the group.

She mentally renamed the group "the Department of Mothers of Handicapped Children." It was a different type of motherhood — more accepting, more loving, more hardworking than the regular kind. It softened and improved one's *middos* and contributed to the shaping of one's personality. As Malka Tova said, a person changes when he experiences a difficult *nisayon*. A window opens in his heart to other people, to different people. He gains new understanding, new acceptance, new capabilities.

Naomi noticed one woman who seemed to be itching to speak. Toward the end of Yossi's and Kreindy's mother's talk, she began leaning forward impatiently. When Yossi and Kreindy's mother paused to think for a moment, the other woman blurted out, "My problem is just the opposite. I have nine children, *bli ayin hara*, and it's my seventh who is deaf. My second child takes everything upon himself. He bears his sister's *tzarah* in a most incredible fashion. He feels it's his responsibility to see to it that she succeeds. And he never allows himself to fail. He once got a 91 on a Gemara test and he ate himself up with grief. He begged his *melamed* to let him take a retest, even though his was the highest mark in the class. He insists on being an overachiever; he doesn't allow himself any slack. I see the tension and pressure he's under, the way he's tearing himself apart, and I try to stop him from being that way, but I can't change his nature."

"Tell me," Reilly said to the woman, "how do you feel about success? About excellence?"

"What do you mean? I like to succeed and excel, of course."

"How important is it to you that your children excel?"

"Very important."

"What do you say to a child when he fails?"

She hesitated. "I don't remember exactly. Maybe that he'll do better next time, or something like that."

"Well," Reilly said quietly, "children absorb what's important to their parents. Your son wants subconsciously to compensate you for your troubles. He's trying to give you what seems to him to be the most important thing to you. There must be an emphasis on excellence in your home if that's the way your son is trying to give you *nachas*."

Reilly paused as the woman pondered the social worker's words silently. "I'm not one hundred percent certain I'm correct," Reilly went on, "but if I were you, I'd take that child for evaluation. Consult a psychologist. It's not healthy for a child's development for him to bear such a heavy burden."

"And what can be done?"

"There are lots of things that can be done. Tell him about your failures, teach him that it's okay to make mistakes and alright to fail, that we're human beings with human weaknesses and limited abilities. Send him the message that success is not everything."

Here Reilly stopped speaking directly to the woman and looked at everyone. "In general, dear mothers, the need for excellence is the scourge of this generation. Raise children who are happy, not achievers! Why should little girls cry about grades that aren't high enough? Why should a child with little scholastic potential be rejected socially? Why should a boy be afraid to show his father a test he didn't do well on? Children are not born to feel scholastic pressure. It is us parents and teachers who are responsible. Why don't you think about that, while we hear from our next mother?"

The woman's words pounded relentlessly in Naomi's brain. *My second child takes everything on himself. He bears his sister's tzarah in a most incredible fashion. He feels it's his responsibility to see to it that she succeeds. He demands the most from himself, with no compromises or shortcuts. I see the tension and pressure he's under, the way he's tearing himself apart, and I try to stop him from being that way, but I can't change his nature.*

That's my Yanky. True, not everything the woman described was mirrored in Yanky's behavior — Yanky never put that great an emphasis on success — but the general picture, the general picture is so similar. Yanky not letting Becky tell me things that would cause me pain. Yanky worried. Yanky tense. Yanky clamping his lips together and remaining silent. Yanky refraining from playing with his friends in order to play with Becky.

Dear G-d in heaven! What can I do to stop it? Until recently, Naomi saw these phenomena as separate and unconnected, but now this woman came and bound it all together. Everything came together like puzzle pieces forming a complete picture: Yanky was bearing a burden too heavy for his young shoulders.

"I have a similar situation at home," Naomi found herself telling Reilly before she could ask another woman to introduce herself. "But my son, Yanky, doesn't set so much store on excellence."

Reilly's pleasant smile broadened. "Of course not. Not everyone considers success to be of the utmost importance. The question is what you find extremely important."

Naomi thought for a moment. "My children's happiness," she said with conviction.

"And do you think they aren't happy?" Reilly asked.

She didn't reply. Were her children happy? "Becky certainly isn't happy, nor is Mindy."

"So," Reilly said slowly, "your Yanky wants to make Becky happy. Understand, dear mothers: Your children absorb whatever message you impart. If you send them the message that your deaf children are to be pitied, that's the way they will feel, and there's a good chance that's what they will be. If you send them the message that they are regular people, that they have a minor problem that can be overcome, that their lives are wonderful — that's what they will believe and feel."

"Messages?" one mother wondered aloud. "How do we send them messages?"

"You transmit whatever it is you really feel, even if you tell your children differently," Reilly explained with a smile.

"That's a real problem," Naomi said heavily.

All eyes turned to her. "Why?" someone asked.

"I don't know about you," Naomi said candidly, "but I feel my children aren't happy, that they're suffering. So how can I send my children a message I don't believe is true?"

"If you work on developing a sense of inner joy," Reilly said, "your dream will come true. You'll achieve what's most important to you in life."

"You mean ..."

"If you're happy, Naomi, your children will be, too."

19

Naomi returned home from the meeting with Reilly with mixed feelings. On the one hand she was confused, scared, lost. She felt she had made a fateful mistake and caused her children — both Becky and Yanky — unnecessary suffering. She didn't know what to think about Mindy.

On the other hand, Naomi was overjoyed. It was as if someone had removed a blindfold from her eyes and she could suddenly see *Hakadosh Baruch Hu's* world spread out before her, with the clear understanding that everything was from Him and that He was at her side always. Once, five years ago, on a day when she'd felt the world was coming to an end, Shlomo had told her something similar. Her fear for the children's future abated then too, but the pain hadn't gone away; it had continued eating away at her insides. Today, listening to Malka Tova talk about coping with adversity, Naomi's world was illuminated.

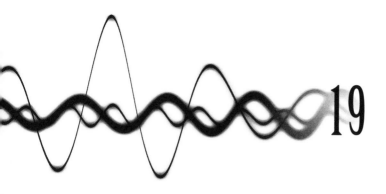

Many people had spoken to her about Hashem's love. After the twins' birth, Naomi went through lots of ups and downs, and Shlomo was always there to encourage her. Her father told her Hashem loved her; her mother hinted gently; even Shaindy, her wonderful cousin, said the same thing. Every time Shlomo spoke to Naomi, a little corner of the dark room she felt she was in was illuminated — but it was with Malka Tova's words that the entire room became flooded with light. So many people had spoken and hinted and explained, but now she finally understood it for herself.

Naomi knew she could do something about the situation; the damage she had caused wasn't irreversible. She returned home determined to change everything. No one would think her children were to be pitied if she didn't think so herself. By the time Naomi arrived home, she was happy and optimistic. Her fear and confusion had disappeared, and she was clear on what she was going to do.

"How was it?" Shlomo asked as he tried to feed Sari. "Was it worth going?"

Naomi's eyes shone. "Definitely," she told him. "I'll tell you about it later."

"Zoom," Shlomo called to Sari, who had sealed her lips firmly. "Look, an airplane!"

Sari smiled, making sure to keep her mouth closed. Naomi chuckled and tickled her under her chin. Sari laughed, but her lips remained clamped together.

"You'll tell me about it?" Shlomo asked, raising his eyes from the spoonful of yogurt for just a moment. Sari batted it out of his hand and onto the floor.

"*Im yirtzeh Hashem.*"

Naomi owed it to him. She was eager to impart her feelings and the new understanding that had finally taken root in her mind after six years of struggling.

In the evening, Shlomo and Naomi spoke for a long time. It was the first time Naomi spoke about Becky and Mindy without crying. Shlomo's eyes shone with joy. "I don't think you caused all that much damage as you seem to think, but even if you went just for yourself, for your own happiness, I thank Hashem for having sent you there."

They discussed strategies for putting Naomi's decision into action, and she went to sleep feeling calm and content.

"Yanky," Naomi said to her oldest son, her little tzaddik, the following morning. "How do you feel about taking a trip to Sabba and Savta?"

"When?" he asked matter-of-factly, unaware of which Sabba and Savta his mother was referring to.

"Maybe in two days from now, maybe in a week we'll see when things work out."

"But Sabba said he was coming to us the day after tomorrow," Yanky said logically. "Why should I go to him?"

Naomi took a deep breath and looked into his eyes. "No, not Sabba and Savta Katz. Sabba and Savta Mandel."

"What?" Thoroughly taken aback, he tried to figure out what she meant. "Where are they coming?"

"They're not coming anywhere. Don't you want to visit them?"

"In Eretz Yisrael?" He was incredulous. "Our family? In Eretz Yisrael? When? Oh boy!" The furrows in his brow, so unusual in a child his age, smoothed out as he grinned broadly. "Why didn't you tell us?"

"I'm telling you now," Naomi said with a smile. "But it's not 'the family' — it's you."

"Me?" His voice rose an octave. "Me? Alone? To Eretz Yisrael?"

"No, not alone. You and me."

"The two of us?" His eyes lit up for a minute, then grew dark. "What about the girls?"

"Which ones?" Naomi asked innocently.

"*Nu*, Becky, Mindy, Sari?"

"Maybe we'll take Sari along; I haven't decided yet. But Becky and Mindy will stay with Sabba and Savta Katz."

"We'll go without Becky?" Yanky said, taken aback.

"Do you want the girls to come along?"

"Not Mindy," he said with rare candor, "but I'd love for Becky to come with us."

"Why?"

"Because we're friends and we'll have fun together."

"Your summer vacation starts soon," Naomi said, "so we'll be able to go together. We'll go toward the end of vacation and return shortly before Rosh Hashanah."

"With Becky?"

"No."

"What a shame."

"Why is it so important to you that she come along?"

He looked at Naomi in astonishment. "Ima, you already asked me that," he said gently. "And I told you that I want her to have fun and that we enjoy being together."

"You want her to have a good time?"

"Yes and besides, how will Becky manage on her own here? She's starting a new school soon, with new friends. I think it would be best if I'm here when she starts the new school year."

"No," Naomi said firmly. "It doesn't work out with the dates."

The fire had gone out of his eyes. "Well then, I think the best thing is if I don't go."

"Really?" Naomi looked at him lovingly. "Why?"

"Because Becky doesn't have a lot of friends. I'm her only friend."

"But she's starting a new school now and we hope she will have new friends, even lots of them."

"And what if she doesn't?" His eyes were troubled.

"Let's hope for the best," she said calmly. "Becky can handle it on her own. She'll manage. It'll be okay."

"Maybe," he said, leaving the room.

Naomi knew what he was thinking: *Who will greet my sister when she comes home, broken and defeated, from her new school? Who will console her and soothe her hurt feelings when the girls laugh at her?*

The answer was: He would.

And that was what Naomi wanted to prevent. Becky was about to cope with one of the most significant situations in her life. Naomi didn't want the person at her side during those moments, be they difficult, exciting or happy, to be a nine-year-old child bearing a burden too heavy for his narrow shoulders. She had to separate Yanky from his sister, and this was the best way to do that.

If Becky was forced to give up her dependence upon her brother when she needed him badly, it would be easier later on. And the same was true for Yanky: If he detached himself from his deep concern for his sister's welfare when she was going through a rough time, he'd find it easier to do so later.

At least Naomi hoped so. She knew that Yanky would pace the floor like a sleepwalker during those few days, that he'd ask to not go to Eretz Yisrael, that he'd plead to remain in New York, even though a trip to Eretz Yisrael was a dream-come-true — so as not to leave Becky alone. But Naomi would see that he would go, and they would manage — each on his own.

Halevai!

In the end, Yanky and Naomi flew to Eretz Yisrael together. Yanky had kicked up quite a fuss, arguing, crying and pleading that Becky should be allowed to come along or that he should stay home, but Shlomo and Naomi remained firm.

"You can choose who you want to go with," Shlomo said to Yanky with a smile. "Ima or me. But Becky stays home. She'll be starting school in the middle of your trip and she can't miss school."

"But my school year's starting too," Yanky said.

"Yes, but you'll be missing only two days and Becky would miss a week. Besides, Becky's starting first grade in a new school, so it's more important for her to start on time than it is for you."

"I don't see the difference," Yanky argued.

Naomi didn't recognize him. Her gentle, quiet, obedient child had never rebelled like this before. He argued and screamed and wept real tears. It was only then that Naomi realized the extent of his sister's dependence on him.

"I won't go!" he shouted. "I won't!"

"And what will you tell Sabba and Savta Mandel? They're waiting for you," Shlomo said patiently.

"Let them invite Becky, too."

"They did," Naomi hurried to explain. All she needed was for him to blame his grandparents. She didn't want him showing up at their house with a sour face.

"So what happened?"

"We don't want Becky to go, period. I don't know why you're arguing with Ima," his father scolded him.

"There's nothing to discuss," Naomi told him on a different occasion, "and that's no way to talk to Abba."

At the beginning of the airplane flight, Yanky sat rigidly in his seat, his muscles tense, but gradually he relaxed. Naomi utilized the long trip to talk to him about what was going on in his life. They discussed his friends and his class, and eventually the conversation turned to Becky and Mindy.

"Becky has a hard life," Yanky said, explaining his position on his sister's situation for the first time in his life. "I want her to be as happy as possible."

"And you are responsible for her happiness?"

"Who then?" Yanky raised his eyes to search his mother's face. His gaze was so mature, so responsible and intelligent that it took Naomi's breath away. "Becky needs me. I'm her only friend."

"*Im yirtzeh Hashem*," Naomi said quietly, "she'll have lots of friends this year."

"A brother is more than just a friend," Yanky said.

Naomi looked at him. "So is a mother," she said quietly, almost inaudibly.

He did not respond. He turned to look out the window at the fluffy clouds below us. When he returned his gaze to Naomi, his eyes were filled with tears. "Ima," he whispered, "you said to Abba ..."

Naomi held her breath and struggled mightily to maintain a look of calm composure on my face. "What?"

"You once told Abba that Becky is completely detached from society, that she's lonely, that she has no one, not a single friend, not a single child her age to play with."

The exact quotation proved how deeply Naomi's words had penetrated her son's heart.

"You said to him, 'How much longer can she go on this way? We must do something!' And then Abba said, 'She has Yanky.' And you said, 'Yanky's her brother; he can't take the place of a friend.' And Abba said, 'Yanky is excellent company for her. Thank G-d for Yanky. He's so sensitive, so understanding and responsible.'"

He fell silent, breathing heavily as if he'd just removed a heavy sack of stones from his back. Naomi was too shocked to react. What a huge responsibility her son had borne on his shoulders all this time, without confiding in anyone!

"Yanky, my dear, dear boy," Naomi said, praying silently to Hashem to put the right words in her mouth, "you must accept that there are some things you're too young to understand. Even if you hear Abba and me talking about something, and you think you understand what we're saying, you're not always right. Or rather, it's very likely you're wrong."

"Wrong?" He looked at his mother in surprise, objection written all over his face. "How can I be wrong? I mean, I speak English."

"Yanky, adults have a language of their own. They have concepts you aren't capable of understanding. Even if Abba said it's a good thing you're Becky's friend, he didn't mean it the way you understood it. He definitely did not intend for you not to play with the boys in your class after school because you have to play with Becky."

Naomi saw his eyes open wide with astonishment at this information. "Neither Abba nor I wanted you to think that you're like her mother, that it's up to you to do everything in your power to make her happy."

"But if I didn't do that," Yanky insisted, "you would be sad, too."

"Parents can accept things more easily than children," Naomi said softly. "A mother is sad when her children are sad, but she absolutely cannot accept that they shouldn't tell her when and why they're sad. Do you see? If a mother were to know that her child is sad and she doesn't know about it, she'd be the saddest ever, do you understand, dear boy?" Naomi held his hand in hers and looked deep into his eyes. "Do you understand?"

He was silent.

"Becky can be friends with other girls," Naomi said encouragingly. "She's starting a new school this year, and with Hashem's help she'll have lots of new friends. We'll tell her she can do it, right? We'll tell her together. We won't tell her, 'You poor thing; you're deaf; you have no friends.' We'll tell her, 'You're smart; you can do it; you'll have lots of friends.' That will be more helpful, won't it?"

Yanky nodded silently.

"We'll do it together, okay?" Naomi whispered. "And promise me that you'll never, ever hide it from me that you're sad, okay?"

He nodded. His eyes closed and he fell asleep. A leftover tear made its way down his cheek. Naomi raised her eyes Heavenward. "Thank you, dear Father," she whispered, "for this wonderful child."

Everything went smoothly at the orientation party. Becky was thrilled with her parents' decision to send her to a school outside the neighborhood. Although Naomi's attempts to arrange for steady transportation hadn't panned out, Shlomo had agreed to make the hour's drive with Becky every day.

At the orientation party, Becky sat in her place, tense as a tightly coiled spring. The teacher, who was the only one the Mandels had let in on the secret, made sure to face Becky the entire time. Becky moved her head from side to side, trying to absorb everything and make sure she missed nothing. She didn't initiate a conversation with anyone; she just sat quietly and listened, in her own way, to the girls' excited chatter.

The next day, Becky went to school with a knot the size of a tennis ball in her stomach. The first-grade classrooms were situated on the second floor. The previous day, at the orientation party, Becky had memorized the route she had to take to get to her classroom, so she wouldn't have to ask anyone for help.

She was the third girl to arrive in the classroom. She placed her briefcase next to the seat she'd been assigned at the orientation: the first in the middle row. The teacher had assigned the seats, and she had tried to make things as easy as possible for her deaf student.

"My name's Becky," Becky said to the two girls who had arrived before her. One of them, a fair-complexioned girl with blue eyes, smiled shyly. "I'm Leah."

"And I'm Miriam," said the other girl. "Leah and I are neighbors. Your voice sounds a little funny, did you know that?"

"Yes," Becky said. "I know."

"How come?"

"That's my voice."

"Which preschool were you in?"

"My teacher's name was Morah Devorah. Do you know that school?"

"Is it in our neighborhood?"

"No, not at all. It's very far from here."

"And there are no elementary schools closer to where you live?"

"There are," Becky said, keeping her cool, "but I wanted to go to this school."

"Why?"

"Just because. Do you know how to play hopscotch?"

"Of course," Miriam crowed, withdrawing a smooth stone from her pocket. "Come, let's mark off a spot in the backyard for ourselves so no one else will catch it. My big sister says that the second-graders always fight with the first-graders over the space in the backyard. They think they're so big. My sister's ten times bigger than them; she's in seventh grade already."

"Wow, you have such a big sister?" Becky marveled. "That must be fun."

Miriam glowed with pride. "How old is the oldest in your family?"

"My brother Yanky. He's only nine. Then comes me, and I have a twin sister. She goes to a different school. And I also have a little sister who's two."

"You have a twin?" both girls asked enviously. "We always wish we could be twins," Leah admitted. Her bashfulness was in sharp contrast to her friend's nonstop chatter.

"That's right," Miriam said in confirmation. "But we don't have twin bothers or sisters. And you're a twin yourself! Is it fun being a twin? Which school does your twin go to?"

Here was an obstacle. Becky didn't want to tell the girls about Mindy's problem, but she didn't want to lie either.

"It's fun being a twin," she said, responding to the non-problematic part of Miriam's question. "My sister goes to a different school. I travel a long way to come here."

"So that's why you came to this school," Miriam said triumphantly. "My mother always says it's not a good idea for twins to be in the same school."

Becky did not deny it. "Wanna play hopscotch? I have colored chalk."

"Oooh!" Miriam and Leah enthused. "Which colors?"

"Purple and yellow. Race you to the backyard!"

The three tore down the corridor, Becky's tension dissipating a bit.

After Becky met and conversed with a number of girls, her self-confidence rose a notch. She was a super hopscotch player, and her friends had admired her colored chalk. She had argued heatedly with some second-graders and secured a section of the yard for her classmates, an impressive achievement by all counts. Becky chalked up mentally her score for the day: one hundred percent success, zero setbacks.

In class, they began to learn the letters. Becky chuckled to herself and whispered to Toby, the girl sitting next to her, that she could read already.

"Really?" Toby was skeptical.

"What did you say, Becky?" the teacher asked.

Becky told her.

"You know how to read?" the teacher asked admiringly. "What a big girl you are! Come read what I wrote on the board."

Becky read what the teacher wrote without any difficulty. The teacher wrote another sentence, longer and more complex, and Becky read this fluently as well. The girls looked on, open-mouthed.

When Becky had finished reading an entire children's book aloud with no mistakes, the teacher declared, "Becky you don't belong in first grade. You ought to skip straight to second grade!"

The teacher was glad to have the opportunity to praise Becky in front of the class. She hoped that would help her gain acceptance and popularity. The child glowed with pleasure, and the rest of the class looked at her admiringly.

"You would all do very well to be Becky's friend," the teacher said. "She can help you be good students."

Then the teacher distributed stencils and instructed the girls to color them. She walked up and down the rows of seats and showed everyone how to color perfectly within the lines. When she passed Becky's desk she stopped and said admiringly, "Here's a very special notebook I can show you all as an example. This is a girl that knows how to color beautifully!" And she lifted Becky's notebook and showed it to the entire class.

"You see? This is the way coloring should be done."

At recess, everyone crowded around her. "Becky, color my picture, too," "Becky, draw me a shofar," "Becky, what letter comes after *lamed*?" "Becky, how do you write '*Shanah Tovah*'?" "Becky, can you show me how to write a W?" "Becky ..."

Becky's eyes shone with joy. "Wait a minute," she said, laughing. "I can't hear this way."

She uttered the sentence with complete naturalness, and it was accepted that way as well. Becky giggled inwardly. She made sure every time to read the lips of the girl who was speaking to her. It was rather easy because she had told her friends she couldn't hear two girls at once. First-graders tend to use lots of body language, and Becky's friends tugged at her hand when she didn't turn around immediately when they called her, helping her greatly.

All the girls in her class were friendly with her. With her natural leadership ability, Becky became the most popular girl in the class within three days. She was charming and friendly, played with everyone equally and gave up her place in line to girls who were "out." She read them long stories from thick books and drew beautiful pictures for anyone who asked. A crowd of admirers followed her wherever she went. There was only one thing Becky still needed: a true, close friend.

20

"I hear my first-grader travels a full hour to school every day," Sabba said, hugging her tightly. "Is that right, little flower?"

"Yes," Becky said, delighted to see Sabba. "I wanted to go to a school where no one knew I was deaf, and I was right, because everyone is my friend."

"And you're managing to keep it a secret?" Sabba asked worriedly.

Becky nodded, her eyes twinkling with pleasure. "So far no one knows anything. I try really hard to lipread fast, and whenever anyone talks to me, I turn my head in order to hear."

"And no one ever called your name and you didn't hear?"

"I think it must have happened," Becky said, thinking aloud, "but Toby always pulls my sleeve and says, 'Hey Becky, don't you hear someone calling you?' It happened a few times already."

"And Toby doesn't suspect anything?"

"No."

"And Abba takes you to school every day? He drives a full hour to bring you to the school you wanted? That's very nice of him."

"He understood that it was important to me," Becky replied earnestly. "And he even told me I was right."

"I think I have a solution to the transportation problem," Sabba said to Shlomo, who walked into the house just then and began throwing little Sari up into the air.

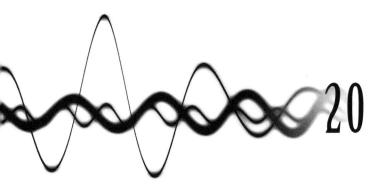

"Hello," Shlomo said to Sabba. "How are you?"

"I hear you drive Becky to school every day and that it takes you an hour to get there. I think I have a solution."

"We're looking for a solution," Shlomo admitted. "Do you know someone who travels to that neighborhood?"

"As a matter of fact, I do," Sabba said, chuckling. "His name is Meir Katz."

"You?" Becky, whose head had been swiveling from her grandfather to her father in order not to miss a word, embraced her grandfather lovingly. "Yes, yes! Sabba, you drive me to school!"

"You're hurting my feelings," Shlomo said with a smile. "Thank you very much for the offer, *shver*, but I think it would be too great an imposition."

Becky didn't like it when conversations took such a turn. "Too great an imposition," and "if it's not too difficult," and "I don't want to trouble you." Such polite, formal words! If Sabba didn't want to take her, he wouldn't offer. And it was hard for Abba to take her. Why should he refuse?

She was silent, because it was forbidden to say differently from Abba, but in her heart she hoped Sabba would insist. And he did.

"Shlomo," Sabba said, "I'm happy to help out however I can. I'm an old man; I can't even concentrate on my learning for many hours at a time. You're an *avreich* whose every free minute is utilized for Torah study. I'd be glad to do it, really."

And so it was settled. Sabba began driving Becky to school every morning. If Becky had known that this was the way things would turn out, she'd have asked to attend the faraway school just for this. It was so lovely! Sabba told her stories, and she confided in him the hardships she had endured in preschool. It was okay to tell Sabba — even Yanky, who had warned her not to tell Ima, had said so. Sabba bought her nosh and never told Ima if she ate more than two sweets at a time.

In school, everything went smoothly. Becky woke up each morning joyfully and went to sleep with a smile on her lips. The sun shone and illuminated the darkest corners of her heart, and her self-confidence blossomed. Sometimes she wondered why she'd ever been afraid of society — what was there to be scared about? She was grateful for every day that passed without her secret being revealed.

The teacher helped her all the time; she tapped Becky on the shoulder whenever someone called her, or, if she couldn't do that, she signaled her with her eyes. She spoke slowly and carefully and, most important of all, she praised Becky in front of her friends every day. She told them what a good student Becky was, how hardworking and bright; she extolled her *middos*, stressing that they ought to learn from her how to share and be patient with others; and she publicly admired Becky's artwork. Everything she said was true. She also awarded Becky the "Best of the Day" prize at least once a week.

Becky was thrilled. Thrilled! She had never been so happy in her life.

Naomi was enormously relieved. She saw her daughter's shining eyes and never stopped praying. Although Becky had never told her what had transpired in preschool, unhappiness had been reflected in her green eyes and her face had worn a perpetually pained expression. Becky had had a hard time in preschool; there was no doubt about that. But in first grade? Her decision proved to have been very wise. In school Becky was happy and Naomi, who knew how transient happiness could be, prayed constantly.

"*Ribbono shel Olam*," she pleaded, "we've suffered so much with this child. She herself has suffered so much, being rejected by her peers through no fault of her own. She's so happy now. Please, let it always be this way. Grant her a happy life."

"IMA," BECKY CALLED as she walked in the door. "Look, I have a list of after-school programs to choose from."

"Great." Naomi was pleased to see her daughter so enthusiastic. "Let me have a look."

Becky handed me a brightly colored flyer adorned with drawings made by the teacher of the art class. "Which class do you think I should take?" she asked.

"Hmmm. That's your decision."

"Of course."

"Aren't you hungry?" Naomi needed time to gather her strength for the scene she knew would be played out in the next few moments. She knew she couldn't distract Becky for longer than a few moments. She was sure to raise the subject of after-school classes again and again until the matter was resolved, but in the meantime Naomi could think what to say.

"Yes, a bit. But Ima!"

"Come eat first," Naomi said, setting a bowl of vegetable soup on the table along with a slice of buttered bread.

Becky washed her hands and sat down near her mother.

"*Nu*, did you read it?"

Naomi nodded. "Did you?"

"Me? A hundred times."

"And have you decided which class you want to take?" Naomi berated herself for asking the question, but her defense was that it was unavoidable.

"Yes." Unable to control her excitement, Becky hadn't yet touched her food. "I know. I want to take portable organ lessons."

"What?" The spoon of soup Naomi had been holding flew out of her hand, hitting the bowl with a clatter and spraying soup all over.

"Portable organ. I want to learn to play." Her eyes were full of innocence. Naomi sighed deeply. She had been bracing herself for Becky's pain over the fact that most of the classes on the list were not viable options for her. She had been planning to speak to her at length about her special mission in this world. She had been expecting questions filled with pain and distress — but this? That Becky would be so unaware of her own situation? That she should think she could learn to play a musical instrument? Naomi hadn't considered such a scenario, and she was greatly surprised. Becky was usually very realistic and down-to-earth.

"Becky," Naomi hesitated. How could she explain without undermining Becky's confidence in what she could do? "Do you realize that it will be hard for you?"

"Why?"

"Because you won't be able to hear what you're playing."

"So what? You play according to notes."

"And how will you hear if you make a mistake?"

"Yanky will tell me."

"Yanky doesn't have that much time, sweetie. He comes home late from cheder, and then he needs to relax a little, to play and read and just be by himself after being away from home all day."

"So maybe Sari?"

"Becky, Sari's two years old!"

"Mindy," she said bitterly. "Mindy will tell me."

Naomi swallowed. "Becky, listen to me," she said softly. "There are other classes. How about gymnastics?"

"Ugh." She grimaced. "I hate gymnastics."

"What about arts and crafts?"

"I don't know."

"Here, look. Art. You love to draw." In art class, Becky could read lips the way she did in school, and most of the class required the use of the hands and the eyes, not the ears. And Becky drew exceptionally well. Naomi couldn't understand why she was resisting. She examined the flyer closely and read aloud: "Portable Organ, Flute, Guitar, Art, Oil Painting, Arts and Crafts, Sewing, Drama, Singing, Dance."

Becky hated sewing, so that was out.

"All my friends are going to take organ," Becky said angrily. Naomi was glad about the "all my friends" part and knew she could handle this small obstacle. Becky's life was full of *nisyonos*, challenges and tests. She had solved her social difficulties by herself in the best way possible. Now she had friends, and it was up to her mother to help her out with this far more trivial problem.

"But Becky ..."

"Oh, alright," Becky said, glancing at the flyer again. She raised her head. "I'll go to dance."

May Hashem protect us, Naomi thought. *Out of the frying pan, into the fire. In the music class she might manage somehow, but dance? How will she hear the music? Will we have to spend hours practicing again in front of a clock until she gets the rhythm right? There are a thousand things more important for her to do with her time.*

"Do you remember the Chanukah party in school last year?" Naomi asked carefully.

Becky's eyes filled with tears. It was a painful memory.

"Yes," she whispered tearfully.

"You don't want to go through that again, do you?" Naomi stroked her cheek.

"No."

"So think what else on this list interests you."

"Drama."

Becky was great at that. She imitated people's facial expressions to a tee. She couldn't imitate people's voices or manner of speech because she had never heard them. She had an inborn talent for drama, but she'd never been able to develop it because of her condition. What a shame. Naomi too had been good at drama as a child. Becky had inherited her mother's talent, but not her ability. Her talent would be lost in the sea of her inability.

"Drama?" Naomi thought aloud. Becky's eyes looked at her pleadingly.

Oh, my dear child, what wouldn't I do so that you could play the organ, dance to a beat, listen and understand? "Okay, we'll see. I'll speak to the instructor of the class, and we'll see what she says."

Becky suddenly burst into tears. Naomi stared at her in helpless astonishment. "Becky, what's wrong?"

"Why?" she wept. "How come with everything I want to do you have to ask if someone agrees? Why can't I be like everyone else and go to the class without asking anyone first?"

It was getting late and Naomi had to go to her clinic. "Becky," she promised her, "we'll talk about it later, okay sweetie? I have to go now. I'll tell you just two things now. First, you can do anything just like anyone else. You're a perfectly ordinary girl, but there are some things you have to work harder at than people who can hear in order to succeed. It's up to you to decide what you want to work hard at. You can succeed at anything you put your mind to.

"The second thing I want to tell you is that you're very talented. Hashem gave you your deafness and He also gave you many talents. There are many girls who aren't as smart as you and can't do many of the things you can. Those girls won't be able to take any lessons they want because they won't pass the tests the school gives. You, *baruch Hashem*, can do well on all the tests because you're so talented, but you have a different problem. Everyone has problems, dear girl, and everyone decides whether to cry about them or try to overcome them."

Becky nodded, her face wet with tears. She went upstairs to her room, only partially consoled. Naomi knew it would take time for her to understand fully what she'd said, and she was glad she'd have some quiet time to mull it over before they spoke again in the evening. Naomi slung her pocketbook over her shoulder and left the house.

BECKY DIDN'T LEAVE her room until evening. Mindy returned home at six, and as soon as she finished eating she ran to her room. Strangely, Mindy loved the room she shared with Becky. She burst wildly into the room the way she always did, kicking the desk and flopping onto her bed. Becky, still moping on her bed, felt a sudden rush of fondness for her twin sister. She approached Mindy and rested her hand on Mindy's. Mindy's hand was stained with magic markers and scarred from knives, peelers, nails and all sorts of sharp objects she managed to get hold of despite the great care her family took to keep them out of her reach. Becky's hand was soft and dainty, and Mindy felt it with unconcealed pleasure.

"Mindy," Becky whispered. "Mindy, look at me, okay?"

Mindy did not so much as glance at Becky. Becky sought a sign of some contact, of intimacy, a spark of something that would indicate her twin shared the same world as her. Mindy, however, did not even raise her head.

"Mindy," Becky pleaded. "Look at me. Look at me, please!" She gripped Mindy's other hand and looked pleadingly at her sister, who remained immobile as a stone.

"Mindy," she wept, the tears coming again. She rested her head on Mindy so that Mindy should be able to stroke her hair, aware that Mindy wouldn't let go of her hair once she got hold of it. Hair always feels pleasant, especially hair as soft and smooth as Becky's and especially to a person who has nothing in this world save for the sense of touch.

Mindy felt the hair and tried to extricate her hands from Becky's. Becky released them and Mindy began pulling Becky's hair gently.

"Mindy, if you won't look at me, at least listen to me," Becky pleaded as if her life depended on it. "I want you to be like me, Mindy," she sobbed. "I won't go to any activities. I won't leave the room. I won't go to school at all. Don't go to school with *goyim*, Mindy; come with me! Come with me to my school." She wept bitterly, but Mindy remained indifferent, playing with her sister's hair in utter silence, her face completely blank.

"Come to our world, Mindy," Becky whispered in a voice thick with tears. "Come to this world. You're my twin and I'll do everything for you. Come, Mindy, come through this door and come into this world where everyone is."

Mindy let go of Becky's hair. Becky sat up and positioned herself opposite Mindy, smiling weakly. She hugged Mindy hard, refusing to let go. Mindy began wriggling in protest, and when that didn't help, she burst into terrifying screeches. Alarmed at Mindy's contortions, Becky relaxed her grip on her twin. The moment she did, Mindy stopped struggling.

"Why did you scream?" she whispered. "What happened to you?

Don't you like it when someone touches you? So how come you like to hug me?

"You know, Mindy," Becky said to her sister, "Ima told me that everyone has problems and everyone decides whether to cry about them or overcome them. Maybe you should try to overcome your problems, Mindy? Everyone can overcome his problems if he tries, everyone."

No response.

"I don't know if I should work hard to play the organ, because I think there are more important things I need to learn to do."

Silence.

"You know, Mindy," Becky said slowly, "I don't know anything about you. Maybe tell me about yourself? Slowly, slowly. You've got to tell me what's going on with you, how you live. What happens in that mysterious world you live in? Do you have fun in school? What do they teach you there?"

"Why are you doing that?" someone asked angrily, clapping a hand on Becky's shoulder. Becky saw Yanky's narrowed eyes and drawn-together eyebrows.

"What?" She hadn't seen the entire sentence.

"Why are you doing that?"

"Doing what?"

"You know she won't answer you."

"Yanky." She turned to her closest friend, her supportive, understanding, wonderful brother.

"What?"

"Why not, Yanky?" her cheeks were wet, and she wiped them. She could see in his eyes that he knew she had cried. "Why shouldn't I talk to her? Why shouldn't I try, at least?"

"Because she's nothing, don't you see?"

"She's not nothing," Becky said, defending her twin. "She's my sister and yours. Why shouldn't we try to help her?"

"Help her!" Yanky echoed bitterly. He sat down on the bed, swinging his feet back and forth. "Hundreds of people have tried to help her and couldn't, so why do you think you can?"

"Because I'm the only one who really understands her," Becky said seriously. After a moment's silence, she added, "And she's the only one who understands me."

Yanky's eyes showed he felt hurt. "And I don't understand you?" he asked angrily.

Becky was silent. She stared at the floor where Mindy's shoes, so similar to her own, were sprawled. They were white sneakers with pink laces and a large pink butterfly on the side. Mindy was her twin. Mindy understood the silent world she inhabited. Yanky shared the normal part of life with her, but Mindy understood the parts of her that were different from everyone else. They shared a bond that was sealed in the silence of a quiet, remote world that only the two of them shared.

Eretz Yisrael 5707/1947

TWO DAYS BEFORE a new moon waxed, four people made their way to the British armory. Meir, who spoke English fluently, was dressed like a British officer. They hoped that no one there knew the names of all the officers and he would not be challenged.

The armory stood there in silence. It was a small structure, surrounded by a few barbed wire fences, and the soldiers patrolling it appeared bored and indifferent. It occurred to Meir that they, too, were not at all pleased to be here and would rather be relaxing at home. *What a strange world,* he thought with a wry smile. *We want to be home and they want to be home. Let every man return to his home, and we won't have to fight them. Eretz Yisrael for the Jews and Britain for the Brits.*

After the other three had left the car, Meir pulled up openly in front of the entrance, trying to attract attention.

"Hey, you!" the sleepy guard awoke from his nap. "Halt! Who are you? Where are you going?"

Meir allowed the light of the guard's flashlight to fall on his face. Upon seeing Meir's uniform with its medals and ribbons, the guard saluted and said courteously, “Papers, please, sir.”

Meir stuck his hand in his pocket and pulled out a document, which he handed to the guard. The guard examined it by the weak light of his flashlight. It appeared to be in order.

“Alright, sir,” he said. “Proceed.”

Meir entered the area illuminated by floodlights. He felt faintly disappointed that it had been so easy. He took his time stepping out of the car and approaching the entrance to the small building. He knew he couldn’t enter until Menasheh and Alon had done their part. He walked to the door of the armory, leaned against it expectantly and waited.

Four strong booms ripped through the sky. The building’s windowpanes shattered. Dozens of panic-stricken soldiers, rifles in hand, sped off in the direction of the explosions.

Meir saw Mickey, the sapper, sprinting toward him. He covered his friend with steady rifle fire, silencing those who would object to Mickey’s entry. Mickey ran up to the door, connected a small detonator and activated the trigger. The tiny, relatively noiseless explosion broke the lock, and they entered the large storeroom, proud of their success.

They heard clearly the crossfire outside between Menasheh and Alon and the British soldiers chasing them. They fired without letup in order to draw the British away from the armory and in their direction. It worked. The British abandoned the armory and headed for a nearby valley.

Mickey used another small bomb to create a hole in the stone wall opposite the spot where Meir had parked his car. Now Meir began piling weapons into the sacks he had brought with him. He tossed the filled sacks quickly through the hole toward his car. The steady thwack-thwack of the sacks hitting the car alerted the British.

Mickey, looking worriedly out the window in the direction of the valley toward which Menasheh and Alon had diverted the British, called to Meir, “They’ve heard us, Meir. They’re coming back!”

"I know." Meir ran to the corner of the room where he found a box marked "Danger! Do not touch!" He nodded to himself. "Mickey, I'm going to explode the fuse box while you jump through the opening in the wall. It'll cut off the electricity to the entire building and the electrified fence. How fast are they coming?"

"They'll be here in five minutes," Mickey said, chewing his nails nervously. "What about you?"

"I'm committing suicide, remember?" Meir smiled, perfectly calm. "Don't worry about me. Jump."

"No..."

"I'm your commander, Mickey," Meir said firmly. "That's an order."

Mickey looked out. The building was only one story high; it wouldn't be a dangerous jump. He looked at Meir and asked quietly, "Do you have your will here?"

"No," Meir laughed. "I gave it to Shaul. Don't open it until you've verified my death beyond the shadow of a doubt. Wait at least two weeks."

"Okay." Mickey threw one final glance at his commander and friend. He couldn't see his face.

Meir was busy fiddling with the wires in the fuse box. He knew that the entire building would go up in flames when the box exploded. He heard the purr of a motor, which meant that Mickey was in the driver's seat. *We've done it,* he thought proudly. *I'll probably die, but we've done it. He closed his eyes and pressed the button.*

HE HAD NO idea how long he'd been unconscious. When he opened his eyes he glanced at his watch, which showed the date as well as the time. He was shocked. He'd been unconscious, hovering between heaven and earth, for more than a month!

"Shalom," he heard a voice next to him say. The Hebrew was perfect but held the trace of a British accent.

"Who are you?" With an effort, he turned his head and saw a

British colonel, his uniform decorated with medals, regarding him with interest.

"Would you care to make my acquaintance? Colonel Thomas Johnson. I've heard a lot about you."

"I'm glad to hear that." Now that the situation was clear to him, Meir's head began to pound. The British were sure to conduct a public trial for him so that he would serve as a lesson for other would-be Jewish fighters.

"Why?"

Meir did not respond. He fixed his eyes on the ceiling and remained silent. The Brit was unimpressed by his silence.

"Would you like me to tell you what happened to you?"

Still Meir was silent.

"You were surrounded by flames. You sustained severe burns and inhaled smoke. The explosion injured you very lightly, but the fire finished the job. Our soldiers, returning to the armory, found the body of a British officer sprawled over the fuse box and understood what had happened. Or rather, they thought they understood what had happened. Your fighters disappeared with most of the weapons in the armory, and our soldiers thought they'd left a British officer to burn.

"They extinguished the fire and rushed you to the hospital. It was your good fortune that you were wearing a British army uniform; they would not have invested that much effort in rescuing you had they known the truth. Now that they've learned who you are, though, they're eager for revenge. Nine British soldiers died the night of the raid."

There was a moment of silence and then the colonel said, "You know, we've been looking for you for a long time."

"I know."

"And we found you in the end. In a most unusual manner."

"Not that unusual for me."

"Yes, we know that such missions are routine for you."

Meir was surprised by the friendly tone.

"Meir, how old are you?"

"Twenty-five," he replied immediately.

"Ah." The colonel mumbled something under his breath. "And do you know what we intend to do with you?"

"Yes."

"Good." He looked at him intently, examining the features that he had come to know so well. The look of youthful innocence on Meir's face touched the commander's heart. "You know, I'm the one in charge of you."

"What do you mean?"

"When I say 'you,' I mean the Jewish fighters. You're in my hands, because I'm the commander of the military unit in Palestine."

"Eretz Yisrael," Meir corrected.

The officer smiled. "Whatever. Do you know how you're faring physically?"

"No." Meir shook his head. "But what difference does it make if I'm only a short while away from death in any case?"

"Not so short," Thomas said quietly. "I've arranged it so you don't get the death penalty."

"You can't do that," Meir said wearily.

"I can, actually. I have connections in high places. I've already done it for you."

"Why?" Meir demanded.

"I was touched by your courage."

Meir was surprised, but he didn't show it. "Why?"

"I know what you did. You agreed to commit suicide so your friends might escape. I don't have a single soldier among my men who would do that." He leaned over and looked into the patient's eyes. "Meir, your courage is extraordinary."

Meir shook his head. He wasn't in the mood to accept compliments just yet. He still had no idea what his fate would be. "How am I doing?"

"If I'd been asked that question while you were unconscious, I'd have said there was no hope."

"And now?"

"You sustained third-degree burns over twenty percent of your body," the colonel replied, "and your lungs nearly collapsed from smoke inhalation."

Meir stared at him intently, willing him to go on.

"Your scars will remain forever," the officer went on, "but that's all."

"G-d watched over me," Meir said, much to his own surprise. He hadn't uttered such words in more than nine years.

"No doubt," Thomas agreed. "Is there anything you want?"

"Yes." Meir closed his eyes wearily. "Would you leave me alone?"

"Certainly." The colonel was unfailingly courteous. "Good night, Meir. I hope to see you again tomorrow."

GRAY WALLS, GLOOMY and terrifying, stretched as far as the eye could see. Meir's trial took place behind closed doors. There was a judge, an attorney for the prosecution, and Colonel Johnson, who acted as attorney for the defense.

It has to be a rigged trial, Meir thought to himself. *What can there possibly be to say in my defense? I once really was a British soldier, serving in His Majesty's army. If only I could call Jim Stuart, my former commander. Maybe he would say something on my behalf.*

Meir didn't even listen to the exchanges between the judge and the attorneys, snapping to attention only when the judge announced his sentence: twenty-five years in prison. It might as well have been a life sentence.

He was led out of the courthouse and back to the penitentiary where he'd been held before the trial. The following day a car with grilled windows pulled up to take him to a large British jail. There were two people in the car: Colonel Thomas Johnson and a taciturn British captain, who Meir recognized as Shaul, the commander of his Jewish fighting group. He retained his composure and gave no sign of recognition.

"Who's that?" he asked Col. Johnson.

"I don't know," he shrugged. "What did you think of the trial?"

"I didn't pay attention," Meir said indifferently. "It was obviously rigged."

"They were talking about the death penalty, Meir," the colonel said. "Then seventy-five years. I brought it down to twenty-five."

Meir said nothing. The colonel was a Brit, and every Brit was his enemy.

The scraping noise of the prison gate as it opened to admit them snapped him out of his reverie. He was led through long corridors, escorted into an empty cell and left alone with the captain.

"Meir, Meir," the captain whispered, his eyes filled with tears. "I never appreciated you properly."

21

New York 5758/1998

There was a gentle knock on the door of Batsheva Tinkelroth's house. She raised a pair of weary eyes from the stencil she was busy preparing and called out, "Gitty, can you answer the door, please?"

"Ima," her sixteen-year-old daughter said, coming into the room, "it's a little girl, probably one of your students. I don't know what she wants."

"Ask her to come in."

Gitty was back a moment later with little Becky Mandel, who was looking around curiously.

"Becky?" Batsheva looked at her student in surprise.

"Yes," Becky said, a bit out of breath. She had obviously walked a long way.

"Come in," she said warmly. "Do you want something to drink?"

Becky shook her head.

"Sit down," Batsheva said, a surge of fondness welling up inside her. She admired the brave little girl who wouldn't allow her handicap to get her down. "Is there anything I can help you with?"

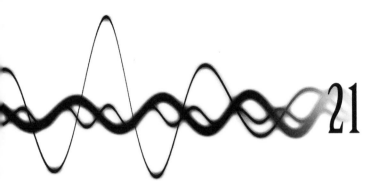

"Yes," Becky said hesitantly. Then she took a deep breath and began. "Today you told us about the Chanukah party we'll be having, with a big play for the whole school, and two girls from every class will be chosen to be in the play."

"Yes," Batsheva said, wondering what Becky was getting at. "That's right."

"I want to be in that play."

Batsheva's astonishment increased. She looked her student up and down quizzically. "Becky, there are tryouts, and the girls that seem most suited to the roles are chosen."

"Yes, I know," Becky agreed. "But I thought ... I'm sick of being scared all the time that my friends will find out I'm deaf. I want to tell them and get it over with so that I won't have to be scared all the time."

"But what does that have to do with the play?"

"If I act in the play, I can show them that a deaf girl can do everything just like a regular girl, and then they won't stop being my friends just because I'm deaf."

Batsheva fixed the child with a penetrating stare. "Is that what happened before?"

"Yes, that's what happened in preschool," Becky said gloomily. "The girls thought I wasn't normal because I couldn't hear. Today the girls don't know I can't hear, and that's why they're my friends. Now that everyone's my friend already, I can stop pretending."

"And you want to do that at the play?"

"Yes. When the play is over, I want to tell everyone, 'You see? I'm deaf, and I acted in the play without anyone knowing that I'm deaf. Deaf people are normal, and they can do everything just like normal people. And not just deaf people — anyone with any kind of problem can learn to overcome it and be normal, but only if everyone else believes they can, too.'"

Batsheva blinked and then, with one swift movement, scooped Becky up in a fierce hug and planted a kiss on her forehead. "Who told you that?" she asked, pushing Becky's shoulders gently back so Becky could read her lips.

"My mother," Becky replied. "She didn't tell me to be in the play.

I want it to be a surprise for her. But she told me, 'Becky, you're completely normal, and there's nothing you can't do.' I was crying because I couldn't go to whatever after-school activity I wanted to, and that's when she told me this. She said I might have to work harder than other people but I could do anything I set my mind to."

Batsheva thought for a moment. "Well," she said, "you have a better reason than most girls to want to be in the play, so I'm willing to try it. Are you sure you can handle rehearsals?"

"I'll try my best, and Hashem will help me. My mother says everyone has talents that Hashem gave him, and even though it's true Hashem made me deaf, He also gave me lots of talents."

Batsheva chuckled.

"Alright then?" Becky asked hopefully.

"We'll see," the teacher replied. "We'll send you to tryouts and see what the play coach says."

ALL THE WAY to the party, Becky seemed to be hiding something. She kept smiling to herself, giggling nervously and trying to conceal her giggles with a series of coughs. She wriggled restlessly about in her seat, jumping up and down as if it had pins and needles in it.

"Did something sting you, Becky?" Shlomo asked from behind the steering wheel, turning his head to the side for just a moment so Becky could see his mouth.

She giggled nervously and blushed. "No."

Shlomo parked the car and Naomi and Becky got out. Becky, radiant, ran ahead while Naomi gathered her things. Shlomo waved good-bye to them, and they joined the stream of women and girls flowing into the building.

They entered a large auditorium. It was a very plain room with yellow plastic chairs affixed to the floor. There was a large stage with a purple curtain in the front of the room.

Naomi looked around for a place to sit down, her hand gripping

Becky's a bit forcefully. Naomi was afraid she'd disappear on her, a rather frightening scenario considering she was deaf. She wouldn't hear Naomi if she called her, and she'd have to work up an awful lot of courage to ask for help.

Naomi spotted two adjoining seats close to the stage. She set her pocketbook down on one of them. "Sit down," she said her daughter.

"No," Becky said, shaking her head. "Just a minute." Her eyes traveled over the room, and Naomi wondered what was going on.

"Who are you looking for?" Naomi wondered aloud.

Becky's eyes lit up suddenly. "Ima," she whispered into her mother's ear, "I have to go now."

"Go?" Naomi stared at Becky in astonishment. "Where?"

"It's a surprise. You'll see."

"And you know how to go wherever it is you're going by yourself?"

"Ima!" She looked at Naomi reproachfully. "Ima, I'm seven years old already and in the middle of first grade," she said in the tone of one stating the obvious.

Naomi nodded apologetically. "Okay, darling, but take care not to get lost."

She darted off like an arrow. Naomi wondered what her shy, quiet little girl had up her sleeve.

The curtain opened, and a choir of about fifty girls began singing Chanukah songs. In honor of Chanukah, Becky's school traditionally put on a big production that involved all the students. Most girls performed in one of the several choirs or dance groups, and only a few were in the play. When Naomi asked Becky what she was in, she evaded the question, and Naomi assumed she had decided not to take part in the production.

The lighting was spectacular, and the girls in the choir came out in matching costumes and sang beautifully. Naomi was sorry Becky wasn't with her. True, she couldn't hear the girls singing, but she would have enjoyed the sight.

The choir came to an end, a dance was performed, and Becky still hadn't returned. Naomi's heart filled with fear. She rose from her place and began looking around for her little girl. Her imagination ran wild. *What if she had lost her way and was now crying bitterly in the middle of a busy street? What if she had somehow wound up in the storage rooms behind the auditorium? What if...?*

From her spot at the back of the auditorium, she saw the curtain rise. The scenery was that of a busy city street. Three girls, twelve- or thirteen-year-olds, stood onstage looking pointedly at their watches. The play had begun.

Naomi heard the patter of small footsteps, and her breath caught in her throat. Becky had walked onstage. Becky had walked onto the stage! Naomi stared at her in disbelief. She was shocked to the core. *My deaf daughter, the apple of my eye and the person I feel I have to protect most, is standing onstage, brimming with self-confidence.*

And she performed. How she performed! She played the part of Shmerel, an eight-year-old orphan from Poland who came to the United States after the war from Switzerland. He arrived with a group of children who were not religious, but he wanted to observe Torah and mitzvos.

My Becky. Naomi's eyes remained glued to the small figure onstage. How had she done it? Who had asked her to be in the play? Why? Who had planned it all? The shock dissipated slowly, and her eyes began to fill with tears. Her lips trembled uncontrollably. She didn't want to take her eyes off Becky, but she could hardly look at her, either.

"Mrs. Mandel?" Someone approached Naomi. She was so worked up that it took her a long moment to recognize who it was.

"Mrs. Tinkelroth? Becky's teacher?"

She nodded. "It must be very moving to see your daughter onstage, isn't it?"

"How did this happen?" Naomi demanded.

"It was Becky's initiative. She heard about the play like everyone else, and she came to ask me if she could try out. She knew only two girls from each class would be chosen, and she wanted to be one of them. She had a reason, she said. I agreed and arranged for her to meet the director of the play, who was absolutely charmed, of course, the way we all are. The director told me that Becky was chosen fairly. She has an unusual flair for drama."

Naomi watched the rest of the play as if hypnotized. Becky performed with grace and charm and true skill, mesmerizing the audience. Of course, a mother's opinion might be the tiniest bit subjective, but the audience cheered so loudly at the end of every scene that she knew she wasn't the only one who thought Becky was spectacular.

Ribbono shel Olam, Naomi prayed from the depths of her heart, *you gave me lofty souls to raise. You gave me this precious child, and I thank You for her every single day. I don't deserve her, but still You chose me to raise her. Help me raise her properly; keep me from damaging her holy neshamah. Please, help her continue to succeed and help me ... help me continue to succeed, too. I see that this method of showing her that she can do anything she sets her mind to is bearing fruit. Yanky is far more relaxed, and Becky is doing so well socially. I thank You for every single day, for giving Reilly the right advice for me, for enabling me to understand and internalize that advice, for granting me success in implementing it, and for the wonderful progress my children have made.*

The play drew to a close amid thunderous applause. The curtain fell and then rose again to reveal Becky standing alone onstage, still dressed as Shmerel. The spotlight fell on her small form, and she raised a hand to quiet the cheering audience.

"I'd like to introduce myself," she said, her voice clear and steady. "My name's Becky, and I'm in first grade."

A murmur of surprise rippled through the audience.

"I'm seven years old, and I have a twin sister. A few hours after we were born my parents learned something very sad: Their babies were deaf. We cannot hear anything at all."

Her words were like an electric current zipping through the room. The murmurs stopped completely, and the auditorium became completely silent.

"My parents decided to do everything they could to help us be like everyone else. My sister Mindy couldn't do it. When she was a little girl the doctors told my parents she was also autistic. So now I'm the only one who can try to be a regular girl. My mother told me that everyone has problems. He or she can cry about them — or overcome them. We, my parents and I, chose to overcome my problem.

"I saw you clapping before. Some people can't even do that. I can tell from your faces that you liked the play; some people can't even understand that.

"I want to ask you something: If you see my sister, don't make fun of her. She's special in her own way, in her own world. And if you see kids like me — regular, smart kids with a problem — don't think they can't do anything. I'm proof. Did any of you know I was deaf? I did everything right. Some kids with disabilities can't do so well, but shouldn't you admire them anyway? People with disablilities should be admired, not pitied. They're much more special than you. They know how to fight; they know how to struggle; they know to thank Hashem for what they have. You have everything; it's no wonder you're happy. We're missing some of the presents Hashem gives most people, and we're happy anyway – isn't that something to admire?

"I wanted to do this to prove that if people give us people with disablilities a chance, we can do so much. Give us a chance. Accept us into your lives. We're not worth any less than other people."

Becky walked offstage to thunderous applause. Naomi ran to her and embraced her so hard she couldn't breathe. Her eyes shone with an otherworldly light.

"Ima," she said with typical simplicity, "why are you crying?"

"I'm thanking Hashem," Naomi told her, "for giving me a daughter like you."

Eretz Yisrael 5707/1947

Many long months passed. Meir learned that prison is not pleasant at all. He thought of Yisrael, his beloved horse, and wondered how he was faring. His friends visited very rarely; most of them were wanted by the British and had to disguise themselves in order to come see him. Meir scolded them for taking unnecessary risks that could cost them their lives, so they did so very seldom.

"Captain," Meir said to Shaul one day when the Jewish commander entered his cell dressed as a British captain, "how is my Yisrael?"

"He's in Erez's stable," Shaul replied. "Erez takes care of him as if he was your only son."

"He is," Meir said sadly. "He's my only friend in Eretz Yisrael. Do you know what I thought when I was alone in the British armory, certain I'd be dying within the next few minutes?"

"What?"

"It occurred to me that it was a good thing I was the one who wouldn't be returning alive. It was a good thing it would be me and not one of the others. No one would cry over my loss. No one would be sorry for my death."

"What!" Shaul said angrily. "What about me? What about your friends? We were — "

"How many fighters were killed under your command?" Meir asked.

"You're not just anyone," Shaul protested. "Not many fighters in my command died, but even if they had, G-d forbid, it wouldn't be the same. I don't equate anyone else with you. I love you like a son, Meir."

"No," Meir said. "I'm not your son. I'm not anyone's son. I have no one in the world."

"I've often wondered about that," Shaul said. "Who are you, Meir Katz?"

"Who am I?" Meir echoed, puzzled by the question.

"What's your past? Where's your family?"

"None of them survived the war."

"You verified that?"

Meir nodded.

"But you left Poland before the war."

"I don't want to talk about it, Shaul; I'm sorry. I can't. The only thing I can tell you is that I have nothing left in the world. I don't love anyone and I have nothing, save for my horse Yisrael and Eretz Yisrael."

"Why do you fight for Eretz Yisrael with such passion?" Shaul tried to understand. "Many people are taking part in this battle, but very few feel as fiercely as you do."

"I thought you'd understand now that I explained how alone I am. Eretz Yisrael is my only friend. Shaul, Shaul, you've lost everything too. Don't you understand me?"

"I've built my home anew, Meir. I didn't see any point in crying over the past and not trying to build everything anew."

"But Shaul, this is our country. We must fight for her. Aren't you afraid you might leave your wife a widow in your struggle for Eretz Yisrael?"

Shaul regarded him silently for a moment. "Meir," he said finally, "I'm not a prophet, and I can't say when this war will be over. I'm doing what I feel is the right thing to do. I'm fighting for Eretz Yisrael because it's important to me, but I don't think it makes sense to postpone building a family because of a lot of 'what ifs.' The young men in Poland never dreamed their wives would be widows a short while after they married them, did they? There are some things that are not in our control, Meir."

"I know," Meir whispered to himself. "There's a Creator Who runs the world."

THE SUN ROSE in the east, tinting the prison walls a rosy pink. Rays of sunshine played across the inmates' faces as they filed out of their cells for morning lineup. Meir left his cell with obvious reluctance. He hadn't had a visitor in nearly a month, and he knew nothing of events in the outside world.

After lineup the inmates were granted permission to stroll around the courtyard briefly. Meir walked alone, his eyes on the ground.

"Meir!" One of the wardens who was particularly fond of him came running up. "Guess what?"

"What?" Meir asked dully. The knowledge that he would spend the next twenty years in jail depressed him terribly.

"It's been approved!"

"What's been approved?"

"Haven't you heard the radio?"

"No. What happened?"

"Mandatory Palestine is free. The British are leaving!"

Two weeks later, the gates clanged shut behind him. He raised his eyes to the blue sky in gratitude, filling his lungs with fresh air, and crouched to the ground. He grasped a fistful of earth and rose slowly to his feet again, allowing the particles to fall through his fingers. The wind blew them away along with all the struggles, the battles, the tears and the despair.

Two hours later, when he mounted his beloved horse, his eyes filled with tears.

"Hashem," he whispered to the darkening sky, "thank you."

22

New York 5759/1999

The claps of thunder did not rouse Becky from her sleep, but the blinding flashes of lightning streaking across the sky did. A glance at the clock on the wall told her it was twenty past six. Still early. Ima wouldn't be coming to wake her soon because it was Chanukah and she had vacation. She could remain cuddled under her warm blanket and daydream if she felt like it.

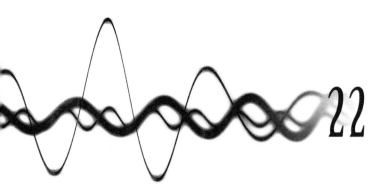

Her daydreams were very pleasant. She thought about the play and how well it had gone. Although she had been eager to reveal her secret so she wouldn't have to be scared all the time that someone might find out that she was deaf, there had been many difficult moments when she doubted she could really pull it off. But she had done a wonderful job. She had asked the lady who wrote the script for the play to help her write down what Becky would tell the audience afterward. Becky had told her what she wanted to say, and the lady had written it in nice words. Becky worked hard to memorize it so she wouldn't forget anything — and she hadn't. Everyone listened carefully, and some of the mothers had even cried. She'd still been a bit worried about what her friends would say, but they were even more eager to be her friend now that they knew she was deaf. They had crowded around her in an admiring circle, and she told them everything: about lip reading and speech lessons and Mindy.

Oops. The happy smile on her lips disappeared, and concern flooded Becky's heart. Mindy. Mindy rolled over in bed. She wasn't on vacation today; her school had normal hours throughout Chanukah. Mindy opened her eyes and leaped out of bed.

Becky stopped her for a good-morning embrace, and her sister's hands tightened around her neck. They made eye contact and exchanged smiles. Mindy's morning smile helped Becky get through the day.

"You like me to hug you," Becky said, thinking aloud, "so how come you don't like when we touch you gently, just like that, for no reason?"

Naomi entered the room. "Good morning, Mindy. Good morning, Becky. Becky, you have vacation today."

"I know, Ima. Ima, what else doesn't Mindy like?"

"Huh?" Naomi seemed confused.

"Mindy doesn't like when we touch her," Becky explained. "Is there anything else she doesn't like?"

Naomi thought for a moment. "She doesn't like to look at the computer," she said finally. "The flickering light seems to bother her. But why are you asking, Becky?"

"No special reason," came the answer. "I was just thinking that it's sad that she has to do certain things even though she doesn't like them."

"What does she have to do that she doesn't like?"

"She doesn't like to wear new clothes, but she does because she has no choice. And I'm sure there are computers in her school and she has to see them, even though she doesn't like to look at them."

"You're right." Naomi, still unsure what her daughter was getting at, looked at her thoughtfully.

"Ima, don't you think it's strange?" Becky asked.

"What's strange?"

"Why does she enjoy it when I hug her, but she doesn't like it when we touch her?"

"Mindy likes it when you hug her?" Naomi looked at Becky for a long time. "How do you know?"

"Can't you tell?" Becky wondered. "She likes it. But she flinches when we touch her, and she doesn't like it when you dress her."

"How did you notice that, Becky?"

"I see her trying to pull her clothes off. She loves to take off her shoes and socks and she hates new clothes because they haven't been washed enough and aren't soft yet. She can't stand labels either. And she likes a ponytail better than loose hair because that way her hair doesn't touch her face."

"Are you sure about all this?"

"Of course. I can tell what upsets her."

"Clothing ..." Naomi murmured to herself. "Mindy doesn't like clothing. Labels bother her. Maybe we should remove them for her? How do you know they bother her, Becky?"

"She comes to me to remove them for her. Ima, didn't you notice that Mindy doesn't like it when we touch her?"

"Yes, I did. So?"

"So that's why she doesn't like labels. It's the same thing. But she does bang her head on the wall and she likes me to hug her hard. Ima, if you didn't like it when people touched you but they did anyway, what would you do?"

"Tell them to stop."

"But if you couldn't do that, 'cause you were deaf?"

A powerful hammer began banging in Naomi's head and she felt very dizzy suddenly.

"What?" she whispered weakly.

"Mindy's deaf, Ima. She can't tell us that she doesn't like it. So what does she do?"

"She has fits," Naomi murmured, thoroughly confused.

"And she hits," Becky added calmly, unaware of the impact her words were having. "Ima, I think that if we don't dress Mindy in clothes she doesn't like and we shut off the lights that bother her — I mean, like shutting the computer when she's around — it'll be easier for her, don't you think so? She can't tell you this, so I'm saying it for her."

"You're a good girl, Becky," Naomi said, stroking her daughter's face tenderly, hopefully. "We'll look into it."

SHLOMO AND NAOMI arrived at Natalie's office with an unconfirmed premise leading to new and unfamiliar territory. When Becky had brought it to Naomi's attention that Mindy couldn't abide skin contact and hated flickering computer screens and neon lights, she had suddenly realized that all this information put together might shed some light on Mindy's condition. She had discussed the situation with a neurologist who knew Mindy, and he had suggested they see an occupational therapist.

Shlomo and Naomi entered Natalie's office. Natalie, the occupational therapist, needed only a brief time with Mindy to diagnose the problem. Much to Naomi's surprise, she succeeded in making contact with Mindy fairly quickly.

"You say your daughter is autistic?" she asked, raising her eyebrows in surprise.

"That's what we were told," Naomi said, her entire body trembling. "Now we suddenly began to suspect that certain sensory stimuli bother her greatly and we thought that might be why she has fits and throws herself sometimes."

"I'd like you to fill out this questionnaire, okay?" Natalie said, handing them a sheaf of papers stapled together in the upper left-hand corner. "Read this and answer the questions as accurately as possible, please," she requested.

Naomi looked at the first page. She skimmed over the introduction: "Questionnaire for parents. Choose one of the following answers: Always, Usually, Sometimes, Seldom, Never ..."

She skipped to the page with the questions.

Does your child:

1. Express discomfort when being washed or groomed?
2. Prefer long-sleeved clothing when the weather is warm and short-sleeved clothing when it's cool?
3. Avoid walking barefoot, especially in the sand or on grass?
4. React aggressively when touched?

React aggressively? Naomi's head pounded. She circled "Always" for every question with no hesitation at all and went on to the next section.

Does your child:

1. Avoid foods or the smell of foods other children are fond of?
2. Agree to eat only certain foods?

Naomi skipped that part. Mindy was not at all sensitive with regard to taste. She skipped the section on "Vestibular Sensitivity" as well and focused on the section entitled "Visual/Auditory Sensitivity."

Does your child:

1. React negatively to loud or unexpected noise? (For example: Does s/he cry or hide when a dog barks, the vacuum cleaner is switched on, or someone uses a blow dryer?)
2. Cover her ears when s/he hears loud noises?

Naomi raised her head. "Mindy's deaf," she said to Natalie, "but instead of crying or hiding from loud and unexpected noises, she gets upset from blinding or flickering lights. The computer, for example, bothers her terribly. She closes her eyes whenever she passes it."

"There's a section that asks about that," Natalie said. "Go on."

Naomi went on reading.

3. React negatively to strong light even after others have already grown accustomed to it?
4. Cover or close his/her eyes in an effort to protect them from strong light?

Naomi finished reading the questionnaire. She had replied "Always" to most of the questions in the sections entitled "Visual/Auditory Sensitivity" and "Tactile Sensitivity." In the other sections her replies varied; there were some "Sometimes," a few "Seldoms," and one or two "Nevers." Unsure what the questions indicated, she looked at Natalie searchingly.

"Your questionnaire underscores the fact that she's overly sensitive to tactile stimulation," Naomi said. "We thought that might be part of her problem, and we want to help her."

"Part of her problem?" Natalie echoed, smiling gently. "It's all her problem. She has a problem modulating sensory stimulation. Mr. Mandel, Mrs. Mandel, your daughter is not autistic."

NAOMI DIDN'T KNOW which was greater: her feeling of gratitude or that of shock. All factors pointed to one very clear fact: Mindy had a sensory problem. Sensory Modulation Disorder, Natalie explained, describes a condition in which one of the senses operates abnormally, either with too great intensity or not enough. And because Mindy was deaf and couldn't express her problem, she'd been mistakenly diagnosed as autistic.

Mistakenly diagnosed! Dear G-d in heaven, my child had been mentally normal throughout all these years, locked in a jail because we hadn't understood her. Naomi couldn't help but berate herself – but how could she have known? She hadn't neglected her daughter; she'd taken her from doctor to doctor, but no one had revealed the true problem. Was Naomi to blame?

"You've got to understand that Sensory Modulation Disorder — SMD — doesn't appear in medical diagnostic books. Many doctors are unaware that this type of disorder exists, so many parents tread a long, exhausting path strewn with errors until they discover the true source of their child's difficulties. Fortunately, awareness of this problem is increasing," Natalie explained.

"What causes the disorder?" Naomi asked. She wanted to know everything. After experiencing a rush of joy and then tortuous guilt, she was eager to actually do something.

"The source of the disorder is most likely in the brain, not the organs. That means there isn't something the matter with her skin that makes her unable to bear tactile stimulation, or a problem with her eyes that makes her overly sensitive to the computer screen. The source of the disorder is the manner in which the brain processes the information it receives."

"Why do you say 'most likely'?"

"Because we can't be a hundred percent sure until we find the area of the brain that's responsible. SMD generally runs in families. Often parents pass it to their children, but we haven't yet isolated the gene that causes it. Contrary to what you may be thinking, SMD is not all that rare. Fifteen percent of the general population experiences this problem — in varying degrees of intensity, of course. Your daughter's disorder is severe."

"And you say her intolerance of strong light is also connected?"

"Yes. The disorder can appear in any of the following areas: visual, auditory, tactile, olfactory, taste and vestibular."

"What does 'vestibular' mean?"

"It refers to a person's perception of his body in space. Let's start at the beginning, alright?"

Naomi nodded wordlessly.

"We're sitting in the same room, on the same type of chair. The temperature is the same for both of us, as is the lighting and the background noise. But the way we perceive our surroundings is different."

"How so?"

"I can tell you're one of those people who doesn't mind the cold. You're wearing thinner, cooler clothes than I am. Why? The weather is the same for both of us. But I feel the cold more intensely than you do. Does the lighting in this room bother you?"

"No."

"It bothers me. I'd love to change the neon lighting for fluorescent. Do you hear the noise filtering in from outside? Is the chair comfortable? We — you and I — would answer these questions differently. How come? We're in the same room, after all. It's because each person perceives his surroundings differently. That much is clear, right? The next step is to understand that a person behaves in accordance with his perception of his surroundings. If you're cold, you'll hike up the heat. If you're bothered by a particular noise, you'll stick your fingers in your ears, right?"

"Right."

"Most people are more or less comfortable in most surroundings. Unless it's extremely hot or cold, the noise level is very loud, or the lighting blindingly bright, they're free to do whatever it is they need or want to: study, read, work, write, whatever. But if they're supposed to study and a flickering light in the room drives them crazy, how can they go on? They get completely distracted.

"Imagine if someone held a flashlight two inches in front of your face and switched the light on and off rapidly. Would you be able to concentrate on a thorny math problem? Of course not! People with SMD have a hard time fulfilling tasks because all their energy is wasted on trying to concentrate despite their surroundings. That's why many children with SMD are diagnosed as having learning disabilities. How can they learn anything when their surroundings are so uncomfortable and even painful for them? Your daughter's case is extreme. She was diagnosed as autistic."

"She was diagnosed as autistic because she was deaf," Naomi fumed.

"Yes. If she hadn't screamed and cried so when she was a little girl, you'd have invested as much effort in helping her as you did with her twin sister, isn't that so?"

Naomi nodded.

"Mindy has two problems," Natalie said. "The first is tactile hypersensitivity and the second is visual hypersensitivity. Interestingly, some people with SMD suffer from hyposensitivity — that means too little sensitivity — in one of the areas I mentioned earlier. But that isn't the case with Mindy — her problem is that she's overly sensitive.

"I diagnosed Mindy with SMD because her sensitivity in these two areas affects her ability to function. I personally don't like neon lighting, but I can handle it. It doesn't distract me. I can overcome my discomfort and go on. Mindy cannot overcome her sensitivity.

"Most children with SMD find it impossible to concentrate and cannot learn properly. As a result, they're often labeled lazy, learning disabled, or hyperactive. Your daughter received a far more severe misdiagnosis: autistic."

Naomi was silent.

"By the way, many autistic people suffer from SMD, sometimes severely."

Naomi didn't want to hear about autistic people. She didn't want to hear about them ever again. "What can we do to help Mindy?"

"First of all: Accept her. The lion's share of her problem is emotional in nature. She was never really autistic; she was misunderstood and therefore misdiagnosed. Now that you know what her problem is, you can understand her better, and that's the most important part in helping her get better."

A chill wind blew through the window. Naomi shivered. "And what can you do to help her?"

"The job of an occupational therapist is to build a suitable environment for the child. Now that I know what Mindy likes, I'll change to softer lighting and shut my computer when she's in my office. I'll lay a soft rug on the floor and buy some soft toys. I'll ask you to buy her clothing made of soft fabrics. Once I earn her trust I'll be able to work with her and introduce her slowly to stiffer, harder textures. She'll never enjoy tactile stimulation, but she'll grow sufficiently accustomed to it so that it won't affect her ability to function. I'll help you create a supportive environment for her at home and in school."

"School?" Naomi asked. "But she goes to a school for autistic children."

"We'll take her out."

"And where will we transfer her to?"

"Keep her home for a while. In the meantime, we'll give her intensive therapy. Bring her here every day."

"How long will it take?"

"I don't know. It could take a long time. Maybe a year."

"If she's so sensitive to touch, why does she like to be hugged hard?"

"It's precisely because of her sensitivity that she enjoys being hugged. A firm hug stabilizes her. She can't handle light, gentle contact but she enjoys a strong, firm touch. You can use this knowledge to help her."

"How?"

"Brush her body with a bristled brush; let her snuggle under a heavy down blanket. Give her a massage with strong, firm strokes. All these are examples of tactile stimulation she'll enjoy. Unfortunately, there isn't any type of visual stimulation she'll enjoy, but you can make things easier for her on that front by installing soft lighting at home, shutting off the computer when she's around, and drawing the blinds so that very little light filters into the house. Once she starts therapy and we stimulate her senses in a controlled manner, she'll find it easier to concentrate even when her surroundings are not ideally suited to her."

"You know something? Mindy used to cry and scream and then suddenly become apathetic, as if she understood there was nothing to talk about."

"Tell me," Natalie said, looking directly at Naomi, "as a baby, did Mindy have crying jags and then suddenly fall asleep?"

Naomi nodded. "Of course. She exhausted herself by crying so much."

"No. She simply gave up. She realized that no one understood her needs and decided to give up. It's a painful decision to make. Babies fall asleep after such a decision, and children become apathetic."

"A painful decision," Naomi whispered. "My child made peace with her autism. She resigned herself to the fact that no one understood her; she accepted the loss of communication with the people closest to her."

She couldn't tolerate the pain. "For six years my daughter was in prison. Six years! For six years she's been crying out in her own way and no one understood her. And I'm her mother. I'm the one who's supposed to sense what my children are going through. I should have felt what she felt. I should have understood her silent cry. Where was I? Where were my maternal instincts? Where was my sensitivity to pick up on my child's distress?"

"Be glad you discovered the problem now," Natalie said soothingly. "She could have grown up and become a woman without anyone realizing she wasn't autistic."

Naomi heart bled. Natalie's words didn't help much. She made an appointment to begin treatment and left the room. Aside from the unbearable pain of learning about Mindy's distress, her sense of herself as a mother had sustained a serious blow. For six years her daughter had been in prison. Six years — and she hadn't had a clue as to her distress.

NAOMI SHOULD HAVE been delighted. Her daughter wasn't autistic! But she wasn't happy. Of course, she was filled with gratitude, but the pain, distress and guilt were so strong she felt she would collapse under their weight.

"This suffering — the six years during which we misunderstood her and failed to communicate with her — was also decreed in *Shamayim* just like the fact that she isn't really autistic," Shlomo said.

"But Shlomo," Naomi answered, tortured by feelings of guilt, "she suffered so much. Much more than if she had been autistic."

"She's been liberated from prison now. After years of suffering and isolation, she's free, and her future is bright. From now on all will be well," he said. "All will be well."

But that wasn't the case.

23

Mindy began going to Natalie for occupational therapy. At first she was suspicious and mistrustful, but gradually she became happy to go there and returned with a smile on her lips and a sparkle of pleasure in her eyes. Natalie spoke to Jenny, Becky's speech therapist, and the two of them worked out a detailed program for communicating with Mindy. Mindy had learned how to communicate her most basic needs at Flowers in the Garden, the school for autistic children she'd attended, but Jenny felt that wasn't enough.

"In school she learned to make eye contact and understand basic instructions," Jenny said. "I want her to communicate like Becky. There's no reason she shouldn't be able to."

"There is a reason," Naomi said quietly.

"There was," Jenny insisted. "Now that reason ought to disappear."

"Ought to," Naomi murmured.

"You're being pessimistic," she chided me. "It isn't like you."

"It is, actually," Naomi said with a bitter smile. "It's true that you insisted on maximal communication with Becky and you achieved outstanding results. But I don't think you can do the same with Mindy."

"Why not?"

"Because a few months have already passed since you began

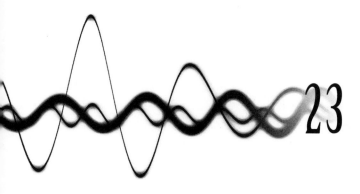

working with her and I don't see any change in the way she communicates with us. I'm afraid all this hard work is for nothing. I'm afraid I've lost her and won't get her back again. I won't get a second chance. Now that I know she's not autistic and success seems so close, I'm terrified of losing her for good."

"Isn't she much calmer than she used to be?"

"Yes. She smiles more often; she's calm and happy. I'm delighted about that — but she hasn't communicated with anyone in a tangible way as I expected her to. I expected her to communicate with us like a regular child. She is one, after all."

"And so?"

"It's not happening, Jenny; it just isn't. You've been working with her for three months. We've been creating a comfortable environment for her and taking care to touch her only in ways she likes. But she isn't responding. She's still so remote, so withdrawn, so isolated and detached."

"Have you consulted with anyone?"

"Yes," Naomi replied in a pained voice. "We went to a specialist in the field of communication. You know what he told me?"

"What?"

"'For six years,' he told me, 'your daughter was in forced isolation. She's grown accustomed to that isolation, made peace with it. For six years she hasn't shared anything with you. She doesn't know how to live differently. What did you think would happen? That the day you discovered she wasn't autistic, she'd open up to the world you live in? She's already locked herself into a different world. She might not be autistic, but her isolation is the same as if she were. How can you expect her to leave her world and enter another?'"

"Naomi," Jenny said, looking at her sternly, "it's true that Mindy has been locked in a jail until now. But now we know she has the ability to leave it. Go to war, Naomi. You know how to do that. Remember how you struggled for Becky's sake. Don't listen to all those experts who would have you give up. Fight all those professionals who tell you it can't be done. Go to war for Mindy's independence. Give the war a name – call it the War of Independence."

Eretz Yisrael 5707/1947

The declaration of *Israel's independence is a remarkable stage in the revival of the Jewish people,* Meir thought. *This land, for which so much blood was spilled, for which we struggled so hard, is now ours. Ours, free and clear!*

Joy bubbled forth and overflowed into the streets. Spirited dancing filled the country, and elation swept away yesterday's sorrow to make room for renewed hope. The bitter *galus*, many people felt, had reached its end. Secular Zionists, and also many religious Jews, too, felt certain the final redemption was upon them. Eretz Yisrael was for *Am Yisrael*; the Jewish State was in Jewish hands. Eretz Yisrael was free from the yoke of strangers and could now begin gathering in lovingly her exiled children after years of suffering and isolation. *Am Yisrael* was finally free, and the future seemed bright.

From now on all will be well, everyone thought. But that wasn't the case.

It wasn't just the air-raid sirens that shattered the euphoria. It was more than the thunder of tanks and renewed battle cries that forced the broken, shattered Jewish people to shoulder arms and set out to do battle again. The men were weary of battle. They loathed the sight of weapons. But they had no choice other than to go to war once more.

Meir was among those who joined the battle.

"This is not the first time I'm fighting," he said candidly to Shaul as the two sat in a military encampment, planning their next attack. "It's the third. But now, I'm tired already. I have no more strength. I'm sick of it all."

"Why?" Shaul looked at him in surprise. "We're almost at the end now. We've already been granted independence; we're fighting now in order to secure our future here."

"If we have one, that is," Meir said quietly.

"Of course we do," Shaul declared. "Now all obstacles ought to disappear."

"Ought to," he murmured.

"You're being pessimistic," Shaul said reproachfully. "It isn't like you."

"It is, actually," Meir said with a bitter smile. "True, I've always been stubborn. True, I struggled mightily so that we might claim this land as our own. I felt that was my purpose in life. But today? I'm not so sure we can achieve that goal."

"Why not?"

"Because the British are gone and we've been granted a trial period. If the world sees that we can't succeed at the relatively simple job of maintaining peace and quiet on our borders, the Mandate will return, even stronger than before. And then I'll know that all our battles were in vain. We won't get Eretz Yisrael again. We won't get a second chance. That's why I'm so scared. Now that I know the British aren't here and success seems so close, I'm terrified of losing Eretz Yisrael for good."

"What do you think will happen?"

"I spoke to Menasheh. Do you know what he said? 'For so many years, *Am Yisrael* was separated from Eretz Yisrael by circumstances not under its control. During those years, the Jewish people grew accustomed to a state of exile and made peace with it. We haven't had a homeland or independence for so long that we don't know what to do with them. Even if we win this war, I fear we might not be able to establish a state; we have no knowledge of how to do so. After so many long years of exile, can the Jewish mentality change? Can we succeed in fighting on our own, as a nation, for the land, and more importantly, if we should win, do we have what it takes to succeed in establishing a state?'"

"Meir," Shaul said, looking at him sternly. "It's true that until now our nation has been in exile. But now we know we have the ability to leave exile. We'll go to war, Meir; we know how to do that. Remember how we struggled to free Eretz Yisrael from the British? We can do it! We're going to fight for independence. We're going to give our struggle a name: the War of Independence."

Eretz Yisrael 5708-5712/1948-1952

The war was over. The price exacted was steep: There had been countless casualties. The fallen were both veteran settlers and newcomers, heads of families and young single men. Some were survivors of the camps who had endured the worst and finally made it to Eretz Yisrael, only to fall in the war.

Meir survived this war just as he had survived his escape from Poland and his ascent to Eretz Yisrael, just as he had survived leaving Eretz Yisrael and traveling to England, just as he had survived fighting in the worst of wars and in the struggle against the British, and just as he had survived the fiery explosion that had nearly transported him to the World to Come.

He had survived it all.

I think I must be immune to death, Meir thought to himself. The Angel of Death had tried to take him, had waylaid him at every step, had tried — and failed. Indifferent as Meir was to death, death was apparently indifferent to him.

Shaul survived, too, but Menasheh had fallen in battle. Meir mourned his friend's passing but felt unable to do anything to perpetuate his memory. He laid a wreath of flowers on Menasheh's grave but felt no satisfaction. He tried to murmur a few chapters of *Tehillim* that he remembered by heart, but the sense of consolation that comes with knowing you've done something to help your friend refused to come.

Eretz Yisrael prepared to absorb an influx of new immigrants. On May 15, 1948, the gates of Eretz Yisrael opened wide. The war had interrupted people's plans to immigrate, but now that it had ended it seemed every Jew in the world wanted to come to the fledgling state in spite of its continuing existential struggle. The state was weak and in shambles as it licked its wounds.

Israel had only seven immigrant houses ready to serve the masses about to flood the country. These immigrant houses were equipped to absorb a few dozen people for an overnight stay. What irony! Facilities for dozens of people to stay for one night when hundreds of thousands were arriving. They called this *aliyat hamachanot* — "the aliyah of the camps," and it very nearly wiped out Eretz Yisrael's social service system completely.

"It is a cloudburst," one of the early Jewish leaders said of this wave of immigrating Holocaust survivors and released Cyprus detainees. "Our tiny state is going to double its population, and we don't have the ability to absorb the newcomers."

Scrambling for a solution, the state cleared the cities of Ramle, Lod and Yaffo, abandoned by franticly fleeing Arabs during the war, and prepared them to absorb the masses.

The *olim*, most of them lonely Jews, Holocaust survivors, cripples, the weak and infirm, found it hard to deal with the difficult conditions but remained nonetheless, burning with love for their country and prepared to struggle if necessary.

The state could not handle the stream of humanity. Before it had a chance to catch its breath and make some sort of order, another wave of aliyah hit, this one known as *aliyat hamaabarot*, — "the aliyah of the transit camps." Although this wave was smaller than the first, it too shook the country to its foundations.

Meir enlisted in this new struggle, assisting the Jewish Agency in providing aid for the *olim*. Now that the gates were open, immigration was legal for the most part, but there was still an illegal channel that smuggled Jews from countries that forbade them to leave, such as Syria, Lebanon and Iraq.

Once the Jews reached Eretz Yisrael, there was still a lot of work to be done. They needed to be settled, they required medicines and medical care, and schools had to be opened and sources of livelihood provided. Once again, the system of social services was in danger of collapse.

Meir watched with mounting frustration as transit camps were built. He objected to this manner of settling people and saw the undercurrent of bitterness among the *olim*. They protested the inhumane conditions and developed a strong animosity toward the absorption officials.

"Why did you bring us here?" they asked bitterly. "If you can't absorb us like human beings, why did you urge us to leave our countries and come to Eretz Yisrael?"

By contrast, David Ben Gurion, the prime minister, was filled with optimism. He spoke passionately of "the miracle of the second aliyah" and lectured euphorically on "the return of the people to Zion." He would not listen to or discuss the difficulties inherent in absorption.

From his position as a board member of the Jewish Agency, Meir began hearing a viewpoint different from Ben Gurion's. Inside conference rooms, people were talking about stemming the flow of aliyah, of filtering *olim*. "We cannot go on absorbing more and more sick people, cripples and people with war wounds," said Meyer Grossman, a board member of the Jewish Agency and the leader of the Jewish State Party. "We must first achieve the conditions of any normal country and only then continue to absorb immigrants."

At first these sentiments were merely whispered in closed meetings. Eventually, though, Grossman decided to speak up. "We must not allow aliyah to endanger us!" he wrote in a strident article in *Hamashkif*. "Since the establishment of the state, more than 160,000 *olim* have arrived without anyone giving a thought as to where to put them or what to do with them. The argument for the rush to bring *olim* was that there was an urgent need for manpower, both for the armed forces and for building the country. That can be understood and even forgiven. Now, a year later, the urgency is gone. The army is strong. We stand on the brink of peace and there is no shortage of labor in Israel. Although there are 40,000 people in the transit camps, and despite the dearth of housing and money, aliyah keeps increasing. It would be criminal to watch these developments calmly and fail to make a determined effort to regulate the process. Instead of a blessing, aliyah can, G-d forbid, bring a curse upon us. We should bring only young pioneers and urge only people of means, who won't be a financial burden, to come here."

The controversy raged. Many people protested the unfair division between the qualified and the unqualified. They were furious at the idea of making things difficult for Jews who wanted to return to the land of their forefathers. There were others, however, who agreed with Grossman that the state was in danger of collapse from having absorbed so many sick and crippled people and felt it was incapable of absorbing anymore.

At a Jewish Agency meeting, members of the board asked for a quarter of a million liras for aid to new immigrants. Grossman's article had apparently made an impact, because the request was turned down.

"I'm asking for a pittance compared to what is really needed!" ranted Yitzchak Rafael, director of the Jewish Agency's aliyah department. "How can you ask me to trim that figure? Do you mean to say we should no longer rescue our fellow Jews seeking to flee persecution and political danger? Whatever happened to 'the ingathering of the exiles'? You want us to allow in only those people we are certain won't become a burden on us?"

Meir was among those who opposed unchecked aliyah. "Mr. Prime Minister," he said fiercely, "the state is on the brink of collapse. We must pick and choose whom to allow in. How will it help the *olim* if the state collapses?"

"I'm concerned about the future," the prime minister objected. "I'm picturing a time when we will ask ourselves where we can find more Jews to bring over here."

"Crisis in Jewish Agency's Absorption System," the headlines blared. "Agency's Coffers Empty; Aliyah Absorption System Deteriorating."

Another conference was held with the participation of board members who lived in the United States. The policy of allowing new immigrants into the fledgling state in huge numbers was criticized sharply. The Americans expressed skepticism regarding the state's ability to cope with the immigrants who had already arrived. The only one who supported encouraging aliyah was Professor Selig Brodetzky, an Englishman, who argued that every Jew ought to make aliyah, qualifications notwithstanding.

Ben Gurion was angry with the talk of restricting aliyah, and he pushed the passage of the Law of Return. On 20 Tammuz 5710/July 5, 1950, in a festive and moving ceremony at the Knesset plenum, Ben Gurion signed the Law of Return, which calls upon every Jew wherever he may be to ascend to Eretz Yisrael. The law opens the gates of the state to every Jew. "This law is the fulfillment of Jewish history. It is the historic right of every Jew, wherever he may be, to return to and settle in Israel, whether because he is stripped of his rights in exile, whether he feels his existence in another country is insecure, whether he suffers persecution, whether he is surrounded by hatred and scorn, whether he is prevented from living the life he wants to live or whether because of his love for Jewish tradition, culture or the sovereignty of Israel."

Despite these emotional declarations, Meir and his friends (the members of the Jewish Agency opposed to aliyah), who were dubbed "the restricters," continued their efforts to categorize potential *olim*. They demanded that only strong young men be allowed entry; they felt the doors should be closed to the elderly, the handicapped, the sick and children.

In an effort to prove that most people felt as they did, they conducted a survey asking the following questions:

A. Do you think unrestricted aliyah should be allowed to continue, or should limits be imposed?

B. Do you feel there is danger inherent in having large concentrations of *olim* in our cities?

C. Should *olim* be pressured to do agricultural work?

D. Who should have priority with regard to assistance in finding housing and employment: former soldiers or *olim*?

The questions were designed to influence people to respond in a certain way, and indeed, 80 percent of those surveyed replied that potential *olim* ought to be selected for suitability and that the state needed time to recuperate before it could absorb more *olim*.

The restricters' demands for a selective immigration law to counter the Law of Return increased steadily. Such a law would screen potential *olim* and grant the privilege of aliyah only to those deemed able to contribute to the state. Understandably, there were many who protested vehemently. Controversy flared.

Although it was Golda Meir's job as the minister of labor to provide sources of income for all *olim*, she supported unrestricted aliyah. "Before aliyah from Romania was permitted," she said, "we wouldn't have dreamed of arguing about cost, qualifications or age. If Russia were to permit its Jews to leave today, I don't believe anyone would be prepared to forgo them. Romania might begin acting like Russia soon. This is not a matter of statistics."

Avraham Ussishkin, a "practical Zionist," on the other hand, argued that "this aliyah was brought here without people's consent ... making Israel a wide open place for the unfortunate, the elderly, the weak, the chronically ill, the crippled and others in need of social services. There are also people who might be healthy physically but are not suited to the country or its way of life in these times ... people who lack the desire to work or the understanding or intelligence necessary to overcome the conditions here. Bringing tens of thousands, if not hundreds of thousands, of unsuitable people to Israel has not enhanced the state's strength nor contributed anything to the Yishuv. It hasn't provided hope for a better future. It hasn't even helped the *olim* themselves, who in many cases are worse off than they were previously."

Overwhelming pressure finally resulted in the passage of the Law of Selective Immigration in November 1951. The law stated that:

A. Eighty percent of immigrants from certain countries (Morocco, Tunisia, Algeria, Turkey, Persia, India, and some countries in central and Western Europe) would be selected from Aliyat Hanoar, professionals up to the age of 35 and families where the breadwinner is younger than 35.

B. Candidates for aliyah, with the exception of people of means who could afford housing on their own, must sign a written commitment to work in agriculture for a minimum of two years.

C. Candidates will be approved for aliyah only after a thorough medical examination under the supervision of an Israeli doctor.

D. *Olim* above the age of 35 may be permitted entry if accompanying families where the breadwinner is qualified to work or if they themselves are trained in a needed work category and will be absorbed by relatives in Israel. This category may not exceed 20 percent of the aforementioned *olim*.

Less than a year later, some changes were made to the law and the following amendment was added:

A. A person may not be prevented from immigrating to Israel barring severe medical or moral problems. This immigration quota applies only to people whose aliyah we subsidize. Jews who pay for their own aliyah may not be prevented from entering, like the 12,000 Jews from Turkey who immigrated recently at their own expense.

B. Any Jew who needs to be rescued may be brought over immediately.

Meir was pleased. His passion to protect Eretz Yisrael was finally fulfilled. The state would not accept more people than it was capable of absorbing, and it would have a chance to recover and grow strong. In another few years it would open its gates anew.

The crippled, the infirm and the handicapped are just a burden, Meir thought to himself, opening a window to let the windy Tel Aviv air in. *Who needs them? We need people who can help develop this country, people who can take the initiative, build things, establish institutions, create opportunities. We can't use cripples now. When you want to build a strong building, you've got to eliminate the weak stones.*

NO ONE PREPARED Meir for what would happen that day. He was feeling good about his work as a member of the Jewish Agency. Now that the Law of Selective Immigration had been passed, he felt new life coursing through his veins. A little voice inside him implored him to have mercy on behalf of those too weak to shout in protest, but he repressed it firmly. This was no time to be a softy. You couldn't hold a surgical scalpel if your hand trembled. Now was the time to fight for the settlement and restoration of Jews in Eretz Yisrael.

He entered his office in the Jewish Agency building. Someone was waiting for him there.

"Meir?" It was Shaul, who was a member of the Jewish Agency as well.

"Yes?"

"There's an important meeting. They want you to attend."

Meir went downstairs and greeted everyone there. On the wall was a map of Morocco. A small red circle marked one of the country's small villages. The men's brows were furrowed as they looked pensively at the map. Meir wondered what it was all about.

"Things are heating up in this settlement in northern Morocco," the chairman said, opening the meeting. "The Muslims living there are fanatics. We fear for the lives of the Jews there. We'd like to bring them over."

Meir's muscles tensed. "So?"

"What do you say?"

"Would bringing them over go against the immigration law?"

The chairman sighed. "Yes. Most of them are children, and some are elderly, crippled or sick. They're all poor. Very few of them are qualified to work."

"The law says we can bring in any Jew who is in danger immediately," Shaul said.

"Yes," the chairman agreed, "but we're not absolutely certain about the danger. We've received only vague reports that trouble is brewing. Is that a clear and present danger?"

"I don't think so," Meir said, warning bells going off in his head. "It's not an immediate danger. If we're going to circumvent the law every time we receive a half-baked report, this country's going to collapse under the weight of the infirm."

"Meir," Shaul said reproachfully, "what if they really are in danger? How can we ignore that possibility?"

"Shaul, we cannot afford to bring every single person who might be in danger to Eretz Yisrael!"

"But this isn't just a stab-in-the-dark 'might'; we have reliable reports."

"You're a soft touch, Shaul," the chairman said. "Probably because of your past."

Shaul paled. Meir felt his heart skip a beat. Shaul was his friend, and he was extremely fond of him. He knew how sensitive Shaul was about his past. He never spoke about Auschwitz or the war. He was angry with the chairman for bringing it up.

The chairman did not notice anything amiss. "Well, what do you say?" he asked.

"What do the others have to say?" Meir asked. The six men sitting around the table had been silent until now, listening to the exchange without comment.

"We'll take a vote," the chairman agreed. A vote was taken and Meir saw, to his consternation, that the results were likely to be tied. There were eight men, including the chairman and Shaul. Four were in favor of bringing in the Jews from the small village in Morocco even though the danger was not clear, and four were opposed, on the grounds that if they brought over every Jew on such flimsy evidence, the immigration law would be useless.

Meir was the last to cast his vote. Despite his certainty in the justice of his way of thinking, he felt a shiver of apprehension. He was about to decide the fate of Jews somewhere in the world. What if he was making a mistake? What if the Muslims harmed them in the end?

"No," he said, his voice trembling slightly. "I don't think they should be brought over."

"The nays have it, then," the chairman said, closing his folder. "We'll relay that to the Aliyah Department. Thank you, gentlemen."

The meeting adjourned. The men dispersed.

Shaul gave him a withering glance. "I wouldn't want to be in your shoes," he said.

Meir looked at him in surprise. "Why?"

"Because if those people are harmed you will bear the blame. I don't know how you can allow the tiniest doubt when it comes to the safety of your fellow Jews. You saw the pain and loss in Bergen-Belsen. You lost your entire family in the Holocaust. Hitler, too, conducted selections!"

"Quiet!" Meir's fist slammed into Shaul's shoulder. The force of the blow sent Shaul reeling to the opposite corner of the room. The two friends regarded one another with a mixture of anger and surprise.

"How dare you?" Meir's voice shook with rage. "Are you comparing our selectivity to what the Nazis did? Have you no shame?"

"I didn't mean that, Meir," Shaul said, sincerely apologetic. "I didn't mean to draw such a comparison. I just wanted to say that you experienced loss, so how can you do this to your brothers?"

"If I thought they would be harmed I wouldn't allow it, of course," Meir replied. "What are you thinking? But I have no doubt that no harm will befall them. The excitement will die down just as it started, and we cannot keep bringing Jews in when we can't absorb them. Don't you understand that?"

"The law says —"

"The law! But this isn't a danger, don't you see that, Shaul? We cannot afford to tremble every time a leaf rustles in the wind. We must bring in only those who will benefit the state, and cripples and sick people do not fit into that category. Anyone who cannot help build the Land should wait patiently until we're strong enough to absorb him."

"Your voice is full of scorn," Shaul said. "If you were motivated only by concern for Eretz Yisrael, I wouldn't hear that note of derision for the sick and crippled."

Meir did not reply. What was there to say? That Shaul was wrong? He was right. That his tone of voice bore no trace of superiority? It was brimming with it. Yes, he saw himself as superior to them because he could create and build, lead and develop, and they could not. Was he better than they? Maybe not, but he could definitely do more.

"The riots began suddenly," the newscaster announced. "A furious mob of Muslims have rioted in the small village of Nera and destroyed almost the whole village. Dozens of Jews have been killed or wounded and hundreds left homeless. Some sought refuge in neighboring towns but were murdered by fanatic, bloodthirsty Muslim mobs there. The Jewish Agency is taking steps to bring the survivors to Eretz Yisrael, but voices are being raised in criticism of those who could have prevented the tragedy and failed to do so. With us here is Labor Minister Golda Meir. Mrs. Meir?"

"I can't even be glad that we were right," Mrs. Meir said, her voice trembling with suppressed anger. "The blindness of those Jewish Agency officials who ended unrestricted aliyah has exacted a heavy toll. We will, of course, demand the establishment of an investigative committee to find out who was responsible; who ignored the warning we received that trouble was brewing and disobeyed the law, which states clearly that any Jew who is in danger must be rescued immediately; whose hard-heartedness was responsible for these deaths and the injuries; who brought a holocaust upon the Jews of Nera. He will pay; that much is certain. But we must also rethink our Selective Immigration Law and consider whether it did not indirectly cause the death of our Jewish brethren."

Meir was on the next boat leaving Israel.

Pain hammered at his heart. His distress was terrible, his guilt agonizing. He had survived everything; he had fought the battles of the young state more bravely than anyone else. But when faced with the real test, he had failed.

You were wrong, Meir, his conscience whispered. *You were wrong to leave your parents' house in Poland, and you were wrong when you made the decision that led to the death and injury of Jews.*

Eretz Yisrael had spit him out.

When the ship left the pier, Meir began to sob uncontrollably – for his past, for the torturous present, for his uncertain future in the United States. He wept for all the mistakes he had made, and true remorse filled his heart.

He left Eretz Yisrael, but he returned to his Jewish roots. For years he had lived as a freethinker, ignoring Hashem's commandments. For years he had ignored his inner self and evaded the piercing question: *Why, Meir? Why?*

Now it was all behind him. The sun was setting. The ship was on its way to America, the magical, golden land. For him, however, America did not signify a chance to grow wealthy. He hoped to establish, finally, a true Jewish home on its soil.

"A national homeland," Lord Balfour had said of Eretz Yisrael, but Meir's home would be built in America. It hadn't been an easy decision, but he had made peace with it. He would never return to Eretz Yisrael, whose sanctity he had profaned with his sins. He would not set foot on its holy soil, which he had sullied with his brothers' blood. He would never again walk its magnificent mountain paths; he was not worthy of them. He would never more gaze at the shining blue sky of the land Hashem watches over from the beginning of the year to the end. He would never enjoy its breathtaking scenery, its ancient buildings, its holy sites. He would never return to the country he loved so fiercely. He would never return to Eretz Yisrael. He was not worthy of her.

24

New York 5759/1999

Becky sensed that something was wrong. When her parents had made the astonishing discovery that Mindy was not autistic, the atmosphere at home had been so happy. The happiness was dissipating gradually, however, and a dark and terrible gloom was taking its place. Ima was crying again and Abba was pale and drawn. They were sad, Becky thought to herself, at how miserable Mindy had been all those years when she hadn't been autistic at all and no one had understood her. But would their sadness help Mindy?

Later Becky understood that it wasn't so simple. Mindy wasn't communicating with others the way they had thought she would now that they knew she wasn't autistic. Yanky had explained to her that because Mindy had been locked up inside herself for so long, she couldn't just leave that jail and begin making progress now.

Becky swung her legs from the side of her bed. What could she do about the situation? She had been so happy at first. Chanukah had been so wonderful, so bright, so filled with hope for the future. But now things looked so bleak. The winter was almost over. Bits of green foliage were already adorning the trees. Purim and Pesach had passed, and summer was peeking through the window already – but Mindy was still the same.

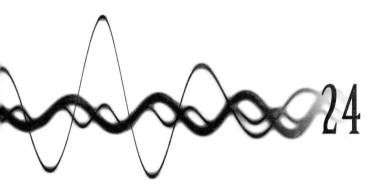

She had returned to Flowers in the Garden. It had been a mistake to take her out. Mindy had taken the sudden transition very hard. After she'd been home for a few weeks it was decided that it would be best for her to go back. The staff there was told about the great changes Mindy had undergone, and they prepared a supportive environment for her. No progress was noted. The staff continued communicating with her the way they had before. When Becky tried to talk to her she met with a stubborn barrier of silence.

"Becky, Mindy needs to go to Natalie today. Can you go with her?" Ima asked her.

Becky agreed, of course. "Sure. I'll be happy to take her."

She and Mindy wore the same outfit. The fact that they looked so similar made Becky even sadder. It was such a shame that she and Mindy couldn't be friends.

Becky grasped Mindy's hand. Mindy grabbed her hard and looked at her angrily. Oh, of course. Now Becky knew that Mindy didn't like to be touched. "Sorry," she said, making sure her face was turned to Mindy, now that Mindy had learned lip reading.

There was no response.

The two girls left the house, walking together yet worlds apart. *There's a strong, thick barrier between us*, Becky thought dismally. The street they were approaching was narrow and usually had very little traffic. Becky looked right, left and right again and signaled to her sister to cross with her. They crossed safely and Becky felt enormously proud. She was so big already!

"Come," she said to Mindy. "Look, here's a park we can cut through to get there faster." Mindy didn't understand, but she followed her twin obediently. They skipped across the grass, Becky taking the lead. The hole in the ground was small, and she didn't see it. Becky tripped and fell with a cry of pain.

It was early evening and the park was empty. Mindy stood near her sister, who was writhing helplessly on the ground in great pain. She looked at Becky, glanced around the park, and then looked at

Becky again. They were alone, she realized dimly. There was no one in the park except for her and Becky.

"Mindy," Becky sobbed. "It hurts! It hurts so much. I think I broke my foot. Go home, Mindy; go call Ima."

Becky regretted the words almost as soon as they were out of her mouth. How could Mindy go home? How was she supposed to know the way? She'd get lost, and she could get hurt. How could she, Becky, have forgotten that?

"Mindy," she called to her sister. "Mindy, help me."

Now a spark of interest flared in Mindy's dull, expressionless eyes, raising Becky's hopes that Mindy would get help. Absorbed in her pain, Becky didn't dwell on the significance of that spark; all she could think about was the fact that she was hurt and all alone.

"Mindy, can't you help me?" Tears streamed from her cheeks. "Please, Mindy, help me."

Mindy crouched down over Becky and, for the first time in her life, communicated with someone. Her lips formed the word "How?"

Becky's heart skipped a beat. Her tears froze. Mindy had spoken to her. Mindy had spoken! She overcame her excitement, afraid that her sister would clam up again if she praised her.

"I don't know," she said. "Maybe you should go call someone."

Mindy rose, her eyes darting all over. There was no one nearby. Becky could see that as well. Mindy's high forehead was furrowed in thought. Suddenly, she bent down and grabbed Becky by both hands, tugged sharply, and brought her to a standing position.

"Ow!" Becky cried out in pain. Mindy's face was an unreadable mask. She supported Becky with her arms around her waist and helped her hop on one foot slowly out to the street. Mindy helped Becky sit down on the curb. The ghost of a satisfied smile played on Mindy's lips.

Someone approached. It was a young woman pushing a baby carriage.

" 'Scuse me," Becky called out. "Can you help us?"

The woman stopped. "What's the matter?"

"I fell, and I think I broke my foot. Can you call my mother?"

"Where do you live?"

Becky gave the woman her address. "We need help. My sister ..." she paused. What should she say? That Mindy was autistic? It wasn't true. That she used to be autistic and therefore didn't speak? What an explanation! She chose to avoid providing an accurate explanation. "She ... she can't go home alone."

"Ah." The woman glanced at Mindy and appeared to understand. There was something about Mindy's facial expression that revealed she was not normal.

"I would go call your mother, but I don't want to leave you two here alone," the woman said.

"It's okay. We can stay here alone. Just go," Becky pleaded. "We'll be alright."

The woman hesitated, but there didn't seem to be any alternative. She nodded and began walking quickly in the direction of the girls' house. Becky and Mindy waited there alone, but Becky was much calmer now. She knew help was on the way. Aside from the pain, she felt the burden of responsibility on her shoulders. She was responsible for Mindy now. Mindy wasn't likely to run away or dart into the street — if she were, Ima wouldn't have let Becky take her anywhere on her own — but she couldn't really be trusted. Actually though, today Mindy had proved that she could be trusted.

Ten minutes later Shlomo's car pulled up alongside them. He and Naomi leaped out of the car and ran to Becky and Mindy.

"Becky! Mindy!" Naomi hugged the two of them together and Shlomo said, "What happened, Becky?"

"I fell, in the park," Becky stammered, exhausted and confused. "There was a hole in the ground and I didn't see it and I think I broke my foot."

Shlomo lifted Becky easily and deposited her in the car. Naomi sat down at her side and held her close. Mindy got in the car by herself, and Shlomo drove off.

"*Baruch Hashem*, Becky," Naomi said, "it doesn't look too bad. We'll go straight to a doctor and see what's wrong with your foot."

Only now that everything was okay did Becky allow herself to burst into tears. She rested her head on her mother's shoulder and wept. Naomi stroked her soothingly over and over again.

"It's okay, Becky," she said. "It's okay, *baruch Hashem*."

They went to the doctor, and an hour later Becky's foot was encased in a large white bandage. Her ankle wasn't broken; she had merely sprained it. The Mandels returned home, and Shlomo placed Becky in the armchair in the living room. Mindy stood in the doorway, her lips pursed as usual. But there was a spark of interest in her eyes.

"Mindy," Becky called. "Come over here. Ima, if not for Mindy we would never have been able to get help. She lifted me up from the ground and helped me walk to the street. If not for her I'd still be lying there, and no one would ever have seen us."

Mindy hesitated. She remained standing in the doorway, leaning against the doorframe.

"Come, Mindy," Becky pleaded. "Come here."

Mindy took a few slow steps forward until Becky could reach her hand to pull her over lovingly. She hugged her tight and said, "Thank you, Mindy. You saved us! If not for you we would have stayed there forever."

Mindy raised her eyes to her sister's face. Naomi held her breath in disbelief, in hope, in prayer, in pain.

"Not forever," Mindy mouthed the words hoarsely and unsteadily. And then her lips curved into a faint smile.

YEHOSHUA CIRCLED THE wall of Yericho seven times before it fell, Meir thought to himself as he sat in the garden, his granddaughters at his side.

"Sabba, tell us a story," Becky requested.

"A story," Mindy echoed. "Okay?"

Meir smiled. A few months had passed since Becky had sprained her ankle, and Mindy had begun to respond. She had continued to make steady, albeit slow, progress since then, *baruch Hashem.*

He opened the book to the story of "The Ugly Duckling."

"And then the duckling looked into the water and saw his own reflection," he read dramatically. "Lo and behold, he was a beautiful, majestic swan. 'Ah,' the ugly duckling realized. 'I'm different from my brothers because I'm handsome; I'm different because I'm not like them. I'm much handsomer. I'm not a small, simple duckling. I'm a swan.'"

The girls read his lips with bated breath.

"Is it a true story?" Becky wanted to know.

"Yes," Meir said, facing the two girls. "Once there were two little girls who were born deaf. At first everyone thought that they wouldn't be able to be like everyone else, that they would always be different. But then they grew up and they saw that they weren't like everyone else, they were better than everyone else. They overcame their problem and became extra special, truly special."

Meir wasn't sure his granddaughters understood him. Becky looked at him with dissatisfaction. "I don't understand," she said.

"Becky," he said, looking deep into her eyes. "You're different, right? You don't hear like everyone else, right? But that's just why you're special. It was you who broke down your sister's barrier of silence, even though you're both deaf."

Becky blushed with pleasure, and Meir was still unsure whether she'd understood.

"But I didn't even mean to do that," she said. "It just happened that I fell and only Mindy was there to help me."

"It wouldn't have happened if you hadn't taken care of her all this time," Meir replied. "If Mindy had not felt that you truly cared about her all these years, she wouldn't have felt that she had to do something to help you, do you see?"

Mindy asked him in her hoarse voice, "Who's the swan? Becky or me?"

Meir assumed she didn't understand the depth of her own question. Hugging her close, he asked, "Who do you think?"

She pursed her lips. "I don't know."

Becky looked at her with a wise expression on her face. "We both are, Mindy," she said. "We're both different but special. Each of us in her own way."

Meir nodded, and Mindy raised her eyes to his.

"Sabba, Becky," Mindy said, "I love you both."

THE PLANE LANDED.

All eight of them filed off: Meir Katz, his wife, and Shlomo, Naomi, Yanky, Becky, Mindy and Sari Mandel. The children were in high spirits, and Naomi felt a sense of freedom and calm envelop her. Her father had retracted his vow never to set foot in Eretz Yisrael again.

Shlomo was lost in thought. His father-in-law had come a long way before reaching this moment. Meir's wife, Naomi's mother, was filled with unadulterated joy. The difficult burden her husband had borne all these years had been alleviated somewhat. The painful memories had abated a bit. He felt lighter, less fettered than before, and she was happy for him.

And Meir? He was devoid of emotion. He disembarked from the plane like a sleepwalker, allowing his daughter and son-in-law to lead him to the bus that took them to the airport building, to the conveyor belt where their luggage awaited them, to the line at passport control, and finally to the soil and air of Eretz Yisrael.

They knew that Meir's son Shmulik, Shlomit and their children were waiting outside to greet them. The children were impatient to greet their cousins. Naomi was longing to see her brother, sister-in-law and nieces and nephews; and Shlomo, too, was eager to see his brother-in-law again. The children's grandmother, of course, couldn't wait to see them as well. And Meir? He felt as though he had stepped outside his body and was watching the proceedings as an observer.

They walked out of the terminal. There was much exuberant hand waving, many emotional embraces and cries of joy. The meeting between the two families was noisy and happy, full of excitement and happiness. Everyone talked and laughed and shouted at the same time, and emotions ran high. After the initial excitement had died down, everyone looked at Sabba in awed silence.

"Fifty years," Meir whispered. "I haven't been here in fifty years."

Everyone fell silent. Mindy squeezed Sabba's hand hard. "Sabba, why? Why didn't you visit Eretz Yisrael for so long?"

"It's an old story, darling," he said, smiling at her fondly. "And I carry it deep, deep inside my heart."

"Like me?" Becky asked.

"Why like you?"

"You once told me that you carry me deep, deep inside your heart."

"Yes, darling, like you."

Looking around him, he saw Eretz Yisrael again: wispy clouds in a blue, blue sky, flowers nodding in the breeze. A tremor ran through his body. He crouched down, lifted a fistful of soil and opened his fingers slowly. The particles of soil filtered through his fingers and blew away with the wind.

He recalled the last time he had done the very same thing, on the day he had left prison. As the gates had clanged shut behind him, he'd raised his eyes to the blue sky in gratitude, filled his lungs with fresh air, and crouched down. Then the wind had scattered the particles of earth he'd sifted through his fingers far away, along with the struggles and battles, the tears and despair.

Everything was so similar now, yet different at the same time. Today he had left a prison of a different kind: a painful memory he had borne in his heart for so many long years. He had thought weak people were of no benefit to anyone. He had thought that the arrival of the crippled and the handicapped would hold back the building of the Land.

But he had been wrong, and not only because the Moroccan Jews had been hurt in the end. No, not only because of that. After many years he had finally understood that handicapped people are special in their own way and that they deserved far greater admiration than normal people. Normal people walk a straight, paved path while the handicapped toil and sweat to carve a path for themselves. They overcome barriers and shatter society-created myths.

"The purpose of creation is to augment *kevod Shamayim*," Meir said to his wife. "Do you know? I always thought that the handicapped couldn't achieve the true purpose of life because in many cases they can't raise families. When you realize what the true goal in life is, you suddenly understand that the handicapped achieve it better than the rest of us. They know how to be truly grateful to Hashem, to thank Him from the bottom of their hearts and to augment *kevod Shamayim*. They are lofty souls that fulfill what they have to do *bishleimus*, perfectly."

She listened in silence.

"Today my granddaughter merited to fix what I damaged," Meir said, stroking Becky's hair lovingly. "And I feel the need to come here and ask forgiveness of the Land that I sullied and stained with blood."

Naomi looked at her father, who seemed suddenly taller than before. "It was Becky, of all people," he said with great emotion, "who succeeded in breaching her sister's barrier. Because she's special in her own way."

Yes, Naomi mused, *Becky has breached a number of barriers. The first is the one that held her prisoner: her deafness. The second is Mindy's. And the third is the jail my father locked himself into because of his agonizing memories.*

Naomi raised her eyes to the blue sky above. She'd been through much in life, just as her children had. She'd endured more than a little suffering, untold anguish, and many moments of hope and happiness. At first, she had locked herself in a prison of silence. Eventually, she had broken free and later she had made peace with her lot — but it was only many long years later that she actually became glad about it. The pain she had endured had taught her a lot about understanding people, and it had forged a close bond between her and her Father in Heaven.

Emotion roiled inside her, setting her soul atremble. When a person leaves a prison, he knows how to appreciate freedom. She inhaled deeply, savoring the wonderful atmosphere of Eretz Yisrael.

Her father had made peace with his painful memory. He felt that Becky was closing a circle he hadn't merited to close. She was a source of inspiration to others with handicaps; she had made a giant step forward for those who are different and special. He sensed that his granddaughter was making amends for what he had damaged. He'd wanted to come to Eretz Yisrael again. He knew how to be thankful for his freedom now, and Naomi did as well.

And Shlomo, Yanky, Mindy and Becky, too — all of them had broken out of an imprisonment of some sort. The same wonderful, majestic melody played in all their hearts: the melody that the free man hums when he is released at last from a prison that was surrounded by seemingly impenetrable barriers.